THE LOOK OF DEATH

THE COLIN BUXTON SERIES
BOOK 2

CC GILMARTIN

CCGILMARTIN.COM

REVIEWS OF ALL MINE ENEMIES
BOOK 1 IN THE COLIN BUXTON SERIES

"A thrilling whodunnit"

"A great read and a terrific debut novel"

"A real page turner"

Copyright © 2023 by CC Gilmartin

All rights reserved.

No part of this book may be reproduced in any form or by any electronic or mechanical means, including information storage and retrieval systems, without written permission from the author, except for the use of brief quotations in a book review.

This is a work of fiction. Names characters, businesses, places, events and incidents are either the products of the author's imagination or used in a fictitious manner. Any resemblance to actual persons, living or dead, or actual events is purely coincidental.

ISBN 978-1-7391362-3-9

❋ Created with Vellum

CONTENTS

Prologue	1

PART 1

Chapter 1	7
Chapter 2	14
Chapter 3	20
Chapter 4	26
Chapter 5	30
Chapter 6	33
Chapter 7	40
Chapter 8	45
Chapter 9	50
Chapter 10	54
Chapter 11	61
Chapter 12	66

PART 2

Chapter 13	75
Chapter 14	82
Chapter 15	87
Chapter 16	94
Chapter 17	100
Chapter 18	111
Chapter 19	116
Chapter 20	122
Chapter 21	128
Chapter 22	133
Chapter 23	140
Chapter 24	145
Chapter 25	151

PART 3

Chapter 26	159
Chapter 27	167
Chapter 28	174
Chapter 29	177

Chapter 30	188
Chapter 31	199
Chapter 32	204
Chapter 33	211
Chapter 34	216
Chapter 35	225

PART 4

Chapter 36	231
Chapter 37	238
Chapter 38	241
Chapter 39	249
Chapter 40	253
Chapter 41	257
Chapter 42	261
Chapter 43	267
Chapter 44	274
Chapter 45	282
Chapter 46	291
Chapter 47	297

PART 5

Chapter 48	309
Chapter 49	317
Chapter 50	323
Chapter 51	331
Chapter 52	337
Chapter 53	343
Chapter 54	349
Chapter 55	354
Chapter 56	361
Available now	367
Coming soon	369
Available for free	371
Acknowledgments	373
About the Author	375

PROLOGUE
SUMMER 1982

Egon's body had been laid out in the dining room, the most cheerless, unloved room, situated at the back of the house. Cold all year round, with its woodchip wallpaper and dark green carpet, it had never felt like part of the inside. Though the jumble of garden furniture and broken bits of bicycles had been cleared, it still felt abandoned. Yet his parents refused to consider a funeral home, saying they couldn't bear to let him go, insisting their son had to be brought home.

Gaze lingering on his twin brother through the open door, Konrad crouched in the hallway, hidden from view. Whereas his own body was lumbering and awkward, prone to fat like his father, his brother had been born with the good genes of his mother: slim, petite, fine-featured. Striking. He couldn't take his eyes off him, and as the undertakers undressed, washed and dried his body in the fading afternoon light, it felt like he was seeing his brother's naked body for the first time.

Of the two of them, Egon was the livewire, the bright spark. Never more so than in the past few weeks, chatting incessantly about the youth theatre show he was about to star in – a musical version of *Sleeping Beauty*. 'I get to wear a navy-blue suit with a rose-coloured shirt, the snazziest of shoes, and because I'm the hero, they'll draw a moustache on me.' He skipped around the house, excitedly reciting passages about everlasting love and how he and his princess were destined to be together.

'Quit prancing!' his father had shouted, slamming the door shut.

'He needs to be word perfect,' his mother yelled back. 'Konrad, help your brother; play the princess.'

Over and over, he'd been forced to repeat lines such as *My hero, I love you, Stay with me forever.*

'You need to say it like you mean it,' Egon insisted. 'It's no good otherwise.'

For hours, Konrad had rehearsed with him, until he too knew the lines off by heart. Soon, he was not only saying the words like he meant them, but had become convinced that he and his brother were the embodiment of those characters.

'See, you're a natural performer – just like me!'

Peering through the crack in the door, Konrad leaned forward as two of the undertakers – both in their fifties, pot-bellied, unattractive – lifted his brother and prepared to dress him.

Egon had been brought home in the outfit he was wearing when he died: his favourite *Rocky Horror Picture Show* T-shirt and high-cut Adidas shorts – scarlet with white piping. But his father had demanded he be stripped and the clothes thrown away. 'They're too sissy,' he bluntly stated. It was true; ask anyone in town and they'd say the same.

'My son should look like a prince,' his mother had sobbed.

At her request, the director of Egon's show had arrived that morning with the navy-blue suit and rose-coloured shirt wrapped in cellophane. 'Help me hang this up,' his mother

The Look of Death

whispered. 'Don't you think your brother will look handsome in it?'

Konrad had shrugged.

It was the third undertaker – a young woman with red hair tied back in a mean little bun – who now drew the sleeves of the freshly ironed shirt onto Egon's arms. Like a puppet, the three strangers pulled and twisted his limbs as each successive item – the shirt, the jacket, the trousers – was buttoned, adjusted and zipped.

Once they'd finished dressing him, a hint of make-up was applied and his hair carefully combed and lacquered. The undertakers paused to examine their work. Nodding in agreement, they each made the sign of the cross, before standing aside, satisfied that everything was in order.

Egon's lifeless body, laid out with such precision, was caught in a moment of serenity, his beauty captured forever. Although they weren't identical, Konrad couldn't help but recognise the similarities – while their colouring was different, they shared the same shape of eyes, the same prominent nose and defined lips. From a certain angle, it felt as though he were looking at himself, and the urge to point this out to his parents was so great, he had to stop himself. All they'd do was disagree and remind him how much more handsome Egon was. Even in death.

Sometime later, after the undertakers had left and candles were lit, Konrad was marched into the back room to pray over his brother's body.

'Kiss him,' his mother instructed.

He looked up, alarmed. 'But he's dead.'

'This is your last chance.' His father's tone suggested there would be consequences if he didn't obey.

Perhaps, he thought, if they'd known who his brother claimed to have kissed the previous week, they wouldn't be so insistent.

It had been late on Tuesday night and Egon had crept into

Konrad's room drunk. 'Koni, you awake?' he'd whispered, stabbing a finger into his back.

'Get off me,' Konrad had cried. 'You stink of beer.'

'Want to hear who I snogged tonight?'

Everyone knew he'd been following Felix Roth around for months like a lost puppy. It would just be like Egon to throw himself at someone so obviously straight and unavailable; Felix had a steady girlfriend and was the captain of the football team.

Konrad pulled the covers over his ears. 'Go away!'

But Egon remained, pressing his body against his. 'When we were standing in the wings – while everyone else was on stage - Felix made the first move, told me how cute I looked in my costume, that I wasn't to tell anyone.' He wrapped his arms around Konrad and squeezed. 'I think I'm in love.'

'Bullshit!' Konrad pushed his brother off the bed and onto the floor. 'Why can't you be normal?'

'That actually hurt.' Egon got to his feet. 'I'm not going to hide who I am. Why should I? It's about time you got used to it.'

PRESSED BY HIS FATHER, Konrad took a small step towards the open coffin. Unlike his brother's usual odour of sweat and *Juicy Fruit* gum, a weird, solvent smell drifted upwards. Suddenly, he'd no idea who this slab of meat was, dressed in a cheap suit, his face a mask.

The weight of his father's hand on his shoulder increased, became insistent.

Up close, the lips appeared odd – cold, pinkish grey in colour – like stone. What lay before him was nothing more than a ghoulish version of Egon.

Before he had time to resist, his head was thrust down and, in an instant, his lips locked with his brother's.

PART 1

1

SEVEN YEARS LATER - NOVEMBER 1989

On that first night, when the Wall collapsed, people were in a frenzy. No one had dared imagine it could come about so quickly. The excitement of two sides of the same city coming together for the first time in over twenty-five years was overwhelming: people poured out onto the streets singing, dancing and drinking until they collapsed; long-lost friends hugged and relatives kissed each other; new bonds were formed, with promises of staying together forever.

Thrilled by the chaos, he watched on as hordes of people helped one another scale the Wall's familiar grey slabs and start tearing them apart. Car horns blared, celebrating this shared act of mass destruction, and he knew the time had finally come. He needed to kill someone.

A couple of days later, on Saturday 11th November, he took the crammed U-Bahn to Zoologischer Garten, where he knew you could buy heroin. Wandering amidst the garish neon lights and the stunned crowds milling around outside the station, it took only a few minutes to find someone willing to sell.

'Twenty Marks,' the man whispered, extinguishing a cigarette and pulling the hood tighter over his shaved head.

He handed over a crisp bank note.

Without a word, the man snapped the note from him and thrust a packet of powder into his hand, before disappearing into the throng of people.

As the winter light faded into late afternoon, he followed the tree-lined route of the Landwehr Canal along the north edge of Schöneberg and into Kreuzberg. Reflected on the water's dark surface, the bare branches seemed to tremble in anticipation of what he'd planned. His chosen destination was *Blue Boy Bar* on Eisenacher Strasse – it was less busy than the other gay bars he'd considered. Most played their music too loud or were stuffed full of clones, making him stand out too much. This place had only a few tables inside with soft jazz playing in the background. A perfect place to pick someone up.

On entering, a barman – looking like Tom Cruise in *Cocktail* with his thick, glossy hair and black button-down shirt – immediately caught his eye and asked what he wanted.

'A beer.'

'New around here?' The barman expertly removed the cap and handed him the bottle.

Pretending not to hear, he leaned in closer. 'How much?' It was better to be aloof than avoid engaging any further. After all, an easily remembered conversation might lead back to him and that wouldn't do. 'How much?' he repeated.

'I take it you've come over from the East?'

'And? Does that matter anymore?

The barman shook his head. 'That's not what I meant—'

'How much?'

'Unbelievable,' the barman muttered. He cleaned down the section of bar and moved onto the next customer. 'Just settle when you leave.'

The Look of Death

He scanned the room, but no one seemed eager to meet his gaze. Considering whether he'd made the right decision, he stood for ten minutes. There were other, more crowded bars; he could go after dark, where he'd be less likely to get noticed. But as he took another mouthful of beer, at the back wall, where the light was broken, he spotted a guy in his twenties sitting on his own, sketching. Tall, with a sweep of red hair, he was most likely an American tourist. His own English wasn't perfect, but he could hold a conversation if he listened carefully. Besides, for what he had in mind, they wouldn't need to talk much.

He checked his hair in the mirror behind the bar, straightened his shirt and approached him. 'Is this seat free?'

'Be my guest.' The guy removed his coat from the chair. 'It's a bit crazy out there – I just needed time away from it all.'

As he sat, their knees brushed against each other under the table. He smiled. 'Yes, it's a little mad, but fun.'

The guy offered his hand, which was thin and cool to the touch. 'Hi, I'm Fraser.'

He had to think for a split second, quickly going over in his head the possible names he could call himself. 'Egon.' He marvelled at his ingenuity.

As their hands parted, Fraser closed over his sketchbook and set it aside. 'As in Schiele?'

'My mother was a fan.' Another lie: she preferred the sweeping romanticism of Germanic landscapes, not the twisted, emaciated bodies of Schiele.

'She'd good taste.'

This man had an interesting face: deep-set eyes, a long nose, full lips, pale, luminous skin. 'I saw you sketching and thought you might be visiting.'

'I'm from Scotland. You know, bagpipes, whisky, the Loch Ness Monster.'

'Ah yes, Nessie.' Egon sipped his beer, then noticed Fraser

was drinking water. 'Sorry, would you like a beer? Or something else, maybe?'

'I'm fine,' he replied.

Their knees brushed against each other again and the warmth felt exciting. 'So, you're here for the celebrations?'

Fraser shook his head. 'Not intentionally. 'I had a study trip planned for a while and hadn't a clue what was happening at first. But I ended up on top of the Wall on Thursday night, which was wild because I'd literally just stepped off the train.'

'History in the making!' He raised his bottle to Fraser.

'To be in the right place at the right time is unbelievably lucky. How often does that happen? I've been sketching everything I've seen.' Fraser picked up the small sketchbook and flicked through to a page titled '9th November 1989'. A pencil drawing showed a group of people tearing down a section of the Wall, and over the next few pages a myriad of grinning faces drawn in graphite and ink celebrated with bottles of beer raised in the air. There was even one of the art-deco fanlight above the bar's entrance.

'You've an eye for detail.'

Fraser closed the sketchbook and set it aside. 'I like to capture what I see around me.'

'So, you're an art student?'

'I'm studying at the University of Munich for a term and only have a few weeks left before returning to Glasgow. This trip was partly for research but also a reward for completing the first half of my thesis.'

'Can I ask what it's about?'

'The visual arts during the Weimar Republic. Kathe Kollwitz, Otto Dix, George Grosz. Those sorts of people.'

Egon nodded appreciatively, though he considered those artists degenerates. 'And you enjoy Germany?'

'I'm stuck in the library most nights, so I've very little free time.'

The Look of Death

'Then tonight we must party.'

'My train to Munich is first thing tomorrow morning, so I might need to take a rain check.'

There was a nervousness to his face when it was at rest, but he became animated and excited when engaged. Leaning forward, Egon touched Fraser's arm and deliberately pressed his leg into his. He smelled clean, like fresh laundry. 'And miss this historic moment?'

'I'll be back in February.'

'Even in a few months the city will have transformed. Two cities will bleed into each other and soon we won't even notice the difference.'

'You say that as if you disapprove.'

'No. It intrigues me.' Another lie. Having moved around the city in recent days, Egon could find nothing to inspire him. The place seemed broken and he felt it would be best if the city were flattened and rebuilt from scratch, but he wanted Fraser to believe the lie that he was looking forward to the changes. 'What do you say we leave here?'

Fraser picked up his glass of water and took a sip. 'Where to?'

'Your place.' He stroked the back of Fraser's hand. 'You want to?'

Fraser replied with an uncertain shrug of his shoulders as though persuading himself. 'I'm staying at a youth hostel on Kluckstrasse, and it's not that welcoming. A bit bare.'

'We can keep the light off, then.'

'I'm not sure.'

'But it's the weekend the Wall came down. If you can't take a risk now, then when can you?'

'That's true.'

'And I promise, you'll remember this night for the rest of your life.'

Fraser smiled. 'What the hell. Why not?'

Careful to avoid the Tom Cruise lookalike, Egon pushed down his cap and settled the bill with another barman.

Outside, the streets were busier than before. A young girl grabbed them to kiss their cheeks, her foul breath chanting slogans about freedom and love. Hippie shit. Then a teenage guy, barely able to stand, offered them a drink of vodka. 'No thanks,' Egon snapped and ushered Fraser round a corner where the street was quieter. 'We can go this way,' he said. 'The U-Bahn isn't far.'

Hemmed in by a concrete cliff of high-rise flats, the roads that converged at Kottbusser Tor were packed in every direction with people. Brandishing their Deutschmarks, visitors from the East filled their bags with knock-off designer wear and exotic fruit. Egon tutted. 'Is this the best they can do with their freedom?'

Fraser playfully nudged his arm. 'They're enjoying the moment.'

'For what? Western junk?'

On cue, a woman eating a burger stopped in front of them and began singing *The Star-Spangled Banner*. Laughing, Fraser joined her in a verse, his voice matching hers in passion and volume. Egon gave them their moment together and stepped back, hiding in the shadow of a shop doorway. As the woman moved on, Fraser joined him. 'Sorry. I couldn't resist. You don't mind?'

'No. It's just not my thing. The last couple of days have been a lot; too much excitement. I'm bored of it all.'

'People are happy, that's all.'

'But what is happiness? A bag of kiwi fruit?'

'What's so wrong with that?'

This guy knew nothing about Berlin – its people, its culture, its history – but he couldn't risk losing him. 'You're right. I shouldn't be so mean. Let's go back to yours and have our own party.'

'It's just…' Fraser bit his lip. 'I'm not very experienced.'

'Is that it?' Egon laughed, drawing him into a hug. 'Is that what concerns you?'

'I mean, I have condoms and stuff, but—'

'You have condoms? Well, that's promising.'

'You seem confident, assured. I'm not.'

Egon felt a shiver run through Fraser. Reaching over to zip up his jacket, he whispered, 'Don't worry, I'll take care of you. I promise I'll be gentle.'

'You're a weird one.'

'A weird one?'

'I mean funny. Unusual. It's not a criticism. I noticed you as soon as you walked into the bar, but you looked right through me. Even when you were waiting for your drink, scanning the room, you didn't see me. You were focused on the guy at the window. But then suddenly, as if I'd appeared out of the walls, you spotted me. How come?'

'Because you looked like someone who needed a friend. Same as me.'

2

'Shh...we don't want to disturb anyone, do we?' Prising the keys from Fraser's fingers, Egon unlocked the door and bundled him into the room. 'Do you remember where the switch is?'

'Left-hand side.'

Egon's gloved hand scuttled across the wall, soon finding it, and an overhead light sprang into life. 'We have light.'

Persuading Fraser to have a drink on the way back to the youth hostel had had the desired effect. One cherry schnapps became several and now Fraser could barely walk in a straight line, let alone string a coherent sentence together. Gripping him under his arms, he'd had to manoeuvre Fraser past the receptionist, a surly guy in his sixties – holding a Budweiser in one hand, a comic in the other – and along the brightly lit corridors of this ugly slab of a modernist building. Finding the right room had taken longer than he would have liked, but he was confident they'd avoided attracting any undue attention.

As Fraser stumbled around the room, pulling a pair of threadbare curtains closed, he took the opportunity to scan

The Look of Death

the room: a single bed positioned under a broad double window, a mean little armchair, a desk, a wardrobe, a kitchenette in the corner and a door which led into a small shower room. Establishing where things were positioned was a useful precaution in case he needed to exit quickly; something he hoped wouldn't be necessary.

'Like I said, it's basic,' Fraser slurred, gesturing at the walls, his arms becoming tangled in his jacket as he tried to remove it. 'Plus, it's got mice.' He pointed to the carpet. 'There are droppings. See?' He threw his jacket onto the bed and began to unbutton his shirt. 'But apart from that, welcome to my humble abode.' He burped before ripping off his shirt and collapsing into the armchair.

Egon unscrewed the bottle of tequila he'd bought, asking, 'Have you had a slammer before?' He wafted the alcohol under Fraser's nose.

'No.'

'Tonight's your lucky night.'

'Oh, look at the tiny sombrero.' Fraser balanced it on top of his head and paraded around the room.

'Hand me those limes.'

Fraser threw them at him.

'Now, all we need are glasses and some salt.' Egon opened the kitchen cupboards. 'Here we go.' He removed his gloves, then taking a Swiss army knife from his rucksack, sliced a lime into quarters. 'You cut it like so, then put salt on your hand here. The idea is to lick, sip, suck. First, you lick the salt off your hand.' He stuck his tongue out and dabbed it against the salt. 'Wow!' The bitterness made him wince. 'Then you knock back a shot of tequila.' After the alcohol left his lips, the heat raced to the centre of his chest. 'Then you finish by sucking on the lime. Easy.'

'I wanna try.' Fraser held out both hands, like a child demanding to be hugged.

'Let me help you.' Egon put a pinch of salt on the back of his own hand and let Fraser lick it off. He smiled as he watched his face scrunch up, before handing him his glass, ensuring he swallowed every last drop of alcohol. After squeezing lime into Fraser's mouth, he placed the finished quarter into his own. Lunging at Fraser, he bared his teeth to reveal the bright green citrus skin. 'I'm coming to get you!'

Fraser darted out the way, scrambling onto the bed to avoid being caught. 'You're mad!'

A sudden bang on the adjoining wall was accompanied by a cry of 'Shut the fuck up'.

Egon put his finger against Fraser's lips. 'Ssh!' Then, removing the lime from his mouth, he threw it onto the floor. 'Again?'

Fraser nodded enthusiastically.

He was careful to ensure Fraser took more shots and bigger measures. When it was his own turn to slam, he took only a small sip but made it appear he was drinking more. 'Maybe we should get another bottle. What time is it?' Fraser stared at his watch, trying to work out the time. 'Quarter to twelve? No? Already?' Unexpectedly, he made a dash to the door and threw it open, but Egon pulled him back inside, clicking the door closed.

'You're too drunk to go anywhere.'

Fraser lay back on the bed and closed his eyes. 'You're right, Egon.' He tapped the mattress. 'Come here, Egon. I love saying your name.'

He joined Fraser, stroking his hair, the soft red tufts slipping easily through his fingers like silk. He was a handsome boy, clear-skinned and innocent. For twenty minutes they remained this way until Fraser fell asleep; it felt soothing, respectful.

Leaving him on the bed, Egon picked up a discarded lime and crossed to the bathroom with his rucksack. Reflected in

The Look of Death

the mirror, he noticed beads of sweat on his forehead. It was now or never. He splashed his face with cold water and looked at himself again. Staring back was a face he barely recognised, as though someone had erased his own.

'I need the toilet.' On the other side of the door, Fraser's voice sounded slurred, sleepy, as he turned the door handle.

Egon slammed his foot against it. 'Give me a minute.' Pressing his back up against the door, he held firm until he heard the sound of Fraser's body collapsing on the bed, followed by a deep sigh, suggesting he was drunk enough for what was to follow.

He set out the equipment on the tiled counter: the tourniquet, the spoon, the lighter, the syringe and the heroin. Coupled with the tequila, he figured a full dose would be enough to knock out six full-grown men let alone a skinny Scots boy. Using a few drops of lime juice to dissolve the heroin, he heated the spoon over the lighter flame and carefully filled the syringe with the solution.

When Egon returned to the bedroom, he was surprised to find Fraser sitting up in bed with a pencil in his hand, trying hard to focus on a page in his sketchbook. He went to write something but dropped his pencil on the floor. 'One more shot,' he cried out.

Egon took the sketchbook from him and threw it on the floor. 'Anything for you.' Holding Fraser's lips apart, he dribbled the last of the tequila into his mouth, then waited. 'Good boy. You enjoyed that, didn't you?'

Fraser lay back and closed his eyes. It took only a couple of minutes for him to drift off, but he didn't want him fully asleep. Not yet.

Stroking the soft skin of Fraser's chest, Egon snuggled into his warm body for a few minutes. 'You're so beautiful,' he murmured. 'I bet you always will be.'

Straddling him, Egon wound the tourniquet around Fraser's arm. The pressure began to wake him up, as he thought it might, so he had to act quickly. Knowing exactly which vein to place the needle against, he was glad he'd practised the sequence before. As Fraser swung to face him, his eyes widened in fear. Instinct took over and he banged hard against the wall and screamed for help.

The voice from before shouted out, 'For fuck's sake' and footsteps rushed into the corridor.

'No need to worry,' he whispered. 'I promise to take care of you.' Puncturing his pale skin with the syringe, Egon watched as Fraser's eyes fell back on themselves and the body below him weakened.

The voice from the next room was now banging on the door, demanding for it to be opened, that he was going to call the police, whilst outside, rowdy crowds of people still roamed the streets chanting *We are the people!*

What a world, he thought.

Without opening the door, Egon shouted at the irate American, 'Why don't you shut the fuck up? We're trying to celebrate here.' He pressed his eye against the spyhole as the guy continued to bang on it – each thump felt like he might actually break through it – until he gave up his protest and returned to his room.

Egon waited until the American guy's door slammed shut, then crossed over to the bed, holding Fraser as the warmth drained from his body. Certain he was dead, he wiped the froth from his mouth, cleaned the surfaces for fingerprints and packed away all his equipment. Scouring the room, he felt confident he'd left no trace.

While things had gone mostly to plan, he found the surroundings increasingly offensive. The bed sheets were shabby and yellowing, and there was a cigarette burn on the edge of the desk. Also, the frayed curtains and worn carpet were distracting – they ruined the whole effect. No one, he told himself, should have to endure the indignity of dying in such pitiful surroundings.

But Fraser was unfortunate that this was his first kill; if there was to be a next time, he'd need to work at the finer details.

3

FIVE YEARS LATER - FRIDAY, 1ST JULY 1994

Colin's morning shift at *Bar Zum Zum* started at eight. Scrubbing and peeling potatoes, chopping onions, grating carrots, making sure the chicken was properly marinated – the list was endless and Hannah was late. Again. He looked over at the clock on the wall: nine-thirty. It was an hour before the place opened and he'd agreed to have coffee with some random Scotswoman visiting Berlin.

'You'll do it. End of,' his mother had insisted, sounding harassed.

Truth be told, he'd better things to do, but rather than start another argument, he gave in. He could doubtless fob the woman off with a few tourist trap ideas and claim he was too busy to join her. 'What's her name?' He'd grabbed a pen but couldn't find a piece of paper.

'Rhona McDougal. Her mum, Iris – poor soul – used to volunteer at the chapel before arthritis did for her. A bit after your time.'

Colin wrote the name on the back of his hand. 'I think I do remember. Wasn't her son—?'

His mother didn't let him finish. Determined to continue

The Look of Death

as the go-between, she demanded he commit to a time and place where Rhona could meet him.

'Friday morning? Half nine at my work?' he suggested. '*Bar Zum Zum*, 139 Prinzenallee. Do you need me to spell it?'

'No,' she said, 'I'm not a complete eejit.'

'But why does she want to see me?'

Not listening, his mother was already yelling, 'Bye.'

'Mum?'

'For Christ's sake,' she snapped, 'you'll find out soon enough, won't you? This call's costing me a pretty penny,' she added before slamming the receiver down.

EARLY SHIFTS WERE his least favourite and lunches on Friday could be busy, so Colin always enjoyed the calm before the customers descended. Most were regulars who'd sit at the bar nursing a beer as they prepared for the weekend, only occasionally ordering food. Staring at his prep, he reckoned it would probably be enough and poured himself a glass of water. The UK suddenly seemed a million miles away. No more having to pretend, no more having to please others, no more walking around with a target on his back, being the subject of endless abuse. Working in a bar in Wedding in the arse end of Berlin suited him fine.

As he started up the coffee machine, there was a knock. 'Hold on.'

He unbolted the heavy wooden doors. Standing on the steps was a small, painfully thin woman. She couldn't be much older than him, but everything about her demeanour – from the bags under her eyes to the hunched shoulders – spoke of exhaustion. 'Come in,' he said.

She smiled weakly and, nodding at his T-shirt, began unbuttoning her heavy overcoat. 'You've the right idea. I always expect Berlin to be like Scotland in July.'

'What? Snow, wind and hail?'

'Hiya. I'm Rhona.' She shook his hand softly but remained standing by the door, waiting for permission to sit.

'Please.' He guided her towards the corner booth – his favourite – away from the blaring jukebox and the smells of the kitchen. 'I'm fixing myself an espresso. Do you want one?'

'If it's not too much trouble.' She settled herself on the cushioned bench and placed her coat to the side. 'It's cosy in here.'

He gazed around at the tired décor and the dusty plastic flowerboxes in the windows. Far humbler than the swish eateries in the city, he supposed in the proper light the place had its charms. If pine-clad chalets were your thing. 'The locals love it.'

He carried on making the espressos, the violent hiss and spit of the machine suggesting it was in no mood to cooperate. After six months, Hannah had only recently allowed him anywhere near it, grudgingly demonstrating how to make each drink. He fiddled with a switch and an enormous jet of steam blasted out. 'Sorry,' he said, 'I'm not quite a barista yet – more of a dogsbody.'

'Don't bother if it's too much trouble.'

He was adamant it wouldn't get the better of him. 'Aha.' He thrust down a lever and the machine quietened, just in time for black liquid to start dripping slowly from the nozzle. He placed a small white cup beneath it, satisfied he'd managed to make one at least. 'Bear with me,' he shouted over, beginning the process again.

'Your mum said you love it here.' He sensed her watch him intently, bemused at his lack of coordination.

Placing the espresso in front of her, he'd still one eye on the machine huffing and puffing in the background. 'So, she wasn't moaning about me abandoning her?'

Rhona grinned and her face finally burst into life. She dropped a lump of sugar into her cup and stirred, before knocking it back in one. 'Perfect!' she gasped. 'She might have

The Look of Death

questioned what you were doing here. And she may have asked me to find out if you were ever coming back.'

'Good. Tell her never – it'll keep her on her toes.' He rushed back to the machine as the first drops of the second espresso appeared. 'One minute. If I don't keep an eye on it, I'm scared it's going to explode.'

Coffee cup in one hand, he offered Rhona a croissant, but she shook her head. Grabbing one for himself he joined her at the table. Taking the first bite, he reckoned spending time with her wouldn't be too onerous; some of the places where parts of the Wall still stood would be an interesting start, places the tourists never visited but were full of interesting details. 'Here, let me get a map.' Jumping up, she stopped him.

'Your mum didn't explain, did she?'

'Shit, she hasn't set us up on a date, has she?' He scoffed the rest of his croissant, watching her reaction, hoping she'd spot he was teasing.

She held up her hand to display the thin gold band of a wedding ring. 'Sorry, I'm spoken for.'

'It wouldn't be the first time. Moira's a terrible one for sticking her oar in where she isn't welcome.'

'It's about Fraser – my brother. I'm looking for your help.'

He remembered gossip spreading around the parish about Fraser a few years ago: that he'd died from a drug overdose and how surprised everyone, including his own mother, had been. 'They're such a well-to-do family and he was such a clever wee thing,' was the general sentiment. Colin had been less shocked; though he didn't know the McDougals, he'd seen firsthand how drugs could destroy any family. And, having served a couple of years in the police by then, he knew that everyone had their secrets. 'Of course. Fire away.'

'He died here in Berlin.'

'Oh – I'm sorry. I'd no idea.' It was all he could think to

say. Rhona's face, he now realised, was still etched with grief. 'But how can I help?'

'Since he passed I've been coming here most years, making enquiries, trying to piece together Fraser's last days. But no one – not the police, not anybody – seems to want to know. On his death certificate it says a heroin overdose, but that's not what happened. I know it in my heart.' She opened her bag and took out a black, leather-bound notebook engraved with gold lettering and passed it to him. 'My brother never touched a drug in his life.'

Colin leafed through the pages of the notebook; on each page were scribbled details of places her brother had visited, with dates beside them. Conversations she'd had with a Kommissar Fink over the years had been meticulously recorded and a few names circled with question marks placed beside them.

'I'd also like you to take a look at this.' She passed him a small sketchbook. 'My brother drew all the time, right from when he was tiny. He bought a new sketchbook before he came to Germany, and sketched every day.'

He looked through what she'd given him. Images of monuments and faces filled half of the book. The last few pages were the most striking: the Wall being torn down, a few ecstatic faces of Berliners enjoying its destruction, some architectural details. The pencil images were incredibly detailed; every nuance of the figures' movements grasping at the Wall had been considered. 'Such beautiful work,' he said, passing both the notebook and sketchbook back to her.

'I'd like you to keep the notebook.' She pressed it back into his hand. 'And this.' She handed him a photograph of a young red-headed man, his arms around what he took to be his and Rhona's mother.

Colin met her eyes, which were insistent. 'Um, sorry, I don't understand.'

'I'm here because I believe my brother was murdered.'

The Look of Death

Colin scanned her face, checking for a sign that might suggest she was deceiving herself or clutching at straws. But she was calm, clear-eyed. 'Go on.'

'Call it what you like – intuition – but I know my brother didn't die of an overdose by his own hand. I can't prove it yet, but what I can say is there are several other men like Fraser who've died under suspicious circumstances.' She corrected herself. 'A number of *gay* men whose deaths in this city have not been properly investigated.'

He opened a page of the notebook. 'The names you've circled?'

She nodded. 'I'm not saying there's been a cover up; nothing as intentional as that. They've just not been seen as important enough to merit a proper investigation. But if you look at the circumstances of each man's death, you begin to see patterns.'

'Like what?'

She took the notebook from him. Flicking through it, she pointed to a description. 'In the summer of 1990, within ten days of each other, two men – Stefan Reis and Ulrich Steiner – were found dead in a cruising area. You can't tell me that's not suspicious. Ulrich Steiner's death was blamed on a heroin overdose – exactly like Fraser. But my brother never took drugs. Ever. And last year there was another man, Martin Engel, found dead in a graveyard. She thrust the notebook back into his hand. 'I need you to tell me I'm not mad,' she begged. 'Please? You used to be a policeman. Can you help me?'

4

A YEAR EARLIER

For an entire month, Konrad had followed Martin Engel, staying at a sufficient distance to avoid detection, but close enough to listen in on conversations, observing him as he carried on his daily life.

He worked in a large clothes shop, so starting a conversation with him was easy. Cringing at the banality of it, he'd enquired about a shirt in his size.

Martin laid out a variety of styles on the counter – all hideous. 'Why not try on these two?' he'd suggested. 'But I think the blue might suit you best.'

He'd thanked him. They'd even exchanged a look, a flirtatious glance some might call it, and as the blue shirt passed between them their fingers brushed against each other, but he'd quickly pulled away. Too clichéd? However, it seemed to Martin's liking.

Choosing a victim took time. He didn't like the loud ones – the boys with sparkly tops who hollered their lungs out for attention, nor the shady ones, with baseball caps lowered over their eyes. He preferred the ones others might not notice at first, who only on closer inspection revealed their true qualities. Those ones were perfect; the hidden beauties.

The Look of Death

He would then research each candidate thoroughly. Name, age, address, occupation, friends, family, lovers, routine, what buses or trams he took, whether he caught the S-Bahn or U-Bahn, which areas of Berlin he frequented, the parks, the cruising spots. It would all be compiled in his head – a mental map of their life.

Most would fail at this point – he'd identify a flaw which would unravel the attraction. But occasionally one would meet his approval. Then the real work began.

On his first official meeting with Martin at the *Wu-Wu* club, pulsing lights encircled the dancers, bodies crushing against each other, swaying to the music. As Donna Summer breathlessly sang, high-octane screeches mimicked her vocals, and faces leaned into each other, the simple lyrics meaningless and meaningful all at once. As expected, Martin was alone, dancing as though no one else mattered. However, as he was about to approach him, give his usual chat-up line of 'Have we met before?', two young guys grabbed his arm and began dancing with him.

Retreating to the edge of the dance floor, he remained staring, until one of his dancing partners nudged Martin and pointed towards him. Before he could leave, there was a split second of recognition, then Martin stumbled drunkenly towards him, arms swinging, finger stabbing him in the chest. 'Two-shirts man.'

'You've got the wrong guy. Sorry.' He went to leave.

But Martin pulled him back. 'I'd recognise you anywhere. Come dance.'

As Martin's friends looked on, he considered what to do. They'd seen his face and could potentially identify him. But it was dark, they were drunk.

'Lose those two and I'll think about it.'

He'd fucked him twice that night in his dreary, little apartment. Through dry, thin lips, he'd mumbled, 'Two-shirts man' before finally crashing out. Certain Martin was asleep, he leaned forward. 'Actually, my name's Konrad Hausmann.'

For hours he watched while Martin slept – his thin chest rising and falling, the regular beat of his heart just visible below smooth skin. What he'd liked most about researching his life was how ordinary it was; he worked in a department store, wanted to be a social worker, coached kids gymnastics at the weekend. And usefully, how little he had to do with his family, who lived in Stuttgart. His looks weren't perfect; but the hint of youthfulness and a sensuality to his lips were enough for now.

The next morning he'd made an excuse about popping to the shops to buy him breakfast, stolen Martin's house keys and got a duplicate set made. A few nights later, as darkness descended, he'd broken into his apartment. It was hot – still twenty degrees. As Martin's cat slinked towards him, curling herself around his leg, he crouched to lift her up, then shut her in the living room.

Opening the bedroom door, the first thing he noticed was the moonlight streaming in through the window. Filling the room with light, it illuminated the bed, where the shape of two bodies lay. Of course, they hadn't discussed being exclusive to each other, but it had surprised him, nonetheless. When he drew closer, he could make out the face of one of the young guys from *Wu-Wu*.

Having to kill a second person was not part of the plan.

He'd wanted to lie beside Martin, feel his breath against his face, get as close to him as humanly possible without touching him. He'd gone through in his head the surprise and confusion on his face, wondering if they'd gone to sleep together. Him lying, saying yes, to go back to sleep, Martin disbelieving, asking him questions he couldn't answer. But with another person to deal with, he couldn't risk it.

The Look of Death

For now, he let Martin sleep and crept from the house.

5

The door to Martin's apartment was open before Konrad had reached it – he must have been watching at the window, waiting for him like some 50s housewife. It was the same devotion he demonstrated by always preparing one of his favourite meals – last night it had been spicy chicken kebabs with a yogurt and mint dressing. He'd even offered to wash his clothes and iron them. Did he crave domestic bliss that much?

As Martin emerged, patting his jacket pockets, he stumbled over his words. 'My keys! I can't find them. Come help me.' He darted back inside.

Konrad followed him in. There was a faint smell of cooking – a tomato sauce perhaps, garlic for sure. The kitchen window was steamed up and a large pan sat on the stove. Pasta. 'Smells good.' He picked up a string of leftover spaghetti and let it slither into his mouth. 'Tastes even better.'

'You know I always leave them in the fruit bowl on the kitchen table,' Martin said, pulling open a drawer and rummaging through it.

'Could they have fallen from out your pocket? Have you checked the bedroom?'

The Look of Death

He watched Martin race to the back of the apartment, past the cat fast asleep beneath a radiator. Rather than pursue him, he paused to rub Heidi's ears. She yawned and purred gently, sliding onto her side to let him stroke her soft belly fur. 'She's taken to me,' he said, but Martin was out of earshot. 'That's right,' he whispered to the cat. 'Not a sound. Hear?'

By the time he entered the bedroom, Martin was already searching under the bed, sweeping his hand back and forth, sending dust flying into the air. 'Here, let me. I've longer arms.' Konrad pushed his arm further under the bed and felt along the carpet. 'Nothing.'

'And you didn't see them when you left this morning?' Martin was frantically scanning the room.

He had. But he wouldn't tell him that. Knowing Martin intended to spend the day at home to clean and tidy the apartment, he'd taken the keys with him and thrown them into the Spree. 'Babe, maybe it's a sign. Why don't we stay in tonight?'

Martin slammed the drawer of the bedside cabinet shut. As evening sunlight streamed though the bedroom window, the freckles on his face were highlighted, making him look like a teenage boy. 'But you're supposed to be meeting my pals. All they've been asking about is Konrad this, Konrad that. Vincent especially – he says you sound hot.'

'I know… but…' He tilted his head and looked down, copying a gesture he'd seen an actor adopt in a film.

A flicker of understanding crossed Martin's face and he wrapped his arms around him. 'Want me all to yourself? That it?'

The sickly-sweet smell of his skin filled his nostrils, but Konrad forced himself to kiss his lips. 'Who can blame me?'

'I suppose.' Martin met his eyes. 'And there's always Frank's party, next week.'

'You don't mind? I've had a stressful day at work. And you know I'm not trying to avoid them?'

'I didn't say you were.' Martin squeezed his shoulders. 'But you shouldn't worry. No one will give a shit.'

He'd made up a story about a divorce, kids and it being too soon to come out, which Martin had bought hook, line and sinker. 'You're right. But the party next week seems a better option. Less stress.' He pulled Martin onto the bed and placed his hand on his upper thigh. His legs were strong from the gymnastics he'd done growing up and Konrad enjoyed pressing against the tensed muscle. 'Tonight, I'd rather snuggle up with you and watch a movie.'

Martin lay back on the bed and sighed. 'They're going to love you.'

'Of course they are. What's not to love?' he said, dragging Martin on top of him.

6

In the moonlight, Konrad watched the minutes tick by on the bedside clock. After an hour, Martin would be in a deep enough sleep, so that when he woke him, he'd be slightly groggy, a bit disorientated. He wasn't interested in seeing his fear; there was no thrill in that. But he was keen to see his expression change as the soothing caress that had helped him fall asleep, became something else: something jagged, abrupt, far from normal.

Counting down the final seconds, Konrad gripped the smooth skin of Martin's inner arm with his thumb and forefinger and dug his nails in deep. Martin woke with a start. Before a cry escaped his throat, with one clean movement, Konrad straddled him and placed the pillow across his face. At first, there was no struggle, a dull questioning perhaps. *Is this a dream? A game?* Only when he pressed harder, held the pillow more insistently, did the resistance begin.

For the briefest second, Konrad lifted the pillow from his face. No time for words or even a scream, just long enough for a gulp of air and for him to register who was doing this before forcing it down again. This time, the struggle intensified.

He lifted the pillow again: Martin's face was crimson, his eyes bulging. The gasp came from deep within his lungs, the arms and legs flailing out in desperation as their strength waned. Once again, he ground the pillow into his face; he wouldn't lift it until he was sure Martin had passed out. He repeated the action again and again, holding the pillow longer and longer, plunging it down each time he showed signs of reviving. Having invested so much, he was determined to have his pleasure – to keep Martin teetering on the edge for as long as possible.

The sudden ringing of the telephone interrupted the silence, and Konrad's body stiffened. It felt as if someone had entered the apartment and caught him in the act. On and on the rings shrieked, reverberating along the hallway and into the bedroom, until the soft mutterings of a message being left could be heard. Jumping off the bed, Konrad moved out to the hallway. The light on the answerphone was flashing, and he pressed play.

'We're bringing the party to yours. Just leaving the bar. Can't wait to meet your man.' Squeals of drunken laughter ended the message.

Heart racing, Konrad ran to fetch the wheelchair hidden in his car. Returning to the bedroom, he tripped over the rug, narrowly missing Martin's arm, as the edge of the mattress broke his fall. Heidi hissed, and he shoved her and the bedding aside. Dragging him into the wheelchair, he pulled a hat over his ears and hid Martin's bloodshot eyes behind a pair of dark glasses. Before wheeling him to the lift, he washed the wine glasses they'd used earlier that evening, placed them back in the cupboard and wiped the surfaces he'd touched.

He looked at his watch. Just after midnight.

In the corridor and downstairs in the lobby, all was still silent. Perhaps Martin's friends had changed their minds, and gone straight to the club instead. He hoped so. Pushing open the front door, the street was pitch black, and the air humid and heavy with the scent of honeysuckle. As he pushed the wheelchair towards the shadowed corner where he'd parked earlier, he stopped for a moment and filled his lungs with the warm air. How wonderful it felt to be alive.

Behind him a squeal of laughter erupted and he glanced over to see a group of five men, dressed to go clubbing, turn the corner. With some difficulty he continued to manoeuvre the unconscious Martin into the back seat of his car, hoping they wouldn't notice. With one almighty shove, he finally collapsed onto the seat and Konrad threw a blanket over him.

'Need any help?'

Konrad recognised the British accent from the voice who had left the message. He banged the backseat door shut and stood in front of it. 'I'm fine.' Wiping his sweaty hands against his jeans, he held one up to prevent the guy moving forward, but the voice was insistent. This must be Vincent, the guy from Devon, whom Martin referred to as Van Gogh, due to the striking likeness.

'Let me help you with the wheelchair. These old ones are a pain.'

'It's my grandmother's,' Konrad explained, glancing over his shoulder. 'She's

exhausted, poor thing.' To ensure Vincent came no closer, he steered the wheelchair towards him. 'It's kind of you to help.'

The others had hurried over to the door of the apartment and were pressing the button of the intercom, calling Martin's name at the same time.

'My mum's been in a wheelchair since I was a kid,' Vincent explained, 'so I'm a dab hand.' Sure enough, with ease, he collapsed the chair and handed it back to him. 'Would you lot be quiet?' he shouted towards his friends. 'You'll wake the dead.'

'Thank you.'

'No problem. Any time.'

Aware Vincent was still lingering, Konrad hurriedly shoved the wheelchair in the boot.

He slipped into the driver's door and closed the door. Just as he was putting on his seatbelt, Vincent came round to his side of the car and tapped on the window. He could ignore it and drive off, but this might attract attention. Konrad unwound the window a little and Vincent leaned towards him; his breath smelt of stale beer and cigarettes.

'Was there something else?' asked Konrad. If necessary, he could step outside the car, concoct another lie, suggest he'd left something back in his apartment. Anything to divert Vincent's prying eyes away from Martin's half-dead body lying under a blanket on the back seat.

Vincent held up a hat. 'You dropped this,' he said, passing it through the window. 'Stay safe.' With a casual wave, he dashed back over to his friends, who were still pressing at the intercom, loudly shouting Martin's name.

As HE DROVE, Konrad wound down the window, filling his lungs with the cool, night air. Each intake gave him a flashback to Martin struggling to stay alive. It was the desperate noises that he remembered: the gasps, the gurgling, and the whistles of breath that slowly ebbed away. He had to savour the memories while they were still real, visceral, because he knew they'd quickly fade.

Continuing through the deserted streets, he became aware of an ache and he glanced at his wrist to see a bruise forming where Martin had held onto him tightly. He rubbed at it, and then realised there was one on his other wrist, too. Taking his eyes off the road, he lifted both hands and stared at the red marks. Martin had been stronger than he imagined, fought longer than he'd expected. If he hadn't pushed more aggressively, perhaps he'd have been overpowered himself.

The Look of Death

A blaring horn forced him to look up. Somehow, he'd steered over to the other side of the road, and quickly swerved to avoid an oncoming car. In a split second, his life could have been extinguished. Pulling over to the side of the road, he switched on the radio and caught the last few minutes of Debussy's *Clare de Lune*. *Stay calm*, he told himself. *This will be over with soon.*

Sophien Kirche Cemetery lay on the north edge of Mitte, in the old East, where remnants of the Wall still loomed over the rambling graveyard. Turning into Bergstrasse, Konrad stopped at a side entrance to the cemetery where a rusted gate hung from its hinges. There were no streetlights. To his left, an abandoned tenement was cloaked in darkness; ahead lay no-man's-land and the ragged void once occupied by the Wall.

He brought the wheelchair round to the passenger side and hauled Martin onto its seat, neatly arranging his arms and legs. Sweating, he stood back and paused for breath. In this lost, forgotten part of the city there'd be no passers-by, but pushing the wheelchair towards its final destination, he knew a shadow would be watching. The rustle of leaves, footsteps in the distance which abruptly stopped; in recent months, the shadow had been following him wherever he went.

His chosen spot – a clearing in the trees – wasn't far. The wheels squeaked as he rolled Martin from the gravel path onto the dewy grass. Around them, like dolls' houses, ivy-clad tombs with little pitched roofs occupied the spaces between the twisted tree trunks. He dragged Martin from the chair and laid him out on a raised, rectangular gravestone.

As a cloud passed slowly overhead, moonlight kissed Martin's skin, which for a second shone like silver. He held the body with care as he bent Martin's arm at the elbow, arranging his fingers delicately to the side of his neck so that he barely touched himself. He stretched his right arm out and downwards, allowing Martin's fingertips to trail the ground in a fey, melodramatic gesture. Discarding the hat and glasses, he smoothed his hair and closed his eyelids. He then tilted his chin slightly to the left, correcting the angle several times, ensuring it appeared as he wanted. He'd come too far to let one wrong detail spoil the effect.

Martin's flawless skin, even paler than before, glistened. A rush of excitement electrified him as he pressed his lips against his, which were cool and dry. Pulling away, he searched Martin's face for any flicker of movement. None. He then kissed him for a second time. As he locked their lips hard together, he transferred his breath into Martin's mouth.

Breathe. Breathe.

By now, there was little life left. He felt his heart pumping faster, knowing only that *his* intervention could save Martin now and bring him back.

Breathe. Breathe. Goddamnit!

He wasn't sure how long he tried. But as he sat on the ground, exhausted, there was one last thing he could attempt. From the back pocket of the wheelchair, he retrieved a rose he'd taken from the park earlier that day and wrapped in tissue to preserve it. It was yellow. He could have chosen red or pink but yellow seemed right for Martin. He plucked a thorn from its stem, then with one clean movement, pricked his thumb; a black dome of blood seeped from it.

Useless; Martin was gone.

As he scattered petals around the body, the wind picked up and blew them away. Intent on a rose remaining close to Martin, he placed the stem in a crevice at the front of the monument and stepped back.

It was now four a.m. Surveying the corpse for the final time, the skin seemed grey not silver, the casual clothes he'd quickly put on him, completely wrong. Even the patch of

The Look of Death

grass now appeared dry and unkempt. He'd gone to all this trouble – and for what?

He quickly folded the wheelchair and walked to his car.

Before leaving the cemetery, he heard footsteps emerge from the bushes and crunch along the gravel, heading towards the body. He grinned at the audacity. But as ever, he wouldn't look back.

If he were to, it would only give his shadow the satisfaction of acknowledgement. And there was no chance of him ever doing that.

7

THE FOLLOWING SUMMER - SATURDAY, 2ND JULY 1994

Colin listened to Bela's heavy snoring. Lately, he'd been coming over twice a week and not simply for sex; they'd been for Sunday brunch, visited a couple of museums together, normal boyfriend stuff, despite neither of them ever using the term. He appreciated how Bela was keen to show him parts of the city that he wouldn't otherwise see; only last weekend he'd taken him out to Wannsee, to the nudist beach. Without a second thought, he'd immediately stripped off, which had emboldened Colin to do the same.

Lately however, they'd fallen into a comfortable pattern: Wednesdays and Fridays, TV on the former, sex on the latter. But he questioned how much they ever listened to each other. Conversations at times seemed one-sided – they shared few interests and certain things had begun to irritate him. Nothing major, but Colin noticed if he ever expressed an opinion, Bela would challenge it immediately, then spout his own.

Perhaps his uneasiness was due to the unresolved feelings he had around the breakup with Lee. At one time, they'd been as close as two people could be. But circumstances had

The Look of Death

made them drift apart, and in the end, when things got rough, neither had fought to stay together.

Whatever his doubts about Bela, perhaps he needed to try harder.

Colin reached over and ran a finger along Bela's spine. His skin was soft and warm, and he moved closer to breathe in his aroma – soapy, with a hint of citrus. As he placed tiny kisses against his shoulder, Bela shifted to the edge of the bed.

'What's wrong?' Colin asked.

'Go back to sleep.' Bela got up and Colin's eyes followed the shape of his slender frame as he left the room and crossed the hall to the shared toilet.

'Are you staying?' Colin called out, but there was no response and he lay back on the pillow, wondering if Bela had heard.

He returned a few moments later and began pulling on his jeans in the dark. 'Have

you seen my socks?'

'That's a no, I take it?'

'I'd tell you if I was staying the full night.'

Colin listened as Bela struggled to find his clothes. 'Want me to put the light on?'

'Sure.'

Colin switched on the bedside lamp. 'You don't have to tell me every time you want to stay over. If you ever feel like it, I won't mind.'

Bela, half-dressed, was darting around the room picking up his socks and trainers, cursing at one point when he hit his toe against the drawers. He sat on the bed chewing his lip. Eventually, he drew nearer. 'Can I ask you something?' He gently coiled his fingers around Colin's hair.

He smiled and leaned into Bela's caress. Whatever their differences, moments like this felt good. *If only it felt like this a little more*, he thought, but then chided himself for expecting too much. 'Ask away.'

'Where did you get that?' Bela nodded over Colin's shoulder towards the bedside table.

Colin looked round: Rhona's notebook. He picked it up and flicked through it. 'Just something someone gave me. It's not important.' The truth was he hadn't yet gone through it in any detail, so couldn't be exactly sure of all its contents. 'Why are you asking?'

Bela rescued his T-shirt from the floor and pulled it over his head. 'Aren't police officers supposed to be more curious? Even ex ones.'

They'd rarely discussed his previous job; once on the first night, when they'd got back to his place, then a couple of offhand remarks from Bela about the police being homophobic thugs. At least this was a topic they didn't disagree on. 'I've not had time.'

Bela took the notebook from Colin. 'There's some interesting stuff in here: names, theories about recent deaths in the city, police ineptitude.'

'So, that's what you were up to while I was in the kitchen making dinner? Rifling through my things?'

'Your room has a trapeze in it and not a single book. I was bored.'

Colin looked up at the trapeze hanging from the barrel-vaulted ceiling. Installed by the room's previous occupant – an Italian acrobat – it was another quirk of this converted hat factory, which, on his floor, had been split into ten separate rooms sharing a kitchen and two bathrooms. He wasn't even sure if every room was occupied and would struggle to identify all his flatmates if asked to.

Bela slipped on his trainers. 'I should have asked. Sorry.' He picked up his leather satchel. 'Next Wednesday evening, as usual? Seven? You'll make your curry?'

'Wait.' Colin got out of bed. 'If you can stay for five more minutes, I'll even make the special daal you love. I don't

The Look of Death

mind that you read it. In fact, I'd be keen to hear your thoughts.'

Bela dropped his satchel, sat on the edge of the bed and picked up the notebook. 'Who gave you it?' he asked, studying it closely.

'A friend.' Colin was hesitant to say more as he'd promised Rhona he'd be discreet, but Bela knew the city inside out, so could possibly help him. 'Since her brother died in Berlin five years ago, she's identified the deaths of several other gay men who've died, in what she believes, are suspicious circumstances. So far, her attempts to get the police to review her brother's death have got nowhere. 'Young men die all the time,' she's been told.'

'Typical,' Bela said. He opened at a page and pointed to a name which had been circled. 'Martin Engel was an acquaintance of a friend of mine.'

'Honestly?' Colin peered at Rhona's scribbled comment: *Similar to Stefan Reis?*

'I only met him once. He worked in a department store.' Bela screwed up his face. 'Not my type. Too...' he searched about for the right word, '...needy.'

Colin ignored the uncalled-for remark. 'Was there anything suspicious about his death?'

'My friend Kim thought so.'

He'd heard Bela speak about Kim before, one of the few people he looked up to and one of the few friends he ever mentioned. She ran a queer youth group in Kreuzberg which Bela had attended when he was younger, then helped run before being asked to leave. He never spoke about the reasons why. Colin picked up a pen. 'Go on.'

'Kim thought the idea of Martin dropping dead for no reason was absurd; he was fit, in the prime of his life. She also thought it unusual for him to be out late in such a secluded part of town. Why would he go there? And the suggestion he'd been cruising was ridiculous – the place he was found is not a cruising area.' Bela flicked through the notebook again. 'Though your friend's information is a bit patchy.'

'I'm not even sure there's enough to start investigating.'

Bela closed over the notebook and handed it back to Colin. 'If you like, I'll show you where Martin was found. I finish work early, so why don't I cycle over to Sophien Kirche Cemetery at lunchtime?'

'Honestly, there's no need.'

'But you need to go to the crime scene.' Bela looked Colin up and down. 'That's what policemen do, no? Be curious, investigate stuff, catch the baddies.'

Colin followed Bela to the door. 'I promised myself I'd look for another job today and I don't want to put you to any trouble.'

'Why would it be any trouble? I'm your boyfriend, right?'

Colin kissed Bela on the cheek and felt him bristle slightly; he realised he should have kissed him on the lips, but the mention of the word *boyfriend* had caught him off-guard.

Stepping into the hall, Bela swung round. 'I've told you before that during sex I don't like my left nipple being sucked. My right one, yes, but never my left.' He then strode off along the hallway and out the front door. 'One o'clock,' he shouted back. 'Don't be late.'

8

Colin took the S-Bahn to Berlin Nordbanhof before walking east to the gates of the Sophien Kirche Cemetery on Invalidenstrasse. Though the distance was short, his T-shirt quickly became stuck to his skin from the heat. During the morning, the sun had intensified and there was now no escaping its ferocity. Even in the shade, beneath the trees, it felt unbearable, the hottest day of the year so far. He was tempted to turn back, go to the Tiergarten and spend the afternoon sunbathing.

His bike neatly chained to a lamp-post, Bela was already at the entrance, leaning against a wall, engrossed in his book. No shorts and T-shirt for him; wearing his usual dark, work suit and a buttoned-up shirt, he made no concession to the sudden heatwave. It wasn't until Colin was standing beside him that he glanced up and tucked the book into his satchel.

'Sorry.' Colin ensured this time he kissed him on the lips. 'You haven't been waiting long?'

Bela pointed at his watch. 'We agreed one o'clock.'

Getting there hadn't been easy – there'd been a signalling failure on the S-Bahn which had caused delays. 'I'm only fifteen minutes late.' He wiped the sweat from his forehead. 'It's not a disaster.'

From his satchel Bela produced a bottle of water. 'Here. You look like you're about to pass out.'

'You're a lifesaver.' Colin took the water and guzzled half of it. 'Shall we?' He replaced the cap and handed it back.

Surrounded by graffiti-scrawled walls and with tall trees forming a dense, canopy overhead, inside the cemetery was immediately cooler. The traffic noise receded to a low hum, with the brittle sound of birdsong suddenly audible above it.

Bela stepped off the main gravel path and led Colin on a meandering, nettle-lined route past ornate gravestones and elaborate family tombs. Many were in obvious states of disrepair; however, some had survived the tribulations of the twentieth century unscathed, boldly proclaiming the importance of those buried below, long after they'd been forgotten. Colin could happily have spent hours exploring the grounds. 'This is some place.' He paused at a particularly impressive mausoleum framed by ivy-clad, fluted columns and topped with a sculpted pediment. Carved in crisp gothic script, the inscription read:

Ferdinand Kollo 1878-1940
Ich bin alt genug, um Ruhe zu wünschen

'What does it mean?' Colin asked.

'I'm old enough to wish for quiet; it's a quote from Goethe,' Bela explained, racing ahead. 'Here it is,' he shouted back, signalling wildly. 'I've found the spot.'

It was unlike Bela to get so animated. On their trips together, he'd usually focus on the detail and offer endless social and historical context in a low monotone. Once, they'd spent an entire afternoon at the Pergamon Museum, where Bela insisted on explaining the significance of almost every artefact to Colin, who had eventually given up and waited on

The Look of Death

a bench beside the exit until he finished. He wasn't sure if Bela had even noticed his absence. But today he was like a deer springing through the shrubbery, desperate for Colin to follow.

When he caught up, Bela was standing in front of a large family tomb. Enclosed on three sides by decorative stone walls about eight feet high, the paved area within was separated from the impending jungle of weeds by a low wrought-iron fence. Inside, four individual box tombs with slab tops faced the sky, their inscriptions charting a family's history from 1799 to 1880.

'This is where they found Martin Engel last summer.' Bela was out of breath and Colin noticed he'd unbuttoned his collar.

Before he could question him, Bela had hopped over the fence and up onto one of the gravestones, where he remained standing like some renegade statue. Colin was taken aback; he'd been brought up to respect the dead, to keep to the pathways and never step on a grave. 'Bela!'

'What?'

'Show some respect.'

Bela stared at him in disbelief, then jumped down before sauntering off to look at a nearby gravestone, muttering about Colin being an uptight Catholic. Adopting the air of an inspector come to check on the cemetery upkeep, he rubbed dirt from its face and translated the inscription. '*Rest in perpetual peace*,' he shouted over. 'How original!'

'It's just an expression,' Colin said, joining him. He was immediately taken by the elaborate carvings. 'There's comfort in it.'

'They're long dead. Who cares?'

As Bela walked off into the dappled shadows to explore further, kicking his feet through the ivy, Colin returned to the spot where Martin Engel had been found. He removed the lens cap from his camera and began to shoot. Almost a year had passed, so any possible clues would be long gone. A bunch of dried-up leaves had gathered in the corners, but apart from that, there was nothing of note. But as he looked closer, at the front corner, wedged into a crack where the low fence met the stone wall, he spotted the cut stem of a flower and wondered who might have left it there, given the date of the last burial. He pulled it out to reveal a rose. Its petals had long withered, but as he rolled the stem between his fingers, one of the thorns pricked his thumb. 'Ouch!' Blood beaded at his fingertip and he sucked on it to stop the bleeding.

He looked around, pulling his T-shirt away from his sides. Even here, in the depths of the graveyard, the heat was beginning to penetrate.

'Colin! Colin!' The explosion of Bela's voice echoed through the trees, sending a flurry of birds into the sky. 'Colin!' he repeated, his voice now much louder, more alarmed.

Running towards his cries, Colin shouted: 'I'm coming.'

Bela's outline appeared in the distance, standing outside another monumental mausoleum. Within seconds, he was beside him. This marble tomb was obviously the resting place of a very wealthy family; it resembled a small pavilion or garden folly, with an intricately domed roof and stained-glass windows.

With a trembling hand, Bela pointed towards the doorway. 'Look inside.'

Making his way up the steps, Colin pushed the heavy bronze door wide open and stepped inside. Initially, he could see nothing. But as his eyes adjusted to the dim light, a shape emerged from the gloom. On a central dais, the body of a young man lay peacefully, as though asleep: eyes closed, head tilted, right hand touching his neck, left arm trailing the ground.

Colin placed his hand on the man's arm and recoiled at the coldness of his skin. The body was stiff, and was already turning blue, which probably meant he'd been dead for at least eight hours.

'I think it's another gay man,' Bela said. 'The T-shirt he's wearing is from a club night at *Wu-Wu's*. I recognised it immediately.'

9

While Bela ran to call the police, Colin remained in the cemetery. There was a threat of thunder as the sky clouded over and mottled rays of sun alternated with sudden shadows.

Scanning the ground outside for anything suspicious, he could see no footprints and nothing to suggest a body had been dragged there. He peered inside the tomb and inspected the interior, but there were no obvious signs of disturbance or violence.

Colin considered the body. In his T-shirt and distressed jeans, he resembled any guy you might see in a gay bar or club. As he watched, shadows played across the young man's face. Moving closer, there were traces of white froth around his mouth and a red scratch on his arm, possibly a puncture mark from a needle, yet no sign of drug paraphernalia.

He was about to check for other track marks when he heard movement and hurried back outside. Bela appeared through the undergrowth, pointing in Colin's direction, pursued by two police officers.

Instructed to stand aside, the sudden flurry of officers and an ambulance crew cut across the tranquillity of the cemetery;

The Look of Death

voices now chatted through radios, equipment was unloaded and set up, tape wound around trees.

He and Bela were quickly separated; Bela was escorted in the direction of the entrance by a short, dark-haired officer, whilst a tall, red-faced officer approached Colin.

'Hello, I'm Sergeant Deichmann.' He spoke English with an unusual accent – American with a hint of German. 'Sir, this way, please.' He pointed to a corner of the cemetery away from the emergency teams.

Colin, a few steps behind, followed him along a path to a shaded area beneath a large oak tree. He looked up through the layers of green, squinting as the sun blinded him.

'Are you OK?' Sgt. Deichmann asked. He met Colin's gaze with cold, blue eyes. They sparkled momentarily in the sunlight, their peculiar brightness disappearing altogether as he looked down; like a switch had been turned off.

'A bit shocked, that's all.'

'Do you need to sit? Can I get you some water?'

Colin shook his head.

Sgt. Deichmann took out a notepad and the small stub of a pencil. 'Sir, I need your name, address and occupation.'

As Colin gave him his details, he wondered if they'd met before. From that first glance, it felt as though they had; the shape of his eyes seemed familiar, or was it his profile he'd seen before? He couldn't work it out.

The crackle of a voice came through on his radio. 'One second.' Sgt. Deichmann moved one step away from him, shifting his body sideways. His broad frame fitted tightly into his tailored, blue uniform – a bit more aesthetically pleasing than the polyester outfit Colin wore when he worked for the Met.

Although his German was basic, Colin understood him explain that he was currently speaking with one of the men who'd found the body and was due to finish his shift. Ending the conversation with a clipped '*Tschüss*'.

As Sgt. Deichmann removed his cap to flatten a stray curl of blond hair he moved closer; he looked even more familiar and smelled earthy. 'Sir, I've more questions, but can I ask you to speak a little slower? My English isn't that great.'

'It's a million times better than my German,' Colin replied, aware that people sometimes found his Scottish accent hard to follow.

'My colleague tells me the man you were with arrived at the cemetery before you – is that correct?'

Colin nodded. 'Yes. He was waiting at the entrance on Invalidenstrasse.'

'Do you know for how long?'

'We arranged to meet at one after he finished work. Perhaps he was here a bit earlier. I'm not sure.' Sgt. Deichmann waited for a more exact answer. When none came, he scribbled a few words on his notepad.

'And the body – you've never seen this man before?'

Colin recognised Sgt. Deichmann's interview technique: alternate between probing and mundane questions, use an even tone to disguise your main line of enquiry, be aware of body language and intonation, and note anything significant.

'Have you?' Sgt. Deichmann repeated.

Colin gazed over at Bela who was deep in conversation with the other police officer. From his body language – leaning over the notepad, pointing at it, shaking his head and making the officer cross out and rewrite – he could see how detailed he was being. 'No. I didn't recognise him.'

Sgt. Deichmann closed over his notepad and tucked it away. 'Sir, I need you to provide a formal statement. Are you happy to accompany me to the police station?'

'Sure.' In fact, Colin wasn't keen, but he knew it was standard procedure. He didn't relish having to explain why he and Bela were in the cemetery in the first place; if there were suspicions over the manner of the man's death, their reason for being there would implicate them both.

The Look of Death

'This way.' He ushered Colin onto the main path. Halfway along, he twisted round to face him. 'Tell me, you didn't notice anyone acting strangely?'

'No. There was no one else around. Just us.' With the highly polished buttons of his uniform flashing in the sunlight, Colin had a gut feeling that Sgt. Deichmann wasn't the type to leave any stone unturned. Every detail would be scrutinised until he was satisfied. But, he rationalised, all he needed to do was tell the truth. It wasn't as if he'd killed anyone.

10

The police station at Hardenbergplatz was far larger than the one he'd worked out of in London. An oppressive 1930s building with a blank façade punctuated by rows of identical square windows, inside it was teeming with officers. Unlike the Metropolitan Police in London, the atmosphere was focused and formal – almost military; there was no jokey banter going on between officers. However, the usual suspects still lined the corridors: drunks, petty criminals, confused-looking tourists. For the first time in a while, Colin felt a pang of regret that he was no longer in the force.

Sgt. Deichmann told him to sit on a wooden bench in front of reception while he checked on the availability of an interview room. There was no sign of Bela. *God help anyone who is guilty*, he thought. He pitied the criminals he'd dealt with in the past, with their improbable alibis and idiotic deflections. He calmed himself, knowing he'd nothing to hide. Keep it simple. Tell the truth. He could do that.

Five minutes later, escorted by the same dark-haired policeman as before, Bela appeared from a side corridor and acknowledged Colin with a slight nod, before being taken through a pair of double-doors.

The Look of Death

Sgt. Deichmann reappeared through the same double doors holding a clipboard and joined Colin on the bench.

'Sir, I've checked your details on the system, and everything's in order.' He fixed his gaze on Colin again. 'I'll take you through to the interview room now if you're ready?'

Colin knew it was best to get this over and done with. 'Lead the way.'

As Sgt. Deichmann stood, he appeared far taller than he had in the cemetery. 'I'll write out your statement,' he explained, directing Colin along the corridor. 'You can then read it through and, if you're comfortable with everything, we'll get it typed up and you can sign it. It shouldn't take long. After that, I can arrange for a car to take you home.'

'There's no need. I can take the U-Bahn.'

'A car is easier. Prinzenalle, isn't it?' Sgt. Deichmann asked.

'Yes. The old hat factory.'

'With the café on the ground floor?'

'Yes.'

Sgt. Deichmann's face softened and he smiled, his eyes sparking into life. 'I live close by. My brother and I moved into an apartment on Wollankstrasse, just beyond the railway bridge, about a month ago.'

Colin knew it well. Its streets were still cobbled and marked the point where the Wall had divided working-class Wedding in the West from communist Pankow in the old East. He looked again at Sgt. Deichmann, wondering whether he recognised him from around the neighbourhood. Or perhaps it was his brother he'd seen before. It was possible. 'Nice area,' Colin said, knowing it was far from the truth.

Sgt. Deichmann waved his outstretched hand. 'So-so, I'd say.' He leaned conspiratorially towards Colin and whispered, 'This is the end of my shift. When we finish, I can take you home myself. I'll be driving right past your address.'

Colin inhaled his earthy scent again. 'Honestly, there's no need.'

'It's no problem.' He greeted an approaching colleague with a brief nod and smile, before returning his attention to Colin. 'It's the least I can do.'

The interview room was typically functional – designed to unsettle people. Lit by a single dirt-spattered window, it was decorated in the sparsest manner with two chairs facing each other across a small table.

Sgt. Deichmann held open the door. 'Tea? Coffee?'

Colin declined, preferring the statement to be over and done with as quickly as possible. The room smelled of burgers and sweat, and the worn carpet disappeared into dark, grimy corners.

Sgt. Deichmann sat on the chair opposite with his back to the window. He smoothed the form pinned to his clipboard and picked up a pen. His eyes were cold and piercing again. Unnerving. 'Age?'

'Twenty-seven.'

For some reason, it took him forever to write this down. Didn't he believe him?

'I understand from my colleague you and Bela Feldner are partners. Correct?'

Colin considered how much detail to offer but opted for the simplest version. 'Yes, that's correct.'

'For how long?'

'Two months.'

'And you live together?'

'No, no. It's more casual than that.'

Sgt. Deichmann once again took his time noting this, then, when he'd finished, looked up. 'OK, tell me in your own words, why were you at the cemetery and how did you discover the body?'

The Look of Death

'Bela had walked off alone. He found the body and shouted for me.'

'And why were you there in the first place?'

'Bela wanted to show me where another man's body – Martin Engel – had been found last year.'

The writing stopped. Sgt. Deichmann stared at him. 'Are you serious?'

Colin explained the background, how Rhona McDougal had come to him with her concerns about her brother's death and how Bela had recognised Martin Engel's name.

As Sgt. Deichmann scribbled this down, there was a knock at the door and a young officer popped his head into the room. '*Kaffee?*'

Colin shook his head. Sgt. Deichmann replied in German that he'd like a black coffee with two sugars. After the door was closed, he read through what he'd written, making some revisions. 'Sir, why would this woman, Rhona McDougal, come to you with concerns about the deaths of her brother and Martin Engel?'

'It's a long story, but until recently I was a police officer in London and she thought I might be able to help her.'

Sgt. Deichmann adjusted himself in his seat. 'So, you're conducting an investigation into these men's deaths?'

Colin shook his head. 'I think describing what I'm doing as an investigation is an overstatement.' Sgt. Deichmann stared at him. 'I was curious. That's all.'

'But your friend doesn't think the German police are doing their job?'

Colin averted his gaze. 'It doesn't sound good when you put it like that, but kind of. I don't mean any disrespect. Rhona's still grieving – coming up with theories about her brother – and I suppose I wanted to put her mind at ease. Bela and I, we got carried away.'

'You both carried someone away?'

'No, no.' Colin explained the expression as best he could.

Sgt. Deichmann frowned. 'I understand.' The young officer entered and placed a coffee in front of him; he continued writing without looking up. 'Tell me, do you know if these deaths – Fraser McDougal and Martin Engel – were both fully investigated?'

Colin shrugged. 'Fraser's definitely was. Martin's – I'm not so sure; I don't know that much detail about the circumstances. But the body found today, we think it's another gay man. Is that not suspicious?'

Sgt. Deichmann pushed back his chair, gripped the clipboard and stood up. His broad silhouette filled the window frame. 'I need to discuss this with my superior. Stay where you are; I'll be back soon.'

Alone in the room, Colin checked his watch and stared out the window at a pigeon which was staring back at him. He'd nowhere else to be but was keen not to be kept too long. Bad memories of two years before, sitting at a police station in Inverness, being questioned about the death of one of Hollywood's biggest film stars, was enough interrogation for a lifetime.

'It'll work out,' Lee, his boyfriend at the time, had insisted. 'You were the one who solved the case, after all.'

Even then, Colin hadn't been so sure.

'The Trial of the 90s' the press had called it, and he'd been unlucky enough to find himself its star witness. Outed by the tabloids and immediately labelled *'The Bent Copper'*, his professional and then his personal reputation had been trashed. Even after the trial ended, the headlines had continued to scream *'PC's Sex Scandal'* and worst of all, *'Homo of the Highlands'*.

'Take time off. Let things settle,' his Sergeant had told him, but he was too keen to get back on the beat.

One Friday evening, he'd been getting into his car when a fellow constable, someone he'd worked with and actually quite liked, shouted 'Shirt-lifter!' at him. Cajoled on by a few

The Look of Death

of his mates, he yelled, 'Which pansy club are you off to tonight?'

Seeing red, Colin had punched the guy, sending him sprawling across the car park, and by the time he got into work on Monday, a complaint had been made against him, with several witnesses attesting to the guy's story.

'You brought this on yourself.' The Chief Inspector wouldn't look him in the eye as he listed his apparent violations. 'You're lucky I don't dismiss you here on the spot. Now, get back to work,' he barked. 'This is a huge red mark against your name, Buxton.'

Colin had tried to discuss the matter with Lee. 'I can't face it anymore,' he told him. 'It's coming from all directions, and it's getting worse, not better. The pointed comments, the graffiti on my locker. It's bullying. I need to leave.'

But Lee was having his own professional issues; it had been his production company Lawrence Delaney had been working for at the time of his death. 'You can't quit,' Lee said. 'If you do, they'll have won.'

But that's what he did: he handed in his notice, then a few weeks later, the pressures having become too much, he broke up with Lee, telling him it was for the best. A week after that, he got on a bus to Berlin.

TWENTY MINUTES LATER, Sgt. Deichmann reappeared and handed Colin his statement. 'Sir, read this for me, please,' he instructed.

Colin read through the statement carefully – it was an accurate representation of what had taken place.

'Is it good?' Sgt. Deichmann took a sip of his coffee and grimaced. 'Shall I type this up, then drive you home?'

'If that's everything?'

'Sure. Just to let you know, I've read through the police reports for Martin and Fraser. Both deaths were thoroughly investigated. Five years ago, Fraser McDougal died of a drug overdose and there were no suspicious circumstances. Martin Engel died last year of a cardiac arrest. The two deaths have nothing in common.' A smile flickered across his face, and his eyes lit up again. 'Perhaps you and Mr Feldner need to stop getting carried away, eh?'

11

Following the interview, Colin was led from the room and escorted to Sgt. Deichmann's desk, which occupied the central part of a vast and noisy open-plan office lined with filing cabinets. Colin watched Sgt. Deichmann as he slowly typed up his statement, an unflattering pair of spectacles perched on the end of his nose. His desk was chaotic, piled high with paperwork and squashed Coke cans – there was nothing personal: certainly no photograph of a wife and kids.

A senior officer approached, interrupting his typing to whisper in Sgt. Deichmann's ear. He listened attentively, nodding along to the hushed mutterings. The officer stood up straight, glanced at Colin, then patted Sgt. Deichmann on the back. As his hand lingered, Colin was surprised to feel a twinge of jealousy which only faded when the officer moved away.

'Does the name Walter Baus mean anything to you?' Sgt. Deichmann continued typing and didn't turn to face him.

'No.' This was the truth – whether he was believed was another matter. 'Is that the name of the man we found?'

Sgt. Deichmann didn't reply. Typing with two fingers, it

took another fifteen minutes for him to finish and pass the statement to Colin.

'There are no spelling mistakes?' He removed his glasses and rubbed his eyes, squinting to adjust.

'I don't think so.' Colin read it through a second time, satisfied it was an accurate account. 'Where do I sign?'

Sgt. Deichmann handed him a pen and pointed to the bottom of the page. 'I'll type up a copy, translated into German. You'll need to sign that later, but you'll have an opportunity to check that it's correct.' He took the signed statement from Colin and placed it in a tray. 'I'll be five minutes. Is that OK?'

Colin nodded. 'Should I stay here?'

'Better if you wait at reception.'

TRUE TO HIS WORD, five minutes later, Sgt. Deichmann appeared, running a hand through his thick, blond hair. Having changed out of his uniform, he now wore a pair of tight-fitting blue jeans, a Metallica T-shirt, a tan leather jacket and an enormous pair of red trainers with blue and white stripes. His transformation into an American rocker was so unexpected it left Colin speechless.

'You ready to go?' Sgt. Deichmann checked his reflection in the window.

Colin stood up, his own reflection appearing malnourished by comparison. 'Sure.'

'Want me to check if your friend's still here?'

'Bela lives in the opposite direction.' This wasn't exactly true, but Colin knew he'd get home safely by himself.

'OK. This way.' Sgt. Deichmann opened the door, allowing Colin to step through first. 'While on duty, I couldn't say. My name's Klaus.' He shook Colin's hand, squeezing it firmly.

'Should I guess which car's yours?' Colin asked, pointing towards a red 1970s Mustang with blue and white stripes along each side, which stood out like an aberration in a car park full of grey Opels and Volkswagens.

Klaus glanced at his trainers. 'Trust me, it's a coincidence.'

Colin followed him to the car. It shared the same earthy, leathery scent as Klaus but, unlike his work desk, the interior was gleaming, as though it had been valeted that morning. 'Were you a fan of Starsky & Hutch as a kid?'

Klaus shook his head. 'That was an entirely different model. This is classier; all original features.' He spread his hand across the dashboard. 'Wood-veneer dash, leather seats, a three-spoke steering wheel with the Mustang logo.'

'Impressive.'

'A twenty-first birthday present from my parents.'

'I got a card with twenty quid inside,' Colin quipped.

Klaus turned the ignition and revved up the engine.

'Even if they'd had the money, I don't think my parents would ever have given me such a fancy present,' Colin shouted over the *Iron Maiden* track which was now blasting out the speakers.

Klaus raced through the scorching streets of Berlin as though determined to recreate the chase-scene from *The French Connection*. He smiled at Colin. 'She handles great, no?'

Colin felt compelled to nod in agreement but was mentally preparing to grab the steering-wheel as Klaus accelerated across the path of a tram and a lorry slammed on its brakes to avoid a collision. Oblivious, he beat his hands against the steering wheel, singing along to the English lyrics. 'Your kind of music?' he yelled.

Colin shrugged, perplexed at his growing attraction. With his mid-Atlantic accent, rocker style and crazy driving, Klaus was not his usual type and how they'd met only added to his sense of confusion.

Ten minutes sooner than expected, Klaus ground to a halt on Prinzenallee and switched off the engine. He unbuckled his seatbelt and faced him.

Unsure if Klaus wanted to talk or if this was a signal for him to leave, after a second's silence, Colin supposed it was and put his hand on the door handle. 'Thanks for the lift.'

'You enjoy staying at the factory?' Klaus pointed towards the tiled archway which led from the street, through two vine-clad courtyards, to the furthest block where he lived.

'Yes,' Colin replied. For very little rent he had an enormous room in an amazing building. The downside was the logistical complexity of having so many flatmates and the inevitable arguments about bills and cleaning. But it had its pluses; it was great sharing with his close friend and work colleague, Hannah, and with a constant stream of new faces at the breakfast table, there were always opportunities to meet interesting people and make new friends. For now, it felt like home. 'You know it?'

'I've been to a couple of parties.' He wound down the window, letting in a much-needed breeze. 'Have you stayed there long?'

Colin couldn't read what lay behind the intensity of his stare. 'Since January,' he said. 'My flat's pretty basic, but it's cheap. I'm on the middle floor, right at the back.'

'There's a British girl, Hannah, lives there? Right?'

He nodded. 'She's half-German actually. So, you've been on our floor?'

'No. But friends have spoken about her.' He smiled. 'She's the girl who likes to party?'

'That's Hannah alright. We work together at *Zum Zum* on the corner.'

'Handy.'

'Too handy. It means I don't look for any other work, which I should. The bar pays a pittance.'

Klaus shifted, his jacket squeaking against the thick leather upholstery. His distinctive scent engulfed Colin again. 'I've friends who have an incredible flat on the top corner.

The Look of Death

They've a sauna and a huge bed suspended on ropes from the ceiling which rocks when you're in it.'

Colin waited for Klaus to elaborate, but when he didn't, he went to open the door. 'I should go.'

'Maybe you know them? Bill and Seb? Bill's an amazing artist, makes these crazy abstract installations about blood and viruses. I think it's all to do with AIDS. Totally wild.'

'Sounds interesting.'

'If you're looking for easy money, he organises life models at an art school, the one near the palace at Charlottenburg. Chat to him; he's a friendly guy.'

Colin pushed open the door. 'And he lives above me?'

'Mention my name. Tell him Klaus recommends you.'

Colin edged out the car. 'Thanks.' He desperately needed extra cash to help with the bills. 'Maybe see you around.'

'Sure thing.' Klaus buckled up. 'Stay safe.'

Colin paused on the pavement to wave him off, but the car remained stationary. Instead, Klaus leaned out of the window and grinned. 'Maybe I'll see you on the walls of a gallery sometime? Like I said, it's easy money.'

12

In the rear courtyard, the central linden tree was already in shadow as the evening light receded. Colin had spent many hours sitting there, watching residents come and go, taking in the buzz of this secret hideaway behind the bustling main street.

The first time he'd viewed the factory, with its yellow brick walls and tall, gently arching windows he recognised there was something special about it, and had looked into its history. In the 30s, it had been seized from a Jewish hat manufacturer by the Nazis. Unclaimed in the post-war period, it lay abandoned and had gradually fallen into disrepair before squatters took up residence. They eventually established a cooperative, or *Genossenschaft*. Over time, they developed the spaces, restoring the building, and creating apartments and workspaces. Most embraced the communal way of life, their whole existence centring on the ethos of the building – cooking together, exchanging skills, holding meetings on the building's upkeep – while some were less engaged, preferring to use it as a crash-pad. Most of Colin's flatmates unfortunately fell into the latter category.

He entered the building and climbed the narrow stairwell.

The Look of Death

Rather than casual vandalism, the graffitied walls were more about artistic expression: slogans opposing the plan to restore Berlin as the capital, a multicoloured reproduction of Brezhnev's famous kiss with Honecker, and a stencilled tank, firing flowers from its gun turret. Each week a new image appeared. Much like the city outside, nothing ever stood still in this place.

Colin arrived at the heavy metal door to his apartment and punched the PIN into the keypad. The building had been a target for break-ins in the past and he despaired at the lack of vigilance amongst his flatmates. Closing the door behind him, he walked along the darkening corridor, reflecting on the day's events. The irony wasn't lost on him; the whole purpose of coming to Berlin was to escape the aftermath of Lawrence Delaney's horrific murder. He didn't know if he could cope with that level of upheaval and distress again.

A light was on in the kitchen and voices echoed along the hall. Laughter, too. Had he missed a house meal? Popping his head inside, Hannah sat at the head of the table holding court, surrounded by a slew of familiar and unfamiliar faces. They were all tucking into large plates of pasta and salad and the table was lined with bottles of wine.

'About bloody time,' she said above the noise, urging him to join them. 'Another plate!'

'I'll get it.' The voice was familiar. His bum was pinched from behind as Bela appeared, handing him a bowl and kissing him on the cheek. 'I've just been saying what an exciting day we've had.' He pulled a seat out from the table and patted it. 'Come on, sit, and tell everyone what happened. They're all intrigued.'

COLIN MADE his excuses after he'd finished eating and retreated to his room. Minutes later Bela appeared, jumping on the bed and assuming a cross-legged position. 'Why did you play everything down like that?' he asked. 'They were all keen to hear about our adventure.'

'Finding a dead guy is not my idea of a fun anecdote.' Colin stuffed a pile of clean clothes away in the chest of drawers.

'They were going to find out at some point.'

Colin closed the drawer. 'So, when did the police let you go?'

Bela swept his hand across the duvet to smooth out a crease. 'I was at the station ten minutes at most.'

Picking up his toothbrush, Colin crossed the corridor to the shared bathroom, hoping Bela would take the hint and leave. He was exhausted and needed to process the day on his own.

'If you keep the door open, we can continue talking,' Bela yelled.

'I was there for hours,' Colin said, his mouth foaming with toothpaste.

Bela pushed open the door, crossed to the toilet and began to pee.

'Can't you wait? I'm nearly finished.' Colin spat a mouthful of foam into the sink and rinsed his mouth with water.

'You Brits are so hung up.' He zipped up his flies. 'Two of the deaths listed in your friend Rhona's notebook took place in Ernst-Thälmann Park. Do you know where that is?'

Colin shrugged. 'No idea.'

Bela looked at him perplexed. 'How long have you been in Berlin? It's a cruising area, east of here, named after a communist politician – there's a huge monument to him. I can show you tonight.' Colin stood aside as Bela turned on the hot water tap, soaped his hands, and like a doctor preparing for surgery, washed them meticulously.

'No thanks. I need to sleep.'

'Both were found near the pond,' Bela continued.

'According to the police, one died from natural causes and the other a drug overdose.'

Colin handed Bela a towel. 'When was this?'

He dried his hands. 'Summer 1990. It's all in the notebook. Anyway, your friend's right. Both were found in similar circumstances to Martin and the man today.'

'And how do you know all this?'

'While you were being held at the station, I continued researching.' Bela smiled. 'My friend Kim knows loads.' He strode back across to the bedroom and undressed. 'I phoned the youth centre when I got home to ask her for more information. Turns out she's in contact with someone who knew Stefan Reis, the first man found in Ernst-Thälmann Park. Long before Martin's death last summer, she'd challenged the police about their investigation into Stefan's death. But God, she's so emotional. When I said we'd found another gay man in the cemetery today she burst out crying, so I could only get the basics.' Stripped naked, Bela slipped between the bedcovers. 'Apparently, when Stefan Reis was found dead, it was awful, but perhaps not so unexpected; he had a health condition – diabetes, or something. It was only when a second body appeared ten days later that people started asking questions.'

'Ten days?'

Bela plumped up the pillow behind him. 'Ulrich Steiner was found in almost exactly the same spot. Well, you can imagine, the gay community went crazy. Everyone felt for sure we were being targeted, that there was some crazy killer on the loose who was picking off young gay men. Kim went to the police, of course, shouting and yelling at them – she's such a hothead – but they shrugged her off, told her Ulrich Steiner wasn't gay and had died of a drug overdose. Case closed.'

'So, other than the location, there's no connection?'

'Well, the police might have concluded that Ulrich wasn't

gay, but that's not to say he wasn't having sex with a man. It's not so unusual.'

'Would she be up for chatting?'

'I'll leave you her number.' Bela pulled the duvet up to his chest. 'Are you coming to bed?'

Colin knew and understood police procedures; any connection between multiple deaths would be investigated. And yet, he reminded himself, in London he'd witnessed casual homophobia where complaints made by gay men to the police weren't taken seriously. He remembered the cases of two older gay men whose bodies had been dragged from a canal in the East End of London a year apart. The official explanation was accidental death, but he and others in the gay community had suspected foul play. The idea of something similar happening here wouldn't surprise him. While Colin had found Berlin more tolerant compared to London, it was also home to groups of skinheads and other extremists, and since reunification the crime rate had soared.

Bela yawned. 'All cops are the same. They don't care about us queers.'

Colin wanted to challenge him but stopped. The homophobia he'd received from many of his own colleagues in the force was real: a daily grind of low level psychological abuse which had left him feeling helpless and, at one stage, suicidal. 'Some do,' he replied, but he could tell Bela wasn't listening.

Colin cleared cushions from the sofa and began to make up a bed for himself.

Bela sat up. 'Aren't you coming to bed?'

'I'm going to sleep on the sofa tonight.' He could feel Bela's eyes follow him across the room as he grabbed sheets and a blanket from the cupboard. 'You're restless when you're sleeping, and I need to get up early.' He stripped to his boxer shorts and stretched out on the sofa. 'Sleep well.'

Before he could close his eyes, Bela had jumped out of bed

and bounded towards him, tearing off the blanket and throwing it on the floor. 'Don't act this way!'

Colin sprung up. 'What the hell are you doing?'

'You take me for granted.' Bela's voice shook. 'I've got feelings, you know.' Standing naked before him, Bela extended his hand. 'Please, come to bed. I promise I'll not disturb you.'

Whatever his reservations – and there were many – Bela was right. He couldn't go on treating him so dismissively. Either he had to say something, or try and make things work between them. 'Come here.'

Bela shook his head. 'You can be mean at times.' He returned to the bed and pulled the duvet over him.

Colin got up. Leaning over him, he brushed his lips along Bela's shoulder. 'Shove up,' he said, before getting into bed and wrapping his arms around him. After the day he'd had, perhaps some comfort wouldn't go amiss.

SOAKED IN SWEAT, Colin woke with a gasp. He'd dreamt that his ex, Lee, had come to Berlin, pleading with him to return to London. They'd walked around the city, arguing for hours, eventually climbing to the top of the Fernsehturn in Alexanderplatz. As Colin had insisted once more that he was staying, Lee ran through a door, and out onto a deck which had given way beneath his feet. Colin could only watch in horror as Lee tumbled through the air.

He sat up and gazed at Bela, who, despite his claims to the contrary, was sleeping like a baby. Typical. Fast asleep, with his milky skin and high cheekbones, Bela appeared oddly serene; there was no trace of his usual antagonism. Colin moved closer and attempted to wrap his arm around him, but he stirred and pushed him away.

Debating whether to get a glass of water from the kitchen and read for a little, he decided it would take too much effort.

Instead, he'd stay put and try to get back to sleep. The day had been rough, and the image of the dead body in the graveyard kept returning each time he closed his eyes. The man had seemed so peaceful, yet Colin suspected the end of his life hadn't been. Whatever the circumstances, he couldn't discount it having some connection to the other deaths.

As he lay back, the hallway light was switched on; a blade of silver bleeding under the bottom of his door. Thinking it was probably Hannah, he decided to get up. A late-night chat would be just the thing to help him sleep. But as he began to slip from the bed, the light clicked off and the front door creaked closed.

Closing his eyes again, the image of the man in the cemetery flashed into his head – only this time it was Lee, bloodied and broken. In an attempt to dispel it, he rolled over, but as he did so, his arm was grabbed. Bela, too, was having a nightmare, muttering Colin's name. *Don't do it*, he whispered, his fingernails digging into Colin's flesh.

'Bela,' he said. But instead of responding, Bela rose from the bed and crossed to the door, opened it and stood peering out into the darkness.

'He's gone,' he said, closing the door and then returning to bed. Pulling the duvet around his shoulders, the immediate snores told Colin he was back asleep.

They could chat about it in the morning, but he'd never known Bela to sleepwalk. Then again, as far as he knew, he'd never found a dead body before.

Staring up at the ceiling, Colin was now wide awake. There was no way he'd be getting any more sleep tonight.

PART 2

13

SUNDAY, 3RD JULY 1994

With sunlight streaming through the window, Colin woke at noon to find Bela gone. Before leaving, he appeared to have tidied the room, sorted his shoes into pairs and rearranged the potted plants on the windowsills. How Bela had managed to do this without waking him, he'd no idea.

Pushing the duvet aside, Colin pulled on his jeans and T-shirt, scanning the room for Kim's contact details at the youth centre. Bela had promised to leave them, but after looking in all the obvious places, Colin reckoned he'd forgotten. He would call and ask later. However, there was something he needed to do first.

He had never been up to the top floor before. Instead of the graffiti-strewn walls he was used to, framed artwork and the smell of fresh flowers greeted him, far preferable to the smell of stale beer and grungy decor below. Separated from the lower floors by a heavy metal door, he was surprised to be immediately buzzed in by a sleepy voice without being asked his name.

He'd debated whether to pursue Klaus's suggestion of modelling at the art school, but the state of his bank balance had convinced him. He had less than one hundred Marks till he got paid at the end of the month, so not pursuing it wasn't an option.

A dishevelled man in his thirties – dark stubble, hair standing on end, and a thin dressing-gown barely concealing his ripped torso – greeted him with a yawn. 'Do I know you?' From his accent, Colin reckoned he must be Spanish or South American.

'I live downstairs.'

With a critical eye, the guy assessed him, apparently unafraid of appearing rude. As he was doing this, a man in his early twenties squeezed by. 'Great night, Seb,' he said, and jumped down the stairs two at a time, waving goodbye.

'Next Saturday,' Seb growled. 'Put it in your diary.'

'Will do,' the guy shouted back, the slam of the metal door reverberating up the stairwell.

From deeper within the apartment, Colin became distracted by three or four guys in various states of undress wandering in and out of rooms. 'Sorry. I've caught you at a bad time.'

Another guy appeared – blond, tall, Germanic – and kissed Seb on the lips. He'd an enormous grin on his face, and none of Seb's world weariness. 'Who's this, then?'

Colin offered him his hand. 'I live downstairs. I'm Colin.'

'Hannah's flatmate?'

'Yes.'

He shook Colin's hand vigorously. 'I'm Wilhelm, but people call me Bill. And this is Seb – my partner.'

Seb took his hand, but didn't meet his eye.

'She's mentioned you loads.' Bill explained to Seb that Hannah was the girl who'd scored them ecstasy the week before.

Seb's face broke into a friendly smile. 'The girl from *Zum Zum* who wears those amazing clothes?'

The Look of Death

'Which reminds me, you need to give her back the scarf you took.'

Seb rolled his eyes. 'Have you seen my Rizlas, babe?' he asked.

'In the kitchen.'

Seb wandered back into the apartment.

'Do you want to come in?' Bill asked.

As The Communards' *Don't Leave Me This Way* began blaring down the hallway, Seb reappeared with a cute guy in a pair of white Calvin Klein's, dancing energetically.

'Sorry, I can't stop,' Colin said, mesmerised by Seb's hip thrusts. 'Look, this might sound a bit odd, but I'm here to ask about life-modelling opportunities at the art school. Klaus mentioned you looked after the models.'

'You're a friend of Klaus?' He called back to the others, 'Colin's a friend of KD's.' A loud whoop erupted through the apartment.

'If you're looking for a pasty-skinned Scottish life-model with zero experience, I'm your man.' He hadn't fully worked out whether he was up for the job or not, but the idea of easy cash overcame any insecurities about standing naked in front of a room full of strangers.

Bill resisted Seb's attempts at pulling him inside to dance, pushing his eager hands away. 'Why don't you come to the art school on Tuesday? Say, after twelve? A few summer classes started last week and I'm sure one of the tutors will be able to fit you in.'

'Seriously?'

'You've come at the right time. Loads of the models are students and leave the city during the summer, so we're always on the lookout.'

'Thanks. And sorry for disturbing your Sunday morning.' Colin went to leave, but Bill called him back.

'And if you don't mind posing for private clients, you can

earn double. A lot of these summer students are loaded and willing to pay for extra sessions.'

Without thinking, Colin nodded. 'Sure. Easy money, right?'

Downstairs, the long corridor leading to the kitchen was eerily silent, and Colin assumed his flatmates were still in bed, sleeping off their hangovers. The debris of dirty dishes in the kitchen suggested there'd been no attempt to clear up. Dragging the green recycle bin towards the table, he dropped a few empty cans and bottles into it. He'd been reprimanded several times by Rita for not rinsing them out before placing them in the bin, but life was too short; besides, he was doing Rita and the rest of them a favour.

'Hey.' Hannah entered, hair unkempt, make-up smudged, skimpy kimono style dressing-gown loosely wrapped around her. 'This place is a pigsty.' She sat at the table with a groan. 'You making me a coffee, honey?' Her voice, an octave lower than usual, sounded rough.

'That was some session you had.'

Hannah gazed up at the clock on the wall. 'I've had two hours' sleep.'

Colin filled the espresso maker and placed it on the hob. 'Don't you have work in half an hour?' He placed the last empty bottle in the bin, then dragged it back to its usual spot by the sink.

'Don't remind me.' Hannah lay her head on the table, pushing aside an ashtray full of cigarette butts.

'Sorry.' He opened a drawer, found a packet of paracetamol and handed it to her. 'I'll get you some water.'

Hannah popped two pills from the packet and put them in her mouth.

'Here.' He gave her the glass of water.

'Thanks.' She gulped it down. 'Never again.'

The Look of Death

He'd heard this too many times to believe her. A party girl through and through, there was seldom a week passed when Hannah wasn't out at least six nights out of seven – clubbing, partying, drinking herself sober – yet somehow she was still able to get up and do her shifts at the bar.

'Better?'

She shook her head.

'You know I'd open up for you if I could, but I need to do a few things before my shift starts at mid-day.' Going through the notebook in more detail was at the top of his list. 'So, what's with the guys upstairs?'

'Which ones?'

'Bill and Seb.'

Hannah raised an eyebrow. 'They'd eat an innocent like you alive.'

'Party boys?'

'You only enter that flat for one thing.' She took a sip of her espresso. 'Sorry, two. Sex and drugs.'

'So, if I were to tell you I was speaking to them this morning?'

'I'd say spill the dirt.'

'But they're good guys, eh? Because I've asked one of them about a job.'

Before she could reply, Hannah rushed out the room, announcing she was going to be sick.

The sound of her heaving in the toilet was enough to force Colin from the kitchen. Returning to his room, he sat his coffee on the window-ledge and picked up Rhona's notebook. Flicking through the pages, he was surprised by how much information he'd already absorbed: a description of the room where Fraser was found, details of the debris found lying on the bed and floor, a witness saying he'd heard someone shouting 'Help', the names of the dead men who Rhona thought were linked. But other than these straightforward facts, Bela was right; her evidence didn't amount to much.

Then again, she wasn't a police officer; she was a grieving sister trying to get to the truth of how her brother died.

On the other end of the line, Rhona sounded happy to hear his voice. 'Have you discovered something?' Pre-empting his response, she babbled, 'Look, I know there's not much to go on in my notebook, but each time I tried to get anywhere I was fobbed off. In all the times I've been to Berlin since Fraser's death, it's the same police officer telling me I'm overreacting.'

'I'm sorry, there's no easy way to say this, but there's been another death.'

'What?'

Colin had weighed up whether to tell her. But from what he knew so far, the guy they'd found was gay, there was a suggestion of drugs, and the potential of foul play: elements which matched her brother's death. 'The police are involved, but after all these years, I think it's unlikely they'll be looking to make a connection with Fraser's death.' There was silence. 'Are you OK?'

'You do believe me, don't you?' she asked.

Colin caught sight of Hannah striding along the corridor, transformed, looking every inch the professional he knew her to be: hair and make-up immaculate, a spray of citrus perfume trailing her. She smiled and slapped his backside before disappearing out of the door. 'It's early days.'

'I thought you might find links where others haven't.'

'It takes time,' he explained. 'Look, I'm calling to ask if you can do something for me.'

'Anything.'

'I know you don't want to part with Fraser's sketchbook.'

'It's one of the few things I have left of his. He didn't have many possessions.'

'Could you photocopy the sketches for me?'

The Look of Death

'Sure, but will they be of any use? Most of them are from the time he spent in Munich.'

'I don't know. Maybe. You said he sketched constantly, so perhaps there's something you've overlooked.'

'OK. I'll find time this week and post them to you.'

Rhona went off to find a pen, and on her return, Colin spelled out his address. 'But I don't want to raise your expectations too much; keep in mind, at the end of the day, this may amount to nothing. You have to be prepared for that.'

'I understand, but if there's one thing I'm certain about, it's this: my brother was murdered and it's related to those other deaths. I'd stake my life on it.'

14

MONDAY, 4TH JULY 1994

Colin took the S-Bahn to Zoologischer Garten, which was teeming with Monday morning commuters. A wall of heat met him as he emerged from the train station onto the street. It was going to be another scorching hot day and he had a long list of things to do: check the newspapers from 1989 onwards, explore if there were any further leads to glean, then return to Wedding for an evening shift at *Zum-Zum*.

He walked the couple of hundred metres to Amerika Haus, keeping in the shade. Opened in the late 1950s, the building's long, glazed façade quivered in the heat haze. Colin headed towards the entrance where a huge red, white, and blue sign thrust out towards the street, announcing the cultural centre's presence to the world. It had become one of his regular haunts; as well as housing a library and hosting cultural events, it held a large magazine and newspaper collection.

In the marbled reception area with its floating staircase, workmen on ladders were hanging Stars and Stripes bunting and banners for a big 4th of July event they'd been advertising for months. Passing through, he arrived in the archive and

The Look of Death

asked a friendly-looking librarian – Jeanette, her name-badge said – if he could look through the local newspapers.

'Is there anything specific you're interested in?' Like everyone else in Berlin, her English was faultless.

Colin briefly explained about the two deaths which occurred during the summer of 1990. 'I know it sounds morbid.'

She laughed. 'Most people are interested in Berlin's historical past, not local deaths.'

'Is it a weird request?'

'I've had weirder. One American guy wanted to find out about every brunette who'd been murdered in Berlin since 1920.'

'And did you get the information?'

'Of course.'

Colin smiled. He'd met his match. 'I do have a problem though – my German's not great.'

'Don't worry, I can help you – it's all part of the service.' She briefly spoke to a colleague before gesturing to Colin. 'Come with me.' She directed him through a glass door into a low, windowless room lined with metal filing cabinets. Two microfiche readers sat facing each other in the centre.

'Give me the details, and let's see what I can find.' She picked up a pen and paper.

'I've two names: Stefan Reis and Ulrich Steiner were found dead in the summer of 1990 in Ernst-Thälmann Park, ten days apart. And Fraser McDougal died in West Berlin on the 11th November 1989.'

'Two days after the Wall came down?'

Colin nodded. 'He was a student, visiting the city for a few days.'

'Poor guy. It shouldn't be too much of a problem.' She showed him what she'd written. 'Is this correct?'

'Yes. But McDougal only has one L.'

'I'll try it with both – see what comes up. Spelling

83

mistakes of foreign names are common. If you take a seat at one of the readers, I'll do an initial search.'

Impressed by her efficiency, Colin watched as Jeanette leafed through a series of folders, before starting to pull microfiches from the filing cabinets. 'Let's start with these – these are the main local newspapers from that summer.'

She quickly discovered one article on Fraser McDougal's death, however it contained no more information than his sister Rhona had provided. She checked two more microfiches. 'No. That's the only article I can find on him.'

Colin thought it sad that Fraser's death merited only a few scant words and a grainy photo. As Jeanette suggested, they'd even misspelt his name: *McDougall* rather than *McDougal*.

Jeanette inserted another microfiche and raced through to July 1990. She flicked between a few articles before turning to face him. 'Nothing on Ulrich Steiner so far.'

Perhaps a drug death didn't merit a mention. Or maybe Bela had been given the wrong information. 'What about Stefan Reis?'

Jeanette swept through another series of pages. 'Here's an article – with a photo.'

'Can I see?'

'That's funny.' Jeanette angled the screen towards him. 'He looks a little bit like you – don't you think?' She magnified the image and together they both examined it: a similar colouring, the same shape of face, he'd even had his hair styled with the same side-parting a couple of years before.

'Weird.'

'Do you want to try and read the story yourself?'

Colin nodded. 'I'll try.' But as soon as he started reading, it was too much; he couldn't understand half the words. 'I think I get the gist of it, but would you mind translating for me?'

'No problem: "*Police have established that there are no suspicious circumstances surrounding the death of 26-year-old Stefan*

The Look of Death

Reis whose body was discovered in Ernst-Thälmann Park on 7th July. Officers were called to the park around 7 a.m. on Saturday when a man walking his dog found the body. An ambulance crew attended; however, he was pronounced dead at the scene. Initially treating the death as unexplained, police maintained a presence at the park for several days and appealed to the public for information. However, following yesterday's post-mortem examination, death from natural causes was confirmed."' Jeanette turned to Colin. 'There's a final sentence: "*A close friend of the deceased, Leon Brauckmann, 30, from Charlottenburg, stressed that while Mr Reis had an underlying health condition, his friends and family were nevertheless shocked and saddened by his sudden death."'*

'What do you think would be the best way to find Leon Brauckmann?'

'Come with me.' Jeanette gestured for him to follow. 'Through this door.'

Half-expecting to be presented to Leon Brauckmann himself, Colin was a little disappointed to be taken into a small office with a long desk and a large window overlooking an internal courtyard.

Sitting, Jeanette pulled out a thick telephone directory and leafed through it. 'Brauckmann is quite an unusual surname, so if he's still living in Charlottenburg, he shouldn't be too difficult to find.'

'You ought to be running your own detective agency.'

'You'll notice I'm resisting the temptation to ask you what this is all about.' She tapped her finger on a name. 'Here we go. I think this must be him.' She picked up the phone. 'What would you like me to say?'

The conversation with Leon Brauckmann had been brief. Jeanette had initially explained the situation to him in German, but it soon became clear he was happy to speak directly to Colin in English. She passed the handset to him.

'Hello. How can I help?' If Colin hadn't known he was German, he would have sworn the guy was British: he spoke English with a perfect accent.

'I know this is totally out of the blue, and I'll understand if you don't want to, but I wondered if I could come and ask a few questions about your friend, Stefan Reis?'

Colin sensed a slight intake of breath, but even without seeing him, he knew Leon had kept his composure. 'Is someone finally taking Stefan's death seriously?'

'It would only be a short chat. I don't want to take up your time unnecessarily.'

'Don't worry, I've plenty to say. First, Stefan did not die of natural causes as described on his death certificate. And two, the police haven't bothered their arses to properly investigate what I believe and many others do too, was murder.'

'So, you're happy to meet?

'Would Wednesday morning suit? First thing?'

15

TUESDAY, 5TH JULY 1994

'I need a life-model in Studio 6 immediately.' Bill's office was tiny and windowless, decorated with hundreds of images of naked bodies. 'The model hasn't arrived and this group of students have paid a fortune. Can you do it?' He sifted through a heap of loose papers on his desk. 'Now, where the fuck did I put that schedule?'

'Sure,' Colin said, stepping out of the way.

Bill found what he was looking for and pored over it. 'Colin, you're a life-saver. You wouldn't believe the unprofessionalism of some people.' He grabbed a pen and scored through a name.

'Where do I go?'

'Sorry. It's not usually like this. Today's been unusually chaotic.' He opened the door. 'Ground floor. Go down these stairs, turn left and it's at the end of the corridor.'

The telephone rang and Bill picked it up, immediately ranting about fuckwits who didn't take their job seriously. Colin wasn't sure whether to wait, but with a swift wave of his hand, Bill ushered him out. 'Good luck,' he shouted as Colin closed the door. 'You'll get paid cash at the end of your shift.'

When he entered the studio, a small group of students were standing behind their easels; a couple were sharpening pencils, whilst others shuffled bits and pieces of drawing equipment around. As soon as he entered, they looked up, ready and eager to start work. A guy in his early thirties, who Colin presumed was the tutor – pony-tail, pointy beard, round, rimless glasses – rushed towards him. A tirade of German poured from his mouth, but the only words Colin understood were *Zieh Dich aus* – get undressed!

He was led behind a screen, and told to be quick. '*Eine Minute,*' the tutor hollered.

As Colin removed his outer clothing, the idea of posing nude in front of a group of strangers suddenly seemed like a bad idea; the waiting silence from the other side of the screen made it even worse. By the time he removed his underwear, a sweat had formed on his brow and his palms felt clammy, but there was no turning back. *Here goes,* he thought. *Think about the money.*

A set of ladders had been placed in the middle of the room, and the tutor motioned for him to climb them.

'All the way to the top?' Colin mimed as best he could climbing the rungs.

The tutor nodded, and he put his first foot forward, aware that as he climbed, there'd be no chance of hiding; everything would be on show.

When he reached the top, the tutor called out a series of instructions which Colin didn't understand. The sweat was now dripping into his eyes. 'Can someone translate for me?' he asked the row of eager students staring up at him.

'He wants you to put your left hand on the top rung, right hand by your side, and look up at the ceiling.' A young guy his age with dark hair and glasses, stood in the doorway. 'It's a standard classical pose.' He crossed to the tutor and spoke to him in German, before taking his position at an easel.

The Look of Death

'*Zwanzig Minuten,*' the tutor stressed, pointing at the clock on the wall.

'Twenty minutes,' the dark-haired guy translated, his nose twitching like a rabbit's.

'And you need to keep as still as you can,' a girl with pink hair and a black top embroidered with the word *Devil* added. 'Then you get a five-minute break, before doing another twenty.'

Colin followed the instructions, but when he did, everyone laughed.

'Sorry. My fault,' the twitchy guy said. 'Right hand on the top rung, left hand by your side.'

Part of him felt he was being made to perform an initiation rite. But as he settled into the pose, he let his mind drift, thinking about the guy he and Bela had found dead and the odd conversation with Klaus outside his apartment, which had led him to this bizarre moment, standing on top of a ladder naked. If his colleagues at the Met could see him now.

The first twenty minutes were soon over and he stepped down from the ladders and was handed a dressing-gown by the girl with pink hair, which he immediately put on. 'Thanks.'

'You did fantastic,' she said. 'Take a look around, if you want.'

She joined the twitchy guy by the coffee-machine, while he took the opportunity to examine the students' sketches. Some had focused on parts of his body, such as the top of his leg or chest, whilst others had completed quick portraits which captured his likeness: the shape of his nose, his Mona Lisa smile as an ex once commented – smiling or frowning? Others had attempted his full body, with some more successful than others at getting his proportions correct. What was apparent however, was that each individual had a unique style of their own; they showed ten entirely different approaches and ways of looking at him.

At the end of the shift, after Colin collected his money at the administrator's office – fifteen Marks – the girl with the pink hair ran after him, followed by the guy with the twitching nose. 'Hold on,' she shouted. 'Can we have a moment?'

Colin, who'd pushed open the door to outside, let it swing shut. 'Is there a problem?'

'It's Colin, isn't it?'

He nodded.

'We thought you might like to grab some food.' The guy's twitching was more pronounced than before, and he pushed his glasses up to his brow, sniffling as he wiped his nose on his sleeve. 'I'm Lukas.'

'And I'm Maryam,' the girl added.

'We got talking during the break and thought you were amazing.'

Their sketches were by far the most interesting. Maryam's had placed the outline of his body in a forest setting, her focus more on the detail of the trees and flowers than his physicality. Lukas on the other hand, was much more intent on capturing his exact likeness, however he'd created a striking effect by superimposing multiple views of his face over each other. 'Where were you thinking of going?'

'The canteen's OK. It's this way.' She pointed toward a corridor. 'The food's so-so, but it's cheap.

Lukas leaned forward. 'And if you're a fan of mayonnaise.'

'I don't mind mayonnaise.'

'Then it's settled.'

THE CANTEEN WAS a cavernous white space with students pressed up against each other at almost every table, buzzing with chat and laughter.

Maryam grabbed his arm. 'Don't touch the goulash!' Her

The Look of Death

voice seemed designed to make everyone in the queue overhear. A few glances their way only made her raise it higher. 'It sucks.'

Colin moved along the line, staring at the bland assortment of food on offer. 'I might try the salad.'

'Me, too.' Colin felt the pressure of Lukas's body against his back, urging him along the queue.

Maryam screwed her face up. 'I forgot. One of the students got sick from eating here last week.'

'Should we go somewhere else?' The last thing Colin needed was food poisoning.

'We're here now, aren't we?' Lukas leaned over the food, taking in their aromas. 'It smells absolutely fine.'

Colin pointed to an assortment of salads which were being dished up by a dour woman behind the counter. However, when he pointed to an assortment of pickled fish, she shook her head, as though warning him this might be the source of the food poisoning.

'No good.' She squeezed her nose with her fingers, then looked over at Lukas and continued in German.

'She's saying it's got too much raw garlic in it. Not good for kissing.' Lukas gazed at him, his face red with embarrassment, the twitching going into overdrive.

They found a table over by a window looking onto an inner courtyard, full of trees in bloom. Summer in Berlin was beautiful. An intense, orange smell filled the streets and the pavements were sticky with the blossom's residue. The smell of sex, Colin always thought. After the dark, freezing months of winter, the city was fully alive.

He glanced around to see if he could spot any faces from the class. Perhaps it might help the conversation a little, as all three were munching their way through their salads, hardly exchanging a word. 'So, you like it here at the art school?'

Maryam, between mouthfuls, shrugged her shoulders.

'The tutor's a wacko, and it's stifling hot. Other than that, it's pretty cool – there's loads of exciting work going on.'

'And I only started yesterday,' Lukas said. 'I missed the first week because of family stuff back east. They're stuck in some Soviet-era dilemma about property they own here in Berlin, or don't own anymore. It's a mess.'

Colin didn't know a great deal about art, but to him, the standard seemed high. 'You were the one who did the great drawing of me from all different angles?'

'I'm an amateur, but I'm keen to try new things; take it more seriously. I didn't have enough time to finish it in class though, which was frustrating.'

'This afternoon, they've got us painting bowls of fruit.' Maryam drank some of her Coca Cola, then wiped her mouth clean before picking at the last of her salad. 'It's so bourgeois. I wanted to opt out, but they don't offer refunds. Fucking thieves!'

'Shall we head to the park instead?' Lukas asked. 'Wouldn't that be more fun?'

Maryam glanced over at Colin, then put down her fork. 'We were chatting during break—' she began.

'About how excellent you were today.' Lukas tapped Maryam's arm, hoping she'd continue.

'You're so much better than the model they gave the class last week. So, we wondered if you'd pose for us? Privately?'

'There's no way I'm drawing bowls of fruit for the next six weeks.' The bright lights of the canteen made Lukas's green eyes shine behind his thick glasses. Colin liked him. He liked them both. The way they finished each other's sentences made them seem like an old married couple.

'You'd be helping out two aspiring artists in their hour of need.'

Colin grabbed a final piece of lettuce from his plate and stuffed it into his mouth, pushing the rest to the side. 'You

The Look of Death

sure? I mean, you saw me today. Don't you think I was a bit useless?'

'Not at all, you're fresh.' A tiny piece of salad was stuck between Lukas's teeth, and his tongue was struggling to extract it. 'Together, we can pay you double what you earn here.' The piece of lettuce eventually came free and he dabbed at it before sticking it back in his mouth and swallowing it.

'This is not us trying it on with you,' Maryam said. 'I mean if it was, this would be a terrible way to chat someone up. Agreed?' She winked at Lukas, who giggled. 'And you're not my type.' She pointed to the woman who'd served them. 'She's more my type.'

Colin gathered the debris from the table onto the tray. 'Can I think about it?' He stacked their empty plates on top of his.

Lukas sneezed, before pulling a hankie from his trouser pocket and blowing his nose. 'Hayfever. Berlin in summer kills me.'

'We can't wait too long.' Maryam dumped her squashed can of Coke on the tray.

'I'm flattered and I suppose I do need the money.'

'It's a no-brainer, then.' Lukas stared at him, his expression serious, urging him to agree.

'OK. I'll give it a shot.'

'I told you he'd say yes.' Lukas grinned, making him far more attractive than Colin had previously thought. Hints of his ex, Lee: smart and tenacious.

Colin picked up the tray. 'Let's talk dates.'

16

After lunch, Colin had rushed back to Wedding to start his shift at *Zum Zum*. He was due to finish at eleven that night, but Hannah needed him to help clear up, so it wasn't until after eleven-thirty he managed to escape.

'Where you off to in such a hurry?' she'd asked. 'Not staying for a drink?'

'Things to do. People to see.'

'What does that mean? Are you shagging someone else besides Bela?'

He tapped his nose. 'That's for me to know.'

'I told you – this is what Berlin does to people—' she shouted after him, as he rushed out the door, 'it sets them free.'

COLIN HAD DECIDED to check out Ernst Thälmann Park where Stefan Reis and Ulrich Steiner's bodies had been found; he needed to get a sense of the surroundings and the types of men who cruised there.

Sprinting to the S-Bahn, he was lucky to catch a train immediately. Sliding into a space in a crowded carriage, he

The Look of Death

caught sight of his sweaty reflection in the darkness of the window and recalled the various images the students had drawn that day. It was fun, he concluded. Something different, much more satisfying than serving rowdy drunks.

On the approach to Greifswalder Strasse station an elderly woman using a newspaper as a fan asked in German if he could open the window above her. She thanked him as he released the catch and cool air poured over them. Moving towards the exit, he noticed a figure in the next carriage staring directly at him. Dressed in a hoodie and dark glasses, their face was in shadow, and the dim lighting made it difficult to get a clear view. Wondering if it was someone he knew, Colin headed along the carriage, but as he did so, the figure spun round, pushing past other passengers as if desperate to avoid him. Before Colin could reach the connecting door, the train drew into the station and came to a stop.

Stepping onto the platform, the figure got off too, only to be immediately obscured by a boisterous group of teenagers. Colin squeezed past them to see the person disappearing down the stairs to the exit. Though not far behind, by the time Colin emerged onto the street, there was no one around. Mystified, he waited to see if the person might reappear, but no one did.

A SHORT WALK brought him to a square with a large bronze bust mounted on a graffitied stone base: the Soviet-style memorial to Ernst Thälmann. Fist clenched and with a hammer and sickle flag as a backdrop, it was far more austere than Bela had described. He walked past the sculpture and into the dark green folds of the undergrowth behind.

Away from the hum of the traffic, Colin was embraced by silence and the warm, heady scent of summer flowers. In the distance, on the far side of the park, lights flickered from the windows of two residential high rises. He continued deeper into the park. To the right, a shape moved in the bushes and the end of a cigarette glowed. Walking towards it, he heard a murmur which might be running water. He remembered Bela said Stefan Reis and Ulrich Steiner had been found lying on a ramp beside a pond.

Out of nowhere, two men appeared from the shadows and stared straight at him. He considered asking if the pond was up ahead but decided that might arouse suspicion and instead nodded and continued walking.

He kept to the path and soon the pond came into view, a still, black mirror reflecting the night sky. A cool breeze kissed his cheeks as he descended towards it and sat by the water's edge. Protected by a dense barrier of trees, the hidden world of the park revealed itself: the rustle of foliage, the movement of silhouettes, whispers and low whistles. In this secret space in the heart of the city, men were meeting other men for one purpose only: sex.

He tried to imagine the two young men whose lives had ended here. Had the promise of anonymous sex brought them to the park? Hopefully his meeting tomorrow with Leon Brauckmann would shed light on Stefan's likely intentions. He needed to build a picture of these men's lives if he'd any hope of answering Rhona McDougal's questions about her brother's death.

'*Zigarette?*'

A slight figure stood behind him, outlined against the dark sky.

'*Zigarette?*' the voice asked again, approaching him.

Stepping from the shadows into the grey moonlight, a young man, no more than twenty and probably Middle Eastern, revealed himself. Though wearing a hoodie, Colin was reasonably certain this was not the person who'd been watching him on the train.

'I don't smoke,' he replied. 'Sorry.'

The boy sat beside Colin, smiled, and offered him his

The Look of Death

hand. 'Ajnur.' Warm eyes peered out from beneath a ragged fringe of black hair. '*Englisch*?'

'Scottish.' Colin was always careful to correct the assumption. 'But I'll forgive you.'

'Cool! Kilts. Loch Ness Monster.'

'And haggis,' laughed Colin, happy to perpetuate the stereotype. 'Nice to meet you. I'm Colin.'

The last time he'd gone cruising – years ago, following a break-up with his ex, Ben – he'd used a false name. Introducing himself as Steve, he told the guy – a Swede working in the city – that he was an electrician. He hated the deceit and the hypocrisy, but it seemed a necessary form of protection. Had the encounter happened an hour earlier, when he was still on duty, the law would have expected him to arrest the man for propositioning a police officer. Yet there he was out of uniform, in the darkness with a stranger, surrendering his body to pleasure and to hell with the consequences.

With a nod towards the bushes, Ajnur smiled again and pressed his shoulder against Colin's.

Despite the temptation, he wasn't there for a hook-up. 'Not tonight. Sorry.'

Ajnur moved closer and placed his hand on Colin's thigh. 'You sure?'

'I should go.' Colin stood. 'Nice to meet you.'

'Stay. Chat with me.' Ajnur reached out for his hand and gently pulled him back. 'Five minutes?'

Colin thought about all the reasons men cruised. For the majority it was sex, but for others it offered connection, a sense of community. Friends of his had been visiting the same cruising grounds for years and would share stories about the many faces from all walks of life that mingled amongst the bushes. The keenest of his friends – Harry – insisted he'd never met anyone at a club, that it was always in the parks. And he was rarely disappointed with the encounters, even if all it entailed was a nice chat with a lonely man complaining that his boyfriend or wife didn't understand him.

'You sure you don't want sex?' Ajnur asked.

'I don't. Sorry.'

From the look on his face, it was clear he wasn't used to being rejected.

'I'm here for another reason.'

'Ah – you're meeting someone?'

'No.' Colin reckoned Ajnur would have been fifteen or sixteen in 1990; likely too young to remember the deaths, but there was a chance he might have heard gossip. 'Two men died here. Did you know?'

'Of course.' Ajnur leaned back and rested on his elbows. 'This is the spot.'

'What? Right here?'

'Yes. The older guys always talk about it, warning everyone, "*Don't go down there.*" They like to spook people.' His expression suggested he didn't listen. Or care.

'What else do they say?'

Ajnur rolled his eyes. He grabbed the crotch of his jeans and stared at him. 'Are you sure you don't wanna play?'

'Positive.'

Sitting forward, Ajnur trailed his fingertips through the water. 'You know everyone thinks they were murdered.'

If that was the rumour, experience had taught Colin there was usually a good reason why. 'One of them died from a drug overdose, didn't he?'

'Maybe – I don't know.' He stared at the water, his reflection shimmering darkly in the water's surface.

'It's odd, isn't it? That both were found dead in the same spot a week apart?'

'Yes, but no one around here thinks they were connected. The oldies, they'd never seen the first guy before. I don't know his name.'

'Stefan Reis.'

The Look of Death

'If you say so. One guy told me his body had been left like a princess in a fairytale.' He laughed and mimed a swooning motion. 'But the second one was apparently here all the time, selling his body for drugs. His body was just dumped.'

Colin made a mental note about the supposed positioning of Stefan's body, and wondered if it mirrored Walter's. 'Can you introduce me to anyone who was around then?'

By the way Ajnur's shoulder's tensed, Colin knew he'd said too much. It had happened before while doing undercover work – the spell quickly broken by one question too many.

Ajnur jumped up and patted the dust off his jeans. 'See you around.'

Colin had to think creatively. 'Stefan Reis was a friend of mine. That's the only reason I'm asking.'

'Whatever.' Ajnur pulled up his hood. 'You sound like the *Polizei* to me.' He ran up the ramp and vanished into the trees.

STICKING TO THE PATH, Colin made his way back to the monument. Devoid of people and traffic, the square and the street beyond were deathly quiet. As he knelt to tie his shoelace, a twig snapped behind him. Looking back at the park, where the wall of greenery melted into darkness, he sensed someone watching him; like on the train earlier. 'Ajnur?' His eyes tried to make sense of the shadows as a light breeze moved through the trees.

He crossed the square quickly, heading back towards the S-Bahn along the pavement which bordered the perimeter of the park. Checking over his shoulder, in the dense undergrowth, he swore he could make out a figure, moving from one tree to the next, attempting to conceal himself, imagining that Colin was oblivious to his presence.

But he was completely aware.

17

WEDNESDAY, 6TH JULY 1994

The sound of hammering on his door woke Colin. He rolled over and squinted at the alarm clock. Six-thirty. Who the hell wanted to speak to him this early? 'Coming,' he croaked, stepping from the bed, trailing the duvet behind him.

He opened the door to find Bela brandishing a brown paper bag. '*Schmalzkuchen.*' He stepped inside, ignoring Colin's groan.

'Who let you in?' He closed the door, and collapsed back on his bed.

'One of your flatmates – the girl with the crazy hair that's not Hannah. She was doing yoga in the courtyard, so when she finished, I followed her upstairs.'

'You mean Rita?' He heard Bela rip open the bag. 'What've you brought?' Colin murmured, lying back on his bed and pulling the duvet over him.

'*Schmalzkuchen* – I've already said. They're little doughnuts. The bakery on the corner makes the best in the city. Fresh every morning. Here, try one.'

Colin peeked out from beneath the duvet to find a

The Look of Death

diamond of deep-fried dough dusted in icing sugar, being dangled in front of him. He reached out and grabbed it.

Bela prodded him. 'It's good?'

'Oh my God! That's delicious.' He put his hand out for another and a second was placed in his palm. Shoving the bedding aside, Colin propped himself up on his pillow. 'Can you open the blind for me?'

Bela pulled the cord and bright sunlight came flooding into the room.

'Why are you here so early?' Colin asked. 'Not just to bring me doughnuts?'

Bela popped a doughnut in his mouth and sat on the end of the bed. 'This is what nice, caring people do, isn't it?'

'At six-thirty in the morning?'

'Why not?'

'But there's things I need to do today.'

'Isn't Wednesday your day off?'

The fact that Bela retained this level of detail about his routine was yet another irritation. 'But I have plans. Oh, and before I forget, you need to give me Kim's number.'

'Haven't I already given it to you?'

'No.'

'I've got her direct number. That's best. But I haven't got it on me.'

'As soon as would be great.' Colin waited for Bela to leave, but he showed no sign of

doing so. 'Well, I really need to get on – start getting ready, you know?' Despite the hint, Bela didn't budge. 'We've arranged to see each other tonight. Remember? I'm cooking curry.'

Bela's screwed-up expression suggested he wasn't about to be fobbed off. 'Have the police been back in touch?'

Colin suspected the question was prompted more by Bela's determination to stay rather than a genuine interest. 'No. What about you?'

Bela shook his head. 'They'll do nothing.'

'I thought they might want to speak to you again since you found the body.'

'No. They're useless. I told you.'

Part of him understood Bela's dismissiveness. He found it strange that the police didn't appear to be making any connection between the recent discovery of the second body in the Sophien Kirche Cemetery and the two deaths in Ernst-Thälmann Park in 1990. To him there seemed a disturbing parallel – or at least something worthy of further investigation. 'I'm meeting a friend of Stefan Reis at eight-thirty,' he said. 'A guy called Leon Brauckmann.'

Bela moved further up the bed. 'So you agree there's something odd?'

'Yes, but I need more proof.'

'I'll come with you.' Bela jumped up and slung his satchel over his shoulder. 'Come on. Hurry up!'

'I'll be fine on my own,' Colin insisted. 'The guy speaks perfect English.'

'But what if he can't understand what you're saying? You mumble and speak too fast. It'll be a wasted journey, and you'll have to do it again. If I go with you, then you'll have the full information.'

Colin knew better than to argue with Bela once he became fixed on an idea. Against his better judgement, he found himself agreeing. 'I need to grab a shower. Why don't you wait in the kitchen?'

'No. I'll sit outside in the sun.' Bela gathered the packaging from the doughnuts. 'But I'll recycle this first.'

Colin took an extra-long shower in the hope Bela might get bored and leave, however he was still in the courtyard when Colin stepped outside half an hour later. With his sunglasses on, gazing up at the sun streaming through the leaves, for once Bela looked relaxed and he was reluctant to

The Look of Death

disturb him. But his usual impatience returned as soon as he heard Colin's footsteps. 'Where are we going?'

'Goethestrasse in Charlottenburg.'

'It'll take thirty-five minutes.' He could see Bela working out the route in his head. 'We have time for a quick coffee. I know a place that does an excellent ristretto.'

'A what?'

'It's like an espresso only better.' Bela stood. 'Let's go.'

'Hold on.' Colin sat on the bench.

Bela removed his sunglasses. 'You don't want me to come, do you? I knew it.'

'That's not true. I'm happy for you to tag along, but you need to let me ask the questions. You need to give me space. I can't have you trying to take charge all the time.'

'That's not fair,' Bela protested. 'I'm trying to help. I'm always trying to help. So, why don't you stop resisting and let me?' He strode off, before looking back. 'Hurry up!'

LEON BRAUCKMANN LIVED in a pristine neoclassical building on the corner of an otherwise unremarkable street. Stone steps led through elaborate wrought-iron gates to a glazed bronze door. In the lobby beyond, a uniformed concierge sat behind an exquisitely-carved wooden reception desk. Colin rang the bell and was buzzed in. 'How the other half live, eh?' 'The vulgar trappings of an imperialist past.' It was the first full sentence Bela had spoken since they'd left; other than the occasional direction, he'd given Colin the silent treatment on the U-Bahn and in the café.

There was an instant hush as they stepped into the lobby, the thick carpet and heavy doors doing a wonderful job keeping the outside world at bay. It was an entirely different Berlin from the make-do-and-mend aesthetic he'd become used to at the *Genossenschaft*.

The concierge pointed them towards a tiny lift which

carried them to the fourth floor. Pulling back the ornate metal grille revealed an expensively understated hall, furnished with a tasteful selection of antiques. There was only one apartment on this floor and Colin knocked on the door.

An immaculately-groomed man in his mid-thirties, wearing a crisp white shirt and black, tailored trousers answered, a broad smile across his face. 'You must be Colin?'

'Thanks for making the time to see me.'

Leon glanced over Colin's shoulder at Bela.

'I hope you don't mind,' Colin said. 'My friend Bela's joined us, in case we need a translator. Is that OK?' He could tell from Leon's expression it wasn't, but he was far too polite to object.

'Come in. Both of you. From your accent, I presume you're from Scotland?'

'From Glasgow originally,' Colin explained, as he and Bela entered the apartment.

'It's different from the Edinburgh accent.' Leon closed the door. 'I studied at the university there for a year.'

'It's a little broader,' Colin conceded, saving Leon the embarrassment of having to compare the two.

'My apologies for dragging you here so early, but I'm leaving for Prague later this morning. I'm speaking at an architectural conference.'

With Bela a couple of steps behind, Colin followed Leon along an opulently panelled hallway punctuated by fan-shaped wall lights. In contrast to the exterior of the building, the interior had an Art Deco feel. 'What a beautiful apartment.'

'I worry it's a little old-fashioned,' Leon confided. 'I inherited it a long time ago from my grandmother and keep thinking I should modernise, but I can't bring myself to. Too many memories, I suppose. Would you like a coffee? Or perhaps a tea?'

'I'll take a tea.'

The Look of Death

'Bela?'

'Not for me.'

Colin glanced at Bela and noticed how awkward he looked. Was he still in a huff, or was it Leon's relaxed, friendly manner that was bothering him? He couldn't tell.

'How do you prefer it?'

'Black – no sugar.'

'A man after my own heart.' He smiled. 'While I prepare a pot, why don't you make yourselves comfortable in the sitting room?' He pointed towards a set of double doors, before disappearing down a corridor.

The doors opened onto a sumptuous living area: the square sitting-room led through an archway to a more formal, double-aspect drawing room which occupied the corner of the building. This, in turn, led through another arch to a dining room with a vast round table. The décor in all three spaces was classic 1930s, with dark parquet flooring, bright geometric rugs, chrome light fittings and low leather sofas, draped in silk throws.

Bathed in morning light, Colin admired a forest of bonsai trees growing in a shallow, porcelain pot on a low, lacquer cabinet at the foot of one of the tall windows. 'This place is something else.'

Bela sidled up behind him and whispered, 'I fucked him three years ago.' He stepped back. 'Big disappointment.'

Before Colin could reply, Leon appeared with a tray. 'Gentlemen, please sit.'

Bela dropped onto one of the cream sofas. Propped up by an abundance of cushions, Colin took a seat on the sofa opposite. 'What an amazing room.'

'Unfortunately, I can't take the credit. Apart from some of the artwork, everything you see was my grandmother's. Please help yourself to tea.'

'Thanks.' Colin poured himself a cup. 'So, you and Stefan were friends?'

'Where to start? He was such a big part of my life. We met in 1985 while he was studying architecture and I was a guest tutor at the university. We got talking and became firm friends. I've always lived alone, but for eighteen months Stefan stayed with me while his own apartment was being renovated. We were never lovers though – it was never about that.' He smiled. 'We were more like brothers than friends.'

'So his death must have come as a shock?'

'It almost destroyed me, to be honest.' Leon stared out the window, wincing at a sudden ray of sun catching his face. He moved slightly to the side, placing him once again in shadow.

'It can't have been easy, to have lost someone so close.'

'To think he's been dead for four years, it's unimaginable. It seems like only yesterday when he was sitting where you are – chatting, gossiping, having fun. Stefan was special – the life and soul of every party.' He set his tea aside. 'Please don't take this the wrong way, but you remind me of him; a similar profile. When you turn to your left, you could be brothers.'

Jeanette from Amerika Haus had mentioned this, too. From the corner of his eye, he noticed Leon look at him more intently, and ignoring it, fumbled in his rucksack to find his notebook. 'Are you OK with me taking notes?'

Leon nodded. 'But I'm intrigued why you've come to ask about Stefan. Why now?'

Colin took a sip of his tea. 'I'm working on behalf of a friend whose brother died unexpectedly in Berlin – I'm trying to determine if the deaths of other gay men in the city might be connected to his.' Colin locked eyes with Leon. 'You mentioned you have suspicions about the circumstances of Stefan's death.'

'Absolutely,' Leon replied. 'Who didn't at the time? It's true Stefan was diabetic; he had been his entire life, but he took his condition seriously. He was meticulous with his diet and medication, and kept himself extremely fit. But no one wanted to hear that.'

The Look of Death

'You mean the police?'

Leon snorted. 'The police treated Stefan's death as though he was a piece of trash, as though it was perfectly natural for a gay man to be found dead in a cruising area. Case closed. Now, by the way, he never frequented that type of place.'

'So, he didn't cruise the parks?'

'Not at all. Stefan was a complete romantic. All he ever spoke about was finding Mr Right. Which is what had happened the final few months of his life.'

'He had a boyfriend?'

'Yes.' Leon's expression suggested he didn't approve.

'Do you have a name?'

'Konrad someone. I never knew his surname.'

'Any other details?'

He shook his head. 'No. Worked in finance, played racquetball twice a week, travelled a bit for work. I never actually met him. And after Stefan died, I discovered no one else had either. Like a phantom, this Konrad guy vanished into thin air. As far as I know, he didn't even turn up at the funeral.'

Colin sat back. 'Didn't you find that odd, given how close you were?'

'In hindsight, yes. We normally told each other everything. But he'd moved back into his own apartment and prior to that we'd been spending all our time together, so I thought he needed a bit of space.'

Colin noticed Bela bristle, and made a mental note to enquire about both the other men's relationship status. He remembered Rhona saying she didn't think Fraser was seeing anyone before he died.

For the next fifteen minutes, Leon continued to fill in more details about Stefan's life, supplying Colin with names of other friends who knew him, from the tennis club he was part of and his gym buddies. However, not one of them, Leon stressed, would be able to tell him any further details about the man Stefan had shared the last couple of months of his life with. 'He treated it as though it were top secret. I assumed he was a closet case.'

Having exhausted all his questions, Colin rose. 'Thank you. Honestly, you've been a great help. I'm trying to build a picture of these deaths to see if a pattern emerges.'

Leon stood up. 'So, you don't yet have a theory or a prime suspect?'

'Not yet, but you're the first person I've spoken to. I mean, it might come to nothing.'

'I'm just glad someone's finally looking into it,' Leon said. 'All I know is that in those last few months, Stefan retreated from the world. When I think about it, he wasn't himself and I keep coming back to this mysterious new lover who no one ever met. I'm no investigator, but that seems sufficiently strange to require some level of investigation.'

'I agree and what you've shared with me today helps a great deal.'

'After all these years, it's good to talk about Stefan.' Leon opened the door. 'I'm back in Berlin next week, so if you need to meet again, please let me know. I'm happy to help in any way I can.'

As they walked back to the front door, Colin took more time to look at the figurative art lining the walls. He was intrigued by the shapes and colours, the contorted torsos and limbs. He paused at one of them, which showed the naked figure of a man, his eyes gazing imploringly from the canvas. The image was arresting and he had to do a double take of Leon, before realising it was him.

'Stefan's family insisted I have them. As you can see, he was an amazing artist, too.' He reached out and touched the jagged ridges of the oil paint on one of the canvases. 'To be surrounded by his work keeps him close to me.'

What had initially appeared as a decadently ostentatious apartment, now felt more poignant.

The Look of Death

Before they left, Leon turned to Bela, who'd remained silent throughout their discussion. 'Have we met? I feel as if I recognise you from somewhere.'

Hoping to avoid this particular conversation, Colin quickly opened the front door. 'Thanks so much for your time, Leon.'

'A Thursday night, the end of summer, three years ago,' Bela stated. 'You picked me up at a bar in Mitte. We fucked at my flat. You said you'd call, but you didn't.'

Leon blushed a deep crimson. 'Sorry. Yes, I remember now. How remiss of me.' Polite until the end, he said a hurried goodbye and closed the door firmly behind them.

'What I didn't add is that he told me he lived outside the city,' Bela said once they were in the lift.

Colin pressed the button to go down. 'You can't help yourself, can you?'

'What? You think I shouldn't have addressed it?'

'What was the point?'

'Because it was true.'

Colin couldn't look at him. 'You seem determined to put everyone you meet on a guilt trip,' he said, staring ahead.

'Well, he should feel guilty. It was very rude of him.'

When the lift reached the ground floor, Bela wrenched open the grille and stormed out onto the street. 'I don't like the guy,' he said. 'He's hiding something. His stiff body language, the polished way he told his story. It's all suspicious. Don't you see?'

'No, I don't. I saw him as helpful, grief-stricken, frustrated. What I'd expect from someone who's lost a close friend.'

'If you can't see he's a liar, you might as well give up now. But then you were too busy flirting.'

'Seriously?' Colin had had enough. 'Give me one single example of how I was flirting with him?'

Bela's facial expressions scrambled around for one. 'Well,

what was that all about – saying you reminded him of Stefan? Creepy!'

Colin knew this relationship with Bela was no longer working for him. They needed to have a conversation, but not right now. It would have to wait until he'd collected his thoughts and found the right words to say. 'I need to take a rain check on tonight.' He strode off in the opposite direction, refusing to look back even as Bela called out his name.

18

Ajnur stood behind the food stall on Maybachufer Strasse, bored to tears. He'd been out since six that morning working at the family's lock-up doing a stock check, alongside his brother, Mustafa, but as soon as they'd arrived at the market and unloaded that day's fresh produce, Mustafa had made a lame excuse about needing to meet a new wholesaler.

'I won't be long,' he'd shouted, a wide grin revealing a set of perfectly white teeth. His Hollywood smile as he liked to call it.

'You're a bloody liar.' Ajnur watched his brother saunter off, knowing it would be hours before he returned.

Catch you later, little brother,' he shouted back, waving as he disappeared round the corner.

It was a good job the market was busy, otherwise he'd have fallen asleep. The night before had been a late one. After the slim pickings in Ernst-Thälmann Park he'd hooked up with a guy he met in the Tiergarten, a Dutch tourist in his thirties who'd taken him back to a hotel overlooking the park.

When he'd crept home well after four, heavy snoring resonated through the house, suggesting Mustafa had successfully covered for him. While he and his brother might not always get on, they had each other's backs – no questions asked. Which was just as well, as he wasn't sure Mustafa would approve of this hidden side of him. And there was no doubt his parents would be appalled – they'd have him on the first plane back to Turkey if they ever discovered where he was going and what he was doing.

The few hours' sleep he'd snatched weren't enough to keep him focused on the hustle and bustle of the market. He couldn't be bothered to write a receipt, let alone haggle with anyone.

Staring towards the Landwehr Canal, he spotted a nice distraction: a guy in jeans and a white T-shirt leaning against the railings. It was subtle, but judging by his body language, he appeared to be on the lookout for some action. Ajnur caught his eye and held it for a second too long. For several minutes they exchanged glances – nothing too overt. Whether the guy was genuinely interested or teasing, Ajnur couldn't tell. He'd have to wait for Mustafa to get back before he could investigate properly. It wouldn't be the first time he'd picked someone up while working at the stall, but he hadn't risked it in ages; it was a bit too close to home.

A middle-aged woman, a froth of white hair heaped like a swirl of candyfloss on her head, approached the stall and blocked his view. 'I'm not sure what I want. Can I taste a couple?' She pointed to the olives.

'Sure.' Without paying much attention, Ajnur took a cocktail stick, pricked the olives, and handed them to her one at a time.

She chewed and swallowed them, throwing the cocktail sticks to the ground. 'What price are they?'

Ajnur referred to the prices written in large letters across each tray. 'You'll not find better.'

'Let me try that one again.' She popped the olive into her mouth, swallowed, then shook her head. 'I can't decide.' On

The Look of Death

a different day, he might have called her out for time-wasting, but today he was happy to play along until she'd had her fill.

'Come back again,' he said with a fake smile as she finally got bored and moved on.

Damn! The guy in the white T-shirt was now further along the canal side, talking to a girl. They were laughing together. Maybe this was who he'd been waiting for. She held up a map – so not a girlfriend, just a tourist looking for directions. A tree was obscuring Ajnur's view and he tilted his head to one side. As he did so, the guy looked towards him. This time, to avoid any ambiguity, he held his stare for five seconds. Soon after, the girl folded up her map and disappeared into the crowd.

Having had a proper look at the guy, Ajnur thought he recognised his face. Had he seen him in Ernst-Thälmann the night before? Or the Tiergarten? Who knew? There were so many potentially available men in Berlin all sending out signals it was hard to keep up. There were some who discreetly smiled at him as they passed the stall, others who approached and chatted as if they were long-lost friends. This guy seemed more like the former – far more reticent – so, probably in the closet.

The guy turned away to face the canal, obviously playing hard to get. The least he could do was come across and pretend to be interested in buying some dolma or halloumi. A bit of a chat and a flirt would be a start.

He checked his watch. Almost mid-day. He was supposed to get his lunch break then. Where the hell was Mustafa? If his brother didn't turn up soon, regardless of how curious this guy was, things wouldn't be going anywhere. Ajnur looked over to the canal again, but the guy had gone. He glanced up and down the stalls; there was no sign of him. Too bad; he'd seemed his type.

True to form, Mustafa arrived after twelve-thirty with an

excuse about having lost track of time. As he leaned in to hug him, Ajnur could smell perfume on his brother's clothes.

'Think I believe you?' Ajnur pushed him away. 'You're the worst liar.'

'Believe what you want, brother, I'm telling the truth.' He kissed the silver ring on his left hand. 'You have my word.'

'And you stink of cheap perfume!'

'Nothing gets by you, eh?' Mustafa grabbed Ajnur in a headlock and ruffled his fringe. 'But there's nothing cheap about my friend.'

'Better not let Mum smell you. She'll disown you.' Ajnur pulled away from his brother's grip and fixed his hair.

Mustafa took another friendly swing at Ajnur, but he ducked, just as the middle-aged woman from before returned. He sprang to attention. 'I take it you've decided?'

The woman ignored Ajnur and asked Mustafa. 'Are your olives fresh?'

'Get out of here,' Mustafa whispered to Ajnur. He then addressed the woman with his Hollywood smile. 'Apologies for my brother's rude behaviour.' He shoved Ajnur out of the way. 'So, what can I do for you today, gorgeous?'

Ajnur passed his brother the moneybag, slapped him on the back, then strolled towards the canal. 'Tell Mum I'll be back at eight.'

'I could give you my friend's number,' Mustafa hollered, laughing as he passed a second olive to the woman.

'Nah, you're alright,' he shouted back. 'I've my own plans.'

Ajnur decided to take a stroll west along the canal. Perhaps the guy from before was still hanging about. But that had been an hour ago, so there was little chance. There was always the Tiergarten, with its non-stop action.

Every week for the last eight years he'd worked on the market, first as a small boy on weekends, helping his dad, watching as he served the customers, picking up the phrases

The Look of Death

that helped clinch a sale, then alongside his extrovert older brother, who could rally a crowd around the stall in seconds if he wished. Eight long years. Was this going to be his life for the next eight? Or eighteen? Or twenty-eight? It didn't bear thinking about.

He focused instead on the rays of sunshine pushing down through the canopy of leaves. Every now and again the full heat of the sun caught his face, warming his soul. It felt delicious to be out and about in the city on a warm summer's day with the rest of the afternoon free to do as he pleased.

Sitting on a bench by the canal's edge, he took a sip from his bottle of water, then leaning back, closed his eyes. Lazing in the park sounded perfect. He'd find a shaded patch, stretch out and let the men come to him. Like bees around honey.

A shadow fell across him, blocking out the light. When it didn't pass, he opened his eyes to find a figure staring at him. He smiled as the features of the guy from before came into focus. So, he'd waited until he was alone. *Sweet*, Ajnur thought. 'Hey,' he said, 'fancy meeting you here. Do you wanna sit?'

'Only if we can introduce ourselves first.'

'I'm Ajnur.'

'Hi Ajnur, my name's Konrad.'

19

FRIDAY, 8TH JULY 1994

Two days of ten-hour shifts at *Zum Zum* had left Colin exhausted. With barely time to draw breath, he'd little opportunity to consider the information given to him by Ajnur, or the idea that someone may have followed him, nor reflect on the meeting with Leon Brauckmann. But at least now he'd a name to work with: Konrad.

Yawning, thinking of an early night, all of a sudden he remembered the arrangement he'd made to sit for Maryam and Lukas. Rummaging through his pocket, he pulled out a napkin with the date and time: Friday, 8th July, 9 p.m.

'Fuck!' he shouted. He quickly jumped in the shower then rushed from his flat, grabbing a falafel at the nearest Imbiss before taking a train to the art school.

He gazed through the window as it snaked its way through the city, the blue and purple hues of the evening sky starting to succumb to black. Cranes filled the horizon in every direction; the city appeared to be one enormous construction site. After the collapse of the Wall, investment had flooded in, with even the most remote neighbourhoods attracting new residents and tourists. Compared to London, Berlin felt

The Look of Death

cosmopolitan and progressive, not held back by prejudice and dumb questions about which school you went to or what team you supported. This was a city in flux, preparing itself for the future whilst shedding the past. New shiny buildings sprang up every day and the character of entire streets could transform overnight. Colin enjoyed the constant sense of change; it felt like the right place for him to be.

The glass doors to the main reception area of the art school were locked when he arrived. After banging on them for a few minutes, he wandered to the side of the building where a side door was open. 'Lukas? Maryam?' he shouted. Hearing no response, he entered, and walked downstairs to the basement. Soon there was music and the unmistakable voice of Nico singing, *I'll Be Your Mirror.*

The studio they'd been allocated was a cavernous space with no windows and glowing strip-lights. A huge table sat opposite the door and the walls were lined with shelves stacked with pots of paint, dirty brushes and a whole range of weird and outlandish props and artefacts. The centre of the room was dominated by two easels, each holding a large canvas, bringing focus to a moth-eaten armchair, from which stuffing spewed in all directions. Looking down, Colin could barely see the floor as it was littered with paint-soaked rags and images ripped from newspapers. The smell of turpentine was overwhelming, making his head spin.

Both Lukas and Maryam were singing at the top of their voices, swaying hand in hand whilst passing a joint and didn't notice him entering.

'Looks like I've missed the party.'

'Christ!' Maryam squealed. 'You gave me a fright.' Looking even more goth-like than earlier in the week, she was wearing thigh-high black boots, a tiny leather skirt, and a skimpy vest with *ANGEL* embroidered across it.

'Come and join us.' Under the stark ceiling lights, Lukas's

green eyes were even more striking, glinting behind his thick lenses. 'Want a beer?'

Scattered around the floor were several bottles; both of them scurried around trying to locate one they'd not already drunk. Eventually, Maryam found a full one tucked behind a canvas. With great dexterity, she hit the cap along the side of a shelf; it popped off easily, flying across the room. 'Here you go, handsome.'

Colin took it. 'Cool space.'

'You mean grim as fuck.' Maryam found another full bottle and effortlessly repeated her opening technique. 'It's the worst. I mean, who has a studio without a window? Bill assigned us this one. You know him, right? He can't stand either of us. Says we're troublemakers because we won't go to their dumb still-life classes.'

Lukas tidied away some of the drawings which were lying on the floor. 'This is some of my shit art. Well, my old stuff. I'm going to destroy the lot.'

Picking up one of the sketches, Maryam held it aloft. 'I'm having this one.' To avoid Lukas grabbing it back from her, she rushed towards Colin, shrieking, 'Take it! He's going to burn the lot. He's not kidding.'

Colin took it from her. An intricate study of birds in flight around the central figure of an angel, the words *Every Angel is Terrifying* had been scrawled across the image with a red marker pen. 'Is that a quote from Rilke?' Colin remembered it from a book of poetry Lee had given him as a birthday present.

'Handsome and smart.' Lukas grabbed it from him. 'For the bin.' He tore it into tiny pieces and threw them in the air. As they fell, he picked up a small sketch from the sofa and handed it to him. 'You can have this.'

It was one of the sketches he'd drawn of Colin that first day: multiple portraits taken from slightly different angles,

The Look of Death

layered over each other. On closer inspection, it was even more impressive. 'Thank you. I love it.'

Maryam grabbed Colin's hand. 'Let's show you what we've been working on this week.' She angled the larger of the canvases to face him. The outline of a figure had been placed in the centre, with thick lines drawn in different shades of pink rippling from it.

'Is it finished?'

She shook her head. 'This is the start of something new. I'm pretty excited by it.'

'Maryam's a genius.' Lukas came up behind them and put his arms around their shoulders. 'Explain it to him.'

'It's all about the masks we wear in different areas of our lives. How we present ourselves to the world in various contexts: our family, our jobs, our everyday journeys. That sort of thing. Take for example the expression on your face at the moment.'

'What? I have a specific expression?'

'Your body language is relaxed, but I'd say your facial expression is a little guarded, but curious. What I do is I take photographs of people in different situations, then slice the images up into separate parts, before reconstructing them in an entirely new way. Look here.' She urged Colin to step closer.

What appeared like abstract lines were in fact tiny collages of body parts: eyes, hands, mouths.

'You get the idea,' she said.

'Wow. That must take forever.'

'Take a look at her other stuff.' Lukas dragged a large black portfolio onto the table and opened it up. 'It's amazing. I'm determined to be as good as her.'

After scanning Maryam's drawings and collages – detailed, sensual, at times provocative – Colin wandered around the rest of the studio. Everywhere, images had been stuck to walls and shelves, whilst dozens of books lay open revealing even more – from antiquity, cinema, exhibitions. 'How do I fit into all this?'

'Well, when you're ready, sit on the armchair and let us do our thing.' Lukas began sorting out his brushes.

'Shall I take my clothes off?'

Both Lukas and Maryam laughed. 'Only if we can strip off, too.' Lukas picked up a paintbrush. 'We're only interested in your head and face, so no need to undress. Well, not this time.'

'I wore my best pants, too,' Colin teased.

'I should ask you what colour – because I do love sexy underpants on a guy. But I promise I'll be on my best behaviour tonight.' Lukas pulled a sheet from the other canvas to reveal more detailed sketches of Colin taped to a clean canvas.

Maryam pointed to a drawing. 'Focus on this one.' She looked around the room. 'What have you done with the joint?'

'I've somehow ended up with it.' Colin handed it to her, moved a pile of magazines from the armchair onto the floor, then sat. 'How do you want me?'

'Stare straight ahead and try not to move,' Lukas said, turning on a couple of angle poise lights and adjusting them. 'Don't worry, we'll only be doing four ten-minute poses. You'll be out of here before ten.'

As stipulated, they stopped every ten minutes, but instead of chatting Maryam and Lukas would look at one another's work, then flick through a book or magazine, rip out an image, and pin it onto a board which already held a collection of torn-out images.

'Inspiration?' Colin asked.

'More like desperation.' Lukas ripped a photo of a body-builder's torso from a health and fitness journal. 'This might work.'

'Don't listen to him,' Maryam said. 'This is a serious exercise. We're creating a common album of images for us both to reference. The idea is to eventually try and work on a single canvas together.'

'It's a way of ridding ourselves of ego; reinventing and losing ourselves,' Lukas added.

After another ten-minute pose, Lukas threw his glasses onto a chair, thrust his face towards his canvas until his nose was almost touching it and scrutinised what he'd drawn. A long sigh followed. 'That's enough for tonight. Maryam? What about you?'

'Drink? That what you're thinking?'

'Colin? Fancy joining us?' Lukas handed him thirty Marks. 'It's Friday, the night is young.'

'But I've only posed for about thirty minutes.'

'Then the first drink's on you. Coming or not?'

20

Ajnur stood on the balcony, gazing at people below strolling in the street – after ten, and it was still as warm as hell. With the temperature having soared to thirty-six degrees during the day, even now it remained in the high twenties, and across from him, balcony doors had been thrown open to allow in some much-needed air.

Since meeting Konrad two days ago, Ajnur hadn't wanted to leave his apartment; light and spacious, it contrasted with the cramped two-bedroom flat he shared with his parents and brother. Here, there was a sense of pared-back luxury, with each object carefully chosen and perfectly placed to show it off; unlike the mish-mash of cheap ornaments and clashing patterns his parents favoured.

He picked up a bronze sculpture from its prime position on the windowsill. Heavy and shaped like a rose, its long stem was elegant and satisfying to touch. The stylised thorns were rough and his fingers lingered over their sharp edges.

'Take the spare keys,' Konrad had said that first day, throwing him a set. 'I want you to think of this as your home.'

'But what do I do when you're not here?' Spending quality time indoors was a novelty. Usually, if he had a

The Look of Death

moment free, he'd head straight to the park and wander through the bushes in search of guys. But now, he had one guy demanding all his attention.

Konrad had kissed him on the lips. 'You'll find something to occupy yourself.'

Replacing the sculpture, Ajnur wandered through to the bedroom and sprawled face down on the bed, inhaling Konrad's scent. In the mirrored wardrobe, he caught his reflection, stroking the silk sheets as though petting an exotic animal. He laughed at how absurd he looked, how happy he appeared. How had he landed here?

At first, Mustafa wasn't keen on covering for him. But when he offered to do the same for him the following week, his brother finally relented, and agreed to tell his parents that he'd gone with some friends to a festival, and would be back at the weekend. They'd apparently pushed for more details, but Mustafa was an expert at placating them, insisting he could cover the stall on his own for a couple of days, that Ajnur needed some time to himself.

The air-conditioning clicked back on, cooling the room. Perhaps he should take a nap. Konrad had told him he'd be home by eight, but it was already after ten. What was taking him so long? Didn't he know he'd been waiting for him all day? How desperate he was to see him? It was true what they said: older guys made better lovers. Konrad knew exactly what he wanted, plus he was super fit, with the stamina to keep going for hours.

'Why do you want to go out with someone so young?' he'd asked Konrad as he lay in his arms that first night. Usually, the age difference didn't matter, but if this was going to last, he needed to know whether he wanted him for who he was, and not because he was nineteen.

'It's the connection that's important. I've slept with lots of different people – older, fatter, men, women – I'm not just into cute twinks, you know.'

'So, you're bi?'

Konrad had fixed him with a look, suggesting this topic was out of bounds.

'Sorry. I'm asking too many questions.'

'No, you've a right to.' He sat up and looked directly at him. 'You deserve the whole truth. I was married for a few years, but we were too young, and neither of us knew what we wanted. Same old story. Anyway, we're getting divorced and it's been pretty messy.' He extended his arms. 'Now, let's get some sleep. You've worn me out.'

The room was still too warm and Ajnur stood on a chair to adjust the air-conditioning. Konrad had shown him how to do it. He'd shown him how to do everything: put on the washing-machine, load the dishwasher, operate the TV and audio system. It made him feel grown-up and he had blushed, thinking how little he did around his parents' house.

At the sound of the key turning in the lock, he ran to the door, arriving as Konrad was pushing it closed.

'You said eight.' Ajnur pouted, pretending to be angry.

'I'm sorry, baby. A work meeting went on forever.' He buried his nose into Ajnur's hair as he hugged him. 'You smell amazing. Like fresh grass.'

Ajnur enjoyed being held this way. It felt safe, different from the swift, unsatisfying hook-ups in the park. 'Are you hungry?'

Konrad kicked off his shoes and threw his briefcase to the side. 'Starving.'

'I went shopping.' Taking Konrad's hand, he led him through to the kitchen. 'So, I've made a few salads.' He opened the fridge. 'These are all my mother's recipes: *zeytin piyazi*, – an olive salad, *kisir* – bulgur wheat and pomegranate, *baba ganoush* – an aubergine dip, and these are *bazlama* flatbreads to mop everything up with.' As Ajnur

The Look of Death

explained each dish, he placed bowls in the centre of the table.

Konrad removed his tie and slung it over the back of his chair. 'Have you been cooking all day?'

'They're easy to make.' He was lying; it had taken hours.

Konrad drew him close, kissed him and murmured, 'You're the best. Stay with me forever, won't you?'

Once they'd entered the bedroom, Konrad lay back on the bed, grinning. 'Can we try something new?'

'What like?'

Konrad sprang up and brought a blue polyester suit wrapped in plastic from out the cupboard. 'Can you put it on?'

Ajnur removed the cover, placed the suit on the bed and began to undress. Without saying a word, he watched Konrad's grin grow wider with each piece of clothing he put on. Fumbling with knotting the tie, Konrad helped him secure it.

'You look good.' Konrad stepped back and admired him.

Ajnur gazed at himself in the mirror. 'I look like I'm going to a wedding.'

'It fits perfectly. Now, lie on the bed.'

'Is that an order?'

'Do as I say.'

Each piece of the outfit – the shirt, the jacket, the trousers, the black socks and shiny black shoes – were slowly removed and carefully folded. The ritual aroused Konrad far more than his naked body ever had.

'I'll be back in one minute. Close your eyes and stay there.'

Once Konrad left the room Ajnur looked at himself in the mirror. He was too skinny compared to Konrad. He needed to bulk up, do more exercise, sculpt his body into that of a man. This would be his next goal. He was fed up with being a boy.

Hearing Konrad return, he closed his eyes as he'd been told. The shock of the wet sponge forced them open, but

Konrad gently closed them again. 'I want to clean you,' he said.

'But I had a shower before you arrived.'

Konrad wasn't listening. Instead, he gently caressed and cleaned every inch of his body, each stroke followed by a series of tiny kisses. Then, after he'd dried him with a towel, he leaned over and kissed him on the lips. 'Goodnight,' he whispered.

'Is that it?' Ajnur asked.

'Why? What more do you want?'

Ajnur slipped from the covers, careful not to wake Konrad, who was curled up at the edge of the mattress, clinging on as though he might fall off. There'd been a couple of times he'd woken to find him whimpering and had gently pressed his hand against him, hoping to silence the cries, but it hadn't worked.

He walked through to the kitchen, poured himself a glass of water, and stepped out onto the balcony. The light breeze was a welcome relief from the stickiness of the last few days and he took a deep breath, letting the night air fill his lungs. As he exhaled, he became aware of a knot deep in his stomach. Why couldn't he just enjoy the moment? Everything was perfect, wasn't it?

He heard Konrad get out of bed and move through to the kitchen. From within the darkness of the apartment, he heard him whisper his name.

Ajnur turned and focused on the shadow inside, dressed in a grey silk dressing-gown which matched the grey silk bedsheets. Through the open door, they observed each other, and Konrad undid his dressing-gown, letting it drop to the floor; his pale, muscular body ghost-like in the gloom. 'Come back to bed,' he murmured.

Ajnur remained on the balcony. What if none of this was

The Look of Death

real? What if it ended in a few days? Konrad beckoned him in, and Ajnur stepped back inside. The room suddenly felt smaller, the ceiling lower and more oppressive.

'Come back to bed, baby,' Konrad pleaded.

'Soon,' Ajnur said. 'I can't sleep. I'm going to watch some TV.'

'Please yourself.' Konrad kissed him on top of the head and returned to the bedroom.

As the flickering screen lit up the room, Ajnur muted the sound. Tomorrow, he'd go home.

21

Colin attempted to keep up with Maryam and Lukas, who'd stumbled out the bar, grabbed a nearby wheelie-bin, and were now pushing it through the streets.

'What are you doing with that?' he shouted, but they weren't listening. Doubting they'd notice, he considered slipping away and heading home; all night, they'd only had eyes for each other. In the bar, both had drunk shot after shot, daring each other to drink quicker. After the first few, Colin had given up. When they'd produced a sachet of speed, he knew it had been a mistake agreeing to come out with them. The *terrible twins* he'd dubbed them, which had amused them no end. Each was as wild as the other; and neither, as he was discovering, seemed to have any boundaries.

'Come here.' Lukas beckoned for Colin to catch up.

As he approached, Maryam had thrown the bin lid open and was attempting to clamber inside. 'Man, it stinks!' she cried.

'Help me steady it,' Lukas shouted, holding onto a corner.

But before Colin reached them, Maryam was standing inside, gripping onto the sides, hollering to the night sky. 'Push me,' she commanded, banging her hands against the metal, like the statue of Victoria driving her bronze chariot atop the Brandenburg Gate.

Lukas pressed his shoulder into the back of the bin, which gathered speed as it rolled down a gentle incline.

'This is not safe, guys,' Colin yelled as the bin hit a kerb and came to an abrupt halt.

'Again! Again!' Maryam screamed.

Colin stopped at a street corner where he knew he could catch a tram. The night was well and truly over. For two hours, he'd been pretending to enjoy himself, resisting the urge to check his watch every ten minutes. 'I'm going home,' he shouted, hoping they wouldn't try and force him to stay.

'But you can't leave us,' Maryam called back. 'You're our mascot. Lukas, tell him he can't go.'

'You can't go,' Lukas said.

For a moment, Colin thought Lukas might be sobering up; of the two, he appeared the more sensible. But he confused Colin: while he didn't come across as a passive person, when it came to Maryam, he seemed to go along with whatever she suggested. She even influenced his art, telling him which brushes to use, what colours to choose, when to hold back or go further. But Lukas appeared to relish his role as a faithful devotee.

'I'm done in,' Colin sighed as he joined Lukas.

'Maybe we should call it a night,' Lukas said, his eyes wavering.

'No way!' Maryam shouted.

Lukas grabbed Colin's shirt. 'Maryam says we need you.'

'It's late. I'm tired. Go off and have fun. I'm being a killjoy.'

'No, you don't understand. We need you,' Maryam interrupted. 'So, buckle up my beauties and keep pushing!'

Reluctantly, Colin grabbed the wheelie-bin. 'Ten more minutes, then I'm off.'

'To the East Side Gallery,' Maryam shouted.

Lukas steered as they began pushing the bin again. With complete disregard for any danger, he repeatedly stepped out in front of traffic to stop it. As horns blared and Maryam shrieked with glee, he waved in faux apology as cars and cyclists swerved to avoid them.

'You'll get us killed.' Colin stood in front of the bin, refusing to go any further. 'Seriously, I'm not playing anymore.'

Both stared at him, their faces shocked by his sudden outburst. Just as he thought he'd got through to them, they exchanged a look and exploded with laughter.

With one huge heave, Lukas steered the bin around Colin and onto a footpath leading to a bridge across the Spree. 'It's this way,' he said.

AT THIS TIME OF NIGHT, free from the hordes of tourists who turned up daily to photograph themselves beside the vibrant images, the East Side Gallery was eerily quiet. A shrine to the new Berlin, this severed stretch of the Wall had been turned into a symbol of the future. Built on love and community, it subverted everything the Wall once stood for.

Colin had a sudden insight into how Fraser must have felt that night in November, five years previously: the excitement of arriving in the city to discover people tearing the Wall down with diggers, hammers, their bare hands. It must have been incredible to witness, to be part of history. In their detail, his sketches gave a sense of how momentous an event it was. No wonder Rhona held onto them so dearly.

'Look at the state of you.' Lukas laughed. 'What's that stuck to your trousers?'

'Who cares?' Maryam manoeuvred the bin up against the Wall and caught her breath.

'Oh my God! It's maggots,' Lukas cried. 'They're wriggling.'

The Look of Death

'Fuck!' Maryam looked down. 'It's rice, you idiot.' She giggled, brushing a few grains off her leg.

'Now, can we go home?' Colin said.

'Not yet.' Maryam pulled off her boots, threw them at Lukas who caught them mid-air, then sprang on top of the bin, almost immediately losing her balance. Only Colin's quick reaction steadied her, but instead of jumping back down, she began pulling herself up the wall. 'Lukas, give me a push.'

Without a second thought, Lukas launched himself onto the bin, and crouched, taking hold of her legs.

'You're insane,' Colin said, pressing his weight against the bin to stop it from rolling away.

'And that's a criticism?' Maryam asked, as Lukas lifted her high enough to let her grip the top of the Wall. She dangled there for a second before propelling her legs upwards; in one elegant manoeuvre she was sitting astride the top, perfectly balanced. 'It's easy,' she said.

'Now, me,' Lukas begged, raising his arms in the air. Maryam grabbed his wrist as he tried to scrabble upwards. 'Colin, can you help?'

Knowing that without him, it would be impossible for Lukas to climb any further, Colin secured the bin by jamming a half brick under the nearest wheel and jumped on top. As he shoved Lukas from below, Maryam grabbed him from above.

'I've got you,' she shrieked.

'Don't let go,' he screamed back.

With a final push, Lukas joined Maryam on top of the Wall and they both whooped with delight.

Legs drumming against the concrete, they hugged each other and sang a German pop song he'd heard on the radio, but didn't know the words to.

'Join us,' Maryam shouted.

'Yes, join us,' Lukas echoed.

Colin shook his head. 'That's my good deed done for the day. Goodnight,' he said, waving as he made his way down the street. He took a final look back as it turned away from the Spree. What he saw almost defied belief. Despite the round edges at the top of the Wall, both had somehow managed to stand upright, and were gripping each other's hands; balanced precariously, preventing each other from falling.

'*Wir sind frei*,' they chanted.

We're free.

22

SATURDAY, 9TH JULY 1994

Colin replaced the receiver. *Damn!* Kim Stroder was proving elusive. Without the promised number from Bela, he'd gone ahead and found a number for the youth centre himself. But having left several messages with the receptionist, so far she'd not called back.

'Was that Lee?' Hannah asked, handing him a tray of dirty plates.

Colin placed the tray behind the bar. 'Nope.'

'He called again last night.' She held up her hand and waved it in his face. 'You need to talk to him.'

'Excuse me.' Colin collected a few empty glasses from a nearby table and stacked them on the counter.

Hannah was still staring at him.

'I will. Honest. I've been run off my feet. And I'm hungover.'

'Have you told Lee about Bela?'

'It's none of his business.' Colin moved past her. 'Anyway, me and Bela occasionally fuck. That's it. So, drop it.'

Since moving to Berlin, communication between him and Lee had been sporadic. And the few times they'd spoken recently, things had been strained. Though what did he expect? Before moving to Berlin, they'd officially broken up and gone their separate ways. Hannah's existing friendship with his ex – and the fact she'd set Colin up with a job and a place to stay when he arrived in Berlin – was an added complication. He knew her loyalties were split.

'I'm not interfering. You know Lee and I never discuss you.'

Colin filled the sink with soapy water. 'I need to find the right moment to have a proper chat with him. That's all.'

'Here, let me do that.' She picked up the glasses and dunked them in the sink. 'You are coming tonight?'

He screwed his face up. Since first thing, she'd been trying to convince him to go along with her to an exhibition launch. 'What about your hot date? I thought you and this new guy were going out for a meal?'

'That'll be over with quick. He's got his kids staying over tonight.'

'You say that now. But once you get your claws into him – kids or no kids – he'll be like putty in your hands.'

'I promise I'll be good.' She held her hands up in prayer, suds dripping from her elbows. 'Don't be a killjoy. Come out with me. It'll be fun. You do remember what fun is?' She splashed some suds at him. 'Please say yes.'

Saying no to Hannah was practically impossible. 'Make it worth my while.'

'There'll be lots of hot guys there.'

'I'll be the judge of that.'

'Free drink.'

'That'll be finished within an hour.'

'The chance of quality time with me?' She tried flicking more suds at him, but he ducked. 'I dunno, it's a fifteen-minute walk from home. If it's rubbish, we can be back and tucked up in bed by twelve.' With a wink, she dived to the end of the bar to serve a customer. 'You're going to give in – I can tell.'

The Look of Death

He was due to finish at seven, so in theory he could dive home, grab a bath, have something to eat and be ready to go out later. 'What sort of event is it again?' He handed her a clean glass.

'It's right up your street, Mister Culture Vulture. A group of sculpture students and performance artists have taken over a venue called *Griechen Fabrik* – it's like our building only much bigger. There'll be installations, DJs, cabaret, the works. And boys. Lots and lots of boys.'

'And if it's rubbish, we leave immediately?'

'Cross my heart.'

'OK. You've convinced me.' He hoped he wouldn't regret saying yes and that he'd be able to keep up. Hannah liked to party hard and could convince anyone to have one more drink or one more dance. Her tough Yorkshire roots on her mother's side, combined with her beatnik German father, had created a party girl with the constitution of an ox, who took pride in always being the last one standing.

'Thank you.' She kissed him on the cheek. 'Now, do me one more favour and serve Jordi. I can't be bothered with his cheesy one-liners today.'

Colin glanced over at the guy sitting at the end of the bar, one of their regulars and originally from Barcelona. With waist-length silver hair and covered in tattoos, he'd come to Berlin twenty years ago, when it was still free and easy, and never left. He tried it on with almost every woman who entered the bar and Colin was always surprised by how many responded to his questionable charms.

As he was about to take his order, the door to the street opened and Klaus entered, in uniform. Colin signalled to Hannah. 'Sorry, can you see to Jordi?'

'Sure,' she said, raising an eyebrow. Without missing a beat, she strode towards him, warning that she wasn't in the mood for any of his nonsense.

Colin's attention shifted to Klaus, whose imposing stature

and blank stare filled the doorway. 'Sir, is now a good time?' he asked blankly.

'Sure, we've a bit of a lull.' Since meeting Bill and Seb, and gaining an insight into life at their apartment, his mind had run riot, speculating about Klaus's relationship with them. 'But I thought we were on first-name terms?'

Klaus smiled, then glanced around the space. 'My first time here. Any good?'

'The best service in the city.' Colin knew his tone was way too flirtatious and felt his cheeks redden. Hoping Klaus hadn't noticed, he picked up a cloth and wiped the counter.

'Is there somewhere private we can go?' Klaus was back to being direct, officious, no hint of warmth.

'There's a room at the back we can use.' Aware this could also be construed as suggestive, Colin hastily folded the cloth and placed it beside the sink. 'Will that do?'

'Lead the way.'

Colin directed Klaus through a narrow doorway and along an unlit corridor to a storeroom with a tiny, barred window which doubled as a Green Room on the nights that bands played. A mess of discarded bottles and pizza boxes, the space stank of stale beer and cigarettes.

'Sorry, it's a bit of a dump.' Colin moved a pile of flyers off the only visible piece of furniture, a stained and sagging sofa. 'Do you want a seat?'

'I'm fine standing.' Klaus produced a notepad from his pocket.

'Coffee? Tea?'

'No thank you, sir. Sorry, Colin.' He flicked open his notepad. 'Don't worry, it's nothing serious. I'm required to give you an update.'

'Phew! So, you've not come to arrest me?'

Klaus took off his hat and flattened his hair. 'One moment, please.' He produced a photograph from his pocket and handed it to Colin. 'As you know, the body of the man you

The Look of Death

and Bela Feldner discovered was thought to be that of Walter Baus. This has now been formally confirmed. He was twenty-five, a nurse living here in Berlin.'

Colin stared at the smiling image; it was hard to connect this person with the lifeless corpse in the graveyard. 'He's got a kind face.'

'Look carefully. You're sure your paths never crossed?'

Klaus's tone was open enough to elicit an honest response but with a hint of accusation. Colin stared at the image. 'No. I'm sure I've never seen him before.' He went to hand the photograph back to Klaus, but dropped it. Bending down to pick it up, he asked, 'Do you know how he died?' It was the only question he could think of.

'A post-mortem's taking place as we speak.'

'And there are no suspicious circumstances?'

'They found several sachets of illegal drugs in his pockets; it looks like an accidental overdose.'

'But the location? It's so close to where Martin Engel was found. Isn't that suspicious in itself?'

Klaus flicked back to a previous page in his notebook. 'The deaths occurred a year apart and there's nothing to connect them. It's a tragic coincidence.'

Colin was tempted to bring up the two deaths in Ernst-Thälmann Park, to draw a parallel between them, but decided against it. He already felt exposed and a little naïve for mentioning Martin's death again. He had to remember that he was no longer a policeman – to Klaus he probably came across like any other member of the public with a wild theory hell-bent on sharing. 'Is that everything?'

'Yes.' Klaus stepped out into the corridor, with Colin following behind. 'There's the possibility we may want to question you again, but your statement matches your friend's, so it's unlikely.' Colin was glad that Klaus had the sensitivity to use the word 'friend' in reference to Bela. He handed Colin a sheet of paper. 'This is the German translation of your original statement. If you want to get a friend to check it before signing, that's fine.'

'No need, I trust you.' Colin signed the statement and handed it back. 'I'll see you out.'

They clumsily exited the narrow door back into the bar. Hannah was still chatting to Jordi, who'd produced a guitar from somewhere and was playing the intro to *Paint it Black* badly. He appeared to have cleared the bar. Hannah caught Colin's eye but looked away immediately.

Official business complete, Colin stood awkwardly, unsure how to conclude things. Was a handshake appropriate? 'Thanks for the tip about the art school.'

'Oh, so you took my advice? I hoped you would.'

'Like you said, easy money.'

Klaus leaned forward. 'I did it once, but sweated so much I never went back.'

They both shared an awkward laugh, and Klaus stepped towards the door.

'You should pop by the bar sometime,' Colin said, 'when you're off duty. It's not usually this quiet.'

'I might do that.' He opened the door, and Colin followed him out onto the street. The scorching sun hit them – it was another day in the mid-30s.

'Christ, it's hot.'

'You don't enjoy?' Klaus ran his fingers through his hair before putting on his hat.

'I'm Scottish – we're built for the cold and rain.'

'Me, too.' He grinned. 'I burn.' He pulled back the cuff of his uniform to show a scarlet wrist. 'Sunbathing in the Tiergarten. I shouldn't, but there's nothing I like better.'

'Looks painful.'

'Nah. I put some cream on it.' Klaus stepped towards his car and smiled. 'See you around, Mr Buxton. Sorry. Colin.'

'Me and my friend, Hannah, you know her – the girl in the bar and from the *Genossenschaft*? We're going to an art exhibi-

The Look of Death

tion tonight. Well, it's more of a performance thing.' Unfiltered, the words were spilling out. 'And I wondered if you'd like to come along. It's at the *Griechen Fabrik*. Do you know it?'

Klaus remained silent.

In that moment, Colin realised Klaus was probably hit on more times in a day than he was in a year. 'It'll be fun,' he added, conscious of how desperate he sounded.

'Goodbye, Mr Buxton.'

As Klaus sped away, Colin remained standing on the pavement, watching his car disappear into the traffic.

'Everything alright?' Hannah was standing at the entrance to the bar.

'If you mean am I a complete idiot, then yes.'

'He seems nice. Handsome, too.'

'You've never seen him around the building? He's friends with Bill and Seb. Says he knows all about you.'

'I've never seen him before in my life. And believe me, I never forget a face.'

Colin knew for a fact this was untrue. Hannah was forever meeting people who remembered her, but swore she'd never met before. 'You think he might be interested?'

'What? Are you sixteen?' She went to go back inside. 'You'll maybe not want to hear this, but Lee's been on the phone. He says he's sick of you not returning his calls, that he's off to Gran Canaria for two weeks, and if you can be bothered, you've to call when he's back.'

Colin barely reacted. Instead, he kept his sight on Klaus's car as it spun round the corner.

23

The *Genossenschaft* was silent when Colin returned home. He supposed the hot weather must have driven people outside to luxuriate in the evening sun, so he had a couple of hours to himself. A leisurely soak would be the perfect way to spend it.

He rinsed out the bath, thinking about Klaus and the clumsy invitation he'd made. What the hell had possessed him? He must have been mortified; there's Klaus trying to do his job and some random guy's making a pass at him. The reality was Klaus had shown zero interest in him; he'd misread the situation, seen signs that weren't there and made a fool of himself. He cringed at his parting words. *It'll be fun.* The entire episode had left him feeling like a soppy teenager asking someone out on a first date. The next time they met – if they ever did – he'd need to find a way to apologise for crossing the line. And yet, images of ripping off Klaus's clothes, their naked bodies thrusting together, raced through his mind. He needed to sort himself out. And fast.

Down the hall, the phone rang. He ignored it. One of the many drawbacks of living with so many flatmates was the phone ringing day and night. Usually night. Drunken voices

The Look of Death

demanding to speak with Max, Nicole, Rita or any of the dozens of residents of the apartment, past and present. To his relief, the ringing stopped.

He spotted a bottle of bubble bath and poured a little into the warm water. It was probably Hannah's, but she wouldn't mind. Besides, she was always pinching his razors, promising to replace them. Not that she ever did. He helped himself to some more and watched the foam rise to the top of the bath. The phone went again. He waited, hoping someone else might answer it. But it seemed the apartment was quiet for a reason; no one else was at home. The phone kept ringing and would probably continue and ruin his bath if he didn't answer.

'Alright, I'm coming,' he shouted, turning off the taps. He let it ring another second before picking up. 'Hello.'

'Colin Buxton?' It was a woman's voice, with a thick, German accent.

'Who's this?'

'Frida Steiner. You leave a message.'

In her notebook, beside Ulrich Steiner's name, Rhona had written an address with another name, Frida Steiner, beside it. Wife? Mother? Sister? Jeanette at Amerika Haus had located her number, and he'd left a message a couple of days before, hoping for the best.

In the background a dog snarled. 'Wauzi! *Platz!*' she instructed. The dog fell silent. '*Braver Hund!*'

Colin waited until the dog had fully stopped barking, though he could still hear a soft growl in the background. 'Thanks for calling back.'

'Be quick. Wauzi is hungry.'

He needed to get her on his side. And quickly. 'What kind of dog it he?'

'A German Shepherd. He's my baby, aren't you?' She drifted away from the phone,

making baby noises at the dog.

141

'Seriously? I have a German Shepherd, too. Zak.' It was the first name that came to mind. 'They're a lot of work.' Lying was not his thing, but needs must. 'What age is he?'

'Five,' she said, her voice instantly softening. 'It's his birthday soon. Isn't it?' Again, more baby noises.

He could hear the slurp of the dog licking her. 'Wauzi! Stop!' Manoeuvring the dog away, she focused her attention back to Colin. 'In your message you say you want to speak about Ulrich. You know my son?' Her tone had become more direct, almost accusing.

'No, but I would like to ask you some questions about him.' In the silence he could hear both her and the dog breathe. 'Is that okay?' A whine from the dog was followed by Frida calming him. 'I could come to your apartment if it's easier.'

'No, no. It's okay,' she finally said.

Colin knew he'd only a short amount of time to get information from her. Her English wasn't great, and so the questions needed to be simple and direct. 'Do you think the police investigated your son's death properly?'

Wauzi growled as Frau Steiner took a pause. 'You are *Polizei*?'

'No.'

Wauzi growling in the background grew quieter, no doubt sensing a shift in the tone of its owner's voice. 'Good. Say your questions.'

'Did you have any suspicions about Ulrich's death?' The silence was so deafening, Colin thought she'd put the phone down.

'*Ja*.'

'And do you think the police conducted a thorough investigation?'

She silenced Wauzi's low growl with a quick slap. '*Die Polizei*? *Nein*. Four years, and I still wait for an explanation. No one calls. They say Ulrich is a drug addict but this is a lie.

The Look of Death

My son is a good boy. A guard. A soldier with a gun. Bang! Bang! You understand? My son is murdered.'

'Yes,' he replied. 'Your English is excellent.'

'Everyone speaks English now. It's the future. Better than Russian.' She made a spitting sound when saying the word 'Russian'.

'Who do you think murdered him? Did he have any enemies?'

'*Nein.* No enemies.'

The next question was difficult. He wasn't sure how to proceed; whether to ask directly if her son was gay and if this may have had something to do with his death. But as he was about to speak, Frida interrupted him.

'My son is not homosexual. The *Polizei* say this. This is a lie. He is popular. Lots of friends. A girlfriend, too. Sophia. Very pretty.'

Her use of the present tense doubled the sense of sorrow. 'I understand.'

'My son is a good soldier. The best. Not homosexual. Strong. No drugs,' she emphasised. 'Never.'

'Are you still in contact with Sophia?'

Frida heaved a sigh. 'Sophia forgets my son. She is married with a baby.'

'So, your son never had a relationship with a man?' She didn't reply. 'Frau Steiner?'

'One time he kisses a man. Only one time. Ulrich tells me everything. He's a good boy. He still loves Sophia.'

'And do you know this man's name? Did you ever meet him?'

The dog barked. This time Frida allowed it to continue as she remained silent.

Colin asked again. 'The man who Ulrich kissed. Can you remember his name?'

'Who cares about this man?' Frida replied. 'It makes no difference. Sophia is still sad. Ulrich is her true love.'

'So you didn't know his name?'

'*Nein.*'

From down the line, Colin heard soft sniffles of tears. 'This must be difficult. I'm so sorry.'

'Sophia might know.'

'Can I speak to her? Do you have an address? A telephone number?'

'Wauzi! *Such meine Handtasche*!' she ordered.

As they both waited for the dog to fetch her handbag, the front door was thrown open and Hannah's distinctive laugh filled the hallway. She was with her new squeeze. Colin pulled his legs out the way to let them past, sneaking a peek as she blew him a kiss. Though undoubtedly handsome, this new boyfriend was practically indistinguishable from the last three she'd dated. 'Decided to eat in?' Colin shouted after them.

'Less of your cheek.' She slammed shut her bedroom door.

The sound of Wauzi galloping back towards Frida echoed down the line.

'*Braver Hund!*' She fussed over the dog before giving him the number. 'Maybe she stays here. Maybe not. But be careful. Her husband is not a good man. A gangster. He kills you if he knows you speak about Ulrich.'

24

'Do you actually know where this place is?' The promised fifteen-minute walk had become thirty and Hannah was looking lost and out of place on a dark side street of low-rise apartments.

'Let me ask this guy.'

Hannah ran across the road and accosted a middle-aged man in shorts and a vest who was walking a yappy spaniel. Within seconds she had him roaring with laughter and was on her knees giving the dog a kiss.

'What a couple of sweeties,' she said, bounding back towards him. 'A slight error on my part – it's back this way.'

'My God, what are you like? Are we anywhere near?'

'Don't be a grouch,' she said. 'I may not have the greatest sense of direction but you're going to have fun tonight if it kills me.' She took hold of his hand. 'And we're nearly there. C'mon, it's five minutes away. Tops!'

'Promise?'

'Promise.' She stopped to take off her shoes. 'These platforms are killing me – I should've worn my DM's.'

'Yes, what's with the whole femme outfit?' Colin teased. 'Trying to impress someone?'

'God! Am I that transparent? As it happens, there is someone I've got my eye on. Tilda. She's organised the whole event.' They turned onto a main road, which was more built up and busier. 'This is more like it.'

'And what about the guy from earlier?

'Eli's a bit of fun.'

'Anyway, what's with him? You know he came in and took a piss while I was in the bath?'

'And?' She pointed to a large industrial building up ahead with people milling about outside. 'That's it!'

'Though he did look hot in his boxers.'

'He's sweet, but going through some awful divorce. Same old, same old. But he's not as hot as your butch policeman with the psycho eyes!'

Colin didn't need reminding about Klaus. The closer they got to the *Fabrik*, the more he began to dread that he might actually turn up, mistakenly imagining it was some kind of beer fest, and they were two straight buddies hanging out together. Then what? Chat about cars all night? Or police work?

Hannah strode on ahead. 'Tilda probably doesn't know I exist,' she continued. 'She's a friend of a friend, so technically I don't know her, but I feel a strong connection. You know what I mean?'

Colin had stopped listening, images of awkwardly sipping a beer with Klaus crowding his thoughts. He looked at his watch. Ten-thirty. 'Why did I ask him?' he muttered. 'I've enough complications in my life already.'

'You're catastrophising. As usual.' Hannah held his arm, balancing as she slipped her shoes back on.

'I'm sweating like a pig,' he said, untucking his shirt from his jeans. 'Look, I'm gonna head back.'

'Uh-uh. You're out and you're staying out.' Hannah clung onto him. 'Besides, it's too hot to sleep.'

The Look of Death

'You've Tilda to chase after. And I feel a complete state – look, I'm soaked through.'

'But what if she rejects me? I'll need a shoulder to cry on.'

'On this sweaty Betty?' He pointed to the damp patches under his arms.

'Gross!'

'Anyway, you won't need me to comfort you – Tilda doesn't know what's about to hit her. She doesn't stand a chance.'

'I need to make an impression tonight; one hour at most to work my magic. Then we can go get some *Currywurst*.' She wrapped her arms around his body, crushing him until he had to pinch her to stop. 'My treat,' she added.

AT THE *FABRIK*, flashing pink neon arrows led them from the street, through a series of courtyards to a vast, double height warehouse, heaving with people. In the centre of the space, on a raised stage, a DJ was blasting out drum & bass. Hannah shouted in his ear to wait, that she'd get drinks, but after fifteen minutes she still hadn't returned.

Typical Hannah, he thought. After waiting another five minutes, he made his way to the bar in an adjoining room, grabbed a beer and decided to go in search of her.

The exhibition proper began in a former workshop, off the main warehouse space. This contained a scale model of the *Fabrik*, and a bronze plaque explaining how the building had operated as a munitions factory in the early 40s. Built like a doll's house, with hundreds of miniature electric lights and populated by an army of tiny workers, sections of the model opened to reveal cavernous halls filled with heavy machinery and a warren of corridors. He leaned in for a closer look, trying to figure out where in the building he was standing.

Ordering a second beer, he followed a group of cute guys through to another room. At the far end of this space, two drag queens in matching blonde wigs and spangly tasselled outfits were performing Dolly Parton covers in German. The atmosphere was both tender and rowdy, as a drunken crowd of about fifty joined in with a sentimental rendition of *Jolene*. Colin was reminded of Glasgow and singing along to Dolly's Greatest Hits tape in the kitchen with his mother; he'd forgotten how good the Queen of Country's back catalogue was. *Old Flames Can't Hold a Candle to You* was his mum's favourite, while he preferred the drama of *Hard Candy Christmas*. And she wondered why he turned out gay.

Abandoning any hope of finding Hannah, he ventured further into the building and continued to drink. Whilst enjoying the architecture, he couldn't make head or tail of the work on display and the performances. In a turbine hall, four naked men in white masks and white body paint hung from ladders. Each took turns to recite a line from a script before striking a new pose. The large audience watching found this hilarious, but Colin struggled to get the joke. The performance concluded with one of the men splaying his legs and, to a chorus of catcalls, pulling a German flag from between his buttocks. In an adjoining nearby space, a girl in a blindfold sat in a rocking chair, knitting a long scarf from wire and in another, a boy with a pencil drew the same straight line on the same piece of paper repeatedly.

He looked at his watch; it was still only eleven-thirty. He continued down a rusted, metal staircase, arriving in the basement. The spaces here appeared to have lain untouched for fifty years; on the walls, there were peeling posters promoting the Nazi war effort, and signs directing workers where to take shelter during air raids. The further Colin explored however, the more he questioned if this was all pretend – contrived as part of the exhibition. As with the rest of the city, it was hard to distinguish the original from reconstructed copies.

The sounds of the event upstairs faded as he made his

The Look of Death

way along an empty passageway. On the verge of turning around and calling it a night, he noticed a pink neon arrow pointing to another staircase which led up to a door.

At the top of the stairs, he pushed it open to reveal a brightly lit L-shaped room with mirrored walls, ceiling and floor. Opposite him, a pink neon arrow flashed on and off, suggesting there was an exit ahead. As he crossed the floor, the door slammed shut and the main lights cut, leaving the space lit only by the quickening pulse of the neon sign, which in the mirrors repeated to infinity. Breathing heavily, he ran to where he thought the arrow was but couldn't find the exit. Increasingly disorientated, and faced with his own panicked reflection, he felt along the walls, searching for a doorhandle, but in the dim light he couldn't even work out where the entrance was. If this was part of the experience, he wasn't enjoying it.

He banged on the walls and shouted for help but couldn't hear any voices or footsteps approaching. Standing in the centre of the room he took deep breaths and tried to compose himself. Sealed in a room with no apparent way out, it felt like a trap had been set for him and he'd walked straight into it.

Suddenly the neon arrow went out, plunging the space into darkness. Colin remained still, unsure what to do next. He'd had a feeling of being followed on the train, and at Ernst-Thälmann Park; was it happening again? A creak of the floorboards suggested someone else was in the room and the sound of heavy breathing, as if someone had recently run up the stairs, appeared to be coming from close by. He couldn't tell if it was real or a soundtrack.

As he raised his fist, having decided that the only option was to smash his way out, the door flew open, and the main lights snapped back on. A group of people barged in, screaming at their reflections in the mirrored walls. One tried to grab him and get him to join them, but he resisted and dived outside.

The claustrophobia had been too much; he sat on the bottom step of the stair, resting his head against the cool, plaster wall and tried to calm himself. The group erupted back out of the room, squeezing past him, still squealing with delight.

It was time to go home.

He followed them out of the basement and within minutes found himself back in the main warehouse space. It was even busier than before and if Hannah was still here the chances of finding her were remote. He skirted around the crowd, leaving the warehouse and arriving in a long corridor. On either side, rooms were packed with people dancing; a frantic spectacle of sweaty bodies throwing themselves against each other. Had he been in the mood, he reckoned the party would have been a blast.

A hubbub of excited voices and a gust of cool air told him he was nearly at the entrance. People streamed past him, their clothes soaking wet. Reaching the main doors, he caught sight of the downpour that everyone was running from. *To hell with it!* As he was about to step out into the rain, a low voice spoke from the shadows.

'Is the party no good then?'

The accent was unmistakable: Klaus.

25

The thunderous noise of the rain hitting the ground was exhilarating; great swathes of water bounced off the cobbled courtyard, washing it clean, whilst people screeched and ran for cover. Huddled together in a doorway, Klaus drew Colin close and kissed his lips. 'You don't mind?'

Colin smiled. 'I didn't think you'd come.'

'I should be catching up on some paperwork, but I couldn't stop thinking about you.' Klaus ran his fingers through Colin's hair.

'I didn't think you were interested,' Colin said. 'I wasn't even sure you were gay.'

'You're kidding? I basically told you I was at an orgy at your neighbour's flat – it's not something I usually mention after I've taken a statement.'

Colin laughed. 'I couldn't be sure that's what you meant.'

'Honestly?' Klaus shook his head.

'I didn't know if I was reading too much into it. Some investigator, eh?'

They kissed again, Colin resisting the urge to tear Klaus's T-shirt off there and then. 'That's the rain stopping,' he said. 'We should start walking.' When Klaus emerged from the *Fabrik's* shadows – tight jeans, broad chest, a big grin on his face – Colin knew without a doubt he wanted him.

Klaus slipped his fingers between his own and gripped his hand. 'Is that okay?'

In the UK, it was rare to see two men walk down the street holding hands. Occasionally, with Lee, if the streets were empty, they'd clasp each other's hands, giddy from the thrill of transgression. But that was the exception. Generally, it felt too risky, an invitation for verbal abuse, or worse. Since coming to Berlin, he'd noticed how common it was, especially amongst women, but with guys of all ages, too. The fact that Klaus, a police officer, was comfortable with it felt like a whole new world opening.

'You don't have to,' Klaus teased. 'I won't be offended. I know how reserved you Brits are.'

Colin squeezed his hand in reply.

Walking through the streets, the air balmy, smelling of wet earth and the pungent odour of ozone, Colin felt a rush of excitement: of getting to know someone new, of taking him home, stripping him, discovering the hidden pleasures of his body.

'I made some enquiries about the other men.' His tone was matter-of-fact, as if Colin had asked him to.

'Okay. Right. That's not why I want to get to know you, though,' he joked.

'Must be my winning personality you're drawn to?'

'Let's see what you've got to offer first.'

Klaus leaned into Colin's shoulder, whispering, 'Hopefully you'll be impressed.'

Could he get any sexier? Had they been closer to home, Colin would have sprinted, dragging Klaus with him.

They walked a little further in silence, enjoying the cool breeze. 'The initial post-mortem results came back for Walter Baus.'

The Look of Death

'Are you able to tell me?' Colin asked, surprised at him mentioning it.

'There was alcohol and drugs in his system – specifically a large amount of speed, but MDMA and heroin too. It seems he was unlucky – taking such a cocktail, and with alcohol, is a gamble. So, it looks like the case is going to be closed.'

'What about Martin? Does no one think it strange, the discovery of Walter so close to where Martin's body was found? And the fact they were both gay?'

'In certain quarters, there's an acknowledgement that it's unusual,' Klaus explained. 'But ultimately, there's nothing to prove foul play, and there's a clear cause of death for each of them.' He let go of Colin's hand and pressed the button at a pedestrian crossing. 'Obviously they're not my cases, but the official line is those deaths were fully investigated.'*'*The sister of Fraser McDougal was liaising with a Kommissar Fink. Do you know him?'

'Unfortunately, yes. Not one of the good guys, I'm afraid.'

'And what are your own thoughts on the deaths? I mean, personally.'

The green man flashed, and they crossed the street.

Klaus's expression changed. 'There's institutional homophobia, for sure,' he said once they got to the other side. 'You have that too in the UK, I guess?'

'I'm living proof of it.'

'There are some contradictions in the evidence collected. For example, one witness at the student hostel said they heard two voices and a scream from Fraser's room. But the receptionist on duty that night, who was considered more reliable, said he'd seen him enter alone.'

'Could you get me the names of the witnesses?'

Klaus shook his head. 'I've already said too much.' He held out his hand for Colin to take. 'I can see there are similarities between some of the deaths. But establishing a pattern of offending is difficult and to then demonstrate those five deaths are connected would require a giant leap. What you're implying is there's a serial killer on the loose.'

Now it had been said out loud, that's exactly what Colin was thinking. 'And one who's targeting gay men; it's terrifying.'

'The guys on Murder look out for connections. If they sniffed something unusual – homophobic or not – they'd act quickly.' He stopped under a street-light, his face cast in shadow. 'And already Ulrich Steiner doesn't fit your pattern – you know he wasn't gay?'

'I got a call from his mother,' Colin said. 'I also spoke to a friend of Stefan Reis.' Revealing so much might be unwise, but he decided it was best to be upfront.

'Oh?' Klaus's expression clouded.

'Ulrich's mother believes he was murdered. She also let slip that he may have been bisexual and that was corroborated by a man I interviewed this week at Ernst-Thälmann Park. Similarly, Stefan's friend, Leon Brauckmann, said that he'd a secret lover at the time of his death and that the police never pursued this as a line of enquiry.' Colin noticed how quiet Klaus had become and that the vein at his temple was throbbing. 'Sorry. We don't have to discuss this.'

'No, no. It's my fault,' Klaus said. 'I brought it up.'

'What's your instinct? Do you think there's anything fishy?'

Klaus smiled. 'Fishy? What does that mean?'

Colin held his nose. 'Like a bad smell – do you think anything's off or odd?'

'Fishy! It's a good expression. I'm going to use that.'

'Has anything been missed?'

'You know how it is with police work. There's always that possibility.' Klaus caressed Colin's back. 'But to be honest, I think you're making connections where there aren't any.'

'So, no one's going to be reinvestigating the deaths any time soon?'

The Look of Death

'I don't think so. Without solid evidence to link them, no one's going to throw money or manpower at it.'

In silence, they arrived at Prinzenallee. The discussion about the case had dampened the mood; despite the obvious sexual tension, whether the night ended here or continued, Colin couldn't tell.

At the archway to the *Genossenschaft*, they paused. Staring at each other, it was Klaus who took the lead, propelling Colin into the shadows, caressing his butt cheeks and biting his neck. Here was a man who could easily switch gears: one minute, stony-faced and measured; the next flushed with excitement and raring to go.

'When you drove me back here, did you think I was interested?' Colin asked.

'Sure. I was hard the entire time. Didn't you notice?'

Admittedly, it wasn't where his attention had been. Reflecting on that first journey – Klaus's crazy driving, his questionable taste in music, the contrast between his personality in and out of uniform – he was amazed they'd managed to end up here, but he put those thoughts aside and enjoyed the feel of Klaus's body against his.

Taking Colin's hand, Klaus placed it firmly against his crotch. 'Look, here he is again – come to say hello.'

Klaus's lines could have come straight out of a bad porno and, resisting an urge to laugh at his corniness, Colin played along. 'Hello.'

Preceded by a deafening rumble of thunder, another downpour began. It felt biblical. They dashed through the archway and ran into the back courtyard, laughing at how quickly they'd got soaked. As they headed for the doorway to the building, a figure shot out from under the tree, blocking their path.

'Bela?' The smell of alcohol was overpowering. 'Is everything OK?' Colin had never seen him drunk before – as far as he knew, Bela was teetotal.

'No one's letting me in upstairs.'

Colin turned to Klaus. 'You remember my friend?'

'Still taking your statement?' Bela mumbled. His body swayed as he reached into his jeans' pocket and pulled out a scrap of paper. 'Here. Kim's direct number. I talked to her. She wants to speak to you as soon as possible.' He shoved it into Colin's hand. 'So, I take it that's us officially over?'

Colin glanced at Klaus, who'd discreetly stepped aside.

'Let's not do this right now—' Colin reached out to touch his arm, but Bela pushed him away.

He then marched off, elbowing past Klaus, and made his way out onto the street. 'Thanks for letting me know,' he called back, his muffled cries reverberating around the courtyard.

'Sorry,' Colin said to Klaus. 'I need to go after him.'

'Go do what you need to do,' Klaus replied. 'We can pick this up another time. There's no hurry.'

'Thank you,' Colin said, giving him another kiss, before sprinting after Bela.

PART 3

26

TWO WEEKS LATER - MONDAY, 25TH JULY 1994

Kim Stroder stood holding a large box of condoms and lube, handing them out to both the familiar faces and the newbies. She had an open-door policy at the Gay Youth Centre and was determined to educate anyone who'd listen. HIV was still rife in the city, and although services were good, a couple of boys from the youth group had still tested positive in the past couple of years. Hence the motto she drilled into them as they arrived each week: *Wrap it up!*

'No flavoured ones?' Christof sniffed a packet before returning it to the box.

'I'll get some next time,' she said, tucking it back into the top pocket of his shirt.

'Plus, I need large,' he announced. With a wink, he threw the packet at Roger. 'These tiny ones will fit you.'

Roger grabbed a doughnut from the table and threw it at Christof.

'Roger! Christof! Enough!' Kim shouted. 'We respect each other here. Now clean that up.' She turned to address the room. 'As Roger has kindly demonstrated, there are drinks and snacks on the table for anyone who wants them.'

Many of the boys who attended the group had known

each other since they were in their mid-teens and over the last eight years since Kim took over its management, there'd been no end of drama: fallings-out, reconciliations, heartbreaks, and recently a marriage proposal.

For the second part of the evening, she'd organised a workshop, but the first half would be the usual catch-up. The aim was to get as much of the gossip out of the way as possible, check in with everyone to gauge how they were doing and highlight if anyone was struggling, plus welcome any new faces into the fold.

The group was open to boys and trans boys aged sixteen to twenty-five. Some referrals came from social work, but mostly boys found out about the group directly through Kim, during one of her regular trawls of the bars and clubs, befriending anyone who looked like they might be underage or vulnerable. The current membership was mixed, and – for now – got along well. Generally, the younger ones kept to one side of the room, and the smaller group of older ones to the other. Kim preferred it that way; it made for an easier life.

'Start moving through to the main hall,' she shouted to the thirty or so who'd shown up. Considering it was summer and a heatwave outside, it was a decent number. 'Roger. Michael. Can you set the chairs out in a circle for me? What's wrong, Christof?'

'No crisps?'

'They're literally right in front of you.' Kim pointed to them. 'Can you ask the two new boys if they want anything?'

'If I have to.' He strolled of in the direction of a few boys loitering at the door.

She looked at her watch. Another five minutes, then she'd start. They'd have to watch their time if they were going to get through everything. Wolfgang, a regular volunteer, would be leading one of his workshops about safe sex and consent, and she didn't want him rushing any of it; it was too important.

The Look of Death

The door flew open and Ajnur appeared.

'Where have you been? I've had to set up without you.' A natural leader, but a bit of a troublemaker when he joined the group, Ajnur had responded well to the responsibilities she'd given him, and over the past few months she'd come to rely on his assistance. 'Did you bring the milk?' she asked, though she could see he was empty-handed.

'When did you ask me to bring milk?' he snapped.

'The last time I saw you. You wrote it on your list. I gave you money.'

He pushed past her.

'Everything okay?'

He shrugged and stepped away. 'I'm not your slave. There're plenty other people you can ask.'

'That's not the point. You told me you'd be here early.'

Ajnur's eyes filled with tears.

'Darling, what's the matter?'

'Leave me alone,' he cried, diving into the toilet.

As she went to follow, Christof strode out of the hall with one of the new boys in tow. 'They're going crazy in there,' he said. 'And Bruno wants hot chocolate, but there's no milk.'

She handed him a few Marks. 'Go get some. And be quick. We'll be starting in two minutes.' Opening the door to the Gents, she shouted, 'Ajnur – don't you dare go anywhere.'

In the hall, a group of boys had found the ghetto blaster and were singing and dancing along to Whitney Houston's *I'm Every Woman*, whilst others were kicking about a ball left by the girls' soccer team. It flew into a stack of chairs, knocking them over. 'Pick those up!' Her booming voice echoed around the hall, and even she winced as it reverberated back at her. 'For once, can you behave like adults?'

With a chorus of sheepish apologies, the boys took their seats. They knew when she meant business.

'Yannick?' She scanned the faces. 'There you are. Can you get things going for me? And to be clear, Yannick's in charge while I deal with an emergency. Any nonsense and he'll tell me – won't you?'

Yannick gave her a thumbs up.

Kim tapped on the cubicle door. 'Ajnur? Are you going to explain what's going on?'

A sniffle came in reply.

'This isn't about a boy, is it?' Silence followed. 'We're not going to resolve anything with you hiding in there, are we?'

The toilet flushed and Ajnur emerged, wiping away tears. He crossed to the sink and splashed water on his face. 'He's not just any boy.'

'Oh, honey.' Kim put out her arms and Ajnur fell into her chest, his entire body heaving with sobs. She'd never seen him like this before. Usually, he had them lining up, could pick and choose. 'So, you've finally had your heart broken, have you?' She sensed a tiny laugh amongst the sniffles.

'Maybe.'

Kim went into the cubicle and brought out a loo roll. 'They're high as kites in there and Wolfgang isn't due for half an hour. Do you want to get yourself together and go grab a coffee at the café on Waldemarstrasse? Here's some cash. I'll come find you once Wolfie gets here and we can talk properly. Yeah?'

Without looking up, he nodded.

Kim constantly worried about Ajnur. She'd first met him at a club in Mitte – he was drunk, and she'd spent several hours talking to him until he was sober enough to be put in a taxi and sent home. While his upbringing hadn't been that strict compared to some Turkish boys, she still felt he had a skewed approach to his sexuality. He was forever telling her it wasn't love he was looking for from men, just sex; that his plan was to fall in love with a woman, get married and have children. She'd spent a lot of time talking to him about understanding himself, thinking about the choices he was making and the impact his actions could have on others, but it mostly fell on deaf ears. Perhaps today was the perfect opportunity for a breakthrough.

His back to the door, Kim spotted Ajnur at the rear of the café. A waitress, leaning against the counter, pointedly ignored her as she flicked through a magazine; otherwise, the place was empty.

'Have things calmed down?' Ajnur asked as she took the seat opposite. Although his eyes were red and puffy, he'd stopped crying and appeared more himself.

'Doing actual back flips would you believe? Wolfgang started the workshop with a game: a *Secret Skills* icebreaker. Turns out at least two of them could've been Olympic gymnasts.' She laughed. 'They were moving onto role-play when I left, but I think he'll have his work cut out with that lot.'

'You can go back if you need to.'

'This is more important.' She spotted his empty cup. 'Do you want anything else?'

He shook his head.

At the counter she ordered a coffee from the sullen waitress, who gave her a look that suggested she was far too busy and could make it herself. 'Black, no sugar,' Kim stressed. The waitress slammed a mug on the counter and filled it to the brim. Kim smiled and said thank you, but it made no difference; the woman's attention was already back on the magazine.

'I'm spilling this everywhere. Can you pass me another napkin?' Kim mopped up the spilt coffee from the tabletop and sat. Without asking, she could already see his defences were back up. 'Someone's upset you, haven't they?'

'Big time.'

'Do I know him?'

'I doubt it.'

As much as Ajnur wanted to appear tough and streetwise, at nineteen, he had a rose-tinted view of life, imagining himself invincible. She knew pushing him wasn't the best tactic; much better to tease the truth from him and offer him the best advice she could. 'I can tell you about my first love.'

'What? Ninety years ago?' he sniped. 'You sure you can remember that far back?'

'Less cheek,' she said, pinching his arm. At least his sense of humour was back. 'Twenty-five years ago, if you must know. First year at university, me and this boy I met through the drama society became best friends. I mean, I *got* him. And he was the first boy I'd ever met who seemed to *get* me, too. We were inseparable. But … do you see where this is going?'

Ajnur rolled his eyes and shifted in his seat. 'God, he wasn't gay, was he? That's so lame.'

'No, not at all. I finally plucked up the courage and declared my undying love for him when we were both drunk. Even though I was given the cold shoulder immediately, I didn't want to hear it and instead kept trying to make him love me. Humiliated myself. Anyway, he fell in love with someone else – a lovely girl – and they became this big thing. And there was me, nineteen-years-old and cast aside, a bit player wishing it was me in the starring role.' She couldn't tell if Ajnur was listening or merely pretending to. 'But you know, I moved on. Reluctantly. I wish I could say he let himself go and lost his looks, but he didn't. What I'm saying is: at the end of the day, I knew I had to let him go or it would eat away at me.'

Ajnur picked up a napkin and began to fold it. 'I think I might be in love. Which is stupid, because I only met him three weeks ago, but I've never felt like this before. He says that I'm the one, that we'll do all these amazing things together.'

'People say things when they're in the first throes that they don't mean.'

The Look of Death

'I'm not stupid.' Ajnur leaned forward. 'This is real. Not some puppy love thing.' He sat back, satisfied he'd said his piece.

'Is this a boy your age, or someone older?'

Ajnur looked down at the floor. 'Older.'

'Straight? Gay? Bi? Married?' She waited until he was ready to answer.

He eventually nodded. 'Separated. And it's complicated.'

'You know it'll only end in tears.' He gazed over at her, his lips trembling. She chose her words carefully. 'If he's going through a messy break-up, perhaps now is not the best time to enter a serious relationship with him.'

Her words were having no effect. She could see Ajnur's eyes drift, considering his next move.

'So, what's upset you?'

He started tearing his napkin into strips. 'All of a sudden, he doesn't want to see me. He asked for his key back, and won't even let me into the apartment. Says his wife's found out about us and won't let him see his kid.'

Kim thought practically. She'd seen it happen many times and knew what to do. 'Have you any belongings there? If so, I can come and help you collect them.'

'Just the medallion my brother gave me last year for my eighteenth.'

'Which you'll want back, I assume?'

'Mustafa would kill me if I lost it.'

'Anything else?'

'A pair of jeans and a few T-shirts.'

'Okay. Then let's leave it a few days. Whatever's going on between him and his wife, maybe he'll talk when things settle. If not, I'll go with you to collect your things. But if you want me to be honest, he doesn't sound as if he deserves you.'

Ajnur thrust his chair backwards and stood. 'I knew you'd say that.' The waitress glanced up momentarily before returning to her magazine. 'This is my fault. It was me who blew it. I was trying to play it cool, pretend I didn't like him as much as I do.'

'I'm sorry Ajnur. And I don't want to sound harsh, but for someone to behave the way he has, you have to question whether they're serious or not.'

'Well, he's amazing.' He wiped away his tears. 'And I have to speak to him. Today.'

'Why today?'

'Because if it's over, I want him to tell me. I need him to say it to my face.' He walked towards the door. 'In fact, I'm going there now.'

Kim followed him. 'I think you should reconsider,' she said, placing a hand on his shoulder.

'I've made up my mind.' He shook himself free and stepped out onto the street.

'Well, if you need to call later, you've got my number,' she shouted after him. 'I'll be home all evening.'

27

Ajnur used the spare key hidden under the plant pot to enter the apartment. He no longer cared about making a fool of himself; if Konrad didn't love him, he could tell him directly. If he heard it straight, then maybe he could move on, but he wasn't going to budge until he got to the truth. Every bone in his body was telling him Konrad loved him; there had to be a solution. Kim might be right: the hysterical ex-wife and her refusal to let Konrad see his son all sounded like he'd a lot going on. But perhaps, rather than end it, he could suggest they take it slower. If Konrad had space to sort things out, then he might change his mind.

As he pushed open the door, Ajnur thought he was in the wrong apartment. 'What the fuck?' he said out loud, moving from the hall to the living room. The place had been stripped clean and was stacked with cardboard boxes. The paintings on the wall, the rugs and ornaments, all the personal touches that made it feel like home, had disappeared. Apart from a vase holding a single red rose, there was nothing to suggest anyone still lived here. Even the walls had been freshly painted white, making the apartment feel cold and sterile, as though what happened between them had never taken place.

Konrad emerged from the bedroom carrying an empty box. 'I asked you not to come here.' Without looking at him, he crossed to the kitchen and began emptying the cupboards. 'Could you leave?'

Ajnur remained where he was, listening as Konrad opened and closed doors. 'Shit!' he shouted and came limping back into the room, dumping the box on the floor.

'What happened?'

'I stubbed my toe.' Konrad sat at the table and rubbed his foot.

Joining him, Ajnur reached out, but Konrad pulled away. 'Why are you being like this? I don't understand. Why won't you even look at me?'

'You don't get it, do you? My wife's told everyone about us – my family, my friends, my colleagues. People I care about, who I wanted to tell in my own time. She's hell bent on ruining my life.'

'People are always telling me it's better that everyone knows; to come out all at once. Like ripping off a plaster.'

Konrad laughed and for the first time since entering the apartment looked at him. His eyes were cold; there was no sign of the affection he once gave him. 'What do you know about anything?' he said. 'You're just a kid, way out of your depth. Now get the fuck out of here.' He stood and kicked a cushion out of his way.

'I'm not some cheap trick you picked up.'

Konrad leaned into his face, spittle spraying from his mouth. 'That's exactly who you are.'

Ajnur pushed him away. 'Where's my stuff?'

'Your jeans and shit?' He shrugged. 'Check the bedroom.'

In a corner of the bedroom, Ajnur found a small box with his jeans and T-shirts neatly folded inside. He noticed they'd been laundered. Underneath was the gold medallion his brother had given to him. He tipped it out, held it in his hand, then with trembling fingers fastened it around his neck.

The Look of Death

His mouth was dry and his stomach ached as he moved into the hallway, any remaining notion he had about confronting Konrad evaporated. What was the point in telling him how hurt he was when Konrad clearly hated him? There was nothing more to say.

As he reached the front door, Konrad ran down the hall shouting, 'Stop!'

Ajnur shrugged him off. 'Why would I stay to be humiliated?'

Konrad pushed the box from Ajnur's hands and pressed his body against his, crushing him tightly against the door. He struggled to breathe and when he tried to speak, Konrad placed a hand over his mouth.

'I'm sorry. You don't deserve this. One last time?' His breathing was erratic, heavy. 'Will you?' With his other hand he tugged at Ajnur's belt, trying to undo it.

He gasped, struggling to escape Konrad's hold, but the more he struggled, the more insistent Konrad seemed to become.

'Do as I say.'

As the pressure from Konrad's body became harder, more unyielding, Ajnur went through in his head all the things that might calm him, but he knew there was only one option that would stop him. The second he stopped resisting, Konrad loosened his grip and pulled him away from the door, dragging his body along the hallway, and pushing him onto the bed.

'I told you. Do as I say.'

Ajnur had begun to understand how much Konrad enjoyed being in control. A few times the sex had reached a point where he'd started to feel uncomfortable, but Konrad had always pulled back. This time was different – the expression on Konrad's face was blank, and Ajnur felt as though he'd never met this man before.

Lying on the bare mattress, he watched as Konrad closed

the blinds. If he made a run for it now, perhaps he could get to the front door before he noticed. But as he went to move, Konrad stepped forward and stood at the end of the bed. Gazing at him he stripped naked, crawled on top of him and grabbed him by the neck. The pressure was greater than anything he'd ever felt before. Konrad was more than angry, he seemed possessed; his face a mask of pure rage.

As he began to pass out, Ajnur thrashed his arms and legs around, trying desperately to find a way to push him off, but as Konrad ejaculated with a groan, he was suddenly released.

Rolling off him, Konrad murmured, 'Did you enjoy that?'

'Sure,' Ajnur whispered, his throat on fire. If this was what he needed to give in order to keep him, then Kim was right: this man didn't deserve him. In that moment, Ajnur made a decision.

Slipping off the mattress, he returned to the hall and picked the box up from the floor. Putting his fingers to his neck, he realised his medallion had fallen off.

'Is this what you're looking for?' Konrad was stood in the bedroom doorway, holding the medallion in his hand. 'Here, let me.'

'I'll put it on later.'

'No, no. I insist.' As Konrad fastened the chain around his neck, he positioned himself

in front of the door, blocking Ajnur's escape.

'Thank you.'

'Honestly, you don't need to go right now. Stay and play some more.'

The affection had come back into Konrad's eyes. His hand caressed Ajnur's cheek and he kissed him as he led him back into the bedroom.

'I don't know what you want from me.' Ajnur went over in his head the multitude of reasons why he should leave and never look back. This guy was fucked up; why hadn't he seen this before?

The Look of Death

'Everything,' Konrad said. 'Now, come on.' He took his hand. 'I'll be gentle. It's just a bit of fun.'

As before, he was made to dress in the blue suit, then undress, and be washed. No words were spoken, and as he lay in the dark, Ajnur knew for certain this was the end. Kim was right, he should have listened to her.

Unsure what time it was or how long he'd been there, he rolled over onto his side. The entire apartment was pitch black, as Konrad had closed every single blind. Beside him, Konrad's breathing was slow and steady. This was his chance to leave. He moved to the edge of the bed and placed one foot onto the floor. As soon as he did, Konrad reached out and pulled him back.

'Where are you going?'

'I need the toilet.' Konrad's hand flopped back onto the bed. He'd blown it. He'd have to wait till he fell asleep again before leaving. 'I'll just be a minute.'

Although not needing to pee, Ajnur flushed the toilet, then let the tap run in case Konrad became suspicious. Pushing the toilet lid down he sat on top and wracked his brain. After being so desperate to see Konrad, Ajnur was now beginning to doubt whether he would ever allow him to leave. But he had to get out. There was only one option left: confront him; show his distaste for what he'd done to him; how he'd treated him.

As he reached for the door handle, he noticed a folded-up wheelchair crammed into the corner behind the door. Unaware of ever seeing one in the apartment before, he wondered how it got there. And for what? Was it another of Konrad's kinks? What was even stranger were a pair of dark glasses and a cap – the sort of things Konrad would never wear – lying on the floor beside it.

'Konrad?' he shouted.

A light went on in the bedroom, and a radio began playing. But instead of being tuned into a station, it remained hissing static.

'Through here.'

'What's with the wheelchair?' He remained in the hallway as the volume was raised on the radio.

Ajnur sensed a hesitation.

'Oh that? A friend asked me to store it for him. Come back to bed.'

'We need to talk.'

'Then let's talk in here.'

There had been one more difference this time during the sex which followed him being washed. After Konrad orgasmed, he forced his mouth closer to his. Ajnur had expected to be kissed, but instead, Konrad exhaled deeply into his mouth, making him gag. Revolted, he'd pushed him away. Out of all the things Konrad had done that night, it felt the weirdest.

'I think I'm going to leave now,' Ajnur called out, trying to sound casual, the noise from the radio now screeching. 'We can meet up and chat another time. Yeah?'

The bedroom light was switched off and the radio went silent.

'Konrad?'

Feeling his way in the dark, Ajnur stepped towards the bedroom. Standing in the doorway, he sensed that Konrad was no longer on the mattress. He moved further inside the room. 'Konrad?' As though being hit by a truck, his body was lifted and thrown onto the bed. 'Konrad!' he screamed.

Within seconds, a pillow had been thrust over his face. His response was immediate, and despite the force, pressing him into the mattress, he was able to push him off.

As he gasped for breath and tried to get to his feet, Konrad leaped on him again, pinning him to the bed, covering his face once more with the pillow.

It became impossible to breathe, to fight, to believe this

The Look of Death

would ever end. With one hand he tried in vain to hold Konrad back, while the other clawed at his body, hoping to hurt him enough to let go. But Konrad seemed immovable, a lead weight squeezing the life out of him.

The pillow was once again removed from Ajnur's face. The ache in his chest made it almost impossible to catch his breath, but he knew his only chance to escape was by screaming as loud as possible. But just as in a nightmare, as he opened his mouth, no sound came out.

This time, as the pillow was ground into his face, restricting his breathing, it felt like the darkness was consuming him. *There's no way back from this*, he told himself.

Why did I trust him? Why is this happening to me? Why isn't someone here to save me?

As he struggled to lift the pillow, push Konrad off, flee, the last words he heard being whispered into his ear were, 'Egon, I love you.'

28

As Konrad pushed the wheelchair holding Ajnur's half-dead body through the Tiergarten, the moon lit his way along a maze of paths and overhanging trees. Despite being after midnight, there was still a warmth in the air, making the park busier than he'd expected. He pulled up his hood, and checked Ajnur was fully covered. He was: blanket tucked up to his chin, baseball cap tipped forward, his eyes hidden behind large dark glasses.

Ajnur hadn't initially figured in his plans, but when he saw him in Ernst-Thälmann Park chatting to Colin, it felt like the stars had aligned. He would use him as a calling card. Or was it an offering? Whatever Ajnur's function, the discovery of his body in the Tiergarten would draw Colin closer, prolong the dance of death he'd unwittingly entered into. He enjoyed being in his life, having the opportunity to gaze at him from close and afar; whether Colin was astute enough to work out that he would be his next victim, remained to be seen. He hoped so. When the time came, it would only heighten the pleasure.

As he was becoming accustomed to, he sensed his shadow – Egon – following him. Like before, he seemed content to observe Konrad's every move, whilst remaining a respectful distance. But tonight, since entering the park, he feared there were more eyes on him. The bushes lining the pathways seemed to be alive: unfamiliar shapes crossed one another in the depths of dense greenery, wriggling in the undergrowth, scurrying between the trees.

He'd chosen the location carefully – the pedestrian suspension bridge spanning the little lake which formed the eastern boundary of the park's main cruising ground. Surrounded by mature trees and with a sinuous pair of bronze lions guarding each approach, the bridge offered drama, secrecy, romance.

As he made the final adjustments to Ajnur's limp body and sprinkled rose petals around him, the sun was starting to rise, illuminating his night's work with pale shafts of golden light. One prick of Ajnur's finger and dark blood oozed slowly down his hand. It took only seconds for the pressure he exerted to wipe the last remaining signs of life from him. Falling to his knees, he kissed Ajnur's lips. This was the closest he'd come to perfection since the first time; much more satisfying than Stefan's or Martin's deaths.

It augured well for Colin.

He took his time walking through the park, enjoying the cool of dawn. On his way out, a couple of beauties caught his eye – men he could happily have spent time with, had he not been satiated. Then, from nowhere, a grotesque man – ugly, feral – staggered from the bushes.

'Where's your patient?' he barked, his body swaying as he pointed to the empty wheelchair.

So, others *had* been watching as he pushed Ajnur through the park and onto the bridge. But this was nothing to worry about. With his reeling eyes, filthy hair and ragged clothes, this was a nobody; a non-person. 'I've released him into the wild,' he muttered, continuing on his way. But as he tried to manoeuvre past him, the man grabbed his arm.

'Why does death so often come at night, when it thinks no one's watching?' He swigged from a bottle of wine, then tapped his finger against his nose. 'Others may not, but I see you. You're no angel, no God. Even in this dim light, I can see the monstrousness of your soul.'

Konrad grabbed hold of his throat and pushed him into the bushes, but as he did so, two guys appeared ahead on the path, and in an instant, the old man pulled away and vanished. Unsure what to do, he waited until the couple passed, then dived into the mesh of branches and thorns, battling through to catch up with him. With each thrash of his arm however, he became more entangled, until he had to admit defeat, skulking back along the pathway to the exit.

As he emerged from the trees with the Brandenburg Gate ahead of him, he breathed a sigh of relief. The city was still wakening and for now his latest sleeping beauty lay undiscovered. Colin wouldn't be able to resist the bait; like the good boy he was, he'd already been chasing clues, compiling theories and getting nowhere.

A car passed, its horn blaring, and a group of youths shouted 'Fag!' in his direction. Shaking his head, he laughed. He could forgive them their error – who else would be walking out of the Tiergarten at this time in the morning?

29

THURSDAY, 28TH JULY 1994

Colin disrobed and walked out from behind the screen. The first few times he'd been self-conscious, but he was now used to the change of atmosphere as the students' attention switched from casual conversations to focusing on him. Rather than being sexualised, the atmosphere was unexpectedly meditative; he'd found it the perfect way to switch off and let his mind drift.

Colin watched Lukas fumble around in his rucksack. 'Has anyone got a charcoal pencil?' he asked. 'I've lost mine.'

Maryam pointed to where his had fallen on the floor. 'Dummy!'

'I'm an idiot,' he said, picking it up.

The tutor shouted '*Ruhig sein!*' and placed a finger against his lips. Maryam and Lukas exchanged a glance, before catching Colin's eye; all three tried to suppress a snigger. Since the drug-fuelled antics at the East Side Gallery, they'd discovered a shared, wicked sense of humour – mostly at the expense of the tutor, who ran the class with military precision. First Colin, then Lukas, had given impersonations of his uptight walk and snippy tone, but it was Maryam who was most able to mimic his intense stare: lingering, indifferent, superior.

The tutor beckoned to Colin and demonstrated how he wanted him to lie: his right arm raised above his shoulder, his head tilted to the side, the angle of his body concentrated to the left. Colin watched attentively, moving into position as requested, checking he was following it correctly. To ensure he'd got it right, he glanced at Lukas and Maryam, who gave him a thumbs up, then settled into the forty-minute pose. With no respite from the heatwave of the last few weeks, it was going to be a gruelling session.

Seconds later, a bead of sweat rolled down his forehead and he flicked it away with a tiny shake of his head. As he did so, another one formed. He'd have to wait twenty minutes for a break to relax his muscles and towel himself dry. Until then, he needed to lie as still as possible, however torturous.

A minute into the pose, in his peripheral vision, he noticed the tutor approach Lukas. He seemed unhappy about something Lukas was doing and kept pointing at his easel and moaning *'Nein'*. As soon as his back was turned, Lukas gave him the middle-finger, forcing an involuntary smile from Colin, which put him off balance. The tutor immediately noticed and shouted an instruction at him, which Colin didn't understand.

Maryam intervened. 'He wants you to raise your right arm an inch more,' she said. Then leaning forward, she lowered her voice. 'The fuckwit needs it to be exact.'

If the tutor was going to be this fussy, maybe he should ask Bill if he could model for another class. Besides, he'd other things to think about: primarily, the force of nature that was Klaus.

'Let me see you strip.' From the start, Colin could see how much Klaus enjoyed giving orders.

He'd removed his T-shirt, which he threw at Klaus, who'd caught and sniffed it.

The Look of Death

'Your jeans, now,' Klaus said. 'Drop them to the floor.'

As he did so, Klaus removed his own T-shirt to reveal a toned hairless torso. He'd clearly spent years at the gym sculpting it, the smooth muscles emphasised by a tattoo of the letters K&H on his left arm.

'The rest,' he'd said, watching Colin's every move.

Only then had Klaus got up from the bed and crossed towards him. 'Tell me exactly what you want me to do.'

The sex was intense, passionate; Colin had never felt so desired by someone. Out of uniform, Klaus gave free rein to his personality; he was uninhibited, curious, experimental. Colin's eyes had been well and truly opened, but it was relentless.

'Can we have one evening when we just watch a movie together?' Colin knew he needed more sleep than he was getting, and couldn't understand where Klaus found the energy.

Klaus unbuckled his belt. 'You've a whole lifetime to watch movies.'

That first glorious week, he'd appeared every night at Colin's, eager to have sex as soon as he arrived. Then around midnight, he'd announce he was hungry, eat something, come back to bed and want more sex.

The second week followed the same pattern. In bed, on the Thursday night, when Colin asked if they could meet at Klaus's for a change, the request was met with a non-committal shrug.

'Who's H?' Colin eventually asked, stroking Klaus's arm. So far, he knew Klaus was a policeman, with a ridiculous American car, who enjoyed having sex, was brought up in Berlin, had parents in Hamburg, and began his training at the Police College once the Wall fell. That was it. There had to be more.

'Hops.' Klaus disappeared into the kitchen, before returning to bed with a bowl of cherries. He spent the next

179

five minutes flicking them into the air, one at a time, and catching them in his mouth. Sucking and gnawing on each one, he let the stone emerge on the tip of his tongue before spitting it into the bowl.

'Is Hops an ex?'

'No,' he said, offering Colin a cherry. 'He's my twin brother.'

'You've a twin?' Colin caught a cherry mid-air and placed it back in the bowl. 'When were you going to tell me?'

Klaus put the bowl aside and thrust his hand down Colin's boxers.

'Are you identical?' Colin asked, removing his hand as Klaus's expression clouded. 'What? Don't you get on?'

'It's complicated. And no, we're not identical. No telepathic connection or anything weird like that.'

'Do you have a picture at least?'

Klaus dragged his jacket up from the floor. From his wallet, he brought out a snapshot of two grinning little boys with gaps in their teeth – one blond, the other dark-haired. 'As kids, we had different interests – I was sporty, he enjoyed music, movies – so we never hung around together. Like chalk and cheese – that's how you say it, no?'

'Then why have you moved in together?'

Klaus shrugged. He then returned the wallet to his jacket, took out a pack of cigarettes and lit up. He opened a window and stood, blowing smoke into the night air.

'I'm interested, that's all,' said Colin. 'I mean, who wouldn't be?'

'We're not close, never have been. And over the last few years, we've barely spoken.' Klaus finished his cigarette and flicked it out the window. 'At the start of the year, my parents suggested we move into an apartment they own. Rent free.' He picked up his jeans and put them on.

'Aren't you staying?'

'Early start.' He pulled on his T-shirt. 'My brother's super-

The Look of Death

smart and I love him to bits, but we're two different people with different interests. What more can I say?' He kissed Colin. 'Maybe one day you'll get to meet him. It's just; I'm not ready for that yet.' He opened the door.

'If I don't see you before, I'll see you Saturday?'

Without answering, Klaus left.

Since that night, Colin hadn't heard anything from Klaus, and he hadn't appeared on the Saturday. The plan had been to go clubbing, and he'd invited Lukas and Maryam along too, as they were eager to meet him. The fact he'd been a no-show had all been a bit embarrassing.

'You sure you told him where we were meeting?' Maryam had asked, ordering another drink at the bar.

Colin looked at his watch. He'd explicitly told him ten-thirty at *Blue Boy Bar on* Eisenacher Strasse before they'd be moving on to the club around midnight.

'Maybe something cropped up at work,' Lukas said, heading off to the toilet.

Maryam waited until Lukas had left. 'And you're sure your boyfriend's comfortable with the whole gay lifestyle stuff? You know, he's with the *Polizei*. Perhaps it's a bit too much.'

'Klaus could teach us all a few tricks, let me tell you.' Colin couldn't work out if he'd overstepped a line by asking too many questions, or if things had naturally fizzled out. If that was the case, then surely Klaus would have said.

THE TUTOR WAS NOW PACING the room, huffing and puffing dramatically, distracting the entire class. He approached Lukas, tapped his canvas twice with a ruler, and once again appeared to reprimand him.

In clipped English, Lukas's voice sliced through the silence of the studio. 'I've paid plenty to do this course and I can do what the fuck I like.' Heads down, the other students did their best to ignore what was going on. After further words were exchanged, the tutor moved on and with a tut, Lukas loudly dragged his easel across the floor until he was sitting directly in Colin's line of sight. He winked, picked up his pencil, and began to draw.

Determined to find his quiet place and time to think, Colin cast his eyes to the floor.

Progressing with the investigation in any meaningful way was proving challenging – what he had were instincts and lots of snippets of information, but nothing concrete to link the deaths other than a strange symmetry between the two deaths in the park and the two in the graveyard. Plus, a recurring theme of an absent boyfriend somewhere in the background.

From the start, Klaus had avoided mentioning Colin's investigation again, other than to warn him off. It was during their first week together, whilst Colin was making a stir-fry, when out of the blue Klaus had come up behind him and said, 'Don't contact anyone about Walter's death.'

'Why?'

Klaus moved closer and whispered in his ear. 'The case hasn't been closed like I thought. But you didn't hear that from me.'

It had been the one and only time he'd brought it up.

The enquiries he'd continued to make about Stefan Reis largely confirmed what Leon had told him: in particular, that he'd been seeing this new guy, Konrad, but none of his friends had met him. However, trawling through the LGBT archive at the Schwules Museum, as part of an article about an AIDS fundraising event, he'd found a photo of Stefan with his arm around a man called Gunther Busch. The headline had been simple to translate: *Künstler gegen AIDS.* Artists against AIDS.

Colin had tracked Gunther down and arranged to meet. As they'd settled into the corner of a bar in Kreuzberg, he

The Look of Death

didn't need any prompts to chat about Stefan; he was easy-going and liked to talk.

'Stefan was a riot,' Gunther said with a smile. 'Artistic, sporty, everyone's friend.' Stefan, he stressed, had brought joy to a lot of people's lives, and his sudden death was felt by many. 'But he'd packed a lot into his life, let me tell you. He was such a livewire, it's hard not to believe there was something odd about the circumstances of his death. I mean what was he doing in that godawful park? It wasn't his style.'

'And do you know anything about the guy he was involved with? Konrad, wasn't it?'

Gunther's reaction was immediate. 'You mean Leon?' He rolled his eyes.

Colin tried to correct him, but Gunther was already in full flow.

'Stefan took everyone at face value, and he was loyal to a fault – he couldn't see how Leon was using him. That man's a control freak. And loaded; a dangerous combination. Leon wanted a relationship with him, but Stefan had no interest whatsoever. You know his ambition was to be a professional artist? That's how we became friends. And he wasn't without talent. Leon made all these promises about how he was going to help him get a show in a gallery through his fancy connections, but he never did. It was just another way to string Stefan along until he gave in. It was cruel, but Stefan didn't want to hear it. He only wanted to believe the best of people.'

He'd also phoned the number Ulrich's mother had given him for his ex-girlfriend. A gruff male voice answered. In faltering German, Colin tried to explain why he was calling, but the phone was slammed down as soon as he mentioned Ulrich's name. After a lot of missed calls, however, he'd finally arranged to meet Bela's contact, Kim Stroder. He was meeting her after the class, to talk about Martin Engel. Getting her perspective would be invaluable.

And despite Klaus's warning, he'd spoken with a friend

who worked at the hospital alongside Walter. She confirmed he'd a history of drug abuse, but had been clean and was having regular counselling as a condition of his employment, and was doing well. Similar to Stefan and Ulrich, she also mentioned he'd been seeing someone new and he'd been excited to introduce him. But, it had never happened, and she didn't know the boyfriend's name.

The first twenty minutes of the pose completed, Colin stretched his back and wiped the sweat from his body. The tutor approached, but Maryam was standing behind him, copying his mannered walk. Lukas was giggling so much he had to leave the room.

'He says because it's so hot you can take a ten-minute break,' she said. 'He must be in a kind mood today.'

Colin pointed to the windows. 'Did you ask if we can open a couple?'

She shook her head. 'Apparently, they don't open. We've made daily complaints. I've asked if we can have some fans, but he does nothing about it.'

Suddenly conscious that they were chatting whilst he was still naked, Colin excused himself, and reappeared from behind the screen wearing his dressing-gown. 'Let's see your sketch.'

'It's not great. I'm too hungover. Me and Lukas were clubbing until six, then we had to get in here for ten.' She flicked to one of the pages. 'You'll find it hard to recognise yourself in this one.' She stepped back with a frown. 'What do you think?'

Though semi-abstract, the resemblance was uncanny. In twenty minutes, she'd not only sketched his face and full body, but captured something of his mood. 'It looks great.'

'You think so?'

'Yes.'

'I don't know how you manage to stay so still. The woman yesterday never stopped moving. I mean, I usually prefer the

The Look of Death

flabbier, older type – there's more to get your teeth into – but give me an average white guy who can stay still any day of the week.'

'I'll take that as a compliment.'

Break over, Colin returned to his pose. He found the second session easier; by then he'd found a way to relax and ignore any distractions. Even with Lukas scribbling and sighing in front of him, he managed to switch off and let his mind wander, fantasising about Klaus reappearing and sweeping him off his feet. More likely, he imagined, he'd never hear from him again. At one point, he wondered if phoning his work on the pretext of enquiring about Walter Baus's case might work, or if that seemed too needy. Fortunately, he'd resisted.

He checked the clock – the final minutes of the pose were dragging, and he was soaked in sweat. The prospect of having to do this again tomorrow seemed like some kind of medieval torture. And he'd promised to do a longer shift at *Zum Zum*, too.

But as he lay there, trying hard not to move, he became hyper conscious of how he'd been positioned. Maryam had mentioned that the poses the tutor chose were all classical. It occurred to him that Walter Baus's body had been found in a similar pose to today's; and according to Ajnur, there were rumours Stefan's body had been oddly positioned. He needed to find out if this was true for the others.

As the students piled out, Colin dressed behind the screen. In his head, he went through the questions he wanted to ask Kim: contacts for Martin Engel, his history, whether he was connected in any way to the other men who'd died, and if he too had a new boyfriend.

When Colin emerged from behind the screen, Lukas was still sitting in front of his easel, Maryam behind commenting on his sketch. 'Do you two wanna grab some food?'

'Sorry, I'm busy.' Maryam pointed at a detail, suggesting Lukas vary the tone more.

'I need to finish this.' Lukas picked up an eraser and rubbed out an entire section.

'You've loads of time this afternoon.' Colin tried to sneak a peek, but one look from Lukas stopped him.

'It's complete crap.' With the eraser, he began taking out an even larger area. 'I take it yours is perfect, Maryam?'

'Well, Colin thinks it's amazing.'

'But he's got no taste.' Lukas stuck his tongue out at Colin. 'Have you?'

'I may be a philistine, but I know what I like.'

'Let's see your masterpiece,' Lukas said.

Maryam turned the easel around and he peered at it, his nose twitching the entire time. 'You had less to drink than me.'

'Yes, but far more drugs.'

Colin gathered his stuff. 'Are we still on for tomorrow night?' He'd promised to sit for them both again.

'Can we make it next week instead?' Lukas crossed to the sink. 'Honestly, you saw the way the tutor was treating me. He absolutely hates my work, and I'm going to have to rethink a few ideas. Maryam, is that OK?'

'I'm free whenever you want me.' She threw some drawing equipment into a large bag and slung it over her shoulder.

Colin looked at his watch. 'Lunch tomorrow if you're both around?'

Together, they both replied 'Sure', but Colin wasn't going to hold his breath. The terrible twins only had eyes for each other these days.

While Lukas washed his hands, Maryam beckoned Colin over, and he managed to catch a glimpse of Lukas's sketch. The first thing that struck him was that the face and body didn't appear to be of him. Instead, he'd drawn a whole series

The Look of Death

of images of someone else's face from various angles, overlapped and intercut across the entire paper's surface. It was technically amazing, and drawn with such style, it forced you to look closely and scrutinise it more. But knowing Lukas, he'd probably rip it up and throw it in the bin.

Lukas grabbed his rucksack. 'Right, that's me. Maryam, are you coming?' He picked up a newspaper lying by his seat and tucked it under his arm.

'Wait!' Colin noticed a photo on the front page. It looked like someone he recognised. 'Can I see that?'

'You can have it if you want. I've already read it.'

As Colin took the newspaper from him, the details of the photograph became clearer. He wasn't mistaken. It was definitely him. He'd recognise that face anywhere. Colin pointed to the article. 'Can you tell me what this says?'

'Some young guy was found dead in the Tiergarten.'

But he wasn't just any young guy. Staring from the pages of the paper was Ajnur, his beautiful smile exactly as Colin remembered it that night in the park.

30

On the platform at Kurfürstendamm, the heat was suffocating and Colin looked around in vain for somewhere to sit. Since seeing the story about Ajnur, his mind had been racing; the idea that the vibrant young man he'd met in Ernst-Thälmann Park was dead seemed incomprehensible. And the fact he should be linked to yet another death was disturbing. The carriage was full, so Colin remained standing on the crowded train, his face thrust into the armpit of his nearest neighbour. At least the windows were open, offering some respite from the sweltering heat. He'd never experienced anything like it; the temperature had hovered around the mid-thirties for weeks and was forecast to continue. Any exertion was a challenge and trying to sleep had become its own form of torture. For weeks he'd lain awake half the night worrying about the case, unable to stop thinking about it, but getting nowhere as his mind went round in circles.

He leaned his head against a pole and closed his eyes, recalling Ajnur by the pond – his curiosity and eagerness to connect – and he couldn't help but feel he'd failed to protect him. That night, he'd been convinced someone was following him, but maybe it was Ajnur who was being followed.

The Look of Death

Regardless, with the discovery of another gay man's body in a city park, surely the police would have to re-examine the other deaths? He opened his eyes and stared out of the window as the pitch-black tunnel walls flew past.

It was a ten-minute walk from Kottbusser Tor station to the imposing red brick building where the Gay Youth Centre was based. In obvious need of major repair, it reminded him of his old secondary school in Glasgow. Like so much of the city, Colin wondered how long it would be before a developer got their hands on it to convert into swanky new apartments. For now, however, it appeared to be a thriving community space at the heart of the local neighbourhood.

To his surprise, he found Bela sitting on the steps by the entrance, staring up at the sky. As he approached, Colin realised they'd not spoken to each other since the night of the *Griechen Fabrik* party. When Colin had caught up with Bela, he had calmed down and seemed more sober, but he didn't want to talk, other than to say he accepted things were over between them, but that it still hurt. Colin's lingering memory of their goodbye was how subdued Bela had been.

'Fancy seeing you here,' Colin said. 'I've been meaning to call.'

'Have you?' Bela removed his sunglasses. 'I find that hard to believe.' Flicking a strand of hair from his eyes he said, 'Kim's had some bad news.'

Despite the initial prickly remark – which he deserved – Bela seemed less intense than usual: he was wearing a trendy pair of shorts and T-shirt and had re-styled his hair. 'I'm sorry to hear that,' Colin said. 'You know I'm supposed to be meeting her?' He instinctually went through a mental list of the things he could do if she cancelled: visit the Tiergarten where Ajnur's body had been found, return to Ernst-Thälmann Park and speak to people who might have known him.

Bela stood. 'One of the members of the youth group was

found dead on Tuesday. She's inside organising a counselling session for members.' He threw his satchel over his shoulder.

Colin's throat constricted. 'Not Ajnur Osman?'

'You knew him?' Bela stared suspiciously at Colin.

'It was in today's newspaper.' He pulled the article from his rucksack.

Bela stepped aside to let a tearful boy pass. 'They're all like that,' he muttered.

'No wonder. Another gay man dead – it doesn't bear thinking about.' Colin hoped the police would ask more questions this time. If not, he'd a moral obligation to keep pushing, force them to pay attention, go to the press if necessary; anything to make them take these deaths seriously.

'Good to know that you and your police officer friend are working so closely together on the investigation.'

Colin ignored the jibe. 'Any word on what happened?'

'The rumour is he was murdered, but no doubt the police will blame it on sunstroke or falling out a tree or something equally ridiculous.' Bela smirked. 'According to Kim, he was found by some tramp who stalks the park begging for drinks.'

'Got a name?'

'Noah something or other.'

'Any suggestion he was involved?'

'Kim's known him for years and says he's weird but harmless.'

'So, where can I find him?'

Bela rolled his eyes. 'The guy was hanging around the Tiergarten cruising ground at dawn – where do you think you'll find him?' He took out sun-cream and dabbed it on his nose.

'You need to put some on your neck.' Colin put out his hand. 'I can do that for you.'

Snapping the bottle closed, Bela threw it back in his satchel. 'No thanks. I've got it.'

The Look of Death

'Do you think Kim'll be able to see me?'

'Ask her yourself.' Bela shrugged and wandered towards the street. Without looking back, he raised his hand to wave. 'Have fun!'

INSIDE, the empty foyer was cool and shaded. The building even smelled like his old school; the floors having soaked up decades' worth of cheap disinfectant. Ahead, a bulletin board was plastered with information about clubs: basketball, sewing, dancing. He glanced around for someone to ask directions before spotting a hand-drawn, rainbow-coloured sign with Kim's name on it pointing towards a whitewashed corridor.

Round the first corner, a group of boys stood outside a door. Clinging onto each other, some wept quietly, while others dried their eyes. He'd a sudden flashback to the Broderip Ward at London's Middlesex Hospital in 1989, where Keith, one of the first friends he ever made in London, had died of AIDS; in the corridors there, similar groups of disbelieving young men held each other up and grieved in much the same way.

A tall boy stepped from the group to light a cigarette.

'Excuse me,' Colin asked. 'Do you know where I can find Kim?'

The boy took a long drag on his cigarette and stared at him. 'Are you Colin Buxton?'

Slightly taken aback, he nodded. 'How do you know?'

The boy offered his hand. 'I'm Christof. Kim asked me to look out for you.' He signalled for Colin to follow him. 'She's in her office.'

'I can come back another time.'

'No,' Christof said. 'She thinks now's best.'

They turned a corner and Christof leapt up a small flight

of steps leading to another cheerless corridor. 'I take it you were friends with Ajnur?'

'Yeah,' he replied. 'He was such a fun guy – always playing practical jokes. I wouldn't be surprised if he suddenly appeared. But I guess that's not going to happen, eh?' At the far end of the corridor, he knocked on a door with another handwritten sign stuck to it: Kim's name surrounded by big gold stars. Pushing it open, he said, 'That guy you're expecting is here.' Ushering Colin in, Christof left and gently closed the door behind him.

Curtains drawn to block out the sunlight, the room was dimly lit and appeared empty. It took him a few seconds to realise that to one side of a cluttered desk, a woman lay on a low sofa, her knees pulled up to her chest in a foetal position. 'Hi,' he began, 'Kim? I'm Colin. I'm sorry to hear about Ajnur.'

She slowly unfurled her limbs. 'Bela's told me about you.' Her voice was deep and resonant.

He doubted this was a good thing. 'Are you sure you want to chat?'

Kim nodded, switched on a small table lamp, and with a cough, drew a hand-rolled cigarette from a tobacco tin sitting beside it. 'Christof?' she shouted.

The boy popped his head around the door. 'Yes?'

She shuffled across the room. Dressed in faded bondage trousers, a long-sleeved *Die Toten Hosen* T-shirt, and chunky, black trainers, her age was impossible to determine; she could have been thirty-five or fifty. 'Have you got a light there, honey?' She took the lighter from Christof's hand and lit her cigarette. 'Thanks, darling. Go tell them I'll be through shortly.'

'Do you want anything – a coffee?'

'No, I'm fine for now.' Pushing back her peroxide blonde dreads, Kim focused her attention on Colin and motioned for him to sit. 'Bela insisted I see you.' She sat behind her desk and unconsciously touched a faded scar which ran down her left cheek. 'He told me you've interviewed family and friends of the men who've died.'

'It's been slow progress. And it's mostly been friends I've spoken to. I've not had much luck tracking down family.'

'You're doing better than the *Polizei* then. As far as I know, they barely questioned any friends. A couple of family members, but that's all. It shows a complete misconception of how gay men live their lives – who they confide in. It's no wonder they claim there's no evidence of wrongdoing. In each of these deaths they've simply gone for the obvious explanation and stopped looking.' She wiped her nose on her sleeve. 'Perhaps if they'd taken more time to investigate Martin's murder and the others, Ajnur would still be with us.' Her voice trailed off and she stared at the door as if expecting someone to enter.

'And you're convinced Martin's death was murder?'

'Martin was a fit, healthy young man.' She took a final drag on her cigarette and stubbed it out. 'The *Polizei* say the official cause of death was cardiac arrest, which I could accept if there was a reason for it – but there's not. Someone did something to cause the heart attack. I'm sure of it. But, Martin's family aren't questioning this, so it's been me pushing for the case to be reopened and they refuse to listen. Had it only been his death, it would have been suspicious enough but there were two similar deaths of gay men prior to Martin's, which I know you're aware of. And now with Ajnur's, there have been two deaths since. How many more gay boys will need to die before they act? I can't believe that no one else thinks there's a pattern here.'

Colin nodded. 'Can I ask how you knew Martin?'

Kim took another cigarette from her tin and lit it. 'He attended the youth group when it first started, but only for a short time. However, a few years later he returned for a summer with us to do a work placement; he wanted to be a social worker. We became friends and he occasionally came back to help. The boys loved him. Here.' She handed him a framed photograph of a fresh-faced young man holding up a trophy whilst a group of young gymnasts surrounded him.

'So, he would have known Ajnur?'

She shook her head. 'I don't think so. Ajnur's only been attending for a year, but Martin would have known a couple of the other boys who've been with us longer – Christof and Roger for definite. I think Christof's in that photo.'

'Can I ask about Ajnur's death?'

Kim took a deep breath at the mention of his name and nodded.

'The police spoke to you about him?'

'Briefly. They were asking a bunch of stupid questions.'

'But this time they think it's murder?'

'I don't know. *I* asked if they did, and they said they were looking at all possibilities – which I took to mean there's something suspicious.'

'Bela mentioned you know the person who found Ajnur's body.'

'I've seen him out and about, but we're not friends. I don't know how to explain it in English – Noah Becker's a bit of a legendary figure on the gay scene in Berlin. Kind of famous. Or maybe infamous is a better way to express it.'

'And what about Ajnur's family? Are you in touch with them? Could I speak to them?'

Kim shook her head vigorously. 'No. I don't think you should do that. I never met them, but I don't think that would be the correct approach. He wasn't out to his family. And Ajnur wouldn't have wanted them being asked about his sexuality. I'm sure of that.'

'But if his body's been found in a gay cruising area, surely they'll work it out?' Kim didn't reply, and Colin decided not to push it. 'Can you tell me, before his death, had Ajnur removed himself from friends? Family?'

The Look of Death

Kim remained silent and continued to smoke her cigarette. He sensed that she might be having second thoughts about agreeing to speak with him.

'Look,' Colin said, 'I'm not the police. Something doesn't add up, and like you, I want to get to the bottom of it.'

She ground her cigarette into the ashtray. 'Ajnur had been having an affair – with a married man by the sounds of it. On Monday, he confided in me. The guy had blown him off and Ajnur was devastated. I gave him some advice: along the lines of *You've had a lucky escape*. When I didn't hear from him that evening, I assumed they'd got back together. As big a personality as he was, Ajnur could be very private. But everyone around here knew his likes – he loved being out in the open, cruising the parks. He found it liberating, but he wasn't stupid or careless and he knew the ropes. Was always safe. This relationship though, it was a new thing for him. A departure.'

'The boyfriend, did Ajnur mention a name, give you any details?'

'Not to me.' Kim lit another cigarette. 'Maybe to one of the boys, but I'd be surprised.'

'And Martin, had he been seeing anyone at the time of his death?'

'Yes. But I never met him.'

'Do you have a name?'

She shook her head. 'Christof might know. I can ask.'

'And was that a new relationship?'

'I think so, but it wasn't so unusual for him to be dating someone new.'

'And the other men who died – were any of them connected to the group?'

'I'm in touch with Leon Brauckmann, Stefan Reis's friend. He says he came to the group with Stefan a couple of times. Years ago. That's significant, don't you think?'

'What, you think someone might be targeting members?'

She stared at him. 'I don't think it's so crazy.'

'But you could equally discover they've all been to the same café or the same club.' 'It's worth considering though, isn't it? I mean, if there's a pattern.'

The room fell silent. Kim seemed set on the idea of the youth group being a target, but Colin wasn't so sure. He rose. 'Well, I'll keep in touch. And again, I'm sorry we had to meet in these circumstances.'

'Why them?' Kim said. 'I keep asking myself that question, when they've been through so much already. Coming out to their families, dealing with AIDS, being vilified by the media. These were young men with so much to offer.'

As Colin walked back along the corridor, he passed an open door. A group of boys sat inside holding hands, heads bowed; their sense of grief palpable. He suddenly felt overwhelmed. How could he, investigating alone in a foreign country, work out how so many men met their deaths? And there was something else playing on his mind – a suspicion that whoever was responsible was treating it as a game, and their actions were becoming more and more audacious the longer the police failed to act.

Christof was standing in the foyer with a second boy, putting up posters on the noticeboard – *Does anyone have any information?* – with Ajnur's name written in large, bold letters. He spotted Colin and smiled. 'Is she OK?'

He nodded. 'Can I ask you something?'

'Sure.'

'Kim says both Ajnur and Martin had started seeing new boyfriends just before they died. Do you know the names of either of them?'

'Not Ajnur's boyfriend.' Christof looked at his friend. 'But with Martin, I've been saying for ages we should have told someone.'

The Look of Death

'So, you've got a name?' Colin asked.

The other boy, who introduced himself as Roger, laid the posters on a table. 'Konrad.'

That name again. 'You didn't tell the police?'

Roger shook his head. 'No one asked.'

'And was it serious?'

'I got the idea they were into each other, but that's all Martin told me. They hadn't been seeing each other for long.'

Colin thanked them. As he headed for the entrance, he felt a tap on his shoulder. 'Yes?' He could see Christof was deliberating whether or not to say something. He kept looking back at Roger, who was trying to avoid looking their way.

'We think we saw him.'

'This guy, Konrad? The one Martin was seeing?'

'We can't be sure, but it was the first night Martin went home with him.'

'Do you have a description?'

Christof shook his head. 'It was dark in the club, with loads of people. Plus, we were drunk.'

'Was he taller than Martin? Bulkier? Thinner?'

Christof shrugged. 'Sorry. He might have been cute, but I wasn't paying that much attention. Plus, I was out of my head on E.'

'Don't worry about it. Having a name helps.' Colin went to leave, but Christof reached out to stop him.

'Roger thinks he saw him afterwards.'

'When?'

Christof looked over at Roger who nodded. 'Can you promise never to tell Kim what I'm about to tell you?'

'Sure.'

'A couple of nights later, Roger and Martin got it together. And because Martin was a volunteer, that's against the rules. Kim would be heartbroken if she knew.'

'Look, Martin's dead, and I believe someone killed him. Any information you might have, will help.'

'Roger was woken up by someone leaving Martin's apartment. So, he got up and looked out the window, and he swears he saw the same guy we saw at the club walking out onto the street.'

'Did he see him any clearer? Could he describe him?'

'No. He only saw the back of him. But he did say he was a big guy – tall and muscular looking. There was something else though which was odd.'

'What was that?'

'He was putting a folded-up wheelchair into the boot of his car.'

Roger crossed and grabbed Christof's hand. 'That's enough. Someone will hear, and we need to sort this poster out. Come on.'

As Christof walked away he said, 'That's all we know. Honestly. Please don't say anything to Kim.'

31

Drunk, Hannah was midway through one of her regular meltdowns when Colin entered the kitchen. This time, the focus of her rage was her latest boyfriend, Eli, who sat staring straight ahead, unmoved by her name-calling. 'Leave her, you dickhead!' she screamed. His lack of reaction was only winding her up more. 'We...are...over,' she yelled, punctuating each word with a poke to his chest.

Their flatmate Rita, barely five-foot tall, tied to pull her to the other side of the kitchen, while the rest of Hannah's friends pretended none of it was happening.

'Save your breath,' Rita insisted. 'He's not worth it.'

Having noticed Colin enter, Hannah grabbed his hand and dragged him across the floor, practically pushing him into the guy's lap. 'Speak some sense to him!' Her words were slurred and she wasn't making eye contact.

'Sorry,' Colin whispered, gripping Eli's shoulder to steady himself. 'She'll not remember any of this.' Luckily, Hannah was out of earshot – otherwise he'd have been in the doghouse, too.

Tirade over, she poured herself a glass of wine and

flopped into a chair by the window. Seconds later she was chatting and laughing with Rita.

'Is that it? Show over?' Eli asked. When he got no response, he turned to Colin. 'Is she always like this?'

'Not always... It's just, sometimes she needs to get things off her chest. I wouldn't take it to heart.'

Eli shook his head, picked up a beer from the worktop and left.

'Good riddance to bad rubbish,' Hannah yelled.

A few minutes later the intercom buzzed. Spotting a chance to escape, Colin sprang up. 'I'll get it.'

'If that's Eli, tell him to fuck off back to his wife.'

Colin ran along the corridor and pressed the button. 'Hello?'

'Colin? It's Klaus.' His voice sounded strained. 'Can I come in?'

After standing him up on Saturday night and not returning his calls, disappointment had been displaced by fury. No games, he vowed to himself. 'Come to question me?' Colin asked, immediately conscious the suggestion could only be construed as game-playing.

'What?'

'You know, about the young guy found in the Tiergarten?'

Klaus muttered something under his breath. It sounded like he'd sworn, but Colin couldn't be sure. 'I'm out of uniform. Can I come up?'

Colin pressed the buzzer and waited at the front door, listening as Klaus's long legs bounded up the stairs two at a time. Sure enough, as he turned the corner, he was wearing his usual tight jeans, a *Van Halen* T-shirt and Adidas trainers. He gave Colin a peck on the cheek as he entered.

'You don't have plans?' he asked.

'Just me and a copy of *Trainspotting*.'

'I need to speak to you. And it's not about any guy found

in a park,' he stressed. 'You're not still poking around?' he added, his expression one of disbelief.

Colin suddenly had no desire to tell Klaus anything. 'Come through.'

Klaus followed him into his room, where he remained standing. Usually, he'd kick off his trainers and flop on the sofa or the bed, but tonight he couldn't stand still, fidgeted constantly and kept glancing at the door, as if he'd a taxi waiting. This was going to be the breakup talk; Colin knew it. 'Do you want to sit?'

'Sure.'

'Tea? A coffee? Something stronger?'

'Do you have whisky?'

Colin brought out his sixteen-year-old *Lagavulin* from the cabinet – a present from his sister before he left London. He hadn't touched a drop yet, but the occasion merited it. If things were going to end, it might as well be with a decent drink in their hands. He poured two glasses and handed Klaus one. '*Slàinte.*'

'*Slàinte,*' Klaus repeated, clinking his glass against Colin's.

He sipped, waiting for Klaus to begin. 'So, what's so important?'

'Wow, this is terrific.' Klaus held it up against the light, pushing a stray curl back from his forehead. At first, Colin had decided it was a nervous tic, but now he feared it was a sign Klaus was lying.

'We waited ages for you at the bar on Saturday,' said Colin.

'Sorry. I should have told you I was going away, but it was all last minute.' He drained his glass. 'There's something I need to explain.'

Colin sipped his whisky, but it tasted too bitter and he set it aside. 'You want to call it quits?'

Klaus placed his glass on the floor. 'No, no. Not at all. Unless that's what you want?'

'I don't get the sense you want much from me. Other than sex.'

'Is that what you think?'

'You left here a week ago and I've not heard from you since. What am I supposed to think?'

Klaus looked at him. 'I should have been straight with you from the start. I had to take a trip to Magdeburg to see my ex.'

'So, you've come to tell me you're back together with your ex? Is that it?'

'God, no. That was finished long before I met you. But he's been going through some personal issues and needed my help.'

Colin waited for him to elaborate. If Klaus was going to be upfront, he needed to tell him everything.

'It's complicated. He had a breakdown a while back and since then I've been keeping an eye on him. All his friends have. But a few weeks ago he took some time off work, and went to recover at his parents' house. Trying to support him has been difficult – it's been hard for both of us to get used to just being friends. I needed to spend time with him – tell him about you – before he came back to Berlin. I didn't want all the good work he's done to be thrown away. I brought him back with me on Monday night.'

Colin picked up his whisky, knocked it back and refilled his glass. 'Why wait till now to tell me?'

'I told you as soon as I could. I promise.'

'And now you have.' He hated being lied to, regardless of the circumstances; his ex, Ben, had been a consummate liar and would spin stories about his whereabouts, who he'd been with, only for it to be revealed he'd been sleeping with other people behind his back. And lying by omission was still lying as far as Colin was concerned. 'OK, thanks for coming to tell me in person. I hope your friend's better now he's back home.'

Klaus stood up. 'Maybe we can do something at the weekend – Sunday brunch, perhaps?'

Colin cleared both glasses away and opened the door to let Klaus out. 'I'll have to see how I'm fixed.' Playing happy families was not on the cards.

Klaus attempted to kiss him on the cheek, but Colin pulled away.

'You've every right to be angry, but don't do anything hasty. We're good, aren't we?'

'I've a lot on my mind,' Colin replied. 'Let's drop it for now.' He could see this wasn't enough for Klaus, but refused to soften his position.

'When I arrived,' Klaus said. 'You mentioned the death of the boy at the cruising grounds in the Tiergarten.'

'Ajnur Osman.'

'I've been told they're treating his death as highly suspicious, probably murder.'

'About time.'

'Whatever information or evidence you've compiled, whatever theories, you should let the police know. They may even consider you a witness.'

After Klaus left, Colin closed the door and sat on his bed.

What had just happened?

Finding out about Ajnur had been the worst possible news, and he still couldn't take it in. There were so many questions he needed answered. But to now discover Klaus had lied. Things were going from bad to worse.

Deciding to call him back, he got up, but stopped. Right now, he didn't feel he could trust him.

32

FRIDAY, 29TH JULY 1994

Colin was woken the next morning, just before dawn, by the sound of someone shoving an A4 envelope under his door. Addressed to him and plastered with stamps, it must have been delivered to the wrong apartment, as there were two other addresses handwritten on it, a question mark, and an arrow pointing to the correct address.

He opened it to discover the photocopies of Fraser's sketches Rhona had promised to send. In all the commotion of the last few weeks it had slipped his mind that he'd asked her to do this. Attached was a note, which read: *Hope these help. I think this is everything from Berlin. Let me know if there's anything else I can do. Good luck, Rhona.*

He glanced through them, remembering the ones which had stood out the first time: rough studies of streets and parks which he vaguely recognised, but couldn't identify; outlines of people and partial portraits. One detailed sketch stood out amongst all the others: a drawing of an art-deco fanlight, which he instantly recognised as part of the entrance to *Blue Boy Bar* in Schöneberg, which he'd visited with Maryam and Lukas on Saturday night.

Diving into a shower, he was out the apartment by six and

took the train to Ernst-Thälmann Park. At the side of the pond, where he'd met Ajnur and the bodies of Stefan and Ulrich had been found, Colin took a few photographs. In the morning light, stripped of its shadows, there was nothing sinister or haunted about the place – it felt open and connected, like any other part of the city. Before he'd managed to question him further, Ajnur had mentioned that whereas Ulrich was a regular at the park, Stefan wasn't. He needed to figure out if this was significant.

Heading back west, he walked through Prenzlauer Berg, crossing the top of Kollwitzplatz before turning onto Schönhauser Allee to pass the locked gates of the Jewish cemetery. It was still early, and the streets were relatively empty. Twenty minutes later, he arrived at Sophien Kirche Cemetery. Though still cool, a threat of the heat to come hung in the air.

Stopping to take a drink of water, he felt a pang of guilt. Maybe he'd overreacted; after all, Klaus had only been trying to help a friend, albeit an ex. But since they'd got together, he'd been unable to shake the feeling that Klaus was holding something back; this proved it. Perhaps a cooling-off period was for the best. Since breaking up with Lee, Colin hadn't been on his own – he'd rushed into something, first with Bela, and now Klaus. Time on his own might do him some good.

The graveyard was a sea of intense greens; the trees were in full leaf, and the scent of flowers and pollen intoxicating. Consumed by tangles of nettles and mare's tail, nature appeared to be swallowing the gravestones and mausoleums whole. Weeds and creepers crowded into the locations where Martin and Walter's bodies had been discovered, as if determined to erase all memory of their deaths. But Colin couldn't forget the image of Walter, draped across the tomb – like a character from a fairytale, lying as if asleep. If Ajnur was to be believed, there was a similarity to how Stefan's body had been left.

He took photos of both spots, trying to imagine the last

moments of each man. According to Klaus, like Stefan and Ulrich, both Walter and Martin had died in the early hours of the morning and it seemed likely Ajnur had too. Similarly, all five men had died during the summer months. The exception to this was Fraser. But, as with Ulrich and Walter, Fraser's death had been blamed on an accidental drug overdose.

Walking the entire length of Invalidenstrasse from east to west, with its gap sites and crumbling buildings, the city felt fragmented. At a break in what had once been no-man's-land, Colin crossed the Spree and arrived in Moabit. Turning south, he followed the brick arches of the S-Bahn along Lüneburger Strasse. Crossing the Spree for a second time, he headed towards the angel, perched in the distance on top of the Victory Column. Glowing golden in the morning sunshine, it brought him to the vast expanse of the Tiergarten. It was now nine-thirty and though the streets were busy with traffic, the park itself was still quiet. The only sights and sounds were a few joggers and a chorus of birds greeting the new day with their sharp tweets. All seemed right with the world.

Leaving the main avenue of trees, he quickly found the small lake and the bridge where Ajnur's body had been discovered. On one of the rare occasions he and Klaus had done something outwith the bedroom, they'd taken a stroll through the park and lazed around on a Tuesday evening. It was buzzing with people throwing Frisbees, joggers, parents pushing prams, and of course plenty of guys eyeing each other up.

'What about him?' Klaus had pointed at a cute guy their age sporting a fantastic Mohican.

'Not my type. You?'

'I'd need to get a closer look. Too muscular and I'm not interested. Too tall and we'd look like a pair of freaks. And if I look into a guy's eyes and don't feel a connection, then it's a no no.'

Klaus lay back, and they'd both enjoyed the leisurely

burlesque of movements and glances going on around them; the secret codes of desire and availability; the cat-and-mouse chase going on under everyone's noses; a parallel world unnoticed by most park goers.

'Come with me.' Klaus took Colin's hand and led him across a pathway and into the bushes, where a couple of guys were buckling their belts and quickly left. Without a word, Klaus led Colin deeper into the mesh of branches. 'Pull down your shorts.'

'Someone might catch us.'

'So?' Klaus grinned. 'No one's watching, are they?'

Colin checked, then did as was told.

Taking his time, Klaus sniffed and licked his entire body – his armpits, his groin, his hair – before pulling his shorts back up, snapping the elastic against his waist.

'Is that it?'

'For now. Let's go.'

Colin remembered they'd crossed the bridge afterwards, holding each other's hands, glowing in the summer night and the warmth of possibilities. Klaus had insisted they take a photo together and they'd posed beside the lion sculptures which guarded each end of the bridge. Klaus let out a roar and pointed at the lions' claws painted with nail varnish, which he found hilarious.

Though still surrounded by police tape, Colin was struck again by the beauty of the location: dappled light fell through tall trees onto a mirror-like lake where brightly flowering rhododendron bushes cascaded into the water. Like Ernst Thälmann Park, this was a well-known cruising ground for gay men and it, too, bordered a pond. However, with its four bronze lions, there was a monumentality about the bridge which echoed the carved headstones and mausoleums of Sophien Kirche Cemetery. But the overwhelming characteristic shared by all three spaces was a sense of tranquillity; all harboured pockets of nature, slightly removed from the commotion of the city. Surely this must be significant, an important choice as part of the killer's ritual?

The youth hostel on Kluckstrasse, a thirty-minute walk away, couldn't have been more of a contrast. A charmless, five-storey 1960s block set back from the road, the only feature shared with the other three locations were the thickets of mature trees, to the north and south of a broad lawn, which framed the facade. Fraser had been found in November, his time of death estimated at between midnight and five in the morning. Though details differed from the other deaths, as the first murder, could it be the killer hadn't fully developed their MO? Or was the explanation simpler: was Fraser's death completely unrelated to the others?

Regardless of his opinion of Berlin's *Polizei*, Colin understood why they might come to this conclusion regarding Fraser. But failing to investigate a connection between the other men's deaths – Stefan Reis, Ulrich Steiner, Martin Engel, Walter Baus and now Ajnur Osman – was a mistake. He was sure of it, but he took comfort that Walter's and Ajnur's deaths were still under investigation. He hoped this might provoke a reassessment of the others.

Before entering the building, he took photographs outside the youth hostel. Inside, a receptionist in his late sixties sat at a desk, reading a comic. He looked up when he saw Colin, but instead of offering assistance, he continued what he was doing. 'Excuse me.' Colin took a ten Mark note from his pocket and placed it on the counter.

The guy looked up and eyed the note. 'Yeah?'

'I'm hoping you can help me with something.'

The guy coughed, caught some phlegm at the back of his throat, swallowed, then rolled up his comic and shoved it in a drawer. 'That depends.'

'In 1989, a Scottish tourist died in one of the rooms here. Do you know which room it is?'

The receptionist pulled his baseball cap over his eyes. 'No

The Look of Death

comment.'

Colin pushed the ten Mark note closer. 'One peek?' Colin held up his camera. 'It would only be for a few minutes. I just want to take a few photographs and I'll be in and out, mate. No one needs to know.'

'Make it a hundred and I might consider it. Anyway, I told the police everything I knew. Case closed.'

So, this was the same person who'd been on reception the night Fraser died. Bingo. 'I'll give you twenty.' Colin rummaged for another ten Marks in his pocket and placed it on top of the other note. 'But that's all I've got.'

The guy leaned over the counter, the smell of stale alcohol on his breath. 'For two hundred, I'll show you the room and tell you anything you want to know.'

'Or maybe you can tell me what you saw that night for twenty Marks.'

'Sorry – can't remember.'

Colin took the cash and shoved it back in his pocket. As he walked towards the exit, the receptionist shouted after him.

'I'll answer one question for twenty.'

'Two questions and you've got a deal.'

'Cash first.'

Colin handed him the money. 'Was he alone the night he died?'

'Yes, he booked in alone and I never saw him with anyone.'

'There's another witness who says there was someone in the room with him – are you saying he's wrong?'

'That American idiot? He stayed here for two weeks smoking pot, never left his room once, trashed the place and complained constantly about noise. Who do you believe?'

OUTSIDE, Colin sat on a concrete bench which formed the base of a brutalist sculpture at the entrance to the hostel. Ahead of him was a bridge spanning the Landwehr Canal. He checked his map; following the canal east would take you to Kreuzberg and the Maybachufer Market where Ajnur worked. Was that significant?

Colin looked at his watch. He'd been up since five-thirty and had walked for miles. It was now ten forty-five and he was starving. He needed to decide whether to go back to the Tiergarten to see if he could locate Noah Becker or try to find a way to contact Ajnur's family.

A movement in his peripheral vision made him turn. A figure stood among the trees, camera held up to his face, taking a photograph. Crossing the lawn, Colin tried to get a better look, but as he drew closer, the shadow retreated deeper into the trees. Stepping under the canopy of leaves, he quickened his pace, as did the figure. Emerging onto the main road, there was no sign of any pedestrians. Colin ran up to the first turning; a walkway led into a central garden around which several medical buildings were arranged. Diagonally across the garden, in the distance, a hooded figure in jeans and trainers with Adidas stripes, was sprinting down a lane. Giving chase, Colin tripped; picking himself up, he ran along the lane, which opened into the backyard of an apartment block. A low passageway led under it and out onto the tree-lined road which followed the canal. There was no sign of the hooded figure in any direction.

Returning to the backyard, he checked behind a row of large, metal wheelie bins, and tried a door which led into the building, but it was locked.

Colin paused for breath. Yet again, someone had been watching him. From now on, he'd need to be more vigilant. Why would they run? If they followed him here, was it from the Tiergarten, Ernst Thälmann Park, or the *Genossenschaft*? And if it was from his building, was it someone he knew, someone close to him?

33

Heading south to Schöneberg, Colin reasoned he'd be able to grab something to eat and ask about Noah Becker in the gay bars – get a better idea of who he was looking for. At *Blue Boy Bar* on Eisenacher Strasse, the barman spotted him as soon as he entered.

'So, what do you fancy today?' His Belfast accent was pronounced, and familiar from a whole cast of Irish uncles, aunties, and cousins on Colin's mother's side.

He ordered a beer. The bar was empty, so he hoped the barman wouldn't mind him asking a few questions. 'Can I ask you something?'

'Fire away.' The barman handed him his drink with a grin. 'I'm Sean, by the way.'

'Thanks Sean.' He tried not to be distracted by his soulful grey eyes. 'I'm looking for a guy.'

'If I'd a dollar.' His grin grew wider. 'Ignore me. What's the fella's name?'

'Does the name Noah Becker mean anything to you?'

Sean feigned astonishment. 'You're kidding me. C'mon, you mean, the shaman guy? How'd you not know him? He's a legend round these parts.' Coming round to Colin's side of the bar, he drew up a stool.

It emerged that Noah Becker was a homeless man who haunted the Tiergarten's cruising grounds. Day and night he could be spotted chancing his luck with whoever crossed his path: the young, the old-timers, those 'visiting for the first time', tourists who stumbled across the area or who'd planned their visit months in advance. Most nights, he'd attempt to join in with couples enjoying a hook-up or guys in group sessions, but he was mostly consigned to the outer edges of any activities; people were put off by his bizarre rants and complete aversion to personal hygiene; hanging around, waiting for an opportunity, watching for a way in – those were the tactics he was infamous for.

'And occasionally, to give him his credit,' Sean said, 'he gets lucky. He was here last night for an hour or two. He's usually here, most Wednesdays, the same time. I think he's got a circuit, mooching around all the gay bars, hoping someone'll buy him a beer or slip him a spliff. Mostly they do, but it's generally to get rid of him. Which is a pity – cos if you get him on a good day – he's an interesting fella.'

'Do you know how I can get in touch with him?'

Sean drew closer. 'Easy! Choose a time. Any time, any day. And hang around the Löwenbrücke – you know the bridge in the park with the lions? A cute guy like you?' He winked. 'Like catnip to him. He'll find you no bother.'

Colin blushed and Sean drew his stool closer. It turned out he was indeed from West Belfast, was training to be an actor, and already had a boyfriend. His eyes glinted when he said it, implying this wasn't a problem. 'Another drink?

'Sorry. Maybe next time?'

'I'll hold you to that.'

'There's one more thing.' Colin brought out Fraser's sketches. 'These are from five years ago. Can you take a look, see if you recognise any of these faces?'

The Look of Death

'I've only worked here a couple of months,' Sean explained. 'But let's see. We've a few regulars who've been hanging around here for years.' He took his time, going through each one in turn, passing them back to Colin. When he got to the sketch of the fanlight, he pointed at it. 'I recognise this, of course.'

'But none of the faces?'

Sean shook his head and continued flicking through the photocopies. He was about to pass them back when he held one up and looked at it more closely. 'Christ! That's Tony.'

'Who's that?'

'My manager. Give me a minute, I'll see if he's back.' Sean shouted through a door behind the bar. 'Tony! You there?'

A guy in a grey suit, tanned, ridiculously handsome with fine, thinning hair, appeared. 'I'm halfway through tomorrow's order – is it important?'

'Take a look at this.' Sean handed him the sketch.

A smile spread across Tony's face. 'Well, that wasn't yesterday. I've a full head of hair.' He handed it back. 'Who drew this?'

Colin introduced himself. 'It's not the cheeriest of stories, I'm afraid. The guy who drew it died later that day.' He handed him the photograph of Fraser which Rhona had given him. 'It was a couple of days after the Wall came down.'

Tony's shoulders slumped. 'I remember him like it was yesterday.' He took another look at the drawing. 'I can picture him that afternoon, sitting in the corner quietly sketching, but I never knew he'd drawn me.'

'Amazing artist, isn't he?' Sean added, looking over his shoulder.

'He was an art student,' Colin explained. 'His name was Fraser McDougal, from Glasgow, and he was visiting Berlin for a few days before heading back home.'

'Tragic,' Sean said. 'What age was he?'

'Twenty-three.'

213

Sean shook his head and went to serve a customer.

'Can you remember anything else about him?' Colin asked Tony. 'Was anyone with him?'

Tony poured himself a glass of water. 'You know, after seeing the newspaper article, I called the police.'

'Why? Did you see something suspicious?'

'Just the guy he was with. In this game, you get a feel for people. You know, spot the dodgy ones, make sure they don't cause any trouble. And this guy wouldn't look me in the eye when I served him.'

'A closet case?'

'You spot those, too. But he was different. Sat over by the window and eyeballed every single guy in here. Skip cap pulled over his eyes, coat zipped up to the top, gave off a weird vibe. He didn't realise, but I watched him the whole time he was here. I got a funny feeling he was up to something.'

'Did you tell this to the police?'

Tony nodded. 'Some police officer said he'd pop by and take a formal statement, but no one ever turned up or left a message, so I forgot all about it.'

'Can you remember the officer's name?'

'From five years ago? I'd have to think.'

'Was it Kommissar Fink by any chance?'

Tony's expression instantly changed. Amazed, he said: 'Yip, that's him. That's what I mean about getting a feel for people. I could tell straight away that the officer wasn't cool with the whole gay thing; just his complete lack of interest in what I was telling him. At the back of my mind, I knew it wouldn't go anywhere.'

'And the weird feeling you had about the guy with Fraser; did anything specific happen?'

'Nope. They chatted, stayed for maybe an hour, then left together. It was about a week later that I picked up a newspaper, and saw Fraser's face. I immediately felt something wasn't right. Drugs, wasn't it? He didn't seem the type.'

'That's the official explanation, but his family think he was murdered.'

'Jesus.' Tony sat on the stool and gazed at the sketch. 'I remember it so vividly. Neo-Nazi attacks were happening, so all the bars were on full alert. I was being extra vigilant, ensuring no one came in who might cause trouble.'

'And can you tell me anything else about the dodgy guy? Height, colour of hair, skinny, fat?'

'There was nothing memorable, to be honest. 'Young guy, average height, slim. But I can tell you one thing.'

Colin leaned forward. 'What?'

'His name was Egon.'

34

Back at his apartment, Colin called Rhona to ask her about the name Egon, and sure enough, she'd never heard it mentioned. He discussed with her the connections he was uncovering between the other men's deaths, but sadly, not with Fraser's. 'At this point, I don't know if there's going to be a fit,' he said. 'I know it's not what you want to hear.'

'We've no expectations,' Rhona replied. 'We're just glad someone's finally listening to us, and doing something.'

'If there's a link, I promise I'll do my best to find it.' Colin knew this was a feeble thing to state, but it was all he could say to reassure her.

Later that evening, feeling refreshed, he returned to the Tiergarten. This time, he'd brought a few bottles of beer in his rucksack. According to Sean, the previous night at the bar Noah Becker had bragged about knowing far more than he'd let on to the *Polizei*, but the first person to "give him a BJ" would be told everything. Colin hoped his stash of beers would be enough.

It was cooler in the park now, but the sky was still bright and cloudless; there were more people around than earlier. The first thing Colin noticed was that the police tape had been removed. He approached the bridge: the pink nail polish on the lions' claws was cracked and fading. *Shame.* Looking for clues, he crossed to the other side and back again. But he knew it was a long shot; the whole area would have been scoured by detectives.

There was nothing unusual on the slats of the walkway or the thick wooden railings. Inspecting each of the lion sculptures in turn, he reached under the belly of the final one and swept his hand to the back. Again, nothing.

With no sign of Noah Becker, he wandered around the park. Where the cruising grounds opened out into more of a meadow, the intense heat meant most guys had stripped off – on closer inspection, it appeared they all had – and were lounging around. Every now and then, heads would appear, bobbing up above the long grass. A sense of innocence and excitement tinged the air, laughter and squeals of delights echoing around the arena of trees. Part of him wished he wasn't there on business, but instead, could throw off his clothes and enjoy the summer warmth.

As he made his way back towards the Lion's Bridge, an emaciated figure – who could only be Noah Becker – came into view. Staggering, he meandered across the pathway, accosting random passers-by, sticking his fingers up at those who ignored him. One person held up his hand to wave; Noah danced with joy and rushed over to high-five him. Sensing trouble, the guy quickly moved on.

Throwing any semblance of self-respect aside, Colin leaned against a tree and tried to strike a nonchalant pose, leading with his crotch. Even from a distance, he could see the hunger in Noah's eyes as his gaze fell on him.

'You've come back to me!' Noah shouted with glee, lurching in his direction with a toothless smile.

Colin maintained eye contact and wondered what the hell he'd let himself in for – Noah cut a terrifying figure. Dressed in a moth-eaten, full-length fur coat, it was hard to tell where the garment ended and his tanned, grizzled chest began. A necklace of blackened teeth hung round his neck and matted grey dreads trailed down his back which he threw from side to side as he spoke. '*Goldelse*!' he exclaimed. 'Where have you been my angel?' he asked in German.

Colin knew from Sean that he spoke perfect English, and introduced himself, asking, 'Can you spare five minutes?'

Noah drew closer, his bloodshot eyes blazing; in the heat, he smelled musky, almost feral. The odour reminded Colin of his early childhood, when his dad still lived at home, and the wild hares he trapped would hang in pairs on the back of the kitchen pantry door, their meat aging.

'Are you looking for something?' Noah nudged him in the ribs, his body language a quixotic, childish flirtation. He opened his coat to reveal a long, semi-erect penis, crowned with a thick Prince Albert ring.

Colin glanced up and noticed the scars and bruising across his chest and abdomen. 'I'm not looking for sex. Sorry. I'd just like to chat.'

Throwing his coat closed, Noah swept off. 'Timewaster!'

Colin raced after him. 'You found the body, didn't you?'

Noah shook his head. 'The gods did.'

'I knew him.' Colin reached out and touched his arm.

Noah grinned, his grimy face wrinkling with pleasure. 'I've men to suck off. Tallyho!' He said this in a perfect upper-crust British accent.

The stench emanating from Noah was so bad, Colin had to take a step back. 'Look, how about we take a seat? There's a bench over there.'

'Piss off!' Noah remained fixed to the spot, his expression suggesting he'd consider other offers.

'What about a drink?' Colin dug into his rucksack and produced two large bottles of beer.

Noah's demeanour softened. 'Angelface, as long as you're paying for it, you can have all the time in the world.' Turning,

The Look of Death

he lifted his coat and, with a wiggle of his bare bum, farted. 'Oopsie,' he whispered, with a coquettish flutter of his eyelashes.

Startled, Colin took another step back. 'Is the bench OK?'

'No. No.' He clapped his hands and stood up straight. 'I've somewhere much cosier we can go. Just you and me.'

Transforming himself into a wilder version of one of the city's official tour guides, Noah beckoned Colin to follow, and set off along a warren of paths. With a lick of his lips, he occasionally turned back to check the beer hadn't disappeared. After giving a full rendition of Sabrina's *Boys, Boys, Boys,* he muttered to Colin, 'Really, I can't remember fuck all. But I'll still get the beer, right?'

'Sure. And I've a few more bottles after these.'

Sean had told a story about Noah: one evening, he'd convinced several people in the bar to buy him drinks, and the drunker he became, the more animated he got. Climbing on top of the bar, he'd refused to come down until he'd recited the Hermann Hesse poem *Stages*. He delivered it with such poignancy it stopped the entire bar. Everyone was entranced by his nuanced, emotional outburst. According to Sean, it was spectacular.

'Give me enough and I'll suck your cock,' Noah shouted back. Obviously, tonight, Colin was receiving a much cruder performance.

'Told you, buddy, I'm fine. But thanks for the offer.'

With a theatrical wink, Noah grinned his gummy grin, suggesting it was an experience those who'd gone before never forgot. 'Over here,' he pointed. 'My kingdom awaits.'

Behind a dense layer of overhanging branches, he revealed a small clearing amongst the trees, only feet from the path. Above head height, to create shelter, a blue tarpaulin had been stretched between several tree trunks, creating a space below with an eerie glow. At ground level the earth was evened out and compacted, and plastic crates had been used to create a sense of enclosure, plus a range of makeshift furnishings. Suspended from the tarpaulin, on threads and rusting wires, were hundreds of small objects which must have been collected from the park: animal bones, bits of plastic toys, small stones, and shards of glass. As he lit candles, Noah gestured to a crate topped by a mouldy pillow and Colin took a seat beside what appeared to be a little cooking area, with a small, cast-iron stove and various pots and pans. To the side of that, wooden pallets had been layered to create a platform – presumably Noah's bed. Piled with clothes, sleeping bags and blankets, it looked more like a nest than a bed. Incongruously, on the edge of this construction, ticking loudly, a large wind-up alarm clock sat. Dozens of bottles were dotted around the encampment; half-filled with what he initially assumed was beer, Colin quickly realised they were most likely Noah's urine. Despite this, there was a homely feel to the place.

Colin opened the first beer. 'There you go.'

Noah grabbed it and took a long slug, finishing it in one. With a gasp and an appreciative smack of his lips, he burped extravagantly. 'Next one, please.'

Colin opened a second bottle.

Taking another long gulp, Noah rummaged underneath a ragged cushion and produced a shallow tin, which he opened to reveal an assortment of drug paraphernalia: a syringe, some bags of white powder, tobacco, a small amount of weed, and a packet of rolling papers. Sitting cross-legged on the ground, he balanced the lid between his thighs and set about making a joint.

'I found one of the other guys who died,' Colin began. By sharing this, he hoped to gain Noah's trust.

'Where?' Not bothering to look up, he kept on rolling, as though this was a conversation he had every day.

'Sophien Kirche Cemetery in Mitte.'

'There's no action whatsoever in that shit-hole. No decent

The Look of Death

ass. *Nichts. Nada. Niente.* Tried it once – wouldn't go back. What sort of ass do you like?'

Ignoring the question, Colin asked, 'Was there anything unusual you noticed about the body?'

'Oh yes. Yes. Yes. Absolutely. He was a beautiful boy. Stunning. With his hands stretched over his chest, I thought he was sleeping. He'd lovely long lashes. At first I thought I'd encountered Titania, the fairy queen. But alas not.'

'People say you saw more. That you were bragging about it in the bar last night.'

'You shouldn't listen to tittle tattle, my angel.' He lit his joint and took a puff, squinting at Colin. 'If you want to know more dearie, you're going to have to suck me.' He finished the second beer and took another puff, exhaling the smoke in Colin's direction. 'What's it gonna be?'

'You know that's not going to happen.' Colin passed him another bottle. 'I've already said.'

'Then, why don't I do you?' He held Colin's eye. 'Drop your trousers. It won't take long.'

Colin shook his head and laughed. 'I told you. It's not happening.'

'You say that now.' He offered the joint to Colin, who declined. 'Good stuff. Some rich dentist gave me it. Laced with a little heroin apparently, to give it an extra kick.'

'Did he give it to you to make you go away?'

Noah coughed, spluttered, and laughed all at once. 'Cheeky fucker. Twenty years ago, I was the darling of this place. Not a punter walked through here that didn't get an eyeful of me. I had my pick.'

Even accounting for the passage of time, Colin doubted Noah's claim. 'Good for you.'

'You don't believe me, do you?' Noah rummaged under his bed and pulled out a mangled old wallet, from which he produced a dog-eared passport photo. 'Feast your eyes on this beauty.'

Sure enough, a bright-eyed youth with a slightly suggestive expression stared back. But the photograph – black and white, taken in a booth – wasn't from twenty years ago, Colin thought. More like forty. 'Handsome.'

'Told you.' Noah took the photo from him and placed it carefully back in the wallet. 'It's true. I confess. I didn't tell the pigs about the flaming chariot.' He shuffled closer, bringing his beer with him and blowing enough smoke into Colin's face to make him feel momentarily high. 'Wanna know more?'

'Sure.' Colin coughed, unsure of how much truth or sense he was going to receive.

'It was infinitely clear. Magical. You could see everything, even after midnight. Full moon. Beautiful. The smell of the earth. The flowers in bloom. The night sky. Moths on the wing. No one else in this place gives a fuck about any of that shit. Only me. People are blind. They never cease to disappoint.'

'Did you see Ajnur?'

'I'd just been fucked senseless by a Japanese tourist. Dom with a capital D, so he claimed. Wanted it rough, and he pushed me around a bit. I mean, he thought he was being rough. But, to be honest, it felt more like tickling, to be honest. He did give me a pill though. Or did I take a pill? It's not important. I was flying high. High! High! Everything was aglow – the trees pulsing, the water luminous, the boys in the bushes radiating light from their fingertips and their throbbing cocks. In-can-de-scent.'

'And the *flaming chariot*?'

'Chariot?' Noah took another puff of his joint, followed by a swig of beer.

'You said a few seconds ago you didn't tell the police about the flaming chariot.'

Noah looked confused. 'I didn't tell the police about the wheelchair, dearie.'

The Look of Death

'You saw someone in a wheelchair?' Colin asked. If so, this was the second mention of one being used.

His eyes glazing over, Noah shouted *Victory!* and rocked back and forwards, as he mimicked riding a horse. This was not going the way Colin needed it to.

'Noah,' Colin said. 'Can you focus on the night you found Ajnur?'

'Ajnur. Aj-nur. Nice name. Means moonlight in Arabic.' Taking another long puff, Noah tried to raise himself from the ground, teetering like a young deer finding its feet for the first time. Performing a full, 360-degree turn, he collapsed back down and thrust his face into Colin's. His breath was rank. 'Someone was pushing the golden chariot, and carrying a long-stemmed rose.' Noah made a whipping gesture, accompanied by a cracking sound. 'I asked him where his patient was.'

'So, you'd seen him earlier?'

'Yes, yes, I told you.' Noah hadn't. 'His patient had sunglasses on. In the middle of the night.' He took another drag of his joint. 'Bit odd, don't you think?'

'What time was this? Two? Three?'

Noah shook his head.

'At the start of the night. End? Can you remember?'

Again, Noah shrugged his shoulders.

'Who was pushing the wheelchair?' Colin asked.

But Noah seemed lost in the memory, trying to grasp it with his hands, as if it were in front of him. 'He'd a checked blanket tucked up almost to his neck, and a funny little hat on. Funny, funny, funny.'

'And this was near the Lion's Bridge?'

'Exactly where you were standing when I saw you this morning with your little camera. Clickety clack. You looked so lost and lonely, glancing around, checking if anyone was about. That's why I waited. I knew you'd be back.'

So, Noah had been watching him that morning, but there

was no way it was him who'd been spying on him at the youth hostel. 'So, you saw a guy pushing someone in a wheelchair?'

'An angel in a golden chariot.'

'Then later, you asked where his patient was. Is that correct?'

'No. He drifted into the trees, up into the skies. His heart flaming. The seven seraphim singing a heavenly chorus of welcome. It was wonderful,' he mumbled.

Noah slumped forward. Shivering uncontrollably, he crawled onto the platform and, sitting on the edge, pulled a threadbare shawl around his shoulders. 'Are you okay?' He was clearly too far gone to make any sense.

'Come sit beside me,' Noah croaked. He opened his shawl and gestured to Colin.

Joining him, Colin tentatively wrapped an arm around him, horrified by how skeletal Noah's body felt through the weight of his heavy fur coat. Up close, the smell was still overpowering, but slightly more bearable; less gamey and more like mushrooms. 'I'll come back another time. Maybe you'll remember more,' he said.

Noah gripped Colin's wrist. 'Death is all around us,' he gasped, before collapsing on the platform and burrowing under a sleeping bag. 'Set it for midnight,' he moaned. 'That's when it's busiest.'

Confused, it took Colin a few seconds to realise Noah was asking him to set his alarm; obviously, he didn't want to miss any of that night's activities.

Emerging from the bushes and back out onto the path, Colin felt disorientated, as if he'd spent the last half-hour in a parallel universe – a nightmarish underworld of which Noah was the master. What journey had brought him to that place, Colin didn't dare to imagine. And while he was confident he'd find him again, he wasn't sure he'd want to.

35

After a quick shower, Colin headed out to *Homo-Bar* to meet up with Hannah. The place was packed, with music blaring, lights flashing, and the heat making everyone sweaty and sticky. Hannah clung onto him, shouting in his ear, 'D'you want a drink?'

'Another beer,' he yelled, gesturing towards the loo. 'I'll be back in a minute.' As she disappeared to the bar, he squeezed through a sweltering crowd of naked torsos, attracting a couple of friendly smiles on the way. A giddy mix of men, booze, and lust – this was the Berlin the gay guidebooks always promised.

The stench of the toilets hit him as the door swung open. He side-stepped a sodden mess of toilet paper stuck to the floor and stood at the urinal; however it was hanging off the wall, the pipes disconnected. He crossed to a cubicle and locked the door.

As Colin tried to avoid inhaling the smells, he heard someone enter the adjacent cubicle. Their breathing was loud – low, rhythmic and sexual. He continued peeing. Seconds later, a voice hissed, 'I'm watching you.' The words were spoken in English but with a distinct German accent. 'But you haven't a clue.' With a bang, the cubicle door was thrown open and someone rushed from the toilets. As quickly as he could, Colin zipped up and followed.

Out in the bar, a large group of leather guys had left, leaving the place far emptier. He scanned the space but saw nothing amiss: no one was out of breath, there were no guilty faces, no boggle-eyed stalkers staring at him. However much he'd drunk, it hadn't been his imagination. He was sure of it.

By now, most people were moving on to the clubs. Hannah, ever the adventurer, was insisting she wanted to be taken to a men-only club night. He'd said there was no way she'd get past the bouncers. But when she'd flattened her hair, put on a baseball cap, and zipped up her tracksuit top, it was uncanny – there was no denying she could pass for a boy. He'd agreed she could tag along, but that once they were in, she was on her own; he was determined to dance till he dropped.

He searched for her among the thinning crowds, but she was nowhere to be seen. It wouldn't have surprised him if she'd latched onto the leather guys and left with them; that was very much her style.

Accepting that she'd ditched him once again, Colin went up to the bar to buy himself another beer. As he waited to be served, he had to do a double take: standing on the opposite side, partially concealed by a column, were Hannah and Klaus, chatting away like old buddies. Was this a set up? Had they organised something together, a pincer movement to force a truce? He wouldn't put it past her to interfere.

Both spotted him at the same time. A flash of a smile from Klaus made his stomach lurch, and he couldn't help smiling back. Klaus was dressed in dark jeans and a white shirt, and under the UV lights he glowed. Hannah was beckoning him over, an excited puppy wanting to show off her new friend. 'Look who I found trying to escape.'

Klaus leaned in to kiss him, his stubble grazing against

The Look of Death

Colin's cheek, familiar and strange all at once.

'Good to see you.' Stepping back, Colin caught Hannah's bleary gaze and knew instantly she'd taken something.

'I was supposed to meet a friend, but he must have moved on.' Klaus put down his empty beer bottle. 'Well, I'll let you two get on with your evening.'

'We're going out dancing. Colin's taking me to a men-only club, aren't you?' Hannah clapped her hands with glee. 'Come with us. It'll be fun.'

'That's not quite true. Once we're in,' Colin stressed, 'we're going our separate ways.'

'Do you think I could pass as a gay guy?' Rounding her shoulders to hide her breasts, Hannah posed in front of Klaus, adopting the look she'd struck before: moody teenager. Klaus grinned. 'You make a super, cute twink. I'm sure you'll be a hit.'

'Would you do me?' She tapped him on the arm. 'Would you?'

'Knock it off, Hannah.' Colin was quickly becoming irritated by their new best friends' shtick.

'Where are you going?' Klaus asked. '*Wu Wu?*'

Colin looked at his watch. It was after one. 'You know what? I've changed my mind. I'm calling it a night.' The freak in the toilet and now this chance meeting was enough for one evening.

Hannah dragged Colin towards her, forcing all three into a tight huddle. 'But you said you were hoping to score.'

Colin wriggled his way out of the tight embrace and gave her the hardest, meanest look he could.

'Why are you staring at me like that? You did.'

'You know that was a joke.'

She held up her hands and slid along the bar.

'I'm heading in the same direction,' Klaus said. 'We can share a taxi if you like.'

Colin glanced around for Hannah, but she was already

deep in conversation with a new group of guys. 'I dunno.'

Like the last two left at a high-school dance, he and Klaus stood in silence, waiting for the other to make the first move. Colin picked up his drink and downed it.

'I called today,' Klaus said. 'But you were out.'

Colin placed his empty bottle on the bar. 'I've been busy. Catch you around?' He went to move off, but Klaus stopped him.

'Stay.'

Colin turned to face him. 'You disappeared for a week. Not a word. Nothing.' He released himself from Klaus's grip. 'Don't you understand how angry I am?'

'I made a mistake.' Klaus was staring at him, his lip trembling. 'I admit it, but I apologised. I thought we were doing OK – better than OK.'

'We barely know each other.' Colin nodded towards Hannah. 'I should see what she's up to.'

'Give me another chance.' Klaus's eyes drilled into him. 'No more secrets. You know everything now. Tell me you'll think about it. Maybe not here, right this minute – I'm not that insensitive. But soon?'

The first night they got together, before having sex, they'd lain for hours talking and laughing. It felt like they'd all the time in the world; a lifetime to spend together. In the morning, he'd woken to Klaus stroking his back, soft touches that tingled through his entire body. Like he already knew it intimately – understood exactly what he needed.

'Think about it, will you?' The confident American drawl had reappeared.

Colin didn't have to think for long. 'Come here.' Wrapping his arms around him, he placed his head against Klaus's chest, inhaling the earthy scent that drove him crazy. How could one person have this effect on him? Klaus gripped him back and squeezed him close. He didn't want to be anywhere else. He didn't want anyone else.

PART 4

36

A FEW DAYS LATER - TUESDAY, 2ND AUGUST 1994

Colin dumped the groceries onto the kitchen counter. This room, like the rest of Klaus's apartment, was in a state of flux; pots of paint and brushes fought for space with suitcases, whilst unopened cardboard boxes, rolled up rugs and framed pictures were stacked against walls. But Colin didn't mind the chaos; it seemed a perfect backdrop to the whirlwind and excitement of the past few days.

Even by Berlin standards, the apartment was big, but for Wedding it was positively palatial. It transpired Klaus's grandmother had bought it as an investment soon after reunification, then died a few months later, and left it to his parents. At first, Klaus hadn't wanted to give up his own apartment in Schöneberg, but this was bigger, and rent-free. 'It's only for a couple of years,' he'd explained.

While Klaus had been out working an early shift, Colin had spent the day lounging in the park and needed to clean off the sun cream. Stepping into the walk-in shower, he heard the front door open and Klaus's voice shout, 'Hi.'

'I've got steaks. Is that OK with you?' Colin yelled back.

But as soon as the words were out his mouth, a semi-naked Klaus appeared, discarding clothes as he approached.

Joining him in the shower, he grabbed Colin's bum. 'Mind if I have mine now?'

'So corny.'

'Yeah? How corny do you want it?' Klaus dropped to his knees and sank his teeth into Colin's buttocks.

LYING IN BED HALF-ASLEEP, as the evening light faded, they watched the shadows of branches quiver across the exposed plaster walls. Using his pinkie, Klaus created a gnarly little shadow puppet. 'Hello, Mr Grumpy Colin.'

'Hello, Mr Grumpier Klaus.' Colin held up his fist and bashed Klaus's hand.

'Does Mr Colin want to have sex again, or does he want to eat?'

'Mr Colin's had too much sex and his tummy's rumbling.'

Klaus jumped up. 'Then let's go eat.'

'And you're sure your brother's not going to suddenly appear and catch us cooking naked in the kitchen?' Colin pulled Klaus onto the bed, his fingers circling Klaus's *K&H* tattoo.

'Didn't I tell you? He's decided to stay in Paris for work, and won't be back in Berlin till next weekend.'

Since getting back together, they'd chatted more than ever. It felt settled, more equal. 'You still haven't told me why you don't get on. Yes, you fought as kids, and I know you had different interests. But what caused the falling out?'

Klaus pulled away and lay back on the pillow. 'OK. Are you ready for this?'

'Hit me with it.'

'When I came out to my parents at the age of sixteen, I sat them down and explained everything. *I'm gay, I like boys, blah blah blah*. Neither was pleased, but they respected my decision, and over the years, it gradually got better, and now they barely even mention it. But when I told Hops, he wouldn't

The Look of Death

speak to me in the corridors at school, refused to share the same bedroom, demanded a bed be set up in the dining-room. I mean, he was a total dick.'

'That must have hurt?'

Klaus shrugged. 'Yeah, for about five minutes. I got on with my life, and he got on with his.'

'What? It didn't improve?'

'No. We both let it drift.'

'So, why move in together now?'

Klaus grabbed a packet of cigarettes from the bedside drawer. He lit up and placed an ashtray on his chest, which he flicked ash into almost constantly. 'Last year, around Christmas time, I got a call from him. And Hops never called. In his head, it would make him seem weak. He was in tears, and wasn't making much sense. But I got snippets of what he was trying to tell me. He finally blurted out he was in love with someone who'd broken his heart. And, after lots more questioning, he confessed that this someone was a guy.'

Colin sat up. 'And this came out the blue?'

'Totally. After the way he'd treated me, I assumed he was a bigot, and that was it. You know, he can be incredibly immature. But when he opened up, I realised how difficult it had been for him. When I came out, I'd been so certain, so eager to tell everyone, that I must have completely missed any of Hops's own struggles. My parents felt the same, told me I needed to look out for him. And the apartment was lying empty – so, it made sense.'

'In the hope of rebuilding your relationship?'

'That's the idea. But you've not met my brother yet. One minute he can be your best friend, then the next, blank you. After that telephone conversation at Christmas, I imagined we'd chat more, sort out our differences, but he didn't want to discuss anything. Even now, if I dare to ask a question, he stares at me as if I've no right. So, I've stopped asking.' Klaus stubbed out his cigarette and kissed Colin's stomach. 'But that's enough about my fucked-up family. I'm going to cook tonight. My treat. Did you get stuff for a salad?'

'Yes – there's plenty,' he said, admiring Klaus's muscular back as he disappeared from the bedroom. 'Is it okay if I help myself to another of your brother's T-shirts?'

'Sure babe.'

Colin hadn't been home in four days. Not even to pick up fresh clothes. Instead, Klaus had suggested he borrow some of his brother's. 'Take what you want,' he'd insisted. 'They're from years ago and they'll suit you better.'

He wandered into Hops's room and switched on the overhead light. Besides a full-length mirror, which leant against a wall, and several boxes Klaus's parents had forwarded from their home in Hamburg, the room was empty. Kneeling on the floor, Colin dragged the biggest box to the centre of the room. It was as if someone had emptied the contents of a wardrobe into it in the 80s, then taped it shut – bundle after bundle of pristine clothes had been kept. Some cool stuff, too. He tried on a *Soft Cell* T-shirt and a pair of Adidas shorts – they fitted perfectly.

Klaus whistled as he entered the kitchen. 'Sexy!'

'Do you think Hops would mind if I wear this T-shirt?'

'Go for it. But put it back afterwards. It's one of his favourites.' He pulled Colin towards him and slid his hand inside his shorts.

'Uh uh.' Colin pushed him away. 'That's a bit weird.'

Klaus grinned. 'Too kinky?'

'Trying to shag your boyfriend while he's dressed as your twin? It's a bit out there even for you.' Colin poured himself some wine. 'You want more?'

'Yes please.'

Colin filled his glass. 'I should go back to mine tonight.'

Klaus attacked both steaks with a meat tenderiser. 'OK. I'll drive, you can pack a few things, then come back here.'

The Look of Death

'Haven't you got an early start?' He sipped his wine. 'Wow. This is delicious.'

'Thirty Marks a bottle. Only the best for my baby.'

'Nothing like the Greek plonk Hannah's been buying in bulk for the bar – I swear it's taking the enamel off my teeth.'

'To your good health.' Klaus clinked against his glass. 'You being here is the best. It gives us a chance to play house together.'

'And you're sure you don't mind me crashing like this?'

'I'd say if I did.'

'And once your brother gets back?'

Klaus grimaced. 'Let's enjoy the time we have on our own. When Hops returns, we can chat more.'

After dinner, they moved through to the living-room, and Colin lit a few candles and settled on the sofa. With its whitewashed walls, furniture covered in dust sheets, bare floorboards and curtainless windows, the room looked neglected.

'You need some big plants in here.'

'I'm not so good with them. They all die after a few weeks.' Klaus flicked through a pile of LP's lined up along the skirting board. 'This is what I was after.' He held up a Miles Davis album for Colin to see. '*Birth of the Cool* – you know it?'

Colin shook his head.

'You're in for a treat.' Klaus blew dust off the turntable.

As the first track crackled through the speakers, Klaus joined him on the sofa. The overlapping rhythms were hypnotic; he rested his head on Klaus's lap and closed his eyes. With his fingertips, Klaus brushed the hairs on his arm back and forth, almost sending him to sleep.

'So, tell me, are you still investigating?'

Colin opened his eyes, surprised Klaus had broached the subject; since they'd got back together, he hadn't asked about it at all. 'Why, do you know something?'

Klaus let him wriggle free. 'Just that Matthias, who works in the murder squad, has got a few suspicions, too.'

'What like?'

'I quizzed him about Walter Baus and this latest case. The boy—'

'Ajnur Osman.' Each time he said his name, Colin felt a pang of guilt.

'Walter's case hasn't been closed yet,' Klaus explained. 'They're confident he died of an overdose, and he had a history of drug misuse, but there's a witness come forward who says they saw him with someone on the night he died.

'And Ajnur?'

'They don't yet have a definitive cause of death for him. But again, rumour has it

that he was a rent boy – turning tricks for a couple of Marks – that sort of thing. I'm sure you know the type?'

Colin reflected on Ajnur's eyes sparkling in the moonlight. As eager as he was, he didn't come across as someone who was selling his body. 'I met him.' Colin said it before thinking, kicking himself as he'd vowed to keep this information to himself, his insurance if necessary.

'Seriously?' Klaus unfurled his legs and reached for his glass. 'When? How?'

There was no way to backtrack. Klaus was on the edge of his seat, eager to hear more. Maybe he needed to trust someone after all, and it might as well be him. 'About a month ago, I visited the spot at Ernst-Thälmann Park where Stefan Reis and Ulrich Steiner's bodies were found. Out of nowhere, Ajnur appeared, and we chatted briefly.'

'And you recognised him as the boy who was found dead?'

'Let's say he made an impression.'

'You had sex with him?' Klaus didn't say this judgementally. But he was scouting for details.

'God, no.'

Klaus swivelled his body, and wrapped his legs around Colin. 'You'll not be surprised to hear, at the station, a Turkish

The Look of Death

rent boy is no one's priority. Matthias is pushing for them to do further tests on the body – his theory is the boy was suffocated – but suffocation's very hard to prove, and no one's listening. That's the culture, I'm afraid.'

'Racism? Homophobia?'

'Basically.' Klaus shrugged. 'It goes deep.'

'And what do *you* think? Are the deaths of Walter Baus and Ajnur Osman related to the other men?'

'I'm increasingly open-minded. Matthias's theory is not dissimilar to yours – sure there are similarities between the deaths, but no consistency.'

'If you take Fraser out the picture, you still have five men dying in the space of four years: all young, all gay, all found outdoors. I'm also beginning to think at least three of them – Stefan Reis, Walter Baus and Ajnur Osman – were posed after they died. That's a lot of coincidences that warrant further investigation'

Klaus yawned. 'I'm not disagreeing.'

'This Matthias – do you reckon I could speak to him? Would he know how Martin's body was found?'

'I dunno. But I can ask, see how he reacts.' Klaus looked at his watch. 'I love you, but it's after eleven and I'm up at four.'

'Sure. Sorry.' Colin's face was burning. Should he say he loved him back?

Klaus leaned over and kissed him. 'You sure you don't want to stay?'

'I'm sure.'

Klaus blew out the candles, and the room fell into darkness, leaving only their shadows. 'I'll speak to Matti first thing tomorrow. He's a good guy. If he can help, he will.' He hauled Colin up from the sofa, clasping him against his chest. 'Please stay,' he said, nuzzling into his neck.

Colin pulled back from him. 'You're insatiable. Get some sleep and I'll see you tomorrow.'

37

Without turning the light on in his room, Colin stripped off his T-shirt and flopped onto the sofa. Exhausted by the pleasures of the past few days, his muscles ached, even his tongue was sore, plus he'd a pounding headache from the wine. Eyelids drooping, he stared up at the shadows which formed jagged shapes across the shallow vaults of the ceiling. Thankfully, the temperature was cooler.

Being apart from Klaus felt weird, like a warm, comfy duvet had been pulled away from him. Over the weekend, it felt like they'd made real progress; it had been good to be able to talk things over and they'd begun to sort out their differences. Klaus seemed prepared to let his guard down, to let Colin in. He was less worried that they were just playing out some sort of fantasy for each other.

Eyes half-opened, he imagined the feel of Klaus's breath against his face, the gentle rasp in his throat as he fell asleep.

EMERGING FROM BEHIND A COAT STAND, Konrad gazed at Colin sleeping on the sofa: torso bare, hand trailing the floor. The rhythm of his breathing, the rise and fall of his chest, the faint

The Look of Death

pulse at the side of his pale neck, all enchanted him. To be in such close proximity to him, to witness his absolute vulnerability, to have such power over him, meant everything. Here was his final *Dornröschen*, his ultimate Sleeping Beauty.

Gently, he opened the window and a soft breeze entered the room. This may waken him, he thought. As Colin stirred and his eyelids momentarily fluttered, he crept towards the door. Now wasn't supposed to be the time. But if he did wake, if Colin were to discover he was not alone, then Konrad was prepared to take action. However, Colin settled back against the cushion, and turned his head away. A relief. Opening the door slightly, he slunk out.

COLIN WOKE WITH A SHIVER. The window was open, and light spots of rain kissed his arm. Groggy and hungover, he stood to shut it, convinced it had been closed when he arrived back. Kicking off his trainers, he stumbled over to his bed and switched on the bedside lamp to find that the duvet had been neatly pulled back, the bed prepared for him to get into; he hadn't done this. Usually, he rolled in and out of it. If he was changing the bedding, he would tuck in the sheet and plump up the pillows. But that was rare. He smelt the pillowcases; they were fresh.

He glanced around the room. A whiff of furniture polish filled his nostrils, reminding him of his mother. He'd only given the room a perfunctory dust a couple of times since arriving in Berlin. Why would someone take it upon themselves to clean?

Opening his chest of drawers, he discovered his socks paired and lined up in rows, his boxer shorts folded, T-shirts arranged by colour. Pulling open the wardrobe door, instead of the charity shop chaos he usually encountered, his jackets, shirts and trousers had been rearranged by type.

The more Colin looked, the more details he noticed. Furniture had been subtly moved, his shoes rescued from the jumble under his bed and organised into pairs, even the dead flies which lined the window ledge had been swept away.

He stepped out into the hallway and listened, but the apartment was silent. He'd have to check if any of his flatmates had a key to his room. But this wasn't their style; this was too much like hard work. If Bela had a key, this was the sort of thing he might do – but, given their current relationship, the idea seemed ludicrous. Anyway, Hannah would need to have let him in, which made no sense.

Like the person on the train, and in the bushes at the park, the man he chased at the youth hostel, and the person who whispered through the toilet cubicle partition, this was targeted. Someone was deliberately messing with his head. But to what end?

Colin returned to his room, grabbed his torch and inspected the window. He cast the beam around the back yard. His room was on the first floor and, due to the surrounding trees and bushes, wasn't overlooked. If you were reasonably fit, you'd only need to drag over one of the larger wheelie bins to be able to reach for the window ledge and hoist yourself up. The latch was old, and could easily be forced open from outside.

He pulled back the duvet. Here was definitive proof that this was not his imagination: white petals lay scattered across the mattress.

38

TWELVE YEARS EARLIER - SUMMER 1982

Whenever necessary, Konrad could turn his face away, step aside and remove himself; blend into the background and become another faceless person in the crowd. How often he'd seen others look right through him, never for a moment imagining what he was capable of. On leaving Ernst-Thälmann Park, he chatted to a man about his dog whilst Stefan's body lay metres away. Yet no one had identified him as being there that morning.

As a child, he'd often imagined himself invisible. Pulling the bedcovers over his body, he would lie motionless, sinking into the mattress, confident that no one would notice. Hearing his mother call on him, he'd remain still as a corpse, listening to her footsteps climb the stairs and enter his bedroom, calling his name, oblivious he was there. The deception thrilled him.

He believed his ability to be absent gave him power, and protected him, too. In those early days, when the older boys teased him about Egon, it became his mantra: turn away, step aside, remove himself.

And at school, it worked also. Whenever faced with a question, he willed himself to not exist and sure enough, the teacher passed him by, looked elsewhere and asked another pupil. He became so good at avoiding the teacher's eye, he couldn't recall ever having to answer a question. Once, his mother came home from a parents' evening to say that his science teacher couldn't remember him. No matter how much she described her son, the teacher was clueless. It didn't bother him – of course it didn't. If anything, it was vindication.

If psychiatrists ever got hold of him, he was sure they'd find it impossible to diagnose why he committed these crimes. His parents were strict but loving, and he didn't want for material possessions. The things he liked to do – reading, running, science, maths – all came easily, but he never excelled. He made sure of that. Everyone noticed the prize-winner, but if you came fourth or fifth, no one gave a damn. It was the same as coming last – everyone fussed over them. So, he avoided that too. Best to fly under the radar; be middle-of-the-road. To him, it represented freedom.

The truth of how he came to kill was too mundane for those trained to peer into the human psyche. He did what he did because he enjoyed it. Had he not discovered that enjoyment, he believed he would never have killed.

The change in his brother started soon after they turned fifteen. Using his birthday money, Egon had bought a box from the chemist and highlighted his hair himself – bright blond streaks declaring his difference. Badges began to appear on the lapels of his blazer, then on his school bag; not the German heavy metal bands everyone else was into, but British musicians like *David Bowie* and groups like *Soft Cell*. Music people said was *gay*.

But Egon was unapologetic and refused to moderate his look; he seemed determined to provoke people. When people accused him of being "a poof", "a faggot", "a queer", he said, 'Yes. So what?'

Despite the punishments dealt out by their parents and

The Look of Death

teachers, despite the abuse and beatings he received from people at their school – amongst them one-time friends – Egon carried on regardless. Konrad was both embarrassed and perplexed by his brother's behaviour, by how unbothered he was by the mistreatment he now received routinely.

'Why do you hang about with those meatheads?' Egon placed his tray on the canteen table and stared at him. 'You're nothing like them.'

It was July and their sixteenth birthday had passed without celebration. Over the past year, he'd publicly dissociated himself from his brother. Everyone at school, including some teachers, now referred to Egon as queer; there were rumours about him eyeing guys up in the communal showers. Choosing to sit at Konrad's table was a daring move; as far as he was concerned, it went contrary to their unspoken understanding.

'Beat it!'

Egon didn't move. Instead, he took out a listings magazine and opened it at a page. '*An American Werewolf in London.* Have you seen it?'

Konrad glanced around, checking no one was looking, that he wasn't being set up. If anyone spotted them together, rumours might fly, and that wouldn't do. He didn't want to be tarred with the same brush. 'No!'

'We've not done anything for our birthday. It's on at the cinema tomorrow night. We should go.' Egon smiled. 'Or maybe you'd prefer *Endless Love?*'

That was a girl's movie. Everyone knew it. Catching Egon wink, he got up from the table. 'You're a pervert.' Egon followed him out the canteen and along the corridor. Konrad didn't look back, hoping he'd give up and go annoy someone else. But as he climbed the stairs towards the English department, he could still hear Egon's footsteps behind him. 'Go away! Leave me alone,' he yelled.

'So, kitty *can* roar.'

243

Though they were not identical twins, there was a resemblance, which made everything so much more humiliating. To see Egon's face up close felt like a betrayal. His eyeliner infuriated him; it was as if he'd deliberately set out to ridicule him.

'Why would I go to the cinema with you?' He could hear his own arrogant tone, copied from the other boys, designed to appear as uncaring as possible.

'Because we're twins? Because it's always been you and me against the world?'

For all their differences, Konrad struggled with this separation from his brother. His mother often commented how, even as a toddler, he'd follow Egon around, crying for his attention. 'So long as we sit apart,' he said, avoiding his brother's stare. 'Agreed?'

The next night, hidden from view in the darkened cinema, Konrad watched Egon from across the aisle, engrossed in the movie. It felt good to be back together, but he worried about what might happen when the lights came on. Would someone say something in the foyer or pick a fight on the walk home? Would Egon refuse to back down, insist on answering back? Why did Egon have to be so much larger than life, so loud, so flamboyant? Why couldn't he be more like him?

The trip to Pfaueninsel had been Konrad's idea. Their grandmother would take him there each Whitsun for a picnic. 'A special treat, for my favourite boy,' she would say. Though Egon had never expressed any jealousy at being excluded, or any interest in visiting, Konrad wanted to do something special to mark the end of the long, hot summer break; just the two of them before the new term started.

It was early September; in less than a week they'd be back at school. But by the time they got to the jetty, it was evening and the ferry had stopped running.

The Look of Death

'We'll have to come back tomorrow.'

'Don't be daft. I'll race you.' Egon dived into the water fully clothed. 'Come on. It's not far.'

Konrad put his shorts, shoes and socks into a plastic bag and carefully placed them in his backpack. Self-conscious, he kept his T-shirt on and lowered himself into the pitch-black water. Despite the summer warmth, the water was freezing and as he kicked out into the channel separating the island from the mainland, he felt the strength of the current tug against his body.

Egon – always the stronger swimmer – had sped ahead, stopping midway to show off by diving under the water and disappearing from view. Seconds later, Konrad felt something grab his ankle and pull him under the water's murky surface. Panicking, he kicked against it and spluttered back to the surface, gasping for air.

Egon emerged beside him grinning. 'Did you know it was me? I bet you didn't!'

'Idiot!' Konrad yelled.

Taking a huge gulp of air, Egon lunged forward and quickly made it to the island. 'I won! I won!' he shouted as Konrad strained to swim the last few metres.

Once on the island, Konrad quietly squeezed the water from his T-shirt and put on the rest of his clothes while Egon stripped to his Y-fronts and ran around making farting sounds with his sodden plimsolls. He prodded Konrad. 'What's wrong with you? You're not mad at me, are you?'

'No,' Konrad lied. He pointed to a gap in the trees. 'It's this way.'

The setting sun cast long, soft shadows as Konrad led Egon along a series of grass-lined pathways, and into a dense area of forest. The air reverberated with the buzz of insects and the violent shrieks of peacocks.

'This place is giving me the creeps.'

'We're nearly there,' Konrad said. 'I need you to close your eyes – don't open them until I say so.'

'Can't you tell me where we're going? I hate surprises.'

'You need to wait.'

Egon did as he was told, but for extra assurance, Konrad placed his hands across his eyes. They both giggled as he propelled him along the path.

'Stand here,' Konrad instructed.

'Tell me when.' Egon's body was shivering from the cold.

'Now,' whispered Konrad, standing aside to reveal an elaborate rose garden, heavy with perfume, the coloured petals still vibrant in the dimming light. 'Special, isn't it?'

'Wow! This is paradise,' a half-naked Egon screamed at the top of his voice. He ran through the bushes, pirouetting as though touched by magic. 'Nana brings you here?'Konrad shook his head. 'She fell asleep on a bench when we came in May. I went off on my own and found it. I wondered what it would look like when all the flowers were out.'

'It looks amazing.' Egon plucked a rose and placed it behind his ear. 'And smells even better. Thanks for bringing me here, I love it.' He threw his arms around Konrad, hugging him tight.

'Okay, okay. No need to be such a poof about it.'

Egon pushed Konrad away. 'Don't call me a poof.'

'Why not? You are, aren't you?'

'Don't be such a shit,' Egon cried, punching Konrad in the arm.

'Don't hit me.'

Egon punched him again. 'Why? You going to go running to Nana?'

Konrad forced Egon into a headlock. 'Say that again,' he yelled.

Egon kicked his legs from underneath him and they both crashed to the grass, wrestling among the fallen petals. He tried to get on top, but Konrad used his weight to press him to the ground, grabbing his wrists and pinning his arms down.

'Let go.'

'You're the shit,' Konrad insisted. 'Admit it.'

'Uh-oh!' Egon started to snigger.

'What's so funny?'

'You are,' Egon panted.

'Don't fucking laugh at me.'

'Why not? I can feel your hard-on poking into my belly. Who's the poof now?'

Konrad felt an immediate rush of adrenaline pulse through his body. He seemed to be floating in the air, as if looking down at himself and Egon lying entwined amongst the rose-bushes. Releasing Egon's arms, Konrad placed his hands around his neck and began to squeeze. Egon punched at Konrad's body; in response, he tightened his thighs and pressed further, using all his strength and weight to smother Egon, to stop the filthy words escaping from his throat. Pushing his face right by Egon's ear, his nostrils filled with the scent of the rose lodged in his brother's damp hair, and he paused. Listening to Egon's gasps and gurgles as he writhed beneath him, he applied more strength, and felt the resistance of his larynx and the solid bone of his vertebrae. He paused again and sat upright, caressing Egon's neck with his fingers. Staring into his brother's eyes, he saw the flicker of recognition – the shared realisation that he wasn't going to stop. Konrad held his breath and gritted his teeth. Tightening his hands again, he felt the muscles in his forearms burn, his nails dig into flesh, felt cartilage fracture under his grip. He watched as the light left Egon's eyes, continuing to press until his arms fell away and his body went limp.

Konrad stood in the thickening shadows and surveyed the garden. It seemed more beautiful than before. Plucking the stem of a rose, he squeezed it tightly in his fist, until he could no longer stand the pain of the thorns against his skin. Drops of blood fell to the ground, mingling with the dark earth, and he breathed in the rich aromas of the roses and the soil all around him. For the first time in his life, he felt alive.

Lying grey and dead against the darkness of the earth, Egon appeared at peace. But something was out of place. Adjusting one arm across his chest, he looked more serene, like the princess from *Sleeping Beauty*. Beautiful. As if death had made him perfect.

Konrad spent hours with the body and it was now pitch dark. Around him, excited by his deeds, howls and squeals emanated from the night forest. 'Wake up,' he whispered to Egon, 'it's time to go.'

But he didn't stir.

If the fairy tale was true, a kiss would revive his brother, but he couldn't bring himself to do it; he felt too ashamed. So instead, he plucked a nearby rose, tore off a thorn, and pricked it against his brother's neck. But only a tiny bead of blood appeared.

It was nowhere near enough to satisfy him.

39

TUESDAY, 2ND AUGUST 1994

Colin woke to the sound of knocking and Hannah shouting his name. Stumbling out of bed, he wrapped a duvet around himself and opened the door.

'Where the hell have you been?' She barged into his room, checking to see if he was alone.

'Good morning to you, too.' He wiped the sleep from his eyes.

'Well?'

'I've been at Klaus's.'

'You dirty stop out.' She thumped her fist against his arm.

'Ouch!' He rubbed his arm. We've sorted things out.'

Lighting up a cigarette, Hannah lay back on his bed, flicking ash on the floor. 'And it didn't occur to you to let me know?'

'What, suddenly you're my mother?' He tried to grab the cigarette from her. 'Remember what we agreed? No smoking in my room.'

'Oh no, you don't.' She blew a puff of smoke in his face. 'I'm seriously pissed off. It's been days!'

'What can I say? I got caught up in the moment. I thought you'd work it out.'

'Then there's all this nonsense.' She handed him a pile of scribbled notes. 'Nearly fifteen messages. If you don't organise a phone line for your room, I'm going to do it for you. Either that or I'm ripping out the one in the hallway. I'm your flatmate, not a bloody answering service.'

'Shit. I'm sorry.' He went through them: one from Lee, two from his mother, one from Rhona, another from his sister, one from Kim, one from Bill, two from Lukas, several more from other artists asking if he was available to pose, and a final one from Bela, with the name *Mustafa* and a phone number beside it; in brackets was written *Ajnur's brother*. 'Thank you.'

'You're such a dickhead, Colin Buxton.' She stubbed out her cigarette in a plant pot. 'It's not like you.'

'What can I say? I'm a twenty-seven-year-old man who's been having lots of great sex. Shoot me.'

She adjusted the pillow. 'I had a long chat with your ex.'

'Which one?'

'Bela.'

'What? He's been here? In my room?'

'No! A few of us were out in the courtyard on Sunday night. He popped by to speak to you and when I told him I hadn't seen you for a few days, he suggested we call the police.'

'The police? Christ! Why?'

'Eh, because of all the murdered men you're investigating.'

'I lost track of time, that's all.'

She gave him a stern look. 'Don't tell me. Tell him.'

Colin flicked through the messages, trying to make sense of Hannah's handwriting. 'Did Lee say anything?'

'Some stuff of yours is still in his flat, and he was wondering whether to send it on or not.' She propped herself up. 'Oh, and by the way, he's got a new squeeze. He sounds happy. That's good? No?'

'I guess,' Colin shrugged.

The Look of Death

'It's all the fun of the fair with you guys; one door closes, another one opens.'

He lay beside her. 'I dunno. It's stupid. With Klaus, sometimes it feels like I'm cheating on Lee. You know what I mean?'

'You're definitely asking the wrong person. I'm juggling two at the moment. I'd always been into the idea, but I hadn't appreciated quite how much energy it actually takes. I'm exhausted.'

'I thought it was just Eli you were seeing?'

Hannah looked at him sheepishly. 'I've been seeing Brad too. I couldn't bring myself to choose.'

'The American guy who comes into *Zum Zum*?'

'He's so sweet.'

'But they look almost identical.' Colin laughed. 'What's to choose?'

'They do not.'

'Are you blind?' Colin cried. 'They're both big blond jocks with weak chins. Like almost every other guy you bring home. You definitely have a type.'

She looked at him quizzically. 'I do not. As long as they've a dick, I'm not fussy. And actually, they don't even have to have a dick. Tilda doesn't – though she is thinking about it.' She bounced off the bed, then swivelled back round. 'Oh, fuck. I was going to say—'

'What?'

'That Kim Stroder woman who rang – how well do you know her? She sounded pretty agitated – and she was kind of abrupt with me – as if she didn't believe I didn't know where you were. She was adamant that you call her back as soon as possible.'

'I'll do it now.' As Hannah left, he shouted her back. 'Has anyone been using my room?'

'Not that I know of.'

'Nobody slept over while I was away?'

'I don't think so. You're the only one with a key.'

'It's just my window was open and all my things had been moved about – tidied up.'

'A burglar with OCD? Exactly what I need.'

'Nothing's been taken. It's kind of weird, don't you think?'

'Maybe you should change the lock? It's part of the reason we got the keypad installed on the outside door – there were always strangers appearing. In the past, when this was a squat, it was pretty casual and because so many folk have passed through, it means there's loads of people out there who have keys or who've kept copies. It's all a bit dodgy. There's a number for a locksmith by the phone. Anyway, I should run.'

'Sorry again for everything.'

'No worries, hun,' she said, shouting *Tschüss* as she ran out the door.

40

Kim insisted they meet away from the youth centre. He suggested a Brazilian coffee-house which Bela had taken him to, not far from the synagogue on Oranienburger Strasse. Set amidst a warren of arcades, and looking onto a beautiful courtyard, it was well insulated from the bustle of the city.

Arriving several minutes late, Colin spotted her through the window. Sitting bolt upright and staring into the distance, she appeared detached from the life of the café around her. There was an iciness about her which he hadn't noticed the last time they'd met.

Colin sat and signalled to the waiter. 'Can I get you anything?'

'No thanks,' Kim said. 'I've ordered.'

He turned to the waiter. 'A black tea.'

Kim looked blankly at him. There were bags under her eyes and her clothes were creased.

'How are you doing? Is everything OK at the youth centre?'

She shrugged.

'I'm glad you called. I was wanting to touch base – update you on a few things.'

The waiter arrived with her order. 'Do you mind?' He shook his head as she attacked a large slice of chocolate cake. 'They make the best Kuchen in the city here.'

Colin began to sweat. Despite the tiled walls and the ceiling fans, the café was stifling hot; it felt more like a sauna than a place to relax and chat. 'I know you advised against it, but I'm meeting Ajnur's brother later.'

Ignoring what he'd said, she scooped up another piece of cake. 'Bela says he's being followed. Did he tell you?'

'No.' They hadn't spoken since meeting at the youth centre. With things going so well with Klaus, Bela felt like a complication Colin didn't need. 'Does he know who it is?' Focused on finishing the cake, Kim shook her head.

'I'm going to call him.' The idea that someone might also be following Bela was alarming. 'Has he reported it to the *Polizei*?'

'The *Polizei*?' She looked at him as if he was an idiot. 'It's probably them; working out how to pin the deaths on him.' She dabbed at the plate with her finger, picking up the final crumbs and popping them in her mouth. 'Anyway, he's gone home to his parents for the rest of the summer.'

Again, as in their previous conversation, he noted a disregard in Kim's tone, which seemed to contradict Bela's view of their cosy relationship. 'Where's that?'

She shifted in her seat, looking towards the door, as if eager to leave. 'Somewhere in the south. Bavaria? I don't know. I don't give him much thought these days. He might come across as someone who means well but he has his own agenda. You must see how he behaves.'

'Sure, he can be a little eccentric, but I can't say I've seen the side you're describing.'

'You know he went behind my back? Tried to take over the running of the youth group; decided that it made more

The Look of Death

sense politically for a gay man to lead it.' She smirked. 'No way was I going to allow that.'

The whirr of the fans got louder and seemed to advance. 'I'm surprised. He speaks very highly of you.'

'Maybe he learned his lesson. For my part, I prefer to keep our interactions to a minimum.'

'I don't suppose you've got a number for him in Bavaria?'

She lit up, retrieving an ashtray from a neighbouring table. 'Sorry. He's no longer on my list of contacts. Anyway, we're getting off subject.' With her large brown eyes, she scanned the room and leaned forward. 'Let's get back to how you're handling this investigation. I've had some time to reflect and do some digging of my own about you, and I don't think you're the right person. Not by a long shot.'

The waiter arrived with his tea and made a fuss of laying it neatly on the table.

'You need to appreciate,' she continued, 'but there are others – professionals – investigating now. This is no longer your case.' She stood, took out her purse and placed ten Marks on the table. 'If you've any respect for the community, you'll step away, leave us alone.' She towered over him. 'Ajnur died while you were pissing about, playing at being a private eye.'

The accusation stung.

'I'll be straight with you. People don't believe you're telling us the whole truth. Leon. Others. And I know for sure you aren't.'

'Leon couldn't have been more helpful when I interviewed him.'

'He's had a change of heart. I think it's now best you let us – the community in Berlin – sort out our own problems. We don't need you throwing your weight around in places you're not wanted. Besides, Stefan Reis's family has hired a private investigator. Leon's helping pay for her.'

Colin shook his head; he'd done hours of work, spent days

going back and forth across the city, made endless phone calls, half of which led to dead ends. 'You're right. I do have information I'm not disclosing. Not for the sake of it. But because I need to protect myself, my sources, the case I'm compiling. And I won't be sharing it till I'm ready. But just so you're aware, I'm getting close. You should let the other investigator know she might not be needed for much longer.'

'If your new boyfriend's helping you, I wouldn't be so confident.'

'What's Klaus got to do with anything?'

'Are you really that naive? Has it not occurred to you what's going on? The *Polizei* aren't incompetent, or understaffed, or whatever pathetic excuse they want to pull out their arses. This is a cover up, pure and simple. They've closed ranks. The killer's a cop.' She picked up her bag and slung it over her shoulder. 'Have you asked yourself what you actually know about Klaus Deichmann? Because I'll tell you what I know. Three years ago, me, Wolfgang and a group of the boys were attacked in a park by a bunch of skinheads. It was a targeted attack – homophobic – there was no doubt. That bastard, Sgt. Deichmann, was first on the scene and fucked up the entire investigation; deliberately as far as I could tell. Wolfgang nearly lost an eye. I had to have twenty stitches.' She pointed to her scar. 'Not a single one of those fuckers was prosecuted, let alone convicted thanks to your bloody boyfriend.'

Having revealed the real reason for their meeting, Kim left without saying goodbye.

41

Mustafa was leaning on the railings overlooking the canal at Maybachufer Markt. Older than Ajnur, with designer stubble and deep laughter lines around his eyes, he had a wide-boy image: leather jacket, stonewashed jeans, white T-shirt with matching Nike trainers, and to complete the look, mirrored sunglasses perched nonchalantly on his brow. Colin watched him from a distance, interacting with other stallholders and passers-by. He seemed a natural entertainer, always ready with a winning smile and a flirtatious comment.

'Hi. Mustafa?'

He stepped forward as Colin approached and grabbed his hand, shaking it eagerly. 'Thanks for getting in touch.'

'Is it good to talk here?' Colin asked. 'We could go somewhere more private if you prefer.'

'No, no, here's good. I can keep an eye on the stall.' His voice cracked. 'I've a new boy who's just started.'

Colin peered over at the young boy serving behind the stall, eagerly serving customers. 'Thank you for agreeing to meet at such a difficult time.'

'You sounded like you cared. No one else seems to. The

Polizei don't – they want to deal with Ajnur's death quickly, sweep it under the carpet.'

'That's my impression, too.'

'I approached the papers – beyond a headline, they're not interested in the death of another Turkish boy.'

'As I said on the phone, this is a private investigation – I'm not working for the police or the press. I want to find out what happened to Ajnur. Same as you.'

'They're saying he was selling his body. If you knew my brother, you'd know how far from the truth that is.' His voice rose, and his chest heaved. 'It's offensive. My brother was a good person. He had his whole life ahead of him. He deserves better.'

Colin decided not to tell Mustafa about his encounter with Ajnur; that would only complicate matters. 'I'm here to help.'

Mustafa took a few deep breaths, focusing on the canal ahead, whispering in Turkish. It took him a few minutes to compose himself. 'I knew my brother preferred men. Ajnur didn't know that, but I've known since he was small. I mean, he did nothing specific to make me guess. It was just how he was, and he was my brother. I didn't care. Less competition for me.' He smiled for a moment before his pained expression returned. 'I wish I'd said something, you know, to make it easier for him.'

'I'm sure he'd have known you accepted who he was,' Colin reassured him. As with all families stuck in silence, no one expressed their true thoughts until their son, daughter, brother, sister chose to make that first step and come out. The fact Ajnur didn't feel able to was a loss, but not unusual. 'You said your family's traditional.'

'Yes. And no.' He grinned. 'I mean, they still think I'm a virgin. Or that's what we all pretend. Ajnur might have assumed if he told my parents, it would have killed them, but they loved him. Sure, they would have had to adjust, but in the end I don't think they would've cared that much. As long as he was happy.'

'He was probably trying to protect them.'

Mustafa wiped his eyes with a crumpled tissue, and blew his nose. 'But it was him who needed protecting.'

Colin waited a few moments for Mustafa to gather his thoughts. 'There's something specific I need to discuss with you – a theory I have about Ajnur's death.'

'Go ahead.'

'There's no easy way to say this – I think your brother may have been murdered.'

Mustafa's reaction was one of relief not shock. 'Me, too. It's the only thing that makes sense.'

'And I believe whoever did it killed other men like your brother.'

'Seriously? And the *Polizei*? What do they say?'

'They're refusing to connect the deaths. Since 1989 four, possibly five, other gay men have been found in Berlin in similar circumstances to Ajnur. So, if you can think – is there anything you know that could help me? Any tiny detail that might point to something out of the ordinary. For example, did he have a new boyfriend?'

Mustafa paused, reflecting on the last few weeks of his brother's life. 'He was restless for sure. Like me, he liked to go off and do his own thing. I'm ninety-nine percent sure he'd started seeing someone regularly. I don't think that had been a thing for him before, to have a serious boyfriend.'

'Did he mention his name? Or the name of anyone new?'

'Not that I can think of. In the weeks before his death, he was very up and down. Not himself. I caught him crying one day, but he said it was nothing – things at home, he was tired – stupid stuff that I knew wasn't the truth. I've been around the block – I can recognise when someone's got it bad. Love, I mean.'

'He never confided in you?'

'No.' Mustafa's eyes welled up. 'I did do something though which he never knew about. I told the *Polizei* of course. But whether they looked into it, who knows?'

'What did you do?'

'I followed him.' Mustafa's face reddened. 'He'd have given me hell if he'd realised, but he was my baby brother. I wasn't gonna let anyone hurt him.'

Colin's heart beat faster. 'Where did you follow him to?'

'To an address in Schöneberg. A few days before his body was found.'

'And can you remember it?'

'I'll never forget.' Mustafa took a pen from his pocket, grabbed Colin's hand, and wrote it on his palm.

42

As Colin was about to leave the *Genossenschaft* that morning, Klaus had called to let him know Matthias had agreed to a meeting and would be at the entrance to Volkspark Friedrichshain, well away from his precinct, at five p.m. Standing by his bike in tight lycra, Matthias was exactly as Klaus had described – tall, bald, and athletic-looking. Dark glasses and a helmet slung over the handlebars completed the stereotypical image of an off-duty copper. Klaus had stressed the need for discretion, and already, even before they spoke, Colin noticed his eyes shifting restlessly.

'Good to meet you.' Colin extended his hand but Matthias shook his head.

'No. No. We can chat over there.' He nodded towards a stone bench which faced a grand water feature. His English was perfect, and like Klaus's, had an American lilt to it.

'Whatever suits.'

'Wait here. Do something until I'm sitting, then come and join me. If someone spots us, it'll look as though we've met by chance.'

Despite the absurdity, Colin played along; if Matthias imagined they were spies in a Cold War movie, he couldn't recall one in which Michael Caine wore figure-hugging cycling shorts.

Making a pretence of tying his shoelace, Colin watched him wheel his bike the few hundred feet to the bench. As instructed, he waited until Matthias was seated, before strolling over to sit beside him. With its cascading pillars of water framed by a monumental colonnade, their meeting place could easily have been a location from the *The Ipcress File*. It was another glorious summer's evening and the warm weather meant the park was still busy with joggers, couples strolling hand-in-hand, teenage boys playing football, all oblivious to the two men's secret rendezvous.

Matthias stared ahead, rubbing his fingers and thumbs nervously. 'If anyone finds out about this,' he stuttered, 'I'll lose my job.'

'I appreciate that, so let's make it quick and cut to the chase.'

Matthias took off his glasses, and placed his helmet on the bench to create a barrier between them. In response, Colin moved an inch or two away, ensuring if anyone noticed them, the impression would be they were both by themselves. Hopefully this would be enough to keep Matthias from bolting.

'Five minutes,' Matthias said. 'That's all I'm willing to risk.'

Klaus hadn't mentioned he might be this nervous. Colin decided to keep it transactional rather than familiar. 'Klaus—'

'No names,' Matthias snapped.

'Okay, no names.' Following his meeting with Mustafa, Colin had been desperate to head straight to the address in Schöneberg. But he knew standing up Matthias wasn't an option. Sitting there in the strangled silence, he hoped he'd made the right decision. 'Should I ask you questions?'

'It's easier if I tell you what I know. When I get up, I'll leave an envelope on the bench.' Matthias patted his backside, suggesting it was stuffed down the back of his padded shorts. 'It's safe for the moment.'

'Thank you for doing this.'

'Anything to help...' He was about to say Klaus's name, but stopped. 'Our mutual friend's a good guy.'

Colin wondered if Matthias had a thing for Klaus. Why put yourself on the line unnecessarily? 'I'll keep staring ahead and you start when you want to. How does that sound?'

Matthias smiled in agreement, his face revealing a boyish handsomeness. 'So, our mutual friend's explained which deaths you've been looking into and the fact that you discovered Walter Baus's body while conducting your investigation. I should say at the outset, the death of Fraser McDougal is not a case I've knowledge of, but the others, most definitely. Following Martin Engels' death last year, I prepared a report which sought to highlight connections between his death and that of Stefan's.'

'Only Martin and Stefan's?'

Matthias nodded. 'My theory was rejected. However, I believe the death of Ajnur Osman strengthens my argument. The information I'm giving you is an extract from that report with some comments I've recently added. I intend to resubmit this shortly, but I suspect it will be rejected again.'

'You don't think there's a connection with Ulrich and Walter?'

'The only common theme between all five is that they died at the locations where they were found. I'm almost a hundred percent certain Stefan Reis and Martin Engel were killed by the same person; there are too many similarities. Although Stefan's death was attributed to his Type 1 diabetes, and the official cause of death for Martin was Sudden Arrhythmic Death Syndrome, I think suffocation should have been pursued as an explanation. Unfortunately, despite my best efforts, that didn't happen. There's also compelling evidence to suggest Ajnur Osman was suffocated. But again, it seems no one wants to hear. Which brings us round to Ulrich Steiner and Walter Baus.'

'For me,' Colin interrupted, 'the proximity to Stefan and Martin of where their bodies were found is a red flag. Have you compared the positions the bodies were found in? Are there any similarities or suggestion any were posed?'

'Given the locations each were discovered in, I can see why you would assume a connection, but I'm still not convinced their deaths parallel the others. If you could prove Ulrich was gay or bisexual, for example, that starts to fit with a broader pattern.'

'I can.' Colin could see him making a mental note of this.

Matthias continued: 'The question of positioning is an interesting one. Again, there were similarities between Stefan, Martin and Ajnur. And you could say the position of Walter's body was broadly similar, but Ulrich's body was different. He was slumped, face down. Also, both Ulrich and Walter lacked a signifying mark that the other bodies had. Plus, they both died of a drug overdose. There's no question about that.'

'Can you tell me what the signifying mark is?'

He tapped his backside. 'All in the report. I don't think those two follow the same pattern as the others, though I could be wrong. But ultimately the problem is an institutional one. My boss – Kommissar Fink – is typical. He only wants to consider the most obvious explanations and focus on the causes of death, not the potential links between them. His starting position is negative: *Why would anyone care about a bunch of dead gay guys?* He's not interested in understanding the lives of these men in any depth. But beyond that, the last thing Berlin wants is a serial killer on its hands. It's not good for business.'

Colin was tempted to ask follow-up questions, but Matthias's focus and rigidity, his almost robotic style of delivering the information, suggested this wasn't an option.

Matthias tapped his fingers against his knees. 'I'm trying

The Look of Death

to make my superiors see sense, but I'm not hopeful. Which is why I agreed to meet you.' Without warning, he stood. 'Once you've looked over the evidence, I need you to destroy it. I don't want to risk it being traced back to me.'

'Of course. Can I ask one last thing?'

'Go ahead.'

'Why are you pursuing this when no one else will?'

Matthias thought for a moment before answering. 'As a gay man, it feels personal. These men were targeted; I'm sure of it. I think they knew their killer, trusted him, may even have been in a relationship with him.' Placing his hand down the back of his shorts, he pulled out a folded brown envelope and dropped it on the bench. In a single movement, he jumped on his bike and within seconds had disappeared from view.

A SHORT WALK from the park, Colin found an empty café and sat outside, ordering a sparkling water. He tore open the envelope to find a single sheet of A4 paper. It was a photocopy, showing small grainy, black-and-white images, numbered one to six which he struggled to decipher. He turned it over. Handwritten in English with a black marker was a list:

1. Thorn from a rose found in the pocket of Stefan Reis
2. Thorn from a rose found in the hair of Martin Engel
3. Thorn from a rose found embedded in Ajnur Osman's left index finger. Petals scattered across body and rose stem discovered wedged under lion sculpture.
4. Both Stefan and Martin had injuries to their index fingers – were any of those caused by a rose thorn?

5. Thin tyre marks found close to Stefan, Martin and Ajnur – a bike? A pram?
6. No sign of thorn on either Ulrich Steiner or Walter Baus. No sign of tyre marks.

Stuffing the piece of paper back in the envelope, Colin took a long drink of water. He'd found a rose tucked away in the tomb where Martin Engel was discovered, and also on the Lion's Bridge where Ajnur was found. The thin tyre mark found close to Ajnur could easily belong to a wheelchair, which would fit with what Noah had told him.

But if the petals he'd found in his own bed were rose petals, then that could only mean one thing.

43

From Nollendorfplatz U-Bahn, Colin walked along Maassenstrasse and turned into Winterfeldtstrasse. Like the rest of Schöneberg the street was quiet and well looked after, alternating between older tenements and modern apartment blocks. It seemed significant that the apartment Mustafa had directed him to should sit at the junction with Eisenacher Strasse, a short walk from *Blue Boy Bar*.

Colin stared up at the building – with long ribbon windows and grey render, it was as architecturally understated as any he'd seen in Berlin. The majority of the apartments were bland and utilitarian, however the corner ones each had large balconies facing the street; the balcony on the second floor was where Mustafa had last seen Ajnur alive.

He'd followed him to the address, with the intention of confronting the guy who'd been messing his little brother around. Concealed on the street below, shortly after he arrived, he'd caught sight of Ajnur shirtless on the balcony. In that brief moment, Mustafa changed his mind. He saw his brother turn and smile to another person inside, and decided he'd got it wrong; his brother appeared happy, so why should he interfere? Seconds later, Ajnur stepped inside and a hand drew the curtains closed.

'Do you think this is the man who killed my brother?'

'It's possible, but I can't be certain. I promise I'll do whatever I can to find out.'

'When you find this monster, let me at him first,' Mustafa said. 'Five minutes. That's all I ask.'

It had taken all Colin's powers of persuasion to dissuade Mustafa from accompanying him to the apartment. Eventually, he relented, accepting that a potential confrontation wouldn't be wise.

A STEEL GATE led Colin from Winterfeldtstrasse into a deserted central garden with a manicured lawn and a single large oak tree. At the angle where the two blocks of the building met, he found the door into the lobby unlocked. Like the exterior, the interior was bland, immaculate and deathly quiet: no screaming kids, no graffitied walls, no one loitering in the stairwell.

He pressed the lift button. If Noah was to be believed, and that was a big if, then Ajnur was in a wheelchair when he arrived at the Tiergarten. That suggested he was in a wheelchair when he left the apartment, and the lift would have been the obvious way to transport it. But to get Ajnur into a wheelchair, he would have to be incapacitated in some way. The lift doors opened, and Colin stepped inside.

But who in their right mind would wheel an injured or restrained person around a major city, knowing they might be discovered at any moment? He tried to imagine the killer's thought processes: alert to possible witnesses, ensuring Ajnur appeared normal, anticipating what other obstacles he might encounter on his journey to the Tiergarten. Was he deliberately courting exposure, to see how far he could take things without being caught?

The Look of Death

Arriving at the second floor, the lift opened onto a low-ceilinged, L-shaped hall with cream-coloured walls, black skirting boards, and a pink terrazzo floor. Four doors, each painted bright red, faced Colin. Judging by the position of the balcony, he determined that the furthest door must belong to the corner flat. Colin walked towards it, assessing his options – should he knock, break in, pretend to be the maintenance man? What would he say if someone was at home – that he'd knocked at the wrong flat? His steps slowed. A dead plant sat to one side of the door and a mat emblazoned with *Wilkommen* lay at his feet.

He listened at the door for any sounds of movement. There were none. He knocked and waited.

Behind the door of the adjoining apartment, the muffled sounds of a TV echoed. Someone was channel-hopping: a quick succession of glitzy game shows and sweeping, melodramatic music interspersed with adverts screaming out the names of German cleaning products.

When no one answered, he crouched and peered through the letterbox. The curtains were half drawn but the apartment appeared to be unfurnished, empty. If the killer had been living here, he wasn't any longer. Relieved, Colin exhaled. He stood and pressed against the solid-looking door, but it was firmly locked: not a millimetre of budge. There was no way he could risk trying to break it down. The neighbours would be out in a flash and before he knew it he'd be the one in cuffs. But apart from the door, there was no other way in, unless he wanted to scale the building and try entering via the balcony. Alternatively, he could try speaking to the neighbours, ask if they'd seen anything unusual, but it was the apartment he wanted to get into.

Reaching up to the small ledge above the door, he felt his way along, gathering a pile of dust and gunk as he did so. No key. He lifted the welcome mat but there was nothing underneath. He checked under the plant pot – bingo! A key.

This felt too easy. All his training was telling him: walk away, don't look back, take what evidence you have, however scant, and pressurise the police, or appeal to a journalist looking for a good story. Just don't put the key in the lock. No one knew he was here, and once inside, there would only be one exit.

A strong smell of bleach hit him as he stepped inside. He closed the door and switched on the bare lightbulb which hung from the centre of the ceiling. A small pile of junk mail lay at his feet, and around him, open doors revealed unfurnished rooms. Whoever had been living here had moved on. But if it was the killer, then surely there must be a trail of evidence: utility bills or a signature on a lease; something concrete that the police could follow up on.

A sudden knock startled him. Snapping off the light, he froze as a German voice shouted through the letterbox, *Hallo.* Terrified to move an inch, Colin felt a bead of sweat trickle down his back. *Hallo* the voice called again.

'Damn it!' Colin muttered. He peered through the spyhole. An elderly man in a pair of shorts and nothing else, his potbelly hanging over the waistband, stood on the other side of the door.

'Ich werde die Polizei rufen!'

Colin opened the door. 'I'm sorry. I don't speak German.' Although he'd understood exactly what the guy had said – that he'd call the police – he needed to act dumb, hoping this would be enough to deter him.

'Englisch?'

'Yes.'

'You live here?'

'I'm going to be moving in.'

The man stopped to consider him, then must have decided he looked legitimate. 'The *Polizei* were here last week, poking around. We don't want trouble.'

Colin reasoned this must have been in response to

Mustafa's statement; so they weren't entirely ignoring his suspicions. 'I'm here to measure up a few things.'

'The last guy was not so good.' The man peered over Colin's shoulder into the apartment. 'But we weren't expecting a new neighbour so soon.' He scratched his groin. 'Let's hope it works out better than before.' The man grasped Colin's hand and shook it. 'You are?'

'Andrew. Andrew Prentice.'

'Herr Brand. I'm your next-door neighbour.'

'Good to meet you.' In an attempt to appear casual, Colin picked up the mail – some fast-food brochures – but nothing with a name on it. 'So, who was it that lived here before? The landlord did say, but I've forgotten.'

'I never met him. He was hardly here. All we heard were strange noises at night.'

'That's weird. Bad neighbours are the worst, aren't they?'

'It disturbed my wife, so I tried knocking on his door a couple of times to complain, but he never answered.' Herr Brand shrugged. 'I don't know what's wrong with people these days. This used to be a friendly place.'

'So you never saw him?'

'I might have seen him once. Well, the back of him.'

'Oh?'

'I mean, who decides to start moving from their apartment at two o'clock on a Tuesday morning?'

'When was this?'

'Last week. The noise woke me up, so I looked through the spyhole to see what was happening. That's when I saw him pushing someone in a wheelchair into the lift.'

'His flatmate?'

Herr Brand shook his head. '*Nein*. As far as we knew, no one else was living there.' 'Gustav!' A ruddy-faced woman in a dressing gown emerged from the neighbouring apartment and eyed Colin with suspicion.

'I'd better go. Like I said, we don't want any trouble. This is a good building, clean, safe.' He shuffled back to his own apartment.

'I'll see you soon,' Colin called to him.

'Come say hello. We can share a beer together,' Gustav hollered in reply, before disappearing inside.

Colin closed the door. Even if it meant telling a few more white lies, it would be useful to interview Herr Brand properly. But for now, he needed to explore the apartment. As he walked along the hall, the noise from the TV next door stopped abruptly for several minutes before starting again. Colin imagined Gustav with his ear to the wall, whispering to his wife about the strange foreigner who was about to move in.

Painted entirely white and with grey carpets in every room, the apartment was devoid of character. Beside the front door was a bathroom, and next to that a large kitchen with a long hatch looking into the living room. It was also generous, with a glass door opening onto a wide, covered balcony. Colin tried the handle, but it was locked. Peering through the window, it also appeared to have been stripped of anything which might identify the previous tenant. A closet in the hallway had been cleared out too, as had a built-in wardrobe in the bedroom.

Colin wandered back through the apartment, double-checking each space and taking photos. He looked out the living-room window, catching his own reflection in the darkening glass. The streets were silent. Apart from the canned laughter seeping through the wall from the Brand's TV, the place felt like a ghost ship.

In the kitchen, he opened the fridge. Like the rest of the apartment, it had been stripped bare and any traces of life forensically wiped from its surfaces. But as he was taking a couple of final photos – doubting they'd be of much use – he noticed something sitting on top of the fridge, in the narrow gap between it and the underside of the kitchen counter.

The Look of Death

Reaching in with his fingertips, he used his nails to gain some traction and retrieved a small cork board, framed and with a string knotted across the back. Pinned to it was a single, square photograph – a Polaroid. The image was grainy, but he could see it was of two people outdoors.

Colin carried the board over to the window and fully opened the curtains. It only took him a few seconds to realise that the photograph was of him and Noah, the day they'd met in the Tiergarten, and the Polaroid was not pinned to the board with a tack or a nail, but with a single thorn from a rose.

This wasn't a trap. This was a clear message. The killer – circling, teasing – was telling him he was one step ahead.

44

With the sun now setting, Colin quickly walked north along a wide boulevard choked with evening traffic. He had to speak to Noah, to pass on the information about the photograph and warn him. If possible, he hoped to convince him to take cover away from the streets, away from any danger. That, he knew, would not be a straightforward task.

As he crossed the Spree, the Victory Column came into view, its crowning angel glowing bright gold against the darkening grey skies. There was a hint of thunder in the air, a heady sense of expectation that the skies might open at any second and bring much needed relief from the oppressive heat.

Cut in two by the road, the Tiergarten emerged before him, cloaked in shadows. At a busy junction, Colin dodged a couple of cars and entered the park along a path where dense thickets of trees came right to the pavement's edge. It was cooler under the canopy of leaves; he buttoned his denim jacket and turned up the collar. Embraced by the darkness, the city felt a million miles away. Heading diagonally across the park, the first fat spots of rain began to drop in earnest.

The Look of Death

Using the Lion's Bridge to orient himself, he checked over his shoulder and followed the intricate network of pathways towards Noah's encampment.

Eyes blinking, an exhausted-looking Noah rose from beneath a heap of sleeping-bags, a snarl etched on his lips. 'Who the fuck's there?' he roared with a shake of his dreads, shining a torch in Colin's face and striking out wildly as he drew closer. 'I'll fucking destroy you.'

Colin jumped back. 'Noah, it's me. Colin Buxton. Remember?' The torch beam moved down his body, lingering on his crotch.

'Well, if it isn't Little Miss Nosy Parker.'

Colin opened his backpack. 'I've brought food this time.' He'd stopped off at a late-night mini-market on the way and picked up a few provisions.

Noah pushed the covers aside and pulled his fur coat tight around his emaciated body, securing it with a silver lamé belt. 'Any more beer?'

'Not this time.'

'Then why'd you fucking bother?' Noah growled, slowly stepping around his shelter, lighting candles.

'Thought I'd drop by and see how you are.' Colin held up a pack of sandwiches. 'Ham and pickle?'

Noah grabbed the packet, tore it open with his painted nails and began devouring the contents. 'Well, now you've done your good deed for the day,' he spluttered between mouthfuls, 'you can piss off.'

Colin remained as he wolfed down the entire sandwich in less than a minute.

'You still here?' Noah wiped his mouth with a matted sleeve.

'Still here.'

'Anything sugary to get my chops around in that pert little satchel of yours?' he asked, placing the sandwich crusts in a plastic bag. 'For the ducks,' he explained.

Colin revealed a chocolate muffin and a bottle of Coke. 'Will this do?'

'You've thought of everything, haven't you, sweet cheeks?' Noah tilted his head coyly. 'Anyone would think it's my birthday.'

'Twenty-five again, Noah. Congratulations.' Colin removed the cellophane and handed the muffin to him.

He grabbed it, then snatched the Coke from Colin and guzzled half the bottle in one go. It was followed by the loudest, longest burp. 'I'll keep the cake for later.' Noah winked, popping it in a tin. 'And think of you as I'm devouring it.'

Colin scanned the den, alert to any sound or shadow. Although the Polaroid had been taken by the Lion's Bridge, the killer might also know the location of Noah's hiding-place. And if someone was watching them before, it was not impossible they could have followed him tonight. 'Can I sit?'

'You can dance a fucking jig for all I care.'

Colin took this as a yes and sat on one of the makeshift chairs, which had acquired a new cushion: green velvet, embroidered in blue thread with an intricate geometric pattern. 'Been shopping?'

'One of those rich poofs left it behind. Hiding out in the long grass, they pretend they've come for a picnic, but they're actually here for a good seeing to, just like everyone else. Pass it over, will you?'

Colin threw it his way.

'You can still smell the sex.' Noah pressed his nose to it and breathed in deeply. 'Spunk, the nectar of the gods!' He primped the cushion and set it on top of his bed. 'It's beautiful, no?'

'It is.' Buried behind the grime and the defensive attitude, there was a part of Noah that was proud of his home. He hadn't simply acquired any old abandoned cushion. It had to be the right colour, the right material, to earn its place among his belongings. However, it was the guys writhing on top who provided the final essential ingredient, enabling it to make the cut and join his pantheon of precious objects.

They sat together in silence for a few minutes whilst Noah rolled a joint. Despite his claw-like hands, his fingers were surprisingly agile as he took his time and perfected his creation. 'Want me to make you one?'

Colin shook his head.

'Who pissed on your parade?'

Hawk-eyed and instinctual, Noah missed nothing; it left Colin wondering how much more he'd actually witnessed the night of Ajnur's murder. 'Someone was spying on us the last time we spoke.'

Noah shrugged. 'It's a free country. Let he who is without sin, and all that.'

'They took a photograph of us.'

'How d'you know?'

'I found it.'

He eyed Colin curiously. 'You got it?'

Colin nodded, fanning away the fog from Noah's joint. 'Wow! That's super strong weed. Is it skunk?'

'It'll make the cake taste sweeter.'

Passing him the Polaroid, Noah examined it, taking his time, moving it into the light, drawing it closer to his face before stretching out his arm, screwing up his eyes to take in every detail. 'Must be an admirer.' He tossed the photograph back to Colin. 'A beautiful young man like you must have lots of them.'

'You must be stoned.'

Noah rummaged in a crumpled plastic bag and pulled out a stack of old black-and-white photographs and handed one to Colin. 'Oh, to be young and beautiful again.'

It was so faded, Colin could barely make out the image. 'Is this—?'

'Yes. Me. Taken in Australia fifteen years ago.'

The image was of a tanned, healthy-looking, muscular

man – a far cry from the photo of a scrawny teenager Noah had previously shown him. 'Did you live there?'

'The guy who took my portrait did. My fella. Brought up on a cattle ranch fifty, sixty times the size of the Tiergarten. Massive it was.' His eyes sparkled at the memory, his arms outstretched, capturing it again in one big hug. 'Simon.'

'A tourist?'

'Was he fuck? An engineer, worked in Berlin. Met him in the dark room at *Tom's Bar*. Now, *he* was a looker. Great muscled thighs from riding those horses. Big, cheerful face. Very kissable lips. The bluest eyes. Fucked every time like it was his last day on earth. Cock as thick as my wrist; like nothing I've ever experienced before or since, let me tell you.'

Colin wondered how much of the story had been embellished over the years, but it gladdened him to know Noah had once loved and been loved, and that he still held onto the memory.

'Twice I visited Oz. Once backpacking when I was twenty-two. Then fifteen years ago, to see if I could make a life with Simon. But it didn't work out. The last I heard he got sick and died soon after. Like so many.' Noah blew a perfect smoke ring which hung in the air for several seconds, before settling his gaze on Colin. 'Spectacular country though. Huge. You can lose yourself there. All those long, empty roads, drifters hitchhiking back and forth. You hear some nasty stories – psychopaths trawling up and down the highways, people disappearing out in the desert.' Noah spat a huge ball of phlegm onto the ground.

'Can I ask you more about the night Ajnur was murdered?'

'What more is there to say? Death's all around us. I sensed it then and I can still feel its presence.'

'How do you mean?

'Someone was destined to get the chop that night. You can sense when a sacrifice is due. And there's more to come. I can

The Look of Death

feel it. I can taste it in the air. I can see it around us. Can't you?'

On cue, a rumble of thunder groaned above them, then a bolt of lightning illuminated the sky. The promised downpour followed.

'I don't think you're safe here,' Colin shouted above the rain. 'The person who photographed us is the same person who killed Ajnur; I'm certain.'

Noah rooted amongst his bedding and turned around brandishing a hunting-knife. 'If death comes for me, I'll gut him from head to toe.'

Sheets of rain poured through the trees, hammering down on the tarpaulin above their heads, creating rivers of mud around their feet. Colin stood. 'I can get you a room for the night.'

'He's slipping through your fingers, isn't he?'

For all the fugue, Noah had an uncanny ability to read Colin's mind. 'For now.'

'I'll let you into a secret. He's circling his prey. That's what a deviant like that does. He lets it build and build, allows the devil to get inside his head, waits for the perfect moment, then pounces. Like an animal.' Noah circled the wet earth with his fingertips, drawing a line across his face and neck. 'Territorial this one. I can sense him around you.' With his index finger he dabbed a spot of mud in the centre of Colin's forehead. 'You need to look within.'

'Stay at my place tonight. Please. I've a sofa you can sleep on.'

His fur coat dragging in the mud, Noah poo-pooed the idea with a wave of his hand and insisted Colin sit beside him on his sleeping platform. 'After you left the last time, the strangest thing popped into my head.'

'What's that?'

'The murder of a young boy. Twelve years ago. Out on the edge of Berlin, in one of those godforsaken towns.'

'You think there's a connection?'

Caught up in the sweep of his story, Noah didn't hear him. 'For some reason, the story came flooding back to me as if it happened yesterday. It was big news – national – for a few days, then forgotten about. But listen to this, my sister lived close by, and that summer I was staying with her. I'd had a relapse – drink, drugs, you name it – I was taking way too much. Complete mess. As a distraction, I began seeing this journalist – a lovely man – but nothing serious, a bit of mutual wanking in the public toilets that somehow developed into a rather sweet little friendship. Well, he was working for the local rag: *Wannsee und Zehlendorf Welt.* This young boy, a teenager, was found dead – murdered – on Pfaueninsel, an island on the Havel. It's a beauty spot. Rather gorgeous. The Prussian royals tarted it up as a playground à la Marie Antoinette, with follies, gardens, that sort of thing. Even a zoo would you believe? Now there are two details which I think you'll find interesting: there was a suggestion at the time that the teenage boy was gay and that there was either a sexual or a homophobic motivation to his killing.'

'And what was the other detail?'

'Other detail? Oh. Yes, what was I going to say? Roses! Roses were scattered around the boy's body. Did I tell you that's how I found Ajnur? Like *Dornröschen.* In fact, when I think about it, the boy may actually have been discovered in a rose garden.'

Could the murders have stretched back that far? 'Noah, tell me everything you know. What? When? Where? Did they get anyone?'

'I don't think they ever caught the bugger. Well, certainly not before the Christmas of that year. I know that. It was out in Wannsee. As far west as you could go in the old days. And the dullest place on earth; I'd have murdered someone myself if I'd had to stay there any longer.'

The Look of Death

Colin clasped Noah with both hands and kissed him on the forehead. 'You're a marvel.'

Noah stared up at him. 'You've lovely lips.'

'Is there anything else you remember? The journalist's name?'

'Now you're asking. He was a little man. Dark, hairy.' He thought for a moment, a smile spreading across his face. 'I've got it. Milo; he had a Greek father. Christ, life used to be so romantic.'

'Can you remember any more details? Anything that didn't make the newspapers?'

Noah sat up straight, his mind whirring like a rusty old machine, the cogs slowly grinding. 'Milo may have talked about another boy being mentioned as a suspect. Apparently, the whole town thought he was guilty, but he'd an alibi.'

'And names? Please Noah, there's so much more cake and Coke if you can remember.'

Noah's eyes narrowed. 'Is that all you think I'm worth?' he snapped. 'No. I won't be used like this. I don't want to think about the past any more. That's all you're getting from me.' He pointed to a plastic bag. 'Now pass me my stash and piss off.'

45

Colin steadied his breathing as the train pulled into Pankstrasse. Exiting immediately, he sprinted up the escalator, taking two steps at a time. Outside on the street, it was still raining heavily. Sticking close to the building line for shelter, he walked quickly to the twenty-four-hour chemist where he dropped off the roll of film he'd taken at Winterfeldstrasse, and collected his prints from the previous week.

Ten minutes later, as he turned into the courtyard of the *Genossenschaft*, he discovered a slight figure wearing a hoodie with the words *Jesus Christ* written on the back, trying to force their way into the building.

'Hey,' he shouted, rushing over and grabbing them.

The figure limply turned around, and Lukas's spaced-out face met his. 'Sorry,' he said, barely able to stand up straight.

'What are you doing?'

Hammering a finger into his chest, Lukas slurred, 'You never turned up to do any more poses.' Each word was spat at him.

Colin couldn't work out if he was truly disappointed or whether it was the drink talking. 'Did you come all this way to tell me that?'

The Look of Death

Lukas looked at him and burst out laughing; thrusting his body at him, he hugged Colin tightly. 'Of course not.'

Colin found it difficult to break free. 'So, why are you here?'

Lukas pulled away from him, dropping a bicycle pump, which he'd been trying to lever the door open with. 'Oh, I didn't tell you. Maryam's gone.' He blew out his cheeks and released a puff of air. 'Vanished!'

Busy with Klaus and the investigation, Colin hadn't modelled at the art school for a week or so. He felt a pang of guilt, as he realised he'd not thought to explain this to either Maryam or Lukas; it had felt like the start of a fun friendship. 'Has she left Berlin?'

'Dunno. The tutor hated both our work so much, she decided she'd had enough. Told him she was leaving. And I haven't since her since.'

'That's terrible. I hope she's OK.'

The sound of someone approaching through the archway made them both turn. A tall figure emerged, and, as it moved into the light, instantly became recognisable as Bill.

'So, the rascal's with you?' Bill laughed as he approached, three pizza boxes piled between his arms.

'Did he escape?' Colin asked.

'He said he was off to explore. That must have been two hours ago.'

'I got locked out, didn't I? Silly me,' Lukas mumbled.

Bill searched for his keys, but Colin pulled out his and unlocked the door.

'We're having a party with some of the students. You should come up. I've called you loads of times.'

Once again, Colin felt guilty; he'd not responded to the many calls asking him to do shifts. 'Things came up,' he said.

'Well, if you're free next week, we'd love to have you back. You were a huge success.'

'I'll give you a call – I promise.'

All three walked into the hallway, but Lukas pulled Colin back as Bill strode up ahead.

'Come and join us if you want,' Bill shouted back. 'No pressure.' His footsteps echoed as he continued to climb the stairwell.

Lukas gripped his arm. 'I've not told you everything,' he whispered.

'What haven't you told me?' Colin asked, supporting him.

'You know we both like you?'

Colin smiled. 'I like both of you, too.' Lukas gazed at him, as if about to say something else. 'What is it?'

Lukas moved in closer and gripped Colin's T-shirt. 'Maryam said she'd like to have, you know, got to know you much better. You know what I mean?'

This had never occurred to Colin, and he wondered if Lukas was actually referring to himself; there'd been the occasional flirtatious remark, but nothing he'd taken seriously. 'You sure?'

Lukas nodded, then stepped away, almost losing his balance on the stairwell. 'Don't ever tell her I told you. Our little secret.'

'It's safe with me. It's just, I didn't realise she was into men.'

'She's not. Just you. She made that very, very clear. Face of an angel, she said. But you don't like her, do you? Not in that way?'

With enough complications going on in his life, Colin was genuinely stumped on how best to reply. 'Are you heading to the party?' he asked.

'Only if you come with me.' Lukas held out his hand. 'I need someone interesting to chat to.'

Colin hadn't the strength or energy to engage in a conversation with Lukas while he was this drunk. He took his hand. 'Tell you what, I'll walk you upstairs, check you don't get lost again.'

The Look of Death

He guided Lukas up the stairwell, ensuring he didn't go wandering elsewhere. But at the top step, he flopped down and refused to move. 'Leave me here.'

'But it's just a few more steps.'

'I'll be fine,' he snapped, as his head drooped downwards and his body went slack.

Pressing the buzzer, Bill opened the door. 'Crashed?' he asked, spotting Lukas slumped against the wall. 'He's a bit of a handful. These East Berliners like to party hard.'

'I'd take him downstairs, but I don't want to confuse him if he wakes and finds himself somewhere strange.'

'It's no problem.' With one heave, he lifted Lukas up and took him inside. 'I'll let him sleep it off. You sure you don't want to join us?'

'Thanks. Another time.'

RETURNING TO HIS APARTMENT, Colin headed straight to his room. Switching on the light, he checked his windows and every square inch of surface for any signs of disturbance. Satisfied all was as he'd left it, he lay on his bed, and allowed the tension to release from his back and shoulders. The Wannsee connection needed to be explored as soon as possible.

Stomach grumbling, he forced himself to his feet and wandered through to the kitchen. As ever, Hannah was there with a group of friends, drinking. A girl, who he assumed to be Tilda, clung to her and sang along in German as one of the boys strummed U2's *One* on the guitar.

'You joining us?' Hannah smiled.

Colin shook his head.

'There's veggie chilli left in the pot and I think there's some rice, too,' she said. 'I finished the guacamole, I'm afraid.'

'No worries.' Colin filled a bowl and helped himself to some bread.

He wandered back to his room and sat on the edge of his bed eating and leafing through the photographs he'd collected, carefully scrutinising each one. Tearing down the posters from the wall opposite his bed, he tacked his map of Berlin to the centre of it and marked each location. Around the edge of the map, he pinned the name of each man who'd died and assembled a group of photos and articles beneath.

On the lower left-hand side of the map, he marked Pfaueninsel with a question mark and stuck the Polaroid he'd found that evening beside the Tiergarten.

If what Noah had told him was correct, this case was bigger than he could ever have imagined. And Noah's suggestion that the killer was circling, waiting to strike, chimed with his own instincts and the growing evidence. It hadn't been paranoia: the interference with his room and the discovery of the Polaroid proved beyond doubt that someone had been following him. The implications were terrifying; it pointed towards the killer having him, or someone close to him, in their sights. But worse than that, based on what he was starting to discern about the killer's MO, it meant it was more than likely he was already in his life. If he'd any hope of solving this, he needed to be objective and dispassionate, to stand back and consider each person in turn.

There was a knock at his door and Hannah's face appeared.

'You okay?' she asked. 'You seemed a bit subdued.'

'I'm fine,' he replied. 'A bit tired and trying to get my head around all this shit.' He nodded towards the wall.

'Jesus,' Hannah cried, stepping into the room. 'Sherlock Holmes, eat your heart out. I didn't realise the police actually did this. Are you going to put up strings to link everything?'

'It's much more of a Jessica Fletcher vibe I'm aiming for.'

'What, does she ever solve anything?'

The Look of Death

'Are you mad? She solves everything.' Colin rearranged a couple of photos. 'Talking of madness, I could do with a sounding board.'

'My Cagney to your Lacey, sort of thing?'

'If you like, but this is serious.' Colin took a deep breath. 'Not to alarm you, but I think the killer is someone I know.'

'Fuck's sake, Colin, shouldn't you go to the police?'

'Not without evidence. Anyway, I don't know if I can trust them.'

'Who are we talking about here? Someone in the building? At work?'

Colin shrugged. 'Kim – the woman from the youth centre who you spoke to on the phone – she reckons the police are covering up for one of their own and she's highly suspicious of Klaus.'

'Klaus? You're joking?'

'Told me things about him that puts him in a new light.'

'But he seems so sound. The idea that he could be a cold-blooded killer – it's absurd.'

'I know. I know. But I think this is how the killer operates; he insinuates himself into the victim's life and then strikes. Several of the men who died had recently started an intense relationship with someone new. Remind you of anyone?'

'Shit. They do say most people are killed by someone they know, don't they?' Hannah squeezed his arm. 'You know you can trust me?'

'I know.' Colin gestured to the wall. 'I've added Bela, too. It was him who proposed going to the graveyard where we found the body of Walter Baus.'

'Christ! Anyone else? Am I on it?'

'Unless you're packing something down there you've not told me about.' Colin laid some of the photographs on the bed. 'A whole load of people are on my list. A guy, Leon, who may or may not have been a good friend of one of the men who died – he's trying his best to side-line me now. There's this sort of artist/tramp weirdo – actually you'd love him – he lives in the Tiergarten, and it was him who found the Turkish boy's body. God, there's even the brother of the Turkish boy, who's basically admitted to leading a double life and let me to a dodgy apartment.'

'And you've been putting all this together on your own?'

'Pretty much.'

The buzzer went.

'That'll be Eli.' Hannah ran to the front door, returning seconds later. 'Colin, you've a visitor.'

Brandishing a bottle of wine, Klaus appeared behind her.

Had they made an arrangement? If so, he couldn't remember doing so. 'Hello.'

Without letting Klaus see, Hannah winked at Colin. 'Are we still going out tonight, then?'

As Klaus looked his way, he held up the bottle of wine. 'Your favourite.'

'We'll do something tomorrow, Hannah.' Colin mouthed 'It's OK' to Hannah as Klaus stumbled to the drawer where he knew the corkscrew lived.

'I'll leave you boys to it.' She closed over the door.

'It's not too late to surprise my favourite man, is it?' Klaus picked up two glasses from the dresser.

'Have you been out?'

'A couple of drinks with workmates. Matti says hi. You made a good impression.'

Colin eyed Klaus with suspicion; his athleticism could overpower someone for sure. And his natural reserve, his understated charm, could easily lull you into a false sense of security. He watched as he pulled out the cork, sniffing it before discarding it in the bin. 'To be honest Klaus, I need to get up early.'

'One drink, then we can go to bed.'

'I've things I want to—'

'Here. You've got to try this.' He handed Colin a large

glass of red wine, clinked his glass against his before kissing him. 'I've missed you.'

'I've missed you too, but I'm busy,' Colin said. 'I'm working.'

'What? You seriously want me to leave?' Klaus's expression clouded.

'Shit,' Colin yelled. He'd spilled wine down his T-shirt; the one he'd borrowed from Hops's wardrobe.

'You've ruined it, babe.' Klaus licked his finger and rubbed at the stain, making it worse.

'Stop! I'll wash it tomorrow.' Colin sat on the sofa, staring at his feet, unable to look up. Why had Klaus turned up out of the blue like this? His knee began to shake and he steadied it with his hand. 'I'd rather be on my own tonight.'

'Wow!'

Colin looked up – Klaus was staring at the wall, swaying slightly.

'I didn't realise you'd done so much,' he said. 'You want to talk me through it?'

'No. It's fine.'

Klaus edged closer. 'No, no – go for it.'

'If I'm being honest, I'd prefer not to.'

Klaus sat beside him. 'I'm trying my hardest to help, Colin, telling you things only the police know.'

Colin waited a second. 'I'm stressed about the case. And the last thing I need is you giving me some sort of crit about my professional methodology.' He couldn't meet Klaus's eyes; in that moment, he felt like a threat. He couldn't shake the thought that the man sitting next to him could be planning to kill him. He felt if he did look up, he'd be able to read this in his eyes.

'I'm not leaving till you tell me what's going on.' His voice was officious, the same tone he used when he was in uniform.

'Please, Klaus. I'll speak to you tomorrow.'

'I'm not leaving.'

Klaus leaned into Colin, filling the space around him, determined to sit it out. Colin's knee trembled again, only this time Klaus's hand reached over to stop it. He then touched his chin and raised his head.

'You don't seem stressed,' he said. 'You seem scared.'

Still unwilling to meet his eyes, Colin tried to stand, but before he could, Klaus's arms wrapped themselves around him and squeezed tight. 'It's going to be OK, babe. I've got you.'

46

TWELVE YEARS EARLIER - SUMMER 1982

Reports in the newspapers continued to claim Egon's body had been 'interfered with' after he'd died. The phrase troubled Konrad – why couldn't they spell it out? Anyhow, they were wrong. He hadn't laid a finger on him. Their endless innuendos about Egon's 'flamboyant character', 'the teenage misfit', and 'the reputed gathering place for homosexuals' were products of their own filthy imaginations. Egon had died pure and innocent. He alone could testify to that. He was tempted to write a letter and set the record straight, expose their lies for what they were. But every time he sat down with a pen and paper, memories of that evening came flooding back; things he didn't want to remember.

A month after Egon's death, two policemen called at the house. His father politely excused himself, but his mother welcomed them in, fussing over coffee and biscuits, and made small talk.

'Frau Hausmann, can we speak to Konrad?'

On cue, he'd appeared; he'd been hiding on the stairs listening to his mother make a show of herself. Entering the room, he sat on his father's chair and hitched up his shorts to accentuate his bulge. It was the sort of thing – provocative, outrageous – that Egon would have done.

The two policemen were handsome – one fair, the other dark, both in their mid-twenties, each with inquisitive, nervous eyes. Only one of them, the dark-haired one, was doing the questioning, whilst the other – the one with the fair hair – noted Konrad's answers.

'Thank you for agreeing to meet with us,' the dark-haired one began. 'We'll try to make this as brief as possible. It must be a very challenging time for you and your family.'

The more Konrad gazed at him, the more he could see the dark-haired policeman's resemblance to Egon – the sculpted lips, the large, doleful eyes, the slightly freckled complexion. Was this a deliberate tactic by the police? An attempt to confuse him? Trap him?

'Can I ask, were you close to your brother?'

'Not especially.'

'But you were twins. That's a special connection, no?'

Konrad shrugged. By being non-committal, he hoped the policeman would get bored and move on. He was only sixteen, so they couldn't push him too much. They weren't there to arrest him; he was confident about that. As far as anyone knew, Egon had been alone that evening like he usually was. Shunned because of his 'sissy ways', they'd find it practically impossible getting anyone to admit even looking in his direction. 'We've always been different. We're not identical, you see.' He watched the fair-haired one carefully write down each word. Konrad thought he looked like one of the slow kids in class, the type who needed to mouth each letter out as they wrote it. 'Did you get what I said?' he asked. 'It's important you write it exactly as I tell you.'

The policemen exchanged a look.

'We've been told you recently went to the cinema together.' The dark-haired one continued.

'Once over the summer, to see *An American Werewolf in*

The Look of Death

London.' Why had he told him? The film couldn't have been gayer – all those nude shots of a boy turning into a werewolf. 'It's great, have you seen it?' Heart racing, he shifted in his seat. It felt like Egon was inside him, trying to take possession of his throat, his tongue, his body. He waited to see if there was another exchange between the two policemen. There wasn't. 'We saw another one, too. I can't remember its name.'

'*Endless Love,*' his mother volunteered. 'Egon had been desperate to see it for months,' she added, dabbing at her eyes with a tissue.

The policemen both smiled sympathetically; however, he knew they'd be thinking for certain he was queer too, just like Egon. Maybe they'd seen it themselves. Maybe they were queer, too. Maybe they were fucking each other. His bulge started to twitch and he adjusted it as discreetly as he could.

'Yes, it's a good movie. Me and my girlfriend caught it,' the dark-haired officer said.

Konrad felt a sudden surge of anger and he imagined squeezing the life out of him, watching him gurgle as he fought for his final breath before he revived him and started all over again.

'So, you wouldn't say you were best friends?'

He shook his head. 'We did our own thing mostly.'

'Konrad's a boys' boy,' his mother interjected. 'Egon was sensitive – an angel.'

The dark-haired policeman nodded. 'What about school? Did you have classes together?'

'Only Art. The teacher moved Egon next to me.' That pervert of a teacher, who got off on seeing them sit together. Konrad could see the way he ogled them: disgusting. Well over forty, with his too-tight jeans and floral shirts, he had the worst breath he'd ever smelt. Every time Konrad asked for help, he'd slither over and press against his leg. He should've reported him. He still might.

293

'Can I ask something?' His mother placed her cup on the table and sat forward.

What the hell is she doing? He stared at her, expressing his disapproval. 'Mum, they've come to speak to me and I'm happy to answer their questions.'

'Are you interviewing everyone in Egon's classes?'

The policemen exchanged another glance. Just for a split second, but enough for Konrad to feel a thrill as their eyes met; they shared a secret knowledge. He'd no doubt his name had been discussed beforehand. Had they considered if he was *the one*?

'We've been conducting interviews at your son's school, but it felt more appropriate to speak to Konrad at home. Understandably he's taken time off school.'

'I don't know how he's going to recover. He's lost so much weight since...' She wiped her eyes again. 'Haven't you, dear? Can't keep anything down, can you? Last week it was coming out of both ends.'

Defiantly, he met both officer's eyes, daring them to laugh or pass comment or show any sign of disgust.

'Our sympathies are with you,' the fair-haired one said.

'How are you feeling now? Any better?' The dark-haired one's accent was melding into Egon's, as if his Sleeping Beauty was there in front of him.

'I'm going back to school tomorrow.'

'Are you?' His mother put down her biscuit, which had been halfway to her mouth.

'I've decided.'

'The teachers have been sending him work, but it's not the same, is it?'

Konrad stared at the soft hairs on his leg; he felt Egon take possession of his fingertips and began to play with them. The fair-haired one noticed and swiftly looked away. *Got you!* He wouldn't even bother trying to revive that one; he'd just take pleasure in seeing the life drain from his body.

The Look of Death

'On the evening Egon disappeared, did you see him at any point?'

He'd lied to everyone that day. His mother, telling her he was off to visit his grandmother, who he then told he'd errands to do for his mother. No one knew about him being with Egon. 'I was at my Gran's.' Even if they questioned her, his grandmother was too senile to remember what had happened that night. He'd already convinced her they'd spent the evening together playing board games, and why would she question her golden boy?

'Yes, you got home quite late,' his mother said.

She needed to shut up, otherwise she'd risk saying something she'd come to regret.

'Gran kept making me eat.' He held his stomach as though still bloated by the imaginary food.

'She spoils him.' His mother offered the officers another biscuit, but they both declined. 'That's probably what made you sick.'

Konrad rolled his eyes at the policemen, and they smiled in recognition. Did women try to mollycoddle them too, he wondered?

The fair-haired one put down his pen and the dark-haired one moved forward on the sofa. 'And you didn't see Egon that night? Even in passing?'

'No. He never came to Gran's and, like I said, we didn't do stuff together.'

'Apart from the cinema?'

'Yeah. I guess. Once, I mean twice.'

'The reason I'm asking is there's a witness who thinks they saw you with Egon at the Pfaueninsel jetty.'

'That's impossible. I was with my grandmother. She'll tell you.'

'Officer,' his mother snapped, 'if Konrad says he was with his grandmother, then he was with his grandmother.'

'Absolutely.' The dark-haired one stood. 'Well, I think

that's all for now. Thank you for your time, Frau Hausmann. Konrad.'

The policemen seemed to fill the room. Konrad liked how their tight uniforms showed off their tall, athletic frames. He'd happily volunteer being interviewed by these dummies again, only next time he'd insist on doing it without his mother being present.

'If either of you remember anything else, please call us. Here's my number.' The dark-haired policeman handed his mother a card.

'Thank you, officers.' She showed them to the front door.

Konrad stood by the window, peering from behind the curtains. As he watched them saunter down the pathway, he pressed his body against the wall, rubbing his crotch against the rough lining of his shorts. The dark-haired one, the one who was the spitting-image of Egon, turned, glanced towards him, and momentarily locked eyes. Playing these sorts of games was far too easy.

47

THURSDAY, 4TH AUGUST 1994

Stepping off the S-Bahn at Wannsee, Colin was soon standing by the edge of the lake, watching small yachts and a pleasure cruiser navigate its broad, glistening surface. Surrounded by shaded forests, the cool breeze coming off the water was a welcome relief from the sweltering city centre. Heading west, it only took Colin twenty minutes to walk into the centre of town.

A church bell tolled nine o'clock. Over the phone, Robert Fischer, the editor of *Wannsee und Zehlendorf Welt* had stipulated that Colin be at his office at nine-fifteen on the dot. Ahead of schedule, he took a seat on a sunlit bench and watched the world go by. Though the main street, Königstrasse, was wide and busy with traffic, Wannsee itself felt sleepy. With low rise buildings and quaint villas set in lush tree-filled gardens, it was more like a village than a town. The thought of Noah ever having lived there seemed incongruous.

That morning, Klaus had been up at four, whispering he was working double shifts over the next two days, so could they meet for breakfast on Saturday? His lips pressed goodbye against Colin's, preventing him replying.

Before they'd gone to bed, the mood between them had been strained. Klaus continued to drink and had clearly been perplexed by Colin's attempts to steer the conversation, to get him to talk more about his background. Once in bed, Colin had feigned tiredness to avoid having sex, but Klaus had clung onto him all night, his body buried deep into his own. It wasn't until after he'd left that Colin was able to relax and sleep properly.

Despite his suspicions, Colin still needed to keep Klaus close. Let him drift, and who knew what might happen.

COVERED IN A DRAB, tweedy material, a line of freestanding partitions divided the shabby offices of *Wannsee und Zehlendorf Welt*. By the door, a woman in her mid-twenties typed furiously at her desk, her fluorescent clothes contrasting with the staid conservatism of her surroundings.

'Colin Buxton?' she asked. 'You're here to see Mr Fischer?'

'We've a nine-fifteen appointment.'

She smiled and ushered him through to the other side of the partition.

Introducing himself, Colin received a curt nod from the editor.

'Please take a seat.' Mr Fischer swivelled from side to side in his high-backed, leather chair behind a vast desk, looking every inch the Bond villain with his pencil moustache and slicked-back hair. 'So, how can I help you?' He momentarily rose to ask his colleague to "type a little more quietly".

Colin waited until he returned to his seat. 'It concerns the murder of a teenage boy which took place here in Wannsee in the early 80s.'

Mr Fischer glanced at his watch. 'Egon Hausmann, I assume? We don't have many murders here,' he explained, plucking a thick, cream sheet of paper from a drawer, and making a note of what Colin was saying.

The Look of Death

'It's part of a bigger investigation I'm working on.' Colin was reluctant to divulge more than he had to. 'I'm working on the theory that the 1982 case may be connected to recent deaths in Berlin.'

'But you're not a policeman or a journalist?' Robert Fischer scrutinized him. 'You're from the UK. Right?'

'Correct.' Colin's foot nervously tapped against the front of the desk. 'I'm making enquiries on behalf of a Scottish family whose son died in Berlin. That's not a problem, is it?'

Robert stopped swivelling. 'And the police, they're conducting their own enquiry?'

'Not into his death, no, but others, yes.'

'It's odd. A few years ago, a young man came into these offices and asked about the case, too. My colleague Milo dealt with it at the time.'

Colin was about to ask for more details when the woman's face appeared at the side of the partition. 'Coffee?'

Colin nodded. 'A black coffee would be great. No sugar.'

'Herr Fischer?'

'Please. And remember, only half a teaspoon of sugar this time.' He waited until she had left. 'I swear she gets it wrong deliberately but it's hard to find decent staff these days. Anyway, as I said, it would have been Milo Savas who did most of the reporting. A capable guy, but unfortunately he died a couple of years ago.'

'I'm sorry to hear that.' Colin made a mental note to pass this news onto Noah.

'If we've time, I can ask Fraulein Weber to do a search of our archive and consult Milo's notes, so if you'd like to leave your number, I can get back to you should she find anything. But I can't make any promises.'

Colin wasn't prepared to be fobbed off. 'I need the information now. It's urgent.'

'That's the best I can do. We're a business, not a library.'

'I need to be discreet, but my research is feeding into the

enquiries the *Polizei* are conducting into the other deaths.' This might be stretching the truth, but Colin reasoned his meeting with Matthias made it partly official.

'Tell me which department you're working with and I'll check with them.' Mr Fischer reached for his phone.

'Don't worry Herr Fischer, I can deal with this.' Fraulein Weber placed two mugs on the table. 'Tomorrow's main feature is typed up and ready for you to proof, and I know the Egon Hausmann case well. I can get Mr Buxton all the relevant information. It won't take long.'

'This is Susannah Weber, our trainee,' Mr Fischer said with a wave of his hand. 'I need you to follow up on those burglaries.'

'I've already done that and written up my notes, and I've scheduled your meeting with the school governor.'

Mr Fischer sighed. 'It seems it's your lucky day, Mr Buxton.'

'If you want to follow me.' Susannah led Colin away from the shaky partition. 'Egon Hausmann went to my school. He was a bit of a loner, but a sweet kid. So tragic.'

'I expect you back at your desk in ten minutes, Fraulein Weber,' Mr Fischer shouted after them. 'This isn't an excuse for slacking.'

'Ignore him,' Susannah whispered. 'He doesn't think he's doing his job properly unless he's yelling at someone.'

'I know the type.'

Susannah led Colin through a door at the back of the office into a small windowless room filled with floor to ceiling steel shelves, stuffed with cardboard boxes. 'Our wonderful archive.' She turned on lights. 'It's not perfect. Five years ago, there was a fire at the paper's previous offices which ruined a lot of it.'

'You said you're familiar with the case. Was anyone ever convicted of the boy's killing?'

'No. There were a couple of theories, but nothing ever

The Look of Death

stuck and then it went cold.' Susannah pointed behind him. 'Could you do me a favour and grab those steps? The files for 1982 are down this row.'

Colin followed her.

'Here we are.' She climbed the steps and dragged a box from the top shelf. 'If you can grab it. Thanks.' Susannah joined Colin on the ground and removed the lid. 'Everything we have is in here: Milo's notes – or at least some of them, transcripts of interviews, a couple of features and some photographs.'

'Does it list the names of any of the suspects?'

'Yes, but there was only ever one suspect that anyone took seriously, though he was never named in the press: Egon's twin brother, Konrad.'

'He'd a twin called Konrad? You're kidding me?'

'Is that significant?'

Colin nodded. 'Do you know what happened to him?'

'The family moved west a few months after the murder. Though Konrad had an alibi, people started putting two and two together. Rumours began circulating – I think they originated from the *Polizei* – about the circumstances of Egon's death. If you read the pathologist's report, what was done to his body post-mortem… Well, there was a level of depravity and it became impossible for the family to remain. Konrad and his parents were basically run out of town.'

'Are there photographs of Egon and Konrad?'

'Let's see. There are definitely photos of Egon. Here.' Susannah handed him a portrait of a dark-haired boy in a school uniform. 'That was the main photo used in the press at the time, though he didn't look like that when he died. I must have been three or four years younger and I remember him clearly. He was different; he stood out. He didn't care what others thought of him, which is unusual for a place like this. He used to drive people crazy by wearing these loud, colourful clothes. He wasn't a big guy, but he could stand up for himself. I don't think it stopped him from being bullied though. You know what kids are like – they can be cruel.'

'And Konrad – what was he like?'

'Sorry, I'm not sure. Quiet. Nondescript. I guess he blended into the background. I remember he didn't look like Egon; they weren't identical, or even that similar-looking.' Susannah sifted through the remaining items in the box. 'I can take photocopies of all of this for you, just don't let Mr Fischer know. How good's your German?'

'Not so good.'

'I'm happy to read through it, let you know if there's anything else that might be of interest.'

'That'd be amazing – I'll give you my number.'

'I've had an idea.' Susannah sprang to her feet and disappeared behind a row of shelves, reappearing minutes later with a slim magazine. 'At the end of the summer term, the school used to publish photographs of each year group.' She opened it to a page and showed Colin. 'This is their year – the photo would have been taken before they broke for the summer holidays – the summer Egon was murdered.' She pointed to a grinning boy with big glasses and highlights in his hair. 'That's Egon. Now let me see if I can find Konrad.'

Colin looked at Egon. Apart from the highlights, it could have been himself at sixteen: same haircut, similar uniform, the shape of face uncannily alike. He felt his heartbeat quicken – this didn't bode well; his resemblance to Stefan and now Egon.

'I think that's Konrad.' She leaned over Colin's shoulder and pointed to a chubby boy with wavy blond hair in the row behind.

'Are you sure?'

'Pretty sure.'

Colin stared at the small, grainy image of the boy. Standing in the back row with the bigger boys, he'd turned his head as the camera shutter clicked, creating a slight distor-

The Look of Death

tion. He asked himself whether the boy could be Klaus. However, there was nothing in the bone structure or in the shape of his head that suggested so. Could it be Bela or Matthias? He thought it unlikely. And yet, the more he looked, the more he became convinced he'd seen this face before.

'Can I have a photocopy of this?'

'Sure.'

As they passed Mr Fischer's desk, Susannah said, 'I'm photocopying Egon's yearbook and a couple of articles for Mr Buxton.'

'So long as you're not taking copies of Milo's notes.'

'Of course not, Herr Fischer.' She winked at Colin and took him to the front of the office. After photocopying everything – including Milo's notes – she shouted over the partition, 'I'll show Mr Buxton out.'

As they spoke on the street, Colin was aware of being watched from inside the office. 'Doesn't he trust you?'

'Not at all. He's scared of any story that might rock the boat. Or anything that might involve a proper day's work. The murder of Egon Hausmann should have been one of the biggest stories ever. It should have been solved at the time, but Fischer, the police, people in this shitty town, weren't that interested at the end of the day in exposing the truth. Whatever happened to him, ultimately they thought he'd brought it on himself.'

The same bullshit he'd been up against. 'You better get back inside, before you lose your job.'

'Don't worry. I'll say I fancied you and was asking for your number. That'll wind him up.'

Colin grinned. He liked her style. 'Where should I write it?'

'Here.' She held out her wrist.

He took out a pen and wrote his number.

'I actually worked with Milo for a few months,' Susannah

said. 'He was a good guy but frustrated and I was sixteen, making coffee, doing the photocopying. Things haven't changed much, eh?' She grinned. 'I did leave, but I came back to look after my mum. She's not well, and it looks like I'm going to be stuck here for a while.'

'That must be tough.'

She shrugged. 'Milo mentioned the case a couple of times, and he tried to follow up on the rumours around Konrad, tried to trace him, but the family had disappeared. There was a suggestion they may have changed their name.'

'So, this might lead to nowhere?'

'You never know, you might get luckier than him.'

'Fischer mentioned someone asked about the case a few years ago.'

'Sorry. I don't know anything about that.' She glanced at the office window and turned her back to it. 'But there was a detail that no one ever knew. It was kept from the public. If they'd known, it was thought it might lead to copycats. So, no one ever reported it. It's there in the notes.'

'Yes?'

'Egon's body had been pierced with rose thorns. There were scars everywhere: in his fingers, on his face, his genitals.' She winced. 'Even pressed into his eyes. It's pretty weird and must have taken hours to do.'

Colin shook his head. 'Call me if you're in the city. Perhaps we can go for a drink.'

'I'll do that and I'll let you know if I find anything interesting in the archive.' Robert Fischer was knocking on the office window, Colin's cue to leave. 'You might even get a scoop out of this,' were his parting words.

'Let's hope you can do it for Egon. Even in death, queer kids are treated badly.'

· · ·

The Look of Death

COLIN DIDN'T MEET another soul on his walk from Wannsee through the forest to the jetty, and on the short crossing, it was only the ferryman and him on the boat. He'd expected Pfaueninsel to be heaving with tourists however, except for the shrieks of peacocks, it was strangely silent.

In the fierce, midday heat, he stood alone at the centre of the rose garden. The bushes were in full-bloom, stalks heavy with flowers shedding petals; the aroma was thick and suffocating, too saccharine, too sweet for him to linger for long. For the first time in weeks, he didn't feel watched and for the first time in the investigation he felt he could solve it.

PART 5

48

SATURDAY, 6TH AUGUST 1994

Colin arrived early at *Café am Ufer* and sat on a bench by the canal, preferring to wait from a distance on Klaus arriving. It was a little after nine and the sun had disappeared behind thick clouds, plunging the surrounding trees into shadow. Around his feet, late sprays of linden blossom had been ground into the pavement, making the surface sticky and pungent. It felt cooler, and in the far distance, thunder rumbled and the air began to hum with static.

When Klaus arrived, he took a seat outside, glanced around before putting on his sunglasses, then sat staring up at the sky. Could he be the killer? Until a few days ago, the idea seemed ridiculous. And while Kim might have her own reasons for planting this seed of doubt, it was Colin who'd cultivated it, testing it against the evidence he'd gathered and what he'd discovered in Wannsee, until it was all he could think about.

As Colin approached, Klaus stood and kissed him on both cheeks. This felt ordinary, like all the times they'd met before. Accepting the gesture, he sat. Not beside Klaus, but opposite. Betraying him, even under these circumstances, felt wrong.

Klaus took a cigarette from his packet and lit up. Was he

nervous, Colin wondered? The double-tap against the ashtray suggested so.

'On Thursday, when I left you,' Klaus began, shifting in his seat to avoid the sun, 'I didn't go to the station. Instead, I phoned in sick.' Colin tried to interrupt, but Klaus stopped him. 'The other night, I couldn't figure out what your problem was, then it dawned on me.'

A waiter appeared, but Colin raised his hand, signalling he shouldn't approach. 'Go on – I'm listening.'

'The bottom line is I don't think you trust me.' Klaus reached for his backpack. 'So, in the spirit of transparency, there's something I want to show you.' He produced a clear plastic folder and placed it on the table.

'What's that?'

'Tell me I'm crazy, but I think you suspect I could be involved in the killing of the men you're investigating.' He took a drag on his cigarette. 'Am I correct?'

A trio of women arrived, their laughter lifting the mood of the café. Behind them, a group of six took their seats outside, and suddenly Colin felt hemmed in. 'Can we go and sit by the canal?' he asked.

No words were spoken as they crossed the road and headed to the canal, and sat on the same bench Colin had sat on earlier. Still clasping the folder, Klaus stubbed out his cigarette and removed his sunglasses; even in the shadows, his blue eyes sparkled with vitality. Since their first meeting, Colin had felt Klaus was hiding things, but might he be entirely innocent?

Klaus handed him the folder. 'Open it. It's what I've managed to gather over the last two days. Go ahead.'

Colin pulled out a collection of photocopies and receipts. 'What is this?'

'When I was getting ready to leave the other morning, I had a good look at the evidence you've compiled. I hadn't realised there was a connection between Ajnur Osman and

The Look of Death

Kim Stroder. I take it you've spoken to her?'

Colin nodded. 'We've met a couple of times.'

'So, she's shared her theory about a police cover up? That they're protecting one of their own?'

'That and her thoughts on your competency, and by association, mine.'

'Fuck. How does she know about us?'

'From Bela; they're friends.'

'That woman hates me. She tried to get me sacked. Something like that could have seriously damaged my career.'

Colin pointed to the papers. 'These are to do with Kim?'

'Yes and no.' He took a photocopy from the top of the pile. 'In the summer of 1990, on the date Stefan Reis was found dead, I was on holiday in Brazil. This is from my passport; you can see my dates of entry and exit clearly stamped.' Klaus handed it to Colin. 'Check it.' The dates tallied. 'What about the other deaths? Ulrich's ten days later?'

'When I returned from Brazil, I was stationed for three months in Leipzig, as part of a training programme with the Federal Police.'

'But Leipzig – that's what, just over two hours away? You could easily have travelled to Berlin and back with no one noticing.'

'Okay, I don't have proof of where I was at the exact time of Ulrich's death, but I'm sure I'll be able to get something – copies of shifts I was working. There will be records.'

'What about Martin Engel's death last year?'

'If you look here, you'll see I was attending my aunt's funeral in Dresden on the day his body was found. I'd travelled there the day before, and here's the order of service with the date. That evening, I was at a family meal and shared a room overnight with my cousin – there are dozens of people who can account for my whereabouts.'

Colin leafed through the documents. Excluding the possibility Klaus was a master forger, it looked plausible. 'Okay, okay, I get it. I'm sorry for doubting you.'

Klaus leaned back in his seat. 'I know how persuasive Kim Stroder can be.'

'It wasn't just Kim, there were other things, too: the intensity of our relationship mirrors the killer's MO. It did cross my mind that the flat in Winterfeldstrasse might have been the one you've moved from, plus you did your disappearing act the week of Ajnur's death.'

'You know I was in Magdeburg.'

'Visiting your ex? I've only your word for that.'

Klaus stared at his feet, his face blushing. 'Shit! I thought you'd work it out.'

'Work out what?'

'Matthias is my ex.'

For a second, Colin though he'd misheard. 'Your ex?'

'I know I should have told you.'

Colin jumped up, scattering the papers on the ground and walked away from the bench.

Quickly stuffing everything in the folder, Klaus chased after him. 'It didn't seem relevant at first but when you two met, it felt too late to get into it, not when things were going so well between us. It was a stupid mistake. I admit it.'

Colin stopped and faced him. 'Did you honestly spend all that time with him or is that a lie, too?'

'Yes, of course I did. Why would I lie about that? He needed my support.'

'I don't know what to believe any more. Are you still with him? Are those documents made up?'

'Of course not.'

'Is the evidence that Matthias gave me real? Is he covering for you? Do you need to confess anything else?' Colin's stomach lurched at the mess he'd found himself in. 'How can I trust you? Every time you tell me the truth, another lie comes out your mouth.'

The Look of Death

Klaus pulled a pen from his pocket. 'I'm going to give you Ramona's number.'

'Who the hell's Ramona?'

'Matthias's sister. She was with me and Matti most of the time in Magdeburg. She returned to Berlin with us, and helped me settle him into his apartment. If you call, she'll vouch for me the evening Ajnur died.'

'This isn't just about Ajnur. How can I trust anything you say?' Colin proceeded up Kottbusser Strasse towards the U-Bahn.

Klaus soon caught up with him, quickening his steps as Colin walked faster. 'Yes, I'm an idiot, and you're right to be pissed, but please hear me out. There's a killer targeting gay men. Agreed?'

'Leave me alone, Klaus.'

'If the *Polizei* were doing their job correctly, there'd be an entire squad out hunting him, with the media biting at their heels for a result. But there's none of that. Just you. Exposed.'

Klaus was right concerning the danger to himself, but Colin wasn't going to admit it. 'I've been careful.'

'Have you?' Klaus clung to Colin's arm, forcing him to stop. He tried to free himself from Klaus's grip, but he was too strong. 'I spoke to Mustafa.'

'When?'

'Towards the end of my shift, Matti asked me to have a quiet word. He'd appeared at the station again on Wednesday afternoon, demanding to know why Ajnur's death wasn't being treated as murder. He's been causing a fuss; threatening to go to the papers, to politicians, saying you're the only person taking it seriously.'

'That's because I *am* the only person taking it seriously.'

'We both know there's a process to good police work.'

'There's a difference between being thorough and scouting around for the most convenient explanation. Your ex basically told me his boss wasn't interested in the truth, only finding a way to wrap up the case with minimal fuss.'

'I know you went to the apartment building on Winterfeldstrasse.'

'And your point is?'

'I checked it out myself. A neighbour gave me your description, even down to the freckle on the side of your neck, said you were in the apartment, that you were acting weird. What the hell were you thinking, Colin? This is a live investigation.'

'What did you expect me to do? Don't forget, it was you who introduced me to Matthias.'

'If you genuinely think for one minute the killer is me, then you're crazy. But I understand why you need to consider it – if you're right about his MO, then yes, you may already know him. I need to make you see though, that it's not safe for you to be doing this on your own.'

Colin pulled free from Klaus. 'Thanks for the concern, but I can handle myself,' he shouted back, dashing across the road.

Klaus followed and was soon by his side, blocking him from going upstairs to the station platform. 'Matthias showed me the evidence he shared with you.'

'There was nothing worthwhile,' Colin snapped, trying to push past him.

'You know that's not true.' Klaus stood firm as Colin continued to shove. 'Stand still for a minute. Please.'

Colin met his eyes.

'The presence of the thorns is evidence that links the deaths. Correct?'

'Not all of them,' Colin answered. 'Not Ulrich. Not Walter.'

'Double murders in the same location,' Klaus said. 'One body pierced with a thorn, the other not. Perhaps it suggests

The Look of Death

the killer is trying to get something right? Maybe it's a mark of importance? One deserves a thorn, the other doesn't.'

A woman squeezed past them, tutting, and Colin moved to the side of the stairwell.

'I don't know all the evidence you've gathered,' Klaus continued, 'but from what I've seen, I'm imagining it's pretty substantial. Am I right? The best thing for you to do would be to pass it over to the *Polizei*.'

What was Klaus's angle? Having shown only fleeting moments of interest before, why was he now a believer? 'I'll share when I'm ready,' he said. 'So, if you'll excuse me.'

'Let me help you, Colin. I have access to resources; I can check things out for you. Please don't do this on your own.'

He waited for Klaus to stop. Searching for a sign that might conclusively tell him whether he was a killer, he couldn't find any. Deep inside, Colin knew he had to take a leap of faith. What was the alternative? Klaus might have lied by omission about Matthias, but that wasn't enough to make him a killer. 'Someone's been following me.'

Klaus's face turned pale. 'You're sure?'

'Yes. And I'm certain someone broke into my room.'

'Why didn't you tell me? Why didn't you call the police?'

'Because I think Kim's theory about a cover up is plausible.'

Klaus leaned against the wall, his shoulders slumped. Perhaps like Matthias, he too had been working behind the scenes, fighting to keep the case open.

'I found a Polaroid of me pinned to a corkboard in the Winterfeldstrasse apartment.'

Klaus looked at him. 'Where was it taken?'

'That doesn't matter.'

'Of course it does.'

'You can't keep information like this to yourself. You know that.'

Colin knew Klaus was right. 'I was in the Tiergarten questioning a witness when it was taken. Close to where we went last month and to where Ajnur's body was found.'

'Christ, no wonder you're paranoid. But ask yourself one question: why would I do this to you? I love you.'

Colin's eyes stung at his own scepticism. But right now, he couldn't be certain.

'I can come with you to the station, help explain what's going on.'

'I need to do this on my own. I need a clear head.'

Klaus took his hand, pressing it firmly within his own. Colin let him hold it for a few seconds before pulling away. 'You can trust me.'

If Klaus's evidence was real, if it proved he'd alibis, then he needed to set that aside from his personal doubts and accept it. He should have been jumping for joy, but part of him felt hollow.

49

FIVE YEARS EARLIER - NOVEMBER 1989

After a seven-year absence, it was Konrad's grandmother who'd brought him back to Wannsee. Her perennial favourite, much to his father's annoyance, she'd given him power of attorney over her estate. With dementia having left her mentally incapacitated, decisions needed to be made; foremost was the sale of her house, now that she was living in a nursing home nearby the Grunewald Forest.

Wannsee looked like a toy town compared to Hamburg, the city where he and his parents had relocated to after Egon's death. No discussion had taken place before the move. One morning, instead of going to school, he'd been told to pack a suitcase, then half an hour later they were in his father's car, driving west on the Autobahn. The contents of their home followed a week later.

Since that day, his parents had never mentioned Egon's name in his presence, never once spoke about the allegations made against him or the series of escalating incidents that drove them from the town: the graffiti on their front door, the excrement pushed through their letter box, the fire set in their rubbish bin. If his parents believed him to be guilty, they never said a word, and their new life in Hamburg trundled on as if nothing had ever happened. As if Egon had never lived.

It was his grandmother who'd confirmed his alibi, who'd gone to the police station with her Bible and sworn that he'd spent the entire evening with her, that it would have been impossible for him to have been on Pfaueninsel at the time of Egon's death. However hard the officers pushed, she was unshakeable in her assertion that Konrad was innocent, that the rumours of his guilt were despicable lies and that the witness – a retired teacher who claimed to have seen Konrad with Egon – was a known paedophile trying to deflect attention from himself. Such was the conviction with which she defended him, Konrad began to believe it himself, and the events of that evening ceased to feel real anymore, becoming more like a dream or a fantasy.

As soon as the family arrived in Hamburg, Konrad was told by his father that he'd be changing his name; he didn't question why and his father didn't offer an explanation. He would take his middle name as his Christian name and adopt his mother's maiden name as his surname. Overnight, he felt reborn.

In many respects, Hamburg proved to be the new start his parents sought: his father secured a well-paid job in the burgeoning computer sector, whilst his mother chose not to return to work, instead committing herself to church and local community matters. He, meanwhile, attended high school. But the sense of unreality around Egon's death infected everything; Konrad walked through life as an observer, detached and aloof, indifferent to the trivialities which seemed to occupy most people.

Whilst not especially academic, his teachers were supportive. Drafted into the athletics team, despite making little effort, he achieved some success. To his surprise, his new classmates appeared to like him too, and he made friends easily with uniformly dull boys obsessed with cars and foot-

The Look of Death

ball. Like his peers, he dated girls indistinguishable from each other, who worried about what people thought of them and wept after drunken sex. At that point, it felt better to pretend, to wear the mask of a normal boy; fitting in, it seemed, was the ultimate disguise. No one was interested in what lay beneath – quite the opposite. Had anyone shown any curiosity, and pulled back the layers, they'd have heard Egon's voice in his head, goading him night and day.

He often spoke to his grandmother on the phone. She was the only person in his life who still called him Konrad, and the only one who ever mentioned his twin. 'Yours and Egon's destinies were entwined from the moment you were conceived,' she'd say. As her mental health started to deteriorate, she increasingly referred to *their little secret, saying boys like Egon weren't tolerated in her day and that Konrad was a good boy who'd protected the Hausmann name.*

As time passed, he developed the sense that people were stupid, that only he possessed insight into how the world actually worked. He alone had superior knowledge of the greatest mystery of life. To feel a person's soul leave this world, to hold onto them as this occurred, and to be the one responsible: no one he knew had experienced this. So, for now, he was happy to play along as the average, dour teenager, knowing that his time would come again.

His return to Wannsee was the turning point; control of his grandmother's finances offered an escape from his parents. Though they objected to him setting foot there again, when he challenged them to explain, neither could voice their opposition. But he was not without his own fears; after seven years of flying under the radar, returning to the town risked his true identity being exposed. As he entered the offices of his grandmother's solicitor, a mere five-minute walk from his old school, his heart was racing. But he needn't have worried, the meeting was entirely professional and half an hour later, with business concluded, he found himself back out on the street.

Emboldened, he walked into the centre of town. Since leaving, his dreams often occupied the lush landscapes of his childhood; unseen, he would float above the lakes and busy beaches, flying amongst the branches of the trees. He rarely dreamt of this winter landscape of bare trees and deserted streets.

Konrad felt a thrill as he watched Julia Grosz through the window of the bakery. She placed four doughnuts in a paper bag for a customer, rang the price up on the till, then rearranged some cakes in the display cabinet. Catching his eye for a second, she smiled at him as if he was any other local out shopping. What a boring life she must lead. He could remember her doing the same thing seven years earlier. Every single day. The idea made him want to vomit.

A young couple with a baby passed – former classmates, he realised – and he adjusted his collar. He needn't have worried however, as the puppy fat from those years was long gone, replaced by a fine-tuned muscular frame. And he'd grown tall. There was no way they'd recognise the dull-looking twin of Egon Hausmann, the most talked-about kid in the town.

He listened to their inane conversation about how beautiful the cakes looked before turning to them and asking with a grin, 'Any recommendations?'

'The Apfelkuchen is best,' the girl replied – Carina, he remembered – as she and her boyfriend entered the shop.

Once on this very street, before his family fled, an old lady he'd never met before, her face scarlet with rage, had appeared out of nowhere and, as others looked on, shouted in his face: *Murderer! Pervert! Devil!* It was the sort of abuse which Egon had received on a daily basis, but to Konrad it felt as though his insides were being torn out. For his entire life, he'd done his best to blend into the background, never

The Look of Death

daring to put his head above the parapet. Egon's death had changed all that forever, or so he'd thought.

Walking into the Post Office, Konrad selected a couple of postcards. He waited in line to be served by Herr Schulz, the Post Office manager, well known as Wannsee's biggest gossip.

'Two stamps please,' Konrad asked.

'Are you visiting?'

The Post Office was quiet. It was mid-afternoon, after the lunchtime rush, the perfect opportunity to take a risk. 'Don't you recognise me, Herr Schulz?'

A flicker of doubt passed across his face. 'Remind me,' he said, scrutinising Konrad's face.

'Elias Muller,' he said. 'I went to school with your son, Reinhart.'

'I'm sorry – I'm usually good with faces.'

'Don't worry. It's been a long time.'

'So, you were friends with Reinhart?'

He shook his head. 'A little, we used to play soccer together.'

'Yes, well Reinhart still loves soccer.' Herr Schulz handed Konrad his stamps and change. 'You should pass by and say hello.'

Outside on the street, Konrad marvelled at the absurdity of people. The idea that the townsfolk of a place on the edge of nowhere, where nothing of note ever happened, would cheerfully welcome a murderer back into their midst and not realise it, beggared belief. Their blind ignorance felt like absolution. He breathed in the air's coldness, holding it in his lungs for as long as possible, conjuring up the image of Egon struggling beneath him, skin against skin, hot and forbidden.

Walking back through the town with his head held high, he bought a bunch of roses from the flower shop. A few times he worried people were staring at him, but at a second glance, he realised they weren't; just as in Hamburg, they were looking by him, beyond him, not seeing him for who and what he was.

There was nothing now to prevent his return to Berlin.

CARVED out of the forest on the edge of town, with its pretty brick church and ornate metal fencing, Wannsee Cemetery felt like somewhere from a fairy tale; an appropriate resting place for Egon. Remembering the exact position of his grave was tricky as he'd been there only once before, for the burial. At first, he took a wrong turn – one step to the right when he should have gone left – but the graveyard was small and the pathway suddenly appeared familiar. At the end, framed by a line of tall conifers, Egon's modest gravestone came into view.

Removing a single rose from the bunch, Konrad ran his index finger down the stem, pressed its tip into the biggest thorn and squeezed hard. A drop of blood trembled then fell to the grass where Egon's body lay beneath. He dropped to the ground and dug the thorn deeper into his flesh, gripping the stem with all his might. How quickly the blood filled his palm; a rose-red fist.

Drained, he rested his head against the smooth coolness of Egon's headstone. Besides the dates of his birth and death, only his name had been engraved on it; there were no other words, no *Beloved son*, no *Dearly missed*.

Using his finger, Konrad trailed blood across the pale, grey marble, writing his own epitaph to his brother. There was only one word which summed Egon up, only one image with which to immortalise him. He should have returned years ago with a hammer and chisel to inscribe it there himself.

The final letter scrawled, he sat back to admire his handiwork:

Dornröschen.

Sleeping Beauty.

50

SATURDAY, 6TH AUGUST 1994

Colin knocked on Hannah's door. Music was blaring – unsettling punk vibes, with a heavy mix of thrash guitar. As he was about to knock again, Rita appeared from her room across the corridor.

'You're wasting your time. I've been banging all afternoon, trying to get her to turn it down.'

'Is something wrong?'

'Search me.' Rita slammed her door shut. Then, as if to outdo Hannah, she cranked up the sound on her decks, to blast out a competing rhythm of electro dance music.

'Hannah!' Colin shouted, thumping his fist against the door. Maybe she'd gone out and left her music on, but as he banged a third time, he noticed an increase in the volume, as if she was deliberately trying to drown him out. 'It's Colin,' he yelled in a final attempt to grab her attention. 'I know you're in there. Open up!'

The music snapped off, and the door flew open. Joint in hand, Hannah leaned against the wall, glancing behind him as Rita's music stopped too. 'Finally! She's been driving me crazy with that bloody racket.' She wiped her eyes and adjusted her kimono. 'What are you doing here? I thought you were with lover boy.'

Surely the expression on his face told her things hadn't gone well, but she seemed unconcerned, distracted. 'Can I come in?' he asked.

For a moment it felt like she was about to slam the door in his face. 'I suppose.' She motioned him inside.

Compared to the utilitarian decor of his own room, Colin envied how beautifully Hannah had furnished her space. Cascades of different coloured fabrics, some opaque and some sheer, hung from the ceiling, dividing the room into distinct sections: a work area with a large trestle desk; bookcases and her own framed artworks that led through to a central sleeping space, with a huge bed, opulently adorned with patterned throws and tasselled, Moroccan cushions; beyond that was a chill out area which overlooked the inner courtyard. He followed her through and collapsed on one of the beanbags; both windows had been thrown open, in anticipation of the approaching thunderstorm.

Hannah sat on a cushion opposite him, a pot of coffee and ashtray within handy reach on a low brass table. She stubbed out her joint and immediately began to roll another one.

'Everything OK?' Colin noticed how shaky her hands were.

'Don't worry about me, I'll be fine.'

Crumpled paper tissues were scattered across the floor and stuffed under her cushion, suggesting she'd been crying. 'You sure?'

'Coffee?'

He shook his head.

She offered him the fresh joint, and for the first time in months, he accepted. The first drag was hot, citrusy and intoxicating. Relaxing back onto the cushion, he took another puff, immediately feeling a rush to his head.

The Look of Death

'Good stuff, isn't it? Helps you forget all the shit going on around you.'

'A bit too strong for me.' He handed it back.

'Lightweight,' she teased, taking a deep, satisfying puff. 'So, tell me everything. Klaus still being weird?'

He shrugged. 'Who knows?'

'But he didn't try to finish you off?'

'Not this time.' He smiled at her ability to make everything seem a joke, unimportant; even the prospect of death. 'But I'm still not sure I can trust him.'

'Sorry to be the bearer of bad news, but on the whole, guys are not reliable.'

'You reckon?'

She wriggled over and nestled beside him. 'In fact, I'd say you're all conniving bastards. Every single one of you. I'm going to run off to become a nun.'

'Why? What's going on with you?'

She plucked a tissue from the floor, blew her nose, and threw it across the room. 'It seems I chose the wrong guy. Well, of course I did, because I'm a fuck up, aren't I?'

'I thought you were hedging your bets these days, what with your two boyfriends and Tilda on the back burner.'

'I had been, but then I decided to make an actual choice for once in my life. It's kind of humiliating, to be honest.' She grabbed a bottle of water and took a mouthful. 'After declaring my undying love to Eli, he's disappeared, done a runner, fallen off the edge of the Earth. No fucking trace.' She lit the joint. 'It's no better than I deserve. I've done it enough times myself, but I foolishly thought we had a chance together.'

'Even though he's got a wife?'

'That's definitely over. They just live together. They're not together, as in having sex and stuff.' She looked at him as though he was an idiot to think otherwise. 'I'd never break up a marriage. What do you take me for?'

'A lovesick fool,' said Colin. 'Like me.'

'He'd been so attentive, so caring. Never tried to make me feel second best. But at the end of the day, I guess I wasn't enough.'

He kissed her on the cheek and stood. 'Let's have a proper chat soon? Right now, I need to sort my own shit out.'

'Good luck with that,' she said, as Colin fought his way through the maze of fabric.'I'll pop by later today or tomorrow,' he called back, stumbling out the room.

In the bathroom, Colin splashed cold water on his face, hoping to revive himself. After a long deliberation, he decided to call the station where Matthias worked. As the line was engaged, he tried the number of Ulrich Steiner's ex and left a message on the answerphone with his details.

He tried the police station again. This time, an operator answered and immediately put him through to Matthias's desk.

'*Hallo?*'

Colin hesitated and Matthias continued, 'Hello? Can I help you?'

Without niceties, Colin blurted out, 'Today. Same time, same place. It's important. I've new information.'

'Colin?' He'd been expecting Matthias to be guarded like last time, but instead he sounded almost cheery, as though he'd been expecting his call.

'Sorry, I didn't know how else to contact you.'

'It's OK,' Matthias said. 'So, you'd like to meet?'

Colin's head was still recovering from the half joint he'd smoked and his mouth was dry, too, making it difficult to get his words out. 'Is that possible?'

'I've a few things to wrap up here, then I'm all yours. Half an hour OK?'

'Great.'

Matthias hung up, leaving Colin wondering whether he'd done the right thing by calling him.

The Look of Death

Realising how stoned he was, he went to the kitchen and grabbed an enormous slice of ham from the fridge and guzzled it down, followed by two glasses of water. He might not trust Klaus when it came to their relationship, but his professional assessment was right; he couldn't do this on his own. And if Matthias was working the case, then it made sense to take everything he'd discovered to him. He was best placed to help, to use the full resources of the *Polizei*. Konrad Hausmann could easily be tracked down by them, whether he was still living by that name or not. This was the right thing to do.

SITTING on the same bench in Volkspark Friedrichshain, knowing what he now knew, Colin thought seeing Matthias again would be awkward. The last time, he'd been nervous, unwilling to look Colin in the eye, so, it was a surprise to see him jogging towards him in running gear with a big grin across his face, waving as though they were long lost friends.

'No bike today?'

'Monday to Fridays only. Then I run at the weekends. It's my routine; keeps me happy,' he said. 'Shall we walk?'

Wandering towards the centre of the park, they followed a path around a large pond. The early evening sun, golden and mellow, lit up the water.

'I've a name that might interest you,' Colin began. 'It relates to a crime in Wannsee in the summer of 1982. A sixteen-year-old boy, Egon Hausmann, was found murdered on Pfaueninsel, in circumstances similar to the deaths here in the centre of Berlin.'

'Go on.' Matthias was listening intently.

'No one was ever convicted, but the prime suspect was Konrad Hausmann, the murdered boy's twin brother. I'd say it's the best lead I've got so far.'

Matthias stopped and stared at the shimmering light on the pond's surface. 'Colin, I need to tell you something.'

It was amazing how a week could transform someone. Before, Matthias's body language had appeared defeated, but now there was a vibrancy. 'Has there been a development?'

'It's time for you to step back.' Matthias's smile widened. 'You've done excellent work. But you need to leave the rest to us.'

'Does that mean the police have reopened the cases?'

Matthias looked up at the sky, bit his lip, then gazed straight at him. 'I'm not saying yes, but neither am I saying no. Hopefully, in the next few weeks, I'll be able to tell you more, but for now, please suspend your investigations. Believe me, it'll all make sense soon enough.' Running off, he shouted back, 'And thanks for the information; that's very useful.'

Before he got too far, Colin decided to run after him. Matthias turned around as he caught up. 'Did Klaus tell you to say this? To try and force me to back off?' Telling Klaus about being followed, the break in, the photograph had been a mistake; Colin could kick himself for having confided in him.

Matthias looked confused. 'I've not spoken to Klaus in days.'

'But you do know about us?'

'Did you assume he wouldn't tell me?'

The taste of the joint still lingered at the back of his throat. Even a couple of puffs had upped his paranoia; never a good thing. 'I wasn't sure.'

'He told me about you soon after you met. It took him a day or two, but I eventually got it out of him.' There was no sense of ill-feeling in Matthias's tone. 'I was – I *am* happy for him – for you both. We're much better as friends; we were no good as lovers. Sad, but true.'

Colin sensed an opportunity – he needed to know if their

The Look of Death

stories matched. 'And how are you now?' A gamble, but he had to take it. 'I don't wish to pry, but—'

'In terms of my recent ill health?' Matthias's body straightened, owning what he was saying. 'Klaus has been very supportive. If it hadn't been for him, and my family, I don't know what would have happened. I was in a bad place for a while.'

'It's great that you're back in Berlin and back at work.'

'Well, I couldn't hide in Magdeburg with my parents forever. Klaus insisted I make a plan to return,' he explained. 'But I'm sorry my problems coincided with you getting together. You shouldn't have had to share him like that. But I'm much better now and being back at work, having that focus, has been better than any pill.' He patted Colin on the arm. 'Honestly, with the case, it's best for you to step back. Take a holiday, go swim in the lakes. Trust me, it's all in hand.'

Seven men were dead. Without a proper explanation, Colin couldn't walk away and forget about it all. 'I can't understand how you can be so emphatic.'

Matthias leaned in to whisper in his ear. 'You've been on the right track all along.' He stepped back and winked. 'There's been an exciting development. You might want to follow the news over the next few days.'

'Have you found the killer?'

Matthias put his finger against his lips. 'I never told you, right?' Without another word he jogged off and was soon halfway out of the park, leaving Colin bewildered.

ON THE TRAIN, a group of skater boys were drinking cans of beer and jumping from seat to seat. Amidst their exuberance, one bumped against Colin's knee. As he was about to challenge him, the teenager stepped back, politely apologised and, with his friends, moved to the far end of the carriage, swinging from the handgrips as they went. At the next stop, Colin watched them saunter off, skateboards in hands.

After Matthias's bombshell, he was in a daze. Could it be true that after all these years, the police had finally realised the deaths were connected? No wonder Matthias was smiling. Despite the doubts and denials of an entire police force, he'd placed his neck on the line and had been proved right.

With the carriage now nearly empty, Colin noticed a lone figure sitting ahead of him, a hood pulled over their head. 'I thought you were in Bavaria,' he said, sitting opposite the figure.

Bela removed his hood. 'I wondered when I might bump into you.'

He'd had enough. 'Have you been following me?'

Bela gazed at him, playing with the zip of his hoodie, yanking it up and down. 'What?'

'In Ernst Thälmann Park? Outside the Youth Hostel. *Homo Bar*?'

'I've no idea what you're talking about. Are you OK? You seem stressed.'

Colin stood as the train pulled into Osloer Strasse. 'This is not my idea of a joke, Bela. You frightened me. I thought someone was out to get me, ready to attack at any moment.' A group of passengers squeezed past him on the way to the door. 'I thought better of you.'

'Me follow you? I'm just back from visiting my family.'

Colin was in no mood for a discussion. Instead, he got off the train and walked along the platform. As the train doors closed, he could hear Bela calling his name, but he ignored him.

Matthias was right; he should take a break. After weeks of investigation, his life had been turned upside down. And now, it seemed, the police had caught their man.

It was time to step back, reflect, and re-evaluate what was important to him. No more chasing shadows.

51

When Colin entered the kitchen, Hannah, Tilda, Rita and a few familiar – and not-so-familiar – faces were sitting at the kitchen table, drunkenly debating the merits of reunification. It was a common theme for discussion and he'd grown weary of hearing the same opinions endlessly expressed about what had and hadn't worked since 1989. Of course, most people supported the changes – no one in their right mind would ever wish for the Wall to return – but there was a hardcore of *Wessis* who still yearned for the West Berlin of old, a place of contradictions which symbolised capitalism and freedom, but in practice was a slumbering backwater into which misfits and miscreants could happily escape from the world.

'Your policeman boyfriend loves the West a little too much, doesn't he?' Rita laughed and nudged the person next to her.

'Sorry? Why are you talking about Klaus?'

'Vulgar,' Rita muttered, loud enough for Colin to hear.

'It's none of your business, but Klaus was brought up in West Berlin.'

This evoked an even louder guffaw from Rita. 'With his accent? I don't think so.'

As he went to leave, Tilda offered him a seat. He shook his head, and caught Hannah's attention. 'Can I have a word?' he yelled over the din, choosing to ignore Rita's follow-up remarks about those from the East being country bumpkins.

'One moment.' Hannah continued making a point to the person sitting beside her about Europe being bigger than individual countries. 'It's all about cooperation,' she said, filling her glass with wine and finally squeezing out from behind the table. 'What's the rush?' she asked, running her fingers through Tilda's hair as she passed.

He beckoned her towards the hallway. 'I need to speak to you. Alone.'

'I don't like that look on your face,' she said, following him out. 'Am I about to get a telling off?'

'I'm not your dad.'

'True. My dad's a pushover compared to you.'

They stood by the telephone.

'It's good news, but you've got to promise you'll keep it to yourself,' he said.

'Of course.'

'I've spoken to the police, and there's been a major development in the case. It sounds like they've got someone.'

'Not Klaus?'

'No. Well, I don't think so,' he said. 'I'm sure they'd have told me if it was.'

'So, you were on the trail of an actual serial killer all along? That's a bit of a head-fuck. You should come and celebrate.'

Colin grimaced.

'Okay. Maybe celebrate's not the right word,' she said, 'but you know what I mean.'

'I dunno. I'm feeling kind of weird about it. What with the

Polaroid and everything. But can you promise not to say anything to anyone?'

'Sure.'

'Shit! There's a message for you,' Hannah interrupted. 'A girl rang while you were out.' Placing her glass by the telephone, she picked up a piece of paper. 'Here you go. It sounded urgent.'

Colin glanced at the message. *Meet me at the Hofgarten Bar on Regensburger Strasse ASAP. Will be there till eleven. Susannah.* He hoped this meant she would be able to flesh out Matthias's cryptic comments.

'Come and have a drink.' Hannah offered him her wine.

'However tempting, I need to meet Susannah; she's the journalist who I met the other day. But save me some food – I'll join you when I'm back.' He read the message again. 'The *Hofgarten*?'

'Classy cocktail place. Lots of sexy women with strong opinions.'

'Sounds like this place.'

'Now flattery, PC Buxton, will get you everywhere.' She blew him a kiss before returning to the kitchen.

FROM THE DOORWAY he spotted Susannah at the bar of the *Hofgarten*, surrounded by a group of friends and holding a drink as colourful as her outfit. She was engrossed in a performance; against the backdrop of the bar's mirrored mosaic walls a woman recited a poem, her rich voice reverberating through the space, as she rotated at least two dozen hula hoops around her torso and limbs. As he squeezed through the crowd of women, Susannah spotted him and signalled that they should talk outside.

Away from the confines of the newspaper offices she seemed different: younger, lighter. 'Good to see you.' She kissed him on both cheeks, then hugged him like a long-lost friend.

'Sorry to interrupt; I don't want to spoil your evening.'

'Don't be stupid. It was me who called you. Look, the poet's about to finish and we're going to stay for a few more drinks. Want to join us?'

'I'd like to, but can I take a rain check?'

'Sure. Let's sit.' Susannah led him over to one of the outdoor tables, set with tealights and a small vase of flowers.

'I'm assuming you've got news about the case?' he asked.

'Yes.' Her face was dancing with excitement. 'You won't believe it.'

'I've got news too, but you go first.'

'What I'm about to tell you isn't official,' she said, her expression suddenly serious in the warm glow of the candlelight. 'It comes from one of my contacts, a friend in the press office at the *Polizei*, so I know I can trust it.'

'They've caught someone, haven't they? My own contact told me as much.'

'Well…' She pulled her chair closer to his. 'Not quite. They've discovered a body.'

For a moment, Colin was lost for words. 'Christ! Another one?'

'A man called Elias Muller.'

He racked his brain, checking to see if he knew the name. But he was sure no one had mentioned it before. 'So, it's another killing?'

'No, no. A suicide. First thing on Friday morning, in the rose garden on Pfaueninsel, they found a man dead. A drug overdose.'

'That's crazy. I went there on Thursday morning, after I left you.'

'How long did you stay?'

'A couple of hours. I left before one.'

'Apparently, he died on the Thursday night. But get this: he left a note, confessing to the murder of not just Egon Hausmann, but six other men.'

It was all making sense. 'Let me guess,' said Colin. 'Fraser McDougal, Stefan Reis, Ulrich Steiner, Martin Engel, Walter Baus and Ajnur Osman.'

'How do you know that?'

'Even Fraser? Wow! Those are the deaths I've been investigating.'

'No way. The police are working on the theory that Elias Muller is the pseudonym of Konrad Hausmann. They've supposedly brought his parents from Hamburg to identify the body.'

Colin sat back, shaking his head. Matthias must have known this information before meeting him; no wonder he was so happy. It was practically unheard of to have a case like this solved with a full confession; it was a police officer's dream. 'Was there anything else in the note, do you know? An explanation?'

'My friend's been told it's several pages long – a kind of deranged manifesto – but she doesn't know the detail. This is going to be massive. Not just in Wannsee, or even Berlin, but nationally. Seven young men, all queer, are killed over a twelve-year period and the *Polizei* fail to make a connection. It's a total scandal.'

'It's not like people weren't telling them. And not just people from the gay community, either. The officer I'm in contact with had previously tried to prove a pattern connecting two of the deaths. If senior officers had listened, how many people could have been saved?' After an initial feeling of euphoria that the perpetrator had been identified and the case closed, Colin felt flat.

Promising to keep in touch, he said goodbye and made his way through the rowdy streets of Schöneberg, unsure which direction to head in. A single thought kept playing over and over in his mind: *I failed Ajnur*. Sitting on a bench, his eyes welled up, and as he wept for the bright young man he'd met, and all those other lost souls denied their dignity and respect for so long, the heavens finally opened; a deluge of rain, washing the streets and the city clean.

52

Soaked through, Colin walked west to Spichernstrasse and took U-Bahn 9 north to Osloer Strasse. The train was packed with people chatting excitedly, invigorated by the sudden downpour which had cut short their Saturday night.

Instead of returning to the *Genossenschaft*, he continued up Prinzenallee, past *Zum Zum* and onto Wollankstrasse, where the neighbourhood bars were beginning to close and customers stagger out onto the pavements. Ahead of him, the railway bridged the street, marking the boundary between West and East Berlin; a void to left and right, shadowing the line of the S-Bahn was all that remained of the space once occupied by the Wall. Overhead, a train screeched and he jumped. Its lights flickered in the darkness. Passing over this dividing line, Colin was forever reminded of the ghosts of past lives; a constant presence in this city.

Continuing for two more blocks, the streets of Pankow were deserted and almost every building seemed to be under scaffolding. Shivering with cold, he arrived at Klaus's newly restored tenement and pressed the buzzer. He waited a minute before pressing it again, but still no one answered. Stepping back, he looked up at Klaus's windows on the second floor; a light was on in the living room. He pressed the buzzer again, holding it for several seconds, but still no reply. Standing on the edge of the pavement, he shouted up at the window. Nothing. Pressing the buzzer one last time, he finally gave up and began making his way back home. He would try again tomorrow.

ALL WAS quiet at the *Genossenschaft*; the kitchen was empty, with no sign of Hannah; the party had moved elsewhere. On the counter, covered by a plate, was a bowl of curry. Beside it Hannah had left a note saying *'For Colin x'*. Too hungry to reheat it, he rinsed a dirty fork under the tap, filled a glass with water and took a mouthful as he walked along the corridor to his room. Pausing at the phone, he considered calling Rhona, but reckoned it was too late; he'd speak to her in the morning when his head was clearer.

Turning the corner, he discovered the door ajar. This startled him, as he was confident he'd locked it. In fact, he'd checked it a couple of times to ensure it was securely locked. He gently placed the bowl and tumbler at his feet, and listened; there were no sounds coming from inside and the room was in darkness. 'Hannah?' he called. 'Are you there?' Complete silence. 'Klaus?'

Colin placed his palm on the door and pushed it fully open; light from the corridor immediately spilled across the floor and onto his bed. Feeling along the wall, he found the light switch and turned it on. At first glance, nothing in the room seemed out of place. To be sure, as he stepped inside, he checked behind the door and inside his closet. Unlike the previous time, nothing seemed amiss – the windows were firmly shut and his clothes and belongings appeared to be as he'd left them. Crossing to the bathroom opposite his room, he flicked on the light switch. It too was empty.

The lock was undamaged, and after what had happened

The Look of Death

before, there's no way Hannah would have let anyone in. But if someone had broken in while he'd been out, what did that even mean? According to Susannah, the killer was dead, wasn't he?

Colin locked his room from the inside, then sat on his bed, picked up the bowl of curry and ate whilst staring at the evidence pinned to his wall: the sketches Rhona had sent, the locations around the city where the men's bodies had been found, notes of the various people he'd interviewed – Leon, Kim, Frida, all the others. No matter how much he looked, trying to connect these fragments together, nothing stood out as being amiss.

Still holding onto the half-eaten bowl of food, his eyes began to close, and he shook himself, trying to keep awake, but it was useless. He was exhausted and needed to sleep. Something still niggled though; there was something he'd missed. But it wouldn't be solved tonight. With a good night's sleep, it might come to him in the morning.

Before getting into bed, he dragged the chest of drawers across the door. If anyone tried to get in, he'd hear straight away. Double-checking the windows were tightly shut, he turned out the light, and lay in the darkness, wondering where Klaus was, and whether he'd somehow played a part in all of this. He couldn't rule out police involvement, but prayed he was wrong. One thing he was sure of though – there were still many unanswered questions.

THE RISING sun woke him early. In the clear light of day, double-checking the room was a priority; to see if he'd missed anything. He worked his way around the space, scrutinising every surface and every object again and again: down the sides of the sofa, under the bed, the mattress. After all, if someone had entered his room, it was for a reason.

About to give up, he spotted a glint of plastic at his feet; a black biro lay camouflaged on the gloss black floor. He picked it up. With its chewed end, it looked similar to his, but it should have been in the zip pocket of his backpack, usually stored on a hook behind the door. He checked it; there was no pen. He thought back, but for the life of him, couldn't remember when he'd last used it.

He pulled his bedside table back from the wall, checking behind it and underneath, pulling the drawer out and emptying the contents onto the floor. Still unsure what he was looking for, nothing seemed out of place; except the pen itself.

He scanned the edge of the bed and the wall behind it. Nothing. Everything was where it should be. Removing the posters and postcards from the wall, he checked if anything was behind them, but it was blank. There must be something. Staring at the images scattered across the bed, his eye caught something; a detail on the sketch Lukas had given him. He gasped. An eye had been drawn in black ink – it hadn't been there when he left to meet Klaus yesterday morning. He was sure of it. Therefore, the man found dead on Pfaueninsel couldn't have done this. Something about his confession didn't add up.

The telephone in the hallway rang. He looked at his watch. Eight a.m. Colin dragged the chest of drawers aside and rushed to answer it.

'Yes?' Half expecting to hear Klaus's voice, he was surprised when Susannah replied.

'Sorry. I know it's early,' she said. 'Did I wake you?'

'No, no. Did you forget to tell me something?'

Susannah sounded excited. Of course she did; like everyone else, she imagined the killer was dead, and the case solved. 'When I got home last night, my contact faxed me a photograph of Elias Muller. We'll wait and see what the police say, but between you and me, I'm sure this is Konrad Hausmann. I thought you might want to take a look.'

Colin didn't have the heart or energy to explain that she,

The Look of Death

the police, everybody, might be wrong, so instead obliged. 'Sure. Absolutely.'

'Are you OK?' Susannah asked.

Should he tell her? She was one of the few people he felt he could trust. But just as he was about to reveal his doubts, he stopped himself. 'Late night, that's all.'

'Do you have a fax number?'

Only Hannah had a fax and it was far too early to wake her. 'Can you do it later? It's in my flatmate's room and I guarantee you she's still asleep.'

'I'm out the rest of the day,' Susannah explained. 'But I could do it tomorrow. There's no hurry.'

'What the hell! Send it through.'

Susannah went on to explain that it might take weeks before information relating to Elias Muller's death would be released. 'There's confusion regarding the authenticity of the suicide note. My contact says there's been a suggestion by the parents that it's not his handwriting.'

Of course it wasn't.

'Keep me posted.' He gave her the fax number and, once again, promised to keep in touch. 'And here's hoping you get to break the story. You never know, it might help you get out of Wannsee,' he added.

There was a chuckle from Susannah. 'I handed in my resignation on Friday. Robert Fischer treated me like shit and he doesn't deserve me. As we speak, I'm flying solo.'

'Good for you.' His instincts were right about her; Susannah was going places.

Walking to the end of the corridor, he pressed his ear against Hannah's door. Other than the soft whirring of the fax machine, there were no other sounds. Maybe she was still out partying. As he was about to knock, someone tapped his shoulder. Turning, he was met by a smiling, naked guy, his torso and arms covered in tattoos.

'Sorry dude, can I get by?'

Colin recognised him as Brad; the boyfriend Hannah hadn't chosen. She must have had a change of heart overnight.

'Sure. Sorry.' He stepped aside to let him through. 'It's Brad, isn't it? Can I ask a favour?'

Brad stared back at him blankly, but before Colin could explain, Hannah's voice, slightly rough, bellowed from the depths of the room. 'Is that Colin?'

Brad drew back the layers of material to reveal Hannah and Tilda's heads rising from their pillows.

'Where's your fax machine?' Colin asked.

'That's what the noise is,' Hannah said. 'Told you I wasn't imagining it.'

'Susannah's sending me through something important.'

'Pass me my kimono.' Brad handed it to her and she jumped out of bed. Pushing aside a pile of clothes, she uncovered the fax machine churning out a grainy black-and-white image. 'Have you patched things up with Klaus yet?'

Colin shook his head. 'I'll explain later.'

Hannah ripped the piece of paper from the fax machine. Looking at it, she seemed confused. 'What the fuck's this? Why's that shit faxing me?'

'Isn't it from Susannah?'

Hannah looked closer. 'It's from a Wannsee number.' She stood still, staring at the image, trying to work something out. 'Why would your journalist friend be sending you this?'

'Susannah's faxing me a photograph of a guy called Elias Muller.'

'Yes. Eli, the bastard who did a disappearing act.'

Colin took the fax from her. 'This is Elias Muller?'

'Or whoever the fuck he is. I found out last night that Sienna from upstairs shagged him too and he told her his name was Konrad.' She went to take the fax. 'Here, give that to me. I want to rip the smug bastard's face to bits.'

Colin held onto it. 'Hannah, we need to talk.'

53

Colin and Hannah went outside to the courtyard, and sat under the tree. The sun had eased, and a light breeze shook spores from the blossom which hung in the shafts of morning light.

Her face was expressionless, drained of blood. Colin held her hand as she repeated over and over, 'I don't understand. I don't understand.'

'Can I get you anything?'

'No,' she replied, staring motionless at the ground. After several minutes of silence, she asked, 'Can I look at the fax again?' He passed it to her. 'Do you really believe he killed all those men?'

'No,' Colin replied. 'Something doesn't add up.'

'So, I'm not crazy? I didn't get conned by some random psychopath?'

'I'm sorry, that's not what I mean; I'm not saying you weren't being used. Elias is Konrad, my prime suspect. And I think there's little doubt he murdered his twin brother Egon in 1982. That killing has particular characteristics which the killings of Stefan, Martin and Ajnur all share: they were probably suffocated and their skin pierced in some way with rose thorns. The other three, I'm less sure of. They don't match the same pattern: they're messier, less consistent, but each successive one increasingly mirrors Elias's kills.'

'But in his suicide note, he's admitted to the other killings?' Her tone had hardened. Any traces of affection for Elias Muller were gone.

'I'm beginning to think he's been murdered, too. And whoever killed him, was responsible for the murders of Fraser, Ulrich and Walter; all of those men died of a drug overdose. There's a second killer – a copycat!'

Hannah's expression changed to one of disbelief. 'If that's what you think, shouldn't you go to the police?'

He dug his hands inside his pocket. 'Yes, but I don't trust them.'

'You're back to thinking Klaus is involved, aren't you?'

Colin exhaled and nodded. 'And I think Matthias might be protecting him.'

'But yesterday, you suggested Klaus was no longer a suspect.'

'While I was out yesterday evening, the copycat was in my room, playing games, messing with my head – he left a sign.'

'What sort of sign?'

Before he could reply, footsteps interrupted their conversation. A young woman – late twenties, wearing stone-washed denims and a grey T-shirt – pushed a pram through the archway. Glancing past them, she focused her attention on the various doorways located around the courtyard, working out which one to take.

'Can I help?' Colin asked.

'Does Colin Buxton live here?' She held up the piece of paper which had his name and address handwritten on it.

'That's me.'

'I'm Sophia,' she said. 'Ulrich Steiner's ex-fiancée.' The baby began to cry and she lifted him out the pram. 'My husband's not happy. A strange man phoning all the time

The Look of Death

asking to speak with me, leaving messages: your address, your name. He doesn't believe I don't know you. You have to stop.'

'I'm so sorry, but thank you for coming to see me.'

Sensing Sophia's awkwardness, Hannah excused herself. 'Come and get me when you're finished, OK?'

Colin nodded and, as Hannah disappeared inside, turned to Sophia. 'Would you like to sit?'

She shook her head, and continued to soothe the baby, who appeared to be on the verge of falling back to sleep. 'I only have ten minutes. My husband is at a meeting nearby and will be finished soon.'

'Is it okay if I ask you some questions about Ulrich? You know I believe he was murdered?'

'Yes,' she said, tears welling up in her eyes. 'I believed that at the time too, but the *Polizei*, they did nothing. Ulrich was a gentle person. He did drugs sometimes but never anything hard. He wasn't stupid.'

'His mother said that shortly before his death he'd been seeing someone else – a man? Do you know anything about that?'

She pulled the baby closer and settled him against her chest. 'After our engagement, Ulrich broke down; he said he thought he was bisexual, that things had happened when he was a soldier, things that caused him to have doubts. Before we got married, we agreed it was something he needed to explore. I wanted him to be sure. I didn't want him to have regrets.'

'And you met the man he was dating?'

She nodded. 'Once – by chance – he was leaving's Ulrich's apartment as I arrived.'

Colin handed her the fax of Elias Muller. 'Is this him?'

Studying the image, she shook her head and handed it back to him. 'No. I've never seen this man before.'

'Could Ulrich have been seeing anyone else?'

'No. I don't think so. There was no one else. He would have told me. He would never have lied to me. I trusted him.'

'So, Ulrich never mentioned an Elias Muller or a Konrad Hausmann? What about Klaus Deichmann?'

'Sorry, no.' She placed the baby back in its buggy. 'The boy I met was called Egon – Egon Hausmann.'

'But that's impossible,' Colin said. 'Egon Hausmann was murdered in 1982. Can you wait a moment?'

Running upstairs to his apartment, Colin met Hannah in the corridor.

'Has Sophia gone?' she asked.

'Not yet.' He pushed open his door and ripped Fraser's sketches from the wall. 'Give me two minutes.'

As he went to head back downstairs, Hannah grabbed him. 'Klaus called, demanding you phone him.'

'Demanding?'

'He says he needs to see you right away.'

'If he calls again, tell him I'll be at his apartment soon.'

Sophia was leaving through the archway when he arrived back in the courtyard. 'One minute,' he shouted, racing towards her.

'Sorry, but I must go. Uwe needs fed.'

'Please. I think I may know who murdered Ulrich.' He handed her the sketches. 'Look through these. Tell me if you recognise Egon.'

Letting go of the pram, she took the sketches and went through them. 'I don't know. It was a long time ago. Most of these aren't finished.'

'Look at them again. Closely.' The blinding sun crept behind a cloud and a gloom fell over the courtyard. 'Is there anything you recognise?'

'Perhaps this one.' She held up a sketch. It was one Colin had returned to again and again. Something about the shape of the eyes and the ridge of the nose reminded him of Klaus. But not enough to convince him. Klaus's face was far more

The Look of Death

rugged, his features more pronounced. These features were far more delicate.

The baby screamed loudly. 'I can't help anymore. My husband left me waiting in the car. Sorry.' Sophia pushed the buggy through the archway and out onto the street.

Left alone with the image, Colin was convinced this was the key. Poring over it for any further clue, at the bottom of the right-hand corner, a diagonal line, as though the original had been folded over, could be faintly made out. He had an idea what it might be, but there was only one person who would know for sure.

Breathless, Rhona answered the phone. 'Apologies. I was exercising along with Mr Motivator,' she said.

'Rhona, do you have Fraser's sketchbook with you?'

'Of course.' She sensed the stress in his voice. 'It's in the dining-room drawer. Do you want me to get it?'

'Could you?'

Seconds later, Rhona returned, her breathing back to normal. 'Have you got any news?'

'Yes,' he replied, 'but I've no time to explain. You need to trust me. Could you turn to a page at the back? There is an unfinished portrait – eyes, nose, a profile – but crucially, I think the bottom right-hand corner's been folded back. Can you check for me?'

Colin tried to breathe slowly, but as the seconds passed, he started to believe he was wrong, that it was more likely a mark caused by photocopying.

'There's a page with a sketch of a man's face,' Rhona said. 'It's on the same page as the art-deco fanlight. Would that be it?'

'Is the corner folded?'

'No.'

'I think the page I'm looking for had three images on it.'

'Hold on.'

Colin held his breath and waited.

When she eventually spoke, Rhona sounded unsure. 'I think I've got it.'

'Is the corner folded over?'

'Yes.'

'Then it's the correct one.

'Phew. I thought—'

'Can you unfold it?'

'One second.' In the time it took Rhona to unfold the corner, Colin's mind raced through all the possibilities, but there was only one word he needed to hear.

'His handwriting was always terrible, but I can just about work it out.'

'So, Fraser wrote something?'

'Egon. Didn't you ask me about that name before?'

54

THREE DAYS EARLIER - THURSDAY, 4TH AUGUST 1994

Konrad lay on the spot where twelve years previously he'd murdered his brother. The smell of the island was exactly the same: an intoxicating aroma of roses mixed with the ozone freshness of the surrounding forests and lake. A unique blend which propelled him back to that night and spoke of transgression, control and death.

He gazed around at the darkening skies. In two days' time he planned to kill Colin Buxton and bring his body back here. Driving from Wedding to Wannsee, he would transfer him onto the small boat that he'd hired and row over to the same spot with the overhanging trees where he was currently moored. By this time of the evening the tourists would be long gone and he'd have all night to spend with the body, undisturbed.

He was confident that Colin Buxton still had no idea who he was, even after weeks of playing cat and mouse. And he'd given him plenty of opportunity to catch him: following him in the park, letting himself get chased outside the youth hostel, leaving the Polaroid in the corkboard, breaking into his room and scattering the petals in his bed. But best of all, being in his life; all the time concealing his true identity.

Konrad took time to clear the area where he planned to lay out Colin's body. Once discovered, it was inevitable that the connection to Egon would be made and that the *Polizei* would finally put the pieces together and realise there could be only one possible killer. The fact he had to point the way, had to solve the crime for them, satisfied him greatly, but he'd have limited opportunity to enjoy their belated realisation: he'd be long gone. A new passport and plane tickets had been bought, his investments cashed in and transferred; a new life, his third incarnation, awaited him in Indonesia where, even if his true identity were ever exposed, no extradition agreement existed. It saddened him that he would never return here to this place where he'd experienced so much pleasure.

Taking a final wander through the rose garden before returning to Berlin, he plucked a rose and inhaled deeply, pressing his finger into the stiffest thorn until the sharp pain receded and all he could feel was the throb of blood, oozing from its tip. He remembered his brother's skin in the moonlight, the joy and terror of uncovering its pale expanses, of pressing thorn after thorn after thorn into his yielding flesh.

A peacock shrieked and a flock of hooded crows flew up into the sky, their silhouettes jet black against the night sky. Konrad peered ahead at the pathway, and sure enough, the outline of a man – his shadow – emerged from the bushes. Was he a figment of his imagination? Konrad didn't know, didn't care, but he found comfort in the fact that this figure was the same height, the same slight build, the same dark colouring as his twin.

He'd first become aware of this shadow after he'd seduced and set free sad, sweet Stefan. Initially a murky presence on the periphery of his vision, over time he came increasingly into focus. It wasn't until the discovery of Walter Baus's body, close to where he himself had laid out poor Martin, that Konrad wondered if his shadow might be a killer too – mimicking his own far superior crimes. In hindsight, it

The Look of Death

seemed strange that the body of a soldier had been found weeks later close to where he'd placed Stefan. And his shadow had been there too, at Ernst-Thälmann Park, watching on as he followed Colin Buxton and witnessed his encounter with Ajnur Osman. The symmetry – reflections within reflections – meant everything to Konrad; but in truth he'd hoped he would appear here in two days' time, rather than tonight.

'You're early,' he called out, bridging the dark space between them.

'I couldn't wait,' the man replied, his voice forceful, confident. This was no mirage. 'I'm such a fan.'

'I'm flattered.' Konrad stepped towards him and switched on his torch.

'You taught me everything I know.'

Konrad had been comfortable so long as this figure maintained a respectful distance; however, it now felt like a line was being crossed. 'What is it you want?'

'I want to know what it's like being you.'

'Why?' Konrad asked.

'To execute your own twin brother must feel like killing yourself. Then to go on living with that thought every day, I wonder how you manage it. So far, nothing you've ever done has brought him back to you though, has it? Well, until now.'

As Konrad raised his torch beam, a trick of the light took place; one he hadn't expected, a shifting of shapes and shadows in the dusk. The man moving towards him bore more than a passing resemblance to his twin, he moved like him too – it was as if the body of his brother had finally risen and was standing in front of him; the likeness was overwhelming. 'Egon?'

'I might be back from the dead, but I'm not here for a reunion. I'm here for revenge.'

Dropping his torch, Konrad stumbled back, falling into a rose-bed. Thorns scratched at his naked arms as he attempted to struggle to his feet, but Egon was on top of him, pinning him to the ground.

'This is the end, Konrad.'

Egon's fist struck the side of his head, and punched his neck. Gasping for air, Konrad scrambled onto his front and tried to crawl away but his face was shoved deep into the earth. The smell of it had never been stronger. Dirt filled his mouth, catching at the back of his throat.

A syringe needle glinted close to his eye. With one heave, Konrad pushed Egon aside, the syringe flying from his hand. Rising to his feet, Konrad tried to steady himself, but Egon grabbed his waist and they both fell, wrestling in the earth, the rose bushes flattening beneath them, the sharp thorns pricking their skin.

Konrad tried to act quickly, to position himself on top. As his hands found Egon's throat and gripped tightly, a familiar thrill overwhelmed him; there was a determination in Egon – which all of Konrad's victims had displayed as they struggled to hold onto life – to fight with all their might. That first time with Egon, he'd tried to scream, fought hard to push him off, before accepting his fate; this time, he seemed more determined to survive.

The sting against Konrad's arm came abruptly and he exhaled, an irresistible force, as if all the oxygen were being sucked from his body. His fingers clawed at the air in an attempt to capture it, but to no avail. A smirk flickering at his lips, Egon pushed him aside and Konrad's arms fell to the ground. A second sting to his neck drew even more breath from his body and it felt as if his lungs might burst.

'Not long now,' Egon whispered. But this wasn't Egon. How could it be? And this person's voice was different: there was a lilt, an American inflection to his vowels which wasn't Egon's. Then again, Egon was dead; he'd killed him years ago, and no matter how much he wanted his brother to return, deep down he knew he never would.

The Look of Death

A third jab was followed by a fourth and Konrad's body began to drift and separate from his consciousness. 'Who ... are ... you?' He couldn't be sure he'd said this out loud, but it didn't matter anymore. *You're not Egon*, was his last thought as night descended.

55

SUNDAY, 7TH AUGUST 1994

'It's Colin. Can you let me in?'

The door to Klaus's buzzed open and Colin bolted up the stairs to the second floor. Konrad's brother, Egon, had died in 1982. That was a fact. So, how come someone calling himself by that name was copying Konrad's kills? The key to it was brothers – or rather twins – and he was sure Klaus had the answer.

On the landing, the apartment door was ajar; stepping inside, he closed it behind him. 'Klaus?'

At the far end of the hall, he could hear movement, as if someone was dragging a piece of furniture across the floor. Walking towards Klaus's bedroom, he passed the living room; the main light was on and a record had finished playing on the turntable – the needle skipping round and around with a rhythmic hiss.

'We need to talk,' he said, entering the bedroom.

The room was in disarray with clothes scattered across the floor and the glass door to the balcony wide open; the muslin curtains which Klaus had recently bought were torn and flapping in the breeze. Eyes closed and head to one side, Klaus lay on top of the bedclothes in his boxer shorts, his right hand trailing on the floor.

'Klaus! What the hell's happened – are you okay?'

As Colin stooped to shake him awake, something hard and heavy hit the right side of his head. His knees went from under him. Ears ringing, he gripped the side of the bed, trying in vain to pull himself upright. A figure in black stepped into his side vision and he heard a rush of air before another blow landed squarely on his back. With a cry of pain, Colin kicked out behind him as his forehead smacked against the wooden floor. Rolling onto his back, he lashed out again as someone loomed over him. Blinded by the blood seeping from a gash on his brow, he ran a hand over his face, trying to focus as he felt someone straddle him and attempt to pin him to the ground.

'Come on Colin, play nice. There's no need to fight,' a familiar voice said.

Summoning all his strength, Colin arched his back, sending his assailant tumbling. Staggering to his feet, he charged and grabbed hold of a wrist and a handful of shirt fabric. He felt hot breath against his face. Eyes still blurred; he shook his head. A sharp pain jabbed at his neck and just before he passed out, a face came into focus.

'Lukas?'

IT WAS GETTING dark when Colin woke. Laid out on the bed, he could hear sounds elsewhere in the apartment: music playing down the hall, footsteps walking back and forth. He looked to the side. The balcony door had been closed, cutting off the city outside; there was no point in shouting for help. His limbs ached and as he tried to move he realised his shirt had been removed and used to tie his wrists to the bedframe.

Klaus lay beside him, his eyes still closed. Colin stared at his chest; from its shallow rise and fall, he was reassured that he was still alive. 'Klaus! Klaus!' he whispered. 'Wake up.'

The music stopped abruptly and the footsteps grew louder. Lukas appeared in the doorway with a bunch of roses. 'Finally, my Sleeping Beauty's awake.' Colin's eyes followed him around the room as he arranged paints and brushes beside an easel he'd set up beside the window. 'Cat got your tongue?' he asked. 'I thought you'd have lots of questions. For someone who's as clever and as perceptive as you, I felt sure you'd have worked out it was me. I gave you enough chances: the time you saw me on the train; or when I tried to freak you out in the toilet at *Homo Bar*.'

'I worked out that the copycat killer was Hops, Klaus's twin.' Colin paused.

'Oh, I'm disappointed. So you didn't work out that little old me – frumpy Lukas – was the mysterious Hops?' He pointed to his twitching nose. 'A childhood nickname from a story we both loved, about a group of feisty rabbits. I can't say I'm not hurt – I thought you might have had a bit more imagination.'

Lukas crossed to the bed and began arranging roses around them. 'It's only when I wear my contacts that people begin to see the resemblance to my beautiful bear of a brother.' Lukas removed his glasses, and sure enough, though his eyes were an entirely different colour, their shape mirrored Klaus's.

'You killed Konrad?' Colin asked. 'And Fraser, Ulrich and Walter?'

'Boring!' Lukas tutted. 'Surely we don't have to do this?' He returned to his easel and adjusted the canvas. 'Now, I need you to lie as still as possible,' he said. 'Imagine you're dead; no sudden movements, please.'

'Are you going to kill us?'

Lukas ignored the question and stared at Klaus. 'You were

always going to go for him, weren't you? Handsome, athletic, dull as ditchwater. Then again, if he wasn't my own brother, I suppose I might fuck him myself. It does get wearing though, the constant comparisons.' He sighed. 'As Egon, I found a different way to be a twin. Konrad showed me the way; I've been obsessed with the case since I was a teenager, sitting in the East, rotating the TV ariel to intercept the channels from the West. Egon's face staring out from the screen turned me on – it was like looking in a mirror. It made me think there was another life. A better life I could be leading.'

'I thought you were brought up in the West?'

'Is that what lover boy told you? Or failed to tell you? Klaus has always been a little economical with the truth when it comes to his origins. So, you see, he's not perfect.'

Lukas continued painting, similar jerks and movements to the ones Colin had seen him make before: tipping his head to the side with a twitch of his nose, standing back and holding his brush up, moving in close to peer through his glasses to understand the details.

'But yes,' Lukas said, 'in answer to your question, I killed Konrad. He had you in his sights and I couldn't let him beat me to it. I've earned it. I've earned you. The student has become the master. If you think about it, it's the natural order of things. And to be honest, he turned out to be a one-trick pony. Whereas me, I'm something entirely different.'

Colin looked around the room for any possible weapon, any means of escape. A jump from the second floor would result in serious injury or death, so that wasn't an option. Making it out of the bedroom, along the corridor and to the front door without Lukas catching him, seemed unlikely. 'It doesn't need to be like this,' Colin said. 'It's not too late to turn yourself in.'

Lukas waved his hand dismissively. 'Don't worry. I'll be finished soon enough. Just putting the final touches to my masterpiece. Who would have thought I had this talent? I only enrolled in the class out of curiosity – to see, and I'm quoting my brother here – "the sexy guy" who found Walter's body.'

'I said you had talent. I love that drawing you gave me.'

'And my recent addition to it? Did you like that?'

'I did,' Colin admitted. 'But how did you get into my room?

Lukas produced a key from his pocket. 'I made a copy while you were staying here.'

'Klaus told me you were in Paris.'

'For a cop, my brother's far too trusting. I couldn't resist popping by when you were both curled up beside each other, fast asleep. But you've been so distracted chasing after Konrad. All that wasted energy. I've been watching him stalk you the entire time. Honestly, you've had so much attention, Colin Buxton. Some might say too much.'

Colin's fingers twitched as he tried to loosen the knot around his wrists. 'I'm surprised though.'

Lukas stopped painting. 'At what?'

'I didn't have you down as a copycat. I thought you were more of an original. A one-off.'

Lukas made short, jagged strokes at the canvas as he glanced at Colin. 'You know, I think that's the most hurtful thing a person could say to a twin. With each kill I feel myself evolving, becoming someone new, someone superior.'

'I didn't mean to offend. I just think there's more to you. You know I do.'

'There are no originals; we're all brothers, variations on a theme. Look at you; you share similarities to Egon. Not as much as me, of course, and none that any run of the mill idiot might notice, but I see it. You share a look: the way your nostrils flare, the distance between your eyes, the proportion of your lips – so kissable.'

Lukas walked over to him and ran his brush down the

The Look of Death

length of Colin's torso; the paint felt cold and slimy against his skin. Leaning over, he kissed him, pressing his lips forcefully into Colin's.

As Lukas locked eyes with him, his face suffused with satisfaction, Colin quickly flicked his neck back and headbutted him hard. Gripping his forehead, Lukas staggered from the bed in shock.

Not letting Lukas from his sight, Colin twisted one hand free from the knotted shirt. As he managed to release his other hand, Lukas grabbed something from the table beside his easel.

Colin gripped Klaus's shoulder and shook him; his eyelids flickered and he whimpered. 'Wake up!' Colin shouted as Lukas lunged at him, brandishing a syringe. Launching himself from the bed, Colin stumbled and tackled Lukas to the floor. Lukas stabbed at him wildly but Colin threw himself backwards, out of harm's way. As he tried to stand, Lukas came at him again, howling maniacally. From a crouching position, Colin hurled himself at Lukas, catching him in the stomach. The syringe thrown from his hand, Lukas clawed at Colin's shoulders. With all the strength he could muster, Colin drove Lukas across the room, ramming him into the easel. Lukas tripped backwards, slamming into the glass door which shattered into a thousand tiny shards. Hands flailing, his trajectory was halted by the wall of the balcony.

'It's over, Lukas.'

From behind him, Colin heard a low groan from Klaus. 'Hops.'

'Every angel is terrifying.' Lukas grinned. 'And I was the most terrifying of all.' His gaze fixed on his brother, in one sudden movement, he climbed on top of the balcony wall.

'No!' Klaus shouted, leaping from the bed and scrabbling to Colin's side, but they could only watch in horror as Lukas threw himself backwards and tumbled into space.

A strangulated cry echoed from below, cut short by a sickening thud. Holding Klaus back, Colin crawled to the balcony's edge. Framed by a burgeoning circle of blood, Lukas's body lay broken below on the courtyard cobbles, his glasses smashed, his eyes fixed and vacant.

56

ONE MONTH LATER

Close to the Tiergarten entrance, Colin sat in the shade of a tree and ripped open a package from Scotland. Inside was a carefully bound volume of A4 sheets with a note:

'Thanks for everything you've done. Fraser never got the chance to finish his thesis, but what he did complete makes for wonderful reading – he had such fresh insights and original ideas. I hope you enjoy. Speak soon, Rhona xx'

He pulled out the manuscript: *Visual Arts during the Weimar Republic* by Fraser McDougal. Leafing through it, some names stood out – Paul Klee, Walter Gropius, George Grosz – but there were many others he didn't recognise.

'What's that?'

Colin stood and gave Susannah a hug. 'Rhona McDougal sent me the first draft of Fraser's thesis.'

'Wow. Can I read it when you've finished?'

'Sure.'

I'm hoping to interview her when she's over in October.'

'Is this for the book?'

'Initial research, yes, but I've not signed a contract yet. There are a few publishers interested, but whoever I end up working with has to understand this story needs to be told in the right way.'

'I can't think of a better person to tell it. I saw you on TV last week, making mincemeat of that interviewer.'

'I was furious; his line of questioning was so sensationalist.' Susannah pointed at a bench. 'Do you want to sit, or shall we chat as we walk?'

'Let's walk – we're heading in this direction.'

Susannah linked her arm through his. 'How have you been?'

'You know, one day at a time. I'm back at work though, doing shifts at *Zum Zum*, but I don't think I'll return to the art school. It'd be too weird. Though Maryam's back in Berlin, begging me to sit for her. She says people will pay good money for my portrait, and we could split the cash.' He smiled. 'I declined.'

'And Klaus? How's he? Have you seen him yet?'

Colin shook his head. 'As far as I know, he's still in Hamburg with his parents. He's on compassionate leave from work but his colleague Matti's in regular contact with him. I've seen him a couple of times, but he says Klaus isn't in a place to speak with me, let alone meet. I'm not sure he ever will be.'

'Poor guy. Where do you begin to make sense of a killer's actions when it's your own twin?'

'I think he feels guilty, complicit; he hadn't realised Lukas was using him to get details about Konrad's MO. And me.'

'Do you think you're going to stay in Berlin?'

'Not for much longer. That's the big news I mentioned on the phone. I'm going travelling; I've booked a ticket to India.'

'That's amazing. It's such a fascinating country – I was there two years ago.'

'You need to tell me all about it. I'm going to travel on my own for a couple of months, then Hannah's joining me. We're going to stay at this Ashram in the north – Uttar Pradesh.'

The Look of Death

'So, it's a spiritual journey?'

'Yes, kind of; for both of us, I guess. She's had a rough time of it, too. Though she has this crazy idea that my ex, Lee – who she's good friends with – should come along too, with his new boyfriend! I swear on all that's holy, that's not going to be happening.'

Susannah laughed. 'Thanks for doing this today. I've been here a couple of times to try to speak to Noah, but I've had no luck.'

'It's weird; he's not the sort of person you could easily miss. It's this way.' Stepping off the path, Colin led Susannah through the bushes. 'Watch your head on this branch.'

Arriving at Noah's den, it was immediately clear he was no longer living there; besides a couple of crates, the site had been cleared of all his belongings. All that remained was a muddy clearing in the trees.

Colin sat. 'This was Noah's home.' Overcome by emotion, his lip began to tremble and his eyes welled up. 'How are you going to tell the story if you can't speak to Noah?'

Susannah crouched beside him and held his hand. 'Don't worry, I'll keep looking for him, and even if I don't find him I can still tell the story.'

'Sorry, I don't know what's wrong with me.' He wiped his eyes. 'The least little thing sets me off. I wanted you to meet him so much.'

'Don't apologise; it's a lot to deal with. And we'll meet another time.'

Colin took one last look at the den. 'Let's get out of here.'

AFTER HE LEFT SUSANNAH, Colin caught the U-Bahn to Kreuzberg. The youth centre was as noisy as ever. A photograph of Ajnur, smiling and goofing around with other members of the group, was pinned to the noticeboard. On the table below, photographs of the others who died had been arranged. At least within this community, these men would never be forgotten.

Though the request to meet had come from Kim, after their last encounter Colin was a little apprehensive. Walking along the corridor to her office, he glanced into the hall; Christof and Roger appeared to be leading some sort of induction for a group of fresh-looking newbies.

Christof spotted him and ran out to give him a hug. 'Thank you,' he cried. 'What you did for Ajnur and Martin and everyone, we'll always remember.'

Colin blushed. He didn't quite see it this way. The investigation had eluded him for so long and only the insights of people such as Noah and Susannah had given him the essential information to piece the case together. 'I saw the noticeboard.'

'That's temporary, we want to do something more special.'

Roger yelled from within the hall that he needed Christof's help.

'I need to go.' Christof leaned towards Colin and kissed him on both cheeks. 'Come back again,' he shouted, running to join his friend.

KIM GREETED him with great affection, and he was surprised when she burst into tears.

'And you're OK? And Klaus too?' she asked, drying her eyes.

This was a side of Kim he'd not expected, but he imagined this must be the person she was to the many dozens of young men who'd walked through the door looking for a space to meet others and be themselves.

'I'm fine. Bruised and battered, but basically okay,' Colin said. 'Klaus, I'm not so sure about.' He spotted more photographs of Ajnur on the wall behind her – this time with

The Look of Death

his brother, Mustafa – and several more of Martin Engel and Walter Baus.

As Colin sat, Kim joined him on the sofa. 'I want to apologise to you,' she said.

'There's no need.' He could see from her expression how much it took for her to say this. 'But I appreciated the invitation to chat.'

'We were convinced – I was so convinced – it was someone in the *Polizei* who was responsible. And when I found out you were with Klaus, I saw red. I was so frustrated and angry. I shouldn't have taken it out on you. I shouldn't have judged you.'

'You were right to be angry with the police. Too many men had died.' He looked at the wall of photographs. 'Ajnur should never have died. I should have put the pieces together sooner.'

Kim shook her head. 'We all missed clues.' She crossed the room and pulled a large photograph album from a shelf beside her desk. 'I've something to show you. To help the boys with their memorial, I've been looking through old photographs to find pictures of Martin.' She sat beside him, opened the album and pointed to an image. 'That's from 1990.'

Colin examined the photo. In the foyer of the centre, a group of a dozen or so boys were crowded around Kim, pulling faces for the camera. On the front row, next to Martin Engel, an expressionless dark-haired boy wearing a *Soft Cell* T-shirt stared into the lens: Lukas Deichmann.

Kim nodded. 'If this has taught me anything, it's that we need to be less judgemental of others.' She closed the album and set it aside. 'You know Bela's back as a volunteer? He's been helping the boys with the memorial.'

'I didn't know that.' Colin laughed, imagining him bossing them around and receiving dog's abuse back, but ploughing on nonetheless. 'I saw it when I arrived. It looks great.'

'God no – that's temporary. He's got big plans – he wants to commission a permanent sculpture for outside in the front garden. Something huge that people can't miss.'

'Well, if anyone's going to make that happen, it's Bela.'

Standing on the packed station platform at Zoologischer Garten, Colin looked around at Berlin, illuminated by the late afternoon sun. It was a city he'd come to love and in lots of ways had thrived in. There was so much in his life to enjoy, he told himself, and he should be grateful.

On time, a crowded train drew in and he stepped back to allow a group of backpackers to board first. A girl squeezed in further to the carriage and beckoned him to step on. 'No,' he said, 'I'm not in any hurry, I'll catch the next one.'

As the train moved off, Colin sat on a bench. He had a few seconds alone on the platform before a new set of passengers arrived. Sure enough, a group of excited, eager teenagers appeared, chatting about where they'd visit: Brandenburg Gate, Checkpoint Charlie. Their energy and enthusiasm was infectious. And suddenly, for the first time in months, Colin knew he was doing the right thing; saying goodbye to Berlin would be tough, but every part of his mind and body was telling him he needed to travel, be lost, wake up and forget where he was.

It was time to move on.

AVAILABLE NOW

All Mine Enemies, **Book 1** in the **Colin Buxton Series**, is available to buy now.

"A thrilling whodunnit"

"A great read and a terrific debut novel"

"A real page turner"

A remote Scottish island… a gruesome murder…secrets waiting to destroy.

Do you love murder mysteries? Are you a fan of Agatha Christie & Lucy Foley? If so, this book is a must-read for you.

On a remote island off the coast of Scotland, a theatre company arrives to rehearse a play starring the Hollywood legend, Lawrence Delaney. But old secrets are waiting to disrupt and destroy this gathering of old friends and foes.

Before a line is spoken, one of the company is found dead. And when the island is cut off from the mainland by the worst storm in a century, the rest are trapped with one deadly secret.

This dark murder mystery will keep you guessing until the very end.

Discover All Mine Enemies, the first in the Colin Buxton crime series by bestselling author CC Gilmartin.

Perfect for readers of Lucy Foley, Rachel McLean, Angela Marsons, and Ann Cleeves.

COMING SOON

Daughter of Enoch, **Book 3** in the **Colin Buxton Series** will be published in 2024.

AVAILABLE FOR FREE

In the Stillness, a **Prequel** to the **Colin Buxton Series**, is available to download for **FREE** when you join the **CC Gilmartin Readers' Club**.

"An intriguing and insightful prequel" Goodreads

Winter 1984. When Colin Buxton hitchhikes from Glasgow to London with his troubled best friend, little does he know that before they reach their destination, their lives will have changed forever.

Making their way along the busy motorways of the North, Colin is led into a world of casual pick-ups and easy money. Confused but intrigued, he chooses to look the other way.

Until a line is crossed.

ACKNOWLEDGMENTS

A huge thanks to the following people for their expertise and input: editors Shelley Routledge and Mary Torjussen; cover designer Stuart Bache; and website designer Stuart Grant at Digital Authors Toolkit.

Special thanks to the **CC Gilmartin Readers' Club** for their support - especially our **ARC Team**.

ABOUT THE AUTHOR

We're Chris Deans and Coll Begg, and together we write as CC Gilmartin.

If you'd like to know more about our books, please visit www.ccgilmartin.com and join the **CC Gilmartin Readers' Club** for **FREE**. As a member, you'll receive your **FREE** digital copy of *In the Stillness*, the **Colin Buxton Series Prequel**, plus regular updates on the progress of the series, as well as our other projects.

We love to hear from our readers. To contact us directly, email: contact@ccgilmartin.com

You can also follow us on social media:

Printed in Great Britain
by Amazon